SHACKLED LILY

T. L. GRAY

Jeanne,

I pray you always find total freedom in Christ. Luke 4:18

Harry

CONTENTS

ACKNOWLEDGMENTS

A special thanks once again to Kristina Krause at Redzenradish Photogray for allowing me to use her beautiful tiger lily photograph.
To Josh Webb of Root Radius, you are a marketing genius. Thank you so much for my amazing book cover and all the marketing direction you have given me.
A special thanks to my dear friend, Angie, who allowed me to brainstorm and fret with her over this book. Your input truly made the final product so much better.
To my sister, Angel, who once again edited my work, encouraging me along the way. Your invaluable input dramatically improved my first attempt.
To some amazing media folks, Brandon and Karen, thank you so much for making the promo video better than I could have ever imagined.
To my faithful beta readers, Abby, Karen and Tonya, thank you so much for your advice and ideas.
And to my wonderful friend, Mandie, who was willing to be the face of Issy for me. You made the character come alive with your beauty inside and out.
Finally, to my amazing husband and children, thanks for supporting my dream world, allowing me to pour my heart and soul into every word.

For my husband, Todd, a man who challenges and
inspires me every day

PROLOGUE

New Year's Day...

They say drowning is a euphoric experience; one where the victim feels complete serenity before death finally takes her. They may be right.

The expanse around me felt airy as it gracefully kept my body suspended. I opened my heavy eyes to look through the nothingness and could see the water's surface above me, ripples gliding in rhythm as my father's face sat distorted by the movement of the water. I reached up for him, but my limbs refused to move. Water...there was so much water. It paralyzed my movement, making me panic until I realized I could still breathe.

My hand suddenly felt warm. Was someone with me? I couldn't see my father's face anymore as I sunk deeper and deeper into the depths. The waves echoed in my ears, enticing me to close my eyes and let go, but I didn't want to sleep...too many dreams...too much pain. I had buried all of them so far below the surface, and now I was trapped there, forced to relive them all over again.

1. MEMORIES

Seven years earlier…
Age: 13

I kissed my father's cheek as I slid out of the passenger side of his black Mercedes. "Bye Daddy!" I beamed, sending him a small wave.

"Don't forget about dinner. I'll be here at six sharp to pick you up. I have a big surprise for you tonight." He seemed excited, and my heart soared at the prospect. "Be sure to wear your new shoes," he continued with a wink.

"Of course! I don't plan to ever take these off." I giggled as I admired my new present. They were the first pair of heels I had been allowed to wear…a gift saved for my thirteenth birthday. The high-end shoes had cost a small fortune, but Daddy said it was worth it to see the smile on my face. Jessica would be insanely jealous when I wore them to school on Monday, and I grinned knowing I would enjoy every second of it. Maybe Tucker Murphy would notice them too and finally ask me to the spring dance in two weeks. He had been hanging around my locker lately, and I was sure he intentionally ran his fingers over my bottom, although he claimed it was an accident.

"Happy birthday, sweetie, I'll see you tonight," my dad called through his open window as he headed down the drive.

I couldn't wait until tonight! Daddy had been hinting to his big surprise all day, and I was sure he was going to tell me that he and my mom were getting back together. He had been coming over several days a week for the last month, and Mom even started getting that sparkle back in her eyes. This morning when he picked me up, they had retreated to her bedroom for over an hour, and her face was flushed when they came out. I may be young, but I was old enough to know that was a good sign.

"Mom!" I called as I shut the front door. "Where are you? You have to see my new shoes!" She wasn't in the living room where she usually sat reading a book, nor was she out in the back yard working on the garden. I ran upstairs to my room and threw the rest of my bags on the bed. The pink flower pattern clashed with the blue from my bags, and I noticed how clean my room looked. Mom must have been in there this morning because everything was perfectly in order, right down to my fuzzy pink and purple rug that had earlier been covered with the latest Teen magazines.

"Mom!" I yelled again, running down the stairs. She hated when I yelled across the house, but I didn't care. I was irritated with her. Not only was she not waiting for me when I got home, but she had been in my room when I specifically asked her not to go in there.

I stormed through her bedroom door and took note of her pristinely made bed. Fresh flowers had also been cut and placed in every available vase around her room. Wow, she really must have been in a cleaning mood this morning.

I sat on the bed and huffed as I looked over to her closed bathroom door. "Mom, I know you are in there. If you don't come out in two minutes, I'm coming in, and I don't care if it is your 'sacred bath time.' You hear me, Mom? I'm coming in!" I was fully annoyed at this point, wanting so much for my mom to see my new shoes. The silence in the room was echoing, and I finally had enough. I stormed to the bathroom and swung open the door, ready to give her a piece of my mind.

The scene before me was paralyzing as I felt my body sway with nausea. The world became a tunnel as the picture before me shifted, coming into focus through the lens of a camera. Blood…there was so much blood.

I heard screaming and turned to see who else was with me, but there was no one…only the haunted eyes of the woman in front me. I backed away, unable to stare at the blood still dripping from her lifeless wrists.

Adrenaline took over as I ran to the phone. It

rang and rang until I heard my father's official voicemail on the other line. I slammed the phone down and called again. He always had his phone.

"What is so important you have to keep calling me?" my dad's voice snapped when he finally picked up on my third attempt.

"Blood everywhere…" I whispered, unable to recognize my own voice.

"Kaitlyn? Is that you?" My dad's voice moved from harsh to concerned in a matter of seconds.

"Blood, Daddy, so much blood. Bathtub. Mom's eyes…" I couldn't speak, my mind only seeing the scene from which I had fled.

"Kaitlyn, stay right there. I'm turning around now and calling 911. Don't go in there again, you hear me?"

I nodded and sunk to the floor, letting the phone slip out of my fingers. The next few hours were like a whirlwind, sirens blaring, my mom's lifeless body being rushed to the ambulance, red stained water making a trail from the bathroom to the front door. I felt weightless as my father picked me off the floor and into his car. The ride was bumpy in the back seat, but I couldn't feel anything so it didn't matter.

The hospital was even scarier. Doctors prodded and poked at me, talking to each other as if I wasn't in the room. They used words such as trauma and shock and placed large blankets around my body. The bed was hard, and the blankets itched my sensitive skin. I just wanted to go home and curl up in my soft pink sheets. I wanted to hold Mr. B., the teddy bear I had had since I was three years old, and pretend this was all a horrible dream.

My father was by my side when I finally woke up. The world was coming into focus again, and I could see the lines on his face as he reached for my hand.

"Kaitlyn, I'm here, baby. Everything's going to be ok," he said softly.

"Where's mom? Is she…is she…" I couldn't finish as the visions of her in the tub came rushing back to my mind.

"Shhh. She's going to be fine. Doctors expect her to make a full recovery. They are just going to keep her here for a few weeks to make sure she gets better."

I knew what my father was saying. They were going to make sure she wouldn't hurt herself again. It didn't make sense. Everything was going so well.

"Why?" I whispered, searching my dad for answers.

"Kaitlyn, sometimes your mom gets sad, but she is going to get better. We are going to make sure she gets some help and never has to feel like that again. Meanwhile, you are going to get to stay with me for a while. Is that ok?" His voice was so soft and comforting, and I reached up to hold him.

"Yes, Daddy, that's exactly where I want to be," I assured him as he stroked my hair. My mom would get better, and he would bring her home too. We would be a family again, and Mom wouldn't be sad anymore.

An hour later, my new shoes sat on my lap as my dad wheeled me out to the car. I didn't know why they were insisting I ride in the wheelchair, but I didn't argue. The Mercedes was a glorious site when the doors opened, and I reached down to put my shoes on, ready to forget this horrible day. My father had sent someone over to my house to pick up my things so I wouldn't have to go back there, allowing us to head straight out to Lake Glenville where Daddy's new house awaited us.

When he and my mom separated last year after "the incident," he had stayed in hotels until he finally purchased his three-story monstrosity just a few months ago. I had been there only one time when he first moved in to pick out my room and meet with the interior decorator who would be furnishing the house. I hadn't wanted a new room and told her to do whatever she wanted. I never saw the final product, but my dad said it was "lovely." Now, I was going to have to stay there for weeks and my stomach turned at the thought.

The trees passed by in a blur as we sat in silence for the duration of the drive. Periodically, I heard my father barking orders to various people on the phone, but I kept my focus on the thin piece of glass which separated myself from the outside world.

We turned the last corner before flying down the long driveway, and I was struck with how much had changed in just a few months. There was now green grass and plush landscaping where dirt and rock had previously been. The house had been repainted a butter yellow color making it look much newer and more welcoming than when I had first seen it.

Daddy parked the car and opened my door, asking me if I could walk.

"I'm not an invalid, Daddy," I huffed, tired of being so coddled. I swung my legs out of the car and found my balance on my new heels. Once stable, I stood with all the grace my mom had taught me to.

My father pulled me in for big hug and muttered, "That's my girl."

He was pulling my suitcases out of the trunk, and I turned to walk towards the front door, when once again the world turned on its axis. This time, the scene was beautiful and came in the form of the most handsome boy I had ever seen. He strolled by me, offering just a slight smile and wink as he approached my dad. I couldn't stop my head from following his movements as I absorbed his flawless frame. Next to my dad, he seemed lanky, but compared to Tucker Murphy…well, there was no comparison. In fact, I was sure that every boy I met in the future would pale next to his tan skin and soft brown hair.

"I'll get that, sir," the boy offered, taking the suitcases from my dad. His voice was as smooth as honey, and I felt it melt into my chest and roll down to the pit of my stomach where little butterflies began to flutter around.

My dad handed him my suitcase and let him finish

unloading the bags. He placed his strong arm around my shoulder and began guiding me to the front door. I subtly looked back at the boy and caught how his muscled arm flexed as he pulled the trunk closed. My cheeks immediately burned when he caught me looking, and I quickly turned my head to see where my dad was leading me.

We stepped into the foyer and my breath caught. It was ghastly! Awful, horrendous, extreme and every other adjective I could find to describe the obsessively ornate décor. What had my father done? The beautiful hardwood floors had been replaced with shiny gold marble and the pristine white walls were now a bronzed plaster with multiple layers of crown molding.

"Beautiful, isn't it?" he asked proudly as I looked around the room.

"What happened to it?" was all I could mutter.

My dad shook his head at me and scowled. "You'll appreciate this stuff more when you're older. Come on, let's go see your room."

I couldn't imagine ever being old enough to like this place. Never, never, never! It was everything my mom hated. There was no way she would live in this…I don't know what my father was thinking!

My room was on the second floor and was more like a suite than a bedroom. I closed my eyes twice when I saw it, hoping the view would somehow improve in those precious few seconds. The walls were an antique white with gold trim around the edges and along the walls forming an ornate lacy pattern. I glanced up at the high, white ceiling and shook my head when I saw a recessed circle painted completely gold with a brown crisscross pattern. In the middle hung a large white chandelier with bulbs made to look like candles.

My dad pushed me into the room despite my protests and walked over to the window to let some more light in. Why he wanted to see this place more clearly was beyond me. It was a toss up which was worse, the ceiling or the large king sized bed which took up a good portion of the room. The headboard ran floor to ceiling in the same white and gold pattern as the walls, only it was adorned with rich silk curtains that came together at the base of a shiny diamond crown.

"What do you think?" my dad asked walking around the room. "I told her you would want some pink." My dad was referring to the hot pink bedspread that covered the gold sheets. It was also the chosen color of each piece of furniture in the sitting area. I hated hot pink. It was a trashy color with no class, and a far cry from the Victoria Secret pink I was used to.

"You want me to sleep here?" I asked incredulously as he approached me.

"Kaitlyn, I know you've been through a lot, but this is your home now. I want you to feel comfortable. A lot of care and thought went into this room. I'd appreciate it if you were a little more grateful."

"Thought and care? By whom, Daddy? Because anyone who knows me would know that I would NEVER like this room!" I stomped my foot while I spoke looking all the spoiled child that I knew I was acting. My dad's face got real tight, and I was sure he was about to scold me when my perfect boy walked through the door to drop off my things. I felt the heat rise to my face again as I watched him walk across the wood floors and over to the round gold and pink rug by my bed. I noted the way he walked, confident and sure, and how he glanced around the room just slightly as he set down my bags. I wondered what he thought of this place, and if he could sense the tension in the room when he walked in.

My dad took his angry eyes off me for one second to address the source of my erratic heartbeat. "Grant, when you're done, I need you to get Wayne Johnson on the phone right away. Don't let him try and push you to his son. I want him…only him. You got it?"

"Yes sir, right away," he answered and rushed back out of the room, but not before momentarily catching my eyes with his. It was less than a second, but the electricity that shot through me in that moment left me shivering well after he was gone.

I spun back around to my dad. "Who is that?"

"That's Grant, my new assistant. His father is an old friend of mine and had to relocate to New York to handle pressing business."

"Why didn't he go with him?" I asked, trying to

sound annoyed by his presence instead of thrilled.

My father let out a sigh and rubbed his chin, realizing I had successfully changed the subject on him. "He's a junior in high school and didn't want to go. He's got his father's entrepreneurial mind and offered to work for free if I would let him stay here and finish out high school. I've been having some difficulty finding an appropriate replacement for Anna, so it worked out well. The kid's a lot smarter than he looks." His voice cracked a little when said the word "appropriate," and I scowled. I hated Anna. She was a witch, a home wrecker, and the trashy blond who had seduced my dad. Good riddance is all I could say on that one.

"Listen, Kaitlyn, I have some really important phone calls to make today, and my day has been completely shot. Make yourself at home here, and I'll see you at dinner tonight. We still have a lot to discuss." He leaned down and kissed my cheek, slightly squeezing my shoulder before he walked out the door.

I stared at him in disbelief. He had just chalked the entire day up to an inconvenience. My mom had bled out in her bathroom, and he was worried about a phone call! The tears started to flow as I looked around the room that was decorated just for me. He didn't know me at all, and the reality of it was plastered all over the room. I burst out of the door and down the stairs. I had to get out of here.

My breathing was labored and shallow by the time

I flew out the back door and down the pier leading to the lake. I took the side steps two at a time and finally collapsed on the sand that ran the length of the property. I watched my dad's shiny red ski boat bouncing in the water at the edge of the pier and could taste the bile in the back of my throat. Tears stung at my eyes, and I missed my mom so bad in that moment I wanted to scream.

I heard footsteps on the pier and turned my head towards the water. If my dad thought he wasn't going to get an earful when he came down here, he had another thing coming. It was my birthday, and he was worried about phone calls! I felt him take up the space next to me on the sand, but I refused to look at him. I didn't want him to see me crying.

"Kind of beautiful out here, isn't it?" The voice didn't belong to my father. Instead, it was the same sweet honey tone I had heard in the driveway. I quickly wiped my eyes and turned to see Grant in all his glory next to me with his elbows relaxing easily on his knees. He turned to look at me and shot me a kind smile, one that reached all the way to his perfect caramel colored eyes. "I'm Grant. You must be the illustrious Kaitlyn I've heard so much about."

I had never been lost for words, but as I looked at him, I could only nod.

He tucked his arm around my shoulder and squeezed it slightly, sending waves of excitement down the length of my body. "Hang in there, kiddo. I know it's a lot to take in at first, but your dad really loves you. You're the only thing that seems to chip at that gruff exterior of his."

He called me "kiddo." Not what I wanted to hear, but he also hadn't moved his arm, so I looked up at him and smiled. We stayed like that for at least ten minutes in silence until Grant's phone beeped at him.

"Duty calls," he stated, jumping up and brushing off his pants. "You gonna be ok?"

"I'll be fine," I whispered, my eyes refusing to break away from his. "Thanks for sitting with me."

"Any time," he said with a wink and then took off in a sprint up the stairs and down the pier.

My arm burned where his hand had been, and I smiled, appreciating the fact that he didn't try and force me to talk. Everyone was always trying to make me talk about my feelings lately. The counselor I went to after "the incident" was always asking me questions like, "How did that make you feel?" or "How has it been with your dad gone?" Blah, blah, blah! It made me feel like crap. I hated my dad being gone, but I wasn't going to tell a perfect stranger that, one who would undoubtedly report all my feelings right back to my parents.

I took off my new shoes, running my hands lovingly over them in the process, and walked down to the water's edge. Maybe I could sleep out here tonight instead of in that room. I shivered as the cold water streamed over my toes. Maybe not.

I touched the spot on my arm where Grant's hand had rested. He was a junior and I was in the eighth grade. That was only four years difference between us. He may see me like a kid now, but with a little makeup and some better clothes, who knows? I smiled as I glanced back at the house, Tucker who?

Dinner started precisely at seven, just as my father had said it would this morning. I met him in the large dining room after meticulously primping, just in case Grant was to join us. My father made his entrance and enveloped me in a bear hug. He was in a good mood, and I loved it when my father had that relaxed look. It warmed up his usually hard face and made my insides feel fuzzy and warm.

"Before we eat, let's go talk in the living room," he said after releasing me. I followed him to the purple couches and sat down. He took a seat on the love seat opposite of me and cleared his throat. I watched as he made a waving motion with his hand and turned to see who he was looking at.

I felt the ringing in my ears the minute I saw her. Flashes of lightning shot before my eyes as anger boiled through every part of my body. Anna was walking timidly towards my dad, her hands fidgeting with each step. I glared as she approached, refusing to hide any of my hatred for her. She sat next to my father, and he wrapped his arm protectively around her. My eyes immediately darted to his hand which was now rubbing the fabric covering her protruding belly.

"Kaitlyn, you remember Anna, my old assistant?" he asked as he turned his attention back to me. Do I remember her? You mean the girl who was naked on your desk when Mom and I walked in your office a year ago? Um yes...I remember her.

My father must have been reading my thoughts because he cleared his throat and continued, "As you can see, Anna and I are going to have a baby. We are getting married in a couple of months and then your new brother will be born this summer." I stared in disbelief, fighting every instinct I had to rip every piece of hair out of her platinum blond head. "Kaitlyn, this is a good thing. Think of it like this, you will get to have two families now instead of one."

My hands were shaking with rage as I watched Anna's hand rub my father's leg. "Does Mom know?" I hissed, trying to get my emotions under control.

"Yes, she knows. I told her a week ago and we talked about it again this morning when I told her that I was telling you tonight," he explained, completely unaware of how close I was teetering on the edge of sanity.

I stood in rage, my whole body shaking with the fury I couldn't control. "This morning? It was your fault!" I screamed, making my father jump. "She did this because of YOU. You cruel, heartless monster...how could you?" I took off running, ignoring my father's screams behind me. I ran and ran until the sand ended, and I hit the edge of the property line where a brick wall blocked my path. I slammed into it hoping it would move out of my way and let me escape my crushing reality. It stood solid, leaving me only to collapse in front of it with my sobs raking every inch of my body. I curled in the fetal position, tasting the sand as it mixed with my tears.

A soft hand began to caress my hair, but I could only make out the knees of my visitor. It wasn't my father, so I didn't recoil from the touch, and let him pull me into his arms while I cried.

"Just let it out, little one," Grant whispered as he held me. "It only gets easier from here." He was rocking me back and forth like a child, and I let him comfort me the way my father never could. When I had finally cried the last of the tears I had been holding onto that day, I sat up and looked at my prince charming. The moonlight only made his features softer and his eyes brighter. He was looking at me like a worried big brother, but I just wanted him to kiss me.

I reached up to touch his cheek, struck by the smoothness of his skin. I felt him hold his breath and then turn away from my piercing stare.

"Lets get you back, kiddo, before your dad starts to hunt you down." He pulled us both up off the sand and kept his arm around me protectively as we walked back to the house. I leaned into him, savoring the way he moved and smelled next to my cheek.

My father was waiting on the pier when we walked up, and Grant pushed me towards him despite my attempts to flee again. He grabbed my wrist and then dismissed Grant, thanking him for finding me. I jerked my hand away and folded them across my chest, staring him down with the same stern look he was giving me.

"What?" I asked rudely as we continued to stare.

"First, young lady, you will never again speak to me that way in my house. Do you understand?" I nodded, still matching his glare. "Second, you will apologize to Anna for your behavior and sit down for dinner with us."

"Never." It was a statement that echoed in the darkness and bounced between us before he finally pulled his eyes off of mine.

"Kaitlyn, Anna lives here. She's going to be my wife, and you are going to have a brother. Those facts are not going to change because you've decided to have a temper tantrum."

"Is that what you told the doctor Mom had this morning? A 'temper tantrum?' God forbid you'd actually take responsibility for what you've done!"

My father turned his steely eyes back to mine, but I didn't flinch. "Go. To. Your. Room," he hissed, fighting to control the anger I saw flash in his blue eyes.

"Gladly," I retorted and stomped off to my room, slamming the door as hard as I could before throwing myself on the hideous pink comforter that signified exactly how dysfunctional my life had become.

It had been three weeks since my birthday and I still hadn't spoken to my dad. I had found that avoiding him in that big house was easy especially with his busy schedule. Anna was gone most of the time with a million appointments to get ready for their wedding—a wedding I had no intention of attending. The school dance had come and gone, and Tucker did finally ask me to go. We had fun, but it was nothing spectacular. Tucker had lost all his charm the minute I saw Grant, who I was convinced was my knight in shining armor.

I would seek him out every day to talk and tease him about his day. When he wasn't swamped with homework or tasks for my dad, we would go out on the boat or play Frisbee in the sand. Grant loved to be outside, so he was easily enticed when I would offer an escape from Daddy's stuffy office.

"You're going to get me fired, kiddo," he had accused one day while we were slicing the boat through the crystal clear lake water.

"Whatever, Grant. My dad knows your dad, and if there's one thing he doesn't take for granted, it's strong business relationships. You would practically have to commit a felony for him to fire you," I assured him.

He laughed and shook his head, sending a stream of warmth down my spine. "You're something else, you know that?"

"That's what they tell me," I replied playfully, trying my best to flirt with him. It was an act I practiced a lot, but never with any headway. Grant saw me as a kid…nothing else. I was determined to change that!

He turned to look out at the water as he drove. He seemed lost in thought and I couldn't help but stare at the way his profile accentuated his strong jaw. I moved to stand next to him, placing my small hand on his back. "Will you teach me to drive this?" I asked, motioning towards the steering wheel in the boat.

He tensed, but moved aside so I could stand in front of him. He showed me the controls and let me take over the steering once I was comfortable with it. At one point, I didn't turn quick enough, and he placed his hand over mine to steer the boat easily to the left. I felt his breath in my ear as he talked me through the turn and actually felt my knees go weak.

The boat had straightened out, but Grant hadn't removed his hand from mine, and I leaned back slightly to put my head on his hard chest. Grant stiffened and moved away from me. "I think you've got the hang of it, Kaitlyn. Let's get back. I still have some things I need to finish up for your father."

That was four days ago, and I had seen very little of him since. He always seemed to have some task from my dad that he had to do. It was the weekend, though, and my dad and Anna were off to New York for a few days. I noticed she never let him out of her sight for long, always tagging along when he went for business trips. That's what happens when you marry a cheater...a life of questions and trust issues. Serves her right.

I hadn't seen Grant since I got home from school, and it was now pushing ten o'clock. I wanted to talk to him. I had decided that I would tell him how I felt about him tonight. I would be going back to my mom's soon, and I didn't want to leave without him knowing how much he meant to me. I couldn't have gotten through these last few weeks without him, and every moment we spent together just reaffirmed that I had fallen hard as a rock for him. I had dreamed of how he would respond. Maybe, just maybe, I would get my first kiss.

I tiptoed to his room and knocked lightly on the door as I opened it up. "Grant?" I asked through the darkness. I heard sheets ruffling as a lamp suddenly switched on revealing all that Grant had been up to.

"Kaitlyn! What are you doing in here?" he yelled, trying to pull up the covers to hide his "friend's" naked body. I gasped at the sight of her, all flushed and disheveled under his sheets and jealousy flamed red hot through my soul. I turned and fled from the scene trying to catch my breath in the process. I was a fool! A complete and utter fool!

I had become just like my mother, reliant on some guy to fill all the holes and hurts in my heart. "Never!" I screamed at the lake, my voice echoing in the darkness.

I wiped my eyes in disgust. There would be no more tears, no more hurting, and no more naive

Kaitlyn. Let someone else have the fairytale. I would be no one's Cinderella!

I heard footsteps behind me and Grant's breathless voice. "Kaitlyn," he said apologetically.

I turned to look at him, my face hardened by the hurt radiating through my entire being. I took note of him, bare chested, wearing nothing but a pair of running shorts I'm sure he threw on in haste.

"I didn't mean to interrupt," I said coldly, making sure my eyes hid everything my heart was feeling.

Grant looked miserable as he stared at me. "We've been together a long time, Kaitlyn."

I raised my hand to stop him and started back towards the house. "You don't owe me an explanation. My father's out of town and you're a guy. I should have knocked," I simply stated as I walked past him.

He reached out and caught my hand before I was out of reach. We stared at each other for what felt like a lifetime—my eyes blank, his full of regret. I pulled my hand out of his and walked away, never looking back.

2. AWAKENING

Present day…

The water was still surrounding me as I watched my thirteen-year-old self fade into the darkness. I was sad to see her go; she represented all the innocence that had been lost that year. The darkness of the water started to feel cold until I could see those caramel eyes everywhere I looked. They displayed every emotion I ever witnessed, sadness, anger, regret, and compassion, always so much compassion. His eyes were penetrating me and I trembled wanting them to go away. I had buried them…why were they back?

The water suddenly began to drain taking his eyes with it. I was falling. I tried to reach out and grab onto anything that would stop the free fall, but the water was gone, and heaviness hurled me down into the darkness. I felt panicked and threw open my eyes right before impact. Fear had labored my breathing making the bright lights that seared into my irises even more painful.

"Kaitlyn? Can you hear me?" a strange voice asked.

I couldn't see anything, just light…too much

light. I blinked, trying to make it go away.

My father's voice came next. "Kaitlyn, can you hear me? Squeeze my hand if you can."

I finally registered his hand in mine and attempted to squeeze it, finding the motion more difficult than I would have expected.

"I felt it," he beamed. "Kaitlyn, can you see me?"

I tried to turn my head, to get my eyes to focus. I could see his shadow, and as I stared at it longer, his features started to come into focus.

"Daddy?" I rasped when I could finally see his blue eyes. They were tired and wet with tears, making him appear softer than I ever remember him being.

"I'm here, baby. I'm here," he assured me. "Can we get her some water?"

Within seconds, I felt a straw in my mouth and drank down the cool liquid that began to ease my scorched throat. Recollection slowly came to me. It was New Year's. Why was my dad here? Where was Jake?

"Why are you here?" I asked hoarsely after taking one more drink of the glorious liquid. "Where am I?"

"You had an accident. You are in the hospital."

Hospital? How? I just went to bed…I remembered it clearly. Jake wouldn't talk to me; he was angry because of Avery, and we had fought harder than ever in our life.

"Where's Jake?" I asked, concerned. Had we driven somewhere?

I watched my father's expression turn into a

scowl. "Jake's fine. He's still at school. Kaitlyn, you are at Duke Medical Center. You've been unconscious for days."

I shook my head. This wasn't possible. It was New Year's. "Why?"

"You had alcohol poisoning, which caused you to pass out. Then you aspirated, and your lung collapsed. Kaitlyn, it's a miracle you are alive, sweetheart."

My head started swimming with the information, and I closed my eyes, unwilling to listen anymore.

"Mr. Summers, that's probably enough talking. She may not be able to handle all this right away. Kaitlyn, do you need anything?" the strange voice asked me.

"Not my name..." was all I could say.

"I'm sorry?" the voice asked again.

I heard my father sigh as he spoke. "She goes by Issy or Isadora," he explained.

"Issy, do you need anything?" the voice asked again.

"Jake...I need to talk to Jake. He's hurting..." I whispered. I felt my eyelids get heavy as I spoke and drifted back to sleep. The dreams came again, haunting me.

Five years earlier…
Age: 15

It had been two years since my world was turned on its axis. My father and Anna had been married in a grand ceremony that was plastered all over the society page in the newspaper. I had initially refused to go, but my father threatened to file for custody if I didn't. He said my mom was unstable, and no judge would stop him if he chose to pursue it. So, I sat there and watched as my father vowed to love another woman. I hated him more than ever for making me witness it. I felt I was betraying my mother just by being there, and was terrified at what I might find when I went home that night.

Grant had come too. He was seated next to his girlfriend, the same one from that horrible night. I watched his features as he sat there, so flawless, and soft and warm in the best kind of way. He had caught me staring and captured my eyes with his until I turned away. I hated him too. I had hardly spoken to him since that night, despite his attempts to talk to me about it. I didn't want to talk; I didn't want to care. Kaitlyn was dead, and Issy didn't cry over boys.

I laid on my bed and stared at the horrible gold ceiling. My father had promised I could change the whole room on my sixteenth birthday. The thought of sleeping in here for another year was nauseating. At least I only had to come every other weekend.

My ears burned as I heard the shrill from that

child's scream down the hall. It was quieted quickly as I knew Rosa would be in there to calm him. Figures my evil stepmother wouldn't bother to raise her own child. The walls were closing in on me again and I needed to get out of there.

I grabbed my robe and headed down the dark staircase and out the back door. It was well past midnight and I shivered as the breeze found its way through my light covering. I watched my feet tiptoe across the wooden pier until I stood facing the water. The moonlight was casting a perfect glow on the waves and each ripple seemed to expand past the unknown.

"Couldn't sleep?" It was Grant's soft voice from the shadows.

"The brat's crying again," I snapped, angry with him for ruining my perfect moment, and even angrier at myself for the butterflies that came at the sound of his voice.

"Yeah, it's hard to get used to, but he's actually a pretty good baby. You might like him if you ever held him." Grant always had something nice to say about everything. I hated that about him. Who was he to lecture me?

"Save it for someone who cares, Grant. Now, are you going to leave or am I? I'm not really in the mood for chit chat." My voice was sharp and flat, an exact picture of what my heart had become.

I heard Grant get up from the chair he had been sitting in and walk over to me. He leaned backwards against the rail and folded his arms, exposing how much he had filled out since starting college. "What happened to you, Kaitlyn?" he asked sadly. "You used to be so sweet."

"Not my name," I responded flippantly, not really addressing his question.

"Oh, that's right. It's Issy now. Well, for the record, I miss Kaitlyn." I could feel his eyes on me, but I refused to meet them. He pushed off to leave when I didn't respond, and I turned to see his retreating figure in the moonlight.

A lone tear fell down my cheek as I realized I missed her too. It didn't matter, though. Kaitlyn was weak and naïve. She would never survive my life.

Sunday finally came, and I packed up to head back to my mother's house. I had seen my father for maybe two hours that weekend, which was pretty much the standard. I still couldn't figure out why he wanted me there when he just ignored me the whole time. It was his form of torture, I decided. One more year…that was all. The thought was almost tangible; I would have my license and could escape this prison any time I wanted to.

Grant was tasked to drive me home. I did my usual and sat in the back seat, texting on my phone to various friends who had spent the weekend going to the movies and the arcade without me. Missy informed me that her brother Max was asking where I was. They were twins and both had hit the genetic lottery. Max played on the junior varsity football and basketball teams. He would be a good peg in my popularity climb so I gave her permission to pass on my phone number.

I ultimately had my sights on Ben Jacobs, a Junior who was known as the school's heartthrob. He lived just down the road from my father's house, which was surprising because our school was a good forty-five minutes away. My high school was the most exclusive private school in the area, though, and Ben's family was in a wealth class with my dad, so it kind of made sense. Dating Ben would immediately put me among the elite, and I had every intention of finding my place at the top of that group.

"Anything interesting to report... *Issy*?" Grant asked from the front seat. I knew he was intentionally being snarky and sarcastic. Grant hated it when I treated him like one of the help, so naturally I had been doing it all morning.

"Aren't drivers supposed to drive in silence? You really need to take your role more seriously, Grant." My voice was playful, but my eyes were sharp when I looked up at him. I knew he saw me through the rearview mirror, and I watched as his neck tensed.

"Your eyes could throw daggers, Issy. You want to tell me why you hate me so much?"

"I don't hate you, Grant. I don't anything you." I responded flatly. My face and words were as cold as my heart felt.

He shook his head, but didn't say anything else the rest of the drive. When my mom's house finally came into view, I felt like fleeing. Despite my attempts to stop it, my palms were sweating, and I had to force myself not to look up and catch Grant's eyes in the mirror. His cologne had drifted from the front seat to the back and affected me far more than I was willing to admit. It was silly that in two whole years, this childhood crush hadn't gone away. Ridiculous. Issy didn't get crushes...she was in control.

"You can take my bags to my room," I dictated authoritatively, trying to mimic the tone I had heard my father use. I noticed a strange car parked in the parking lot and glanced up at the porch.

"Jake!" I screamed when I saw him standing there. I hadn't seen him in years, but always loved when our moms got us together. My aunt Kathy was my mom's younger sister and a favorite of mine. I ran up the stairs and threw myself into his arms. He hugged me back, and I was struck by how thin he had become. I leaned back and took a good look at his face. There were large circles under his eyes and his cheeks had sunken in tremendously since the last time I had seen him. "What happened to you?" I asked before I could put a filter on myself.

He smiled in response, but it was hollow, so different from the lively cousin I remembered. "It's good to see you too."

Grant passed by me with my bags and set them down on the porch. "I think you can manage these from here," he said coldly. "Its nice to see that you aren't a complete brat to everyone."

I glanced up in shock. He had never talked to me like that before. I stared into his eyes as he glared back at me. His stare made me shiver. The look was one I'd never seen before, and if I didn't know better, I'd almost think he was jealous. Jake's eyes grew cold as I felt his arm grip protectively around me.

"I think you're done here," Jake announced harshly.

Grant simply nodded and got back in the car, slamming the door aggressively before peeling out of the driveway. I felt a smile creep onto my face. I had gotten to him, and the feeling of satisfaction made the horror of the weekend slip into oblivion.

"So, how long are you here for?" I asked Jake playfully. "Hopefully long enough for us to get into plenty of trouble."

"How's forever sound?" he asked apprehensively.

"Are you serious?" I squealed. He answered with a nod, and I jumped back into his arms. It was the best news I had ever heard. I wasn't alone anymore. "Oh watch out, North Carolina, Issy just got a sidekick," I kidded.

"If you ever refer to yourself in the third person again, I will personally beat your booty." I watched as Jake's previously dead eyes started to get a little spark in them. They were just like mine, emerald and intense, and I felt an immediate kinship. I could tell he felt it too.

"So, do you drive yet?" I asked as he grabbed my

bag.

"Yep."

I clapped my hands together as I thought of all the mischief we could get into with that one piece of metal. The possibilities were endless. My jubilation ended abruptly, though, when I went inside and saw my aunt Kathy lying on the couch. She had wasted away to almost nothing, her frail frame so emaciated that I could see her bones protruding through her shirt. I looked up and caught my mother's eyes. There was a silent warning in them that I immediately heeded.

"Kathy and Jake are going to stay with us for a while," she said pleasantly, as though it was the most natural thing in the world.

"Fantastic," I lightly agreed, skipping over to where my aunt Kathy laid. I leaned in to whisper in her ear, "You've always been my favorite, anyway." She responded with a smile that seemed as weak as her body. I turned to look at Jake, and we silently exchanged all the hurt and fear we both had suffered since seeing each other last. Ok, so maybe I could love at least one person again. From that moment, I knew Jake would be forever embedded in my heart.

3. PHONE PRIVILEDGES

Present Day...

I was getting irritated with this place. I had been awake for three hours now, had eaten the terrible food they insisted on, walked up and down the hall three times and had even let them monitor me using the restroom. Yet, despite my complying with their every demand, my father still refused to let me call Jake. His way of asserting control over my life, as usual. I pouted and huffed, but to no avail. He insisted that I needed sleep and no emotional stimuli. Whatever.

"So Daddy, you must have a ton of work to do since you've been stuck here with me," I said sweetly, hoping he would miss my ulterior motive. "I would totally understand if you needed to head back to the office. Seriously, the nursing staff has it covered."

He looked up at me from his laptop and seemed conflicted. My dad's buttons were so easy to push. Rule number one: always use work to get his attention. Rule number two: talk about subjects he wanted to avoid. Rule number three: make him think it was his idea. I'd have him out of here in no time.

"I was kind of thinking I may call in the chaplain anyway. I've been having all these thoughts of Mom and the breakup. I don't know, it's just getting to me," I said in a sad tone.

My dad immediately stiffened and started to rub his neck. "You know, it may not be a bad idea to head out for the night. You probably will sleep better if I'm not around anyway."

"I think you are absolutely right, Daddy." I batted my eyes and shot him my sweetest smile, knowing I was putting the last nail in the coffin.

"Ok, I'm going to get going, then. You have the nurses call if you need anything, you hear?" He leaned in and kissed my forehead before rushing out of the room.

I felt relief cascade through my whole body, and I wasn't the only one. The nurses also seemed visibly happier to have my father gone.

"So can I get a shower and into something besides this gown?" I asked the one named Jackie when she came in to check my vitals.

"Of course, dear. That would probably make you feel a lot better." She walked to the sitting area and pulled out a bag that I immediately recognized. "I think your dad packed you some stuff you may want in here."

She left the room, and I threw open my bag, searching all the contents. No way my father packed this bag. The person who did so knew me well. It was most likely my roommate, Avery. All the clothes were folded way too perfectly to have been Jake. I silently thanked her as the bag had all the essentials I could ever want and to my pure joy, I found my phone and charger sitting at the very bottom. Plugging it in, I felt slightly more lighthearted and headed to shower for the first time in days. My mind still couldn't wrap around the fact that it was the fifth of January. I had lost days of my life, well actually I had almost lost my entire life. It was a thought too heavy to process so I quickly pushed it aside.

My mind then wandered to Grant as I wondered what he thought of my accident. Did he still care? I was once again annoyed that I wanted him to. I had successfully put him out of my mind after seeing him at Thanksgiving. Ben's party had been a very effective mind eraser in that respect. Now it seemed I couldn't get the memories of him out of my head. It was all those stupid dreams.

I had to get out of here. I was suffocating in the silence and felt almost panicked at the idea of spending another second alone. I felt the tangles pull as I brushed through my long black hair, leaving droplets of water on my soft flannel pajamas. It felt so good to be clean.

My phone was charged enough to turn it on and soon came an onslaught of messages and voicemails, over a hundred to be exact. I smiled to myself...I wasn't forgotten. I didn't bother with any of them. Only one person really mattered in my mind.

His phone barely rang before I heard his panicked

voice. "Issy?"

"In the flesh," I answered playfully. "Or should I say in the voice? I don't know. Either way, it's me."

Jake was laughing, almost hysterically which seemed odd to me. "Issy, you have no idea how much I wanted to hear your voice. Are you ok?"

"If you call being held captive in a stark white hospital room with no friends being ok, then yes, I guess so. When are you going to come break me out of here?"

Jake laughed again, heartier than the first time, and I laughed with him as the feeling of comfort started to flow all through my body.

"I'd be there in a flash, Issy, if your dad hadn't practically threatened me the last time we spoke. I would have told him exactly where to go except that he reminded me he could pull you from Winsor in a second. I agreed to stay away at that point."

"That jerk. He knows everyone's weakness," I huffed, irritated that Jake wasn't here with me and it was all my father's doing.

"Hey Issy?" Jake asked apprehensively.

"Yeah."

"I'm really sorry. I said horrible things, and I didn't mean any of them. I couldn't have made it this far without you. Please don't ever scare me like that again."

I heard Jake's voice quiver and felt the tears come to my eyes. Darn him for almost making me cry. "Jake, not another word. We're family. That gives us a stupid pass every now and then," I assured him, trying to pull as much humor to my voice as I could. I found the self-control I was searching for and then continued to bombard him with questions about what had been going on the last few days. He didn't mention Avery, and I didn't ask. That was a dysfunctional relationship if there ever was one. Jake broke her heart, then fell in love with her. Only problem was that she was now in love with someone else. Jake wasn't ready to believe it, but it was crystal clear to me. Parker and Avery were meant to be together. I just wondered how long it would take and how much pain he would have to feel before he accepted it.

I didn't know what Jake was thinking. Our family was cursed when it came to love. We had made a pact in high school to never fall in love, as we both saw first hand what it did to our mothers. Stupid, stupid, stupid.

We talked a little longer and then got off the phone. I tried to call my mom, but it went straight to voicemail. Odd. I left her a message. I wanted to call Avery, but suddenly felt so exhausted, I had to lay down. Sleep overtook me quickly, and I sunk back into the world I vowed I'd forget.

Two years earlier…
Age: 18

It was finally my senior year, and I loved every second of it. I had permanently established myself as the queen of the school, an honor bestowed on me almost immediately after Ben and I started dating. My mom had busied herself with caring for my aunt Kathy, so I no longer felt the need to babysit her whenever Anna's picture would show up in the society page.

Ben and Jake both being at Winsor was the only downfall in the equation, but we saw each other often enough. When Jake wasn't home, Ben usually was, and I had learned the art of finding a good party anywhere in the city.

It was my weekend at my dad's again, and while I dreaded two days with my stepmother and her son, it did make it easier when Ben was in town. He was taking me to dinner and out to a local club that turned a blind eye to minors. I hadn't seen him in weeks and couldn't wait until he got here.

I tiptoed into my dad's liquor cabinet while I waited and found the stash I was looking for. Another positive thing about coming to my dad's house was that I discovered how numbing alcohol could be. The combination of neglect and easy access made hiding it a piece of cake, leading me to have multiple private drinking parties while trapped in the house. Grant had caught me on numerous occasions, and while he took it out of my hands and sent me to bed, he never told my dad about it.

Grant had changed in the last year or so. He had broken up with his girlfriend and was starting to lose that boyish softness I liked so much. Personally, I thought he looked miserable, so I refrained from torturing him too much. We had learned to exist without interacting, which was a good thing since I still would get butterflies whenever his hand would accidently brush mine. More than once, I had caught him staring at me, looking conflicted as to whether or not to say something. The moment usually ended with one or both of us walking the other way, leaving a silent tension hanging unresolved in the air.

I continued to drink until my teeth felt numb and thoughts of Grant slipped from my mind. By the time Ben showed up, I was well past sober, a fact I was grateful for after only ten minutes with him. College had changed Ben too. While arrogant and stuck up in high school, he was still funny and charming, but now he was just rude to everyone and seemed to only care when he could party next. Ben had moved from alcohol to weed and then on to some heavier stuff since going to Winsor. I wanted nothing to do with any of it, which annoyed him when he came home.

By midnight he was bored and wanted to leave. I, on the other hand, was having the time of my life dancing with various people in the club. The bartenders had been very kind to me as they went on and on about how beautiful my eyes were. Ben had only danced with me twice and spent most of the night in the corner texting on his phone. I was starting to wonder if I should rethink this dating thing as his stock was seriously starting to plummet.

I reluctantly agreed to leave after he growled at me for the fifth time. The room was starting to spin anyway, so it was probably a good thing. Ben dropped me off in front of my house and peeled out of my driveway with barely a goodbye. My inebriated state was likely the only thing keeping me from driving to his house and busting out one of his headlights.

Good riddance, I thought, and headed through the house and out to the lake. The sand felt cold on my feet, and I watched as the water stayed eerily still as I approached it. I could hear it beckoning me, calling me to it. It was the Lady of the Lake and her voice was hypnotic as I slowly removed my dress. The icy water burned my feet as I walked forward, but it didn't deter me. In fact, I relished it, that feeling of numbness that blocked out any and every emotion I didn't want to feel. By the time I was waist deep, I could no longer feel my legs and slowly let myself sink down until I felt the surface of the water against my neck and then my forehead. I closed my eyes and let the sound of the water rock me to sleep as I sunk lower into the depths.

A minute later I was floating. The water was gone, but the movement continued, comforting me as I tumbled towards sleep.

"What is wrong with you?" a terrified voice asked

in the distance. It was honey sweet and electrified every one of my senses. I felt warmth envelope me as his voice continued, "I need you to open your eyes, just for a second so I know you're still with me, ok?"

I loved his voice, every word like fire to my frozen heart. I opened my eyes as he requested and stared lovingly at his beautiful face. I caressed his cheek, feeling his light stubble that always showed up at the end of the day. It was the first touch we had shared in months, and I knew my fingers would remember the feeling long past that moment. His expression was soft, reminding me of the boy who held me as I cried so many years before. He held me now too, wrapped up in a blanket as the fire cast an orange glow over his tan features.

I snuggled back into him, enjoying every moment of this wonderful dream, and was weightless once again. His arms were so tight and snug against my body that I almost felt disappointed when my mattress gave under my weight, and my soft sheets were pulled over the blanket. I felt his hand on my cheek, his thumb ever so lightly following the contours of my lips. I wanted to open my eyes, but they were too heavy to move, so I lay motionless as his touch left a trail of fire on my skin.

"So beautiful," he whispered. "Like the forbidden fruit put here just to torture me."

His heavy sigh echoed in my room before I felt the bed shift and the door close with one simple click.

I bolted out of bed, my pajamas soaked and my breathing shallow. Was that a memory or a dream? I remembered Ben and the club, even the lake, but had never remembered anything past that. I pulled myself out of bed and splashed cold water on my heated face. This had to stop! I never dreamed, ever. It was always just dead time when I slept. Of course, it had been years since I was sober this many days in a row, a problem I would need to remedy quickly. This couldn't go on. Every time I closed my eyes, I saw *him*, and it was killing me.

I looked over to the clock. It was one in the morning, but there was no way I was sleeping. I dialed Jake's number. Voicemail. My irritation started to boil. My mom hadn't called me back either. I tried her again, but got the voicemail again. I slammed the END button and pouted. I wanted out of here. Finally, I calmed and called Avery's phone. She was typically an early to bed type, but was usually pretty good about waking up to talk to me. It rang and rang, and just when I thought it would go to voicemail, I heard Avery's voice.

"Hi!" she yelled into the phone so loud that I had to pull it away from my ear. "How are you?"

She sounded like a teenager who just got caught making out by her parents. "Wow, Avery, you're like breathing heavy. What did I interrupt?" I asked playfully.

"Nothing! Jake and I were just celebrating your waking up!"

At that point I knew Avery had been drinking and I scowled knowing that Jake was the reason. "Have you been drinking?" I asked, trying to sound lighthearted. "And with Jake of all people?"

"Just a couple of glasses of champagne, nothing big."

"Avery, champagne is the worst. No wonder you are slurring your words. What happened to Parker?" What had I missed in five days?

"Nothing! Jake and I are just friends."

Just friends? Yeah right. I shook my head and cursed Jake a little. I knew exactly what he was doing. I thought about New Year's and the look on Jake's face when Avery left the apartment with Parker. I hadn't even shut the door before I saw Jake's fist hit the wall, sending white powder everywhere. His eyes were wild, desperate. I hadn't seen that look since his mom died, and it scared me. I was suddenly worried for Avery. She was no match for Jake. He had mastered the art of manipulating girls to get what he wanted. I knew how he worked, mostly because I would do the same thing to men, and I suddenly felt very protective of Avery.

"Avery, I love Jake, you know that. But he cannot be trusted with you, ok? He's not there out of friendship. You didn't see him last night…I did. I mean New Year's, whatever. Anyway, Parker is a good guy, and I've seen the way you are with him.

You need to really think this through." I didn't know how to be more clear and hoped she would at least stop and think.

"It's good to see you are back to your old, opinionated self," she said after a stretch of silence. Her voice was more reserved now...a good sign.

"Would you expect anything less?" I asked and then continued, "Hey, since he's there, will you let me talk to him for a minute? I can't seem to get ahold of my mom. I'm guessing my dad verbally accosted her pretty well."

"Yeah, he's pretty efficient at that," she blurted out and my anger burned.

"You too? Man, he's a piece of work. Every nurse on my floor shakes when he's around!" How could my dad yell at Avery? There wasn't a sweeter person in the world. I was about to continue on my rant until I heard sniffles in the background. "Avery, what's wrong? Are you crying?"

"Maybe," she sniffled. "I'm just so glad you are ok. I don't know what I would have done if anything happened to you."

I felt myself tear up for the second time tonight and irritation consumed me. "Avery, this here is why you stay away from champagne! Give me Jake," I demanded.

I heard shuffling and then Jake's hearty voice. "Hey sweetie, what's up?" He sounded distracted, no doubt watching whatever Avery was doing.

"What are you doing?" I scolded.

"I'm having a drink with a friend. Goodness Issy, is your confinement starting to get to you?"

"Jake, don't treat me like I'm stupid. Avery is dating Parker. You need to leave her alone."

I heard his voice change as his anger was clear even through the phone. "A minor problem that will be remedied soon. Probably already would have been if not for your impeccable timing."

"Jake...hear me when I tell you this. She is in love with Parker, whether she realizes it yet or not. You need to let this one go."

"Like hell she is!" he screamed into the phone. "He's just the rebound guy!" I jumped from his voice. I was actually navigating new territory here with Jake, leaving me a little unclear as to how to deal with him. I couldn't see him, so I didn't know how close he was to losing it.

"Fine, whatever," I relented. "Have you talked to Mom? She's not answering my calls."

"Yeah, I talked to her after you called. Your dad had already told her you woke up."

"What? She knows and she didn't call me?" Our relationship had been strained since aunt Kathy died, but this was ridiculous. "What did she say?"

"Nothing really, just that she was glad your dad was there."

I let out an audible growl. Since when did they team up?

"Listen, Issy, can I call you later? I'm kind of in the middle of something here," Jake asked, his voice distracted again.

"I bet you are," I whispered and then hung up the phone. I looked around my empty room and grabbed my slippers to head out the door. There had to be someone on duty I could talk to.

4. FIRST KISS

Last Summer…
Age: 19

It had to be the worst summer on record, I decided. My aunt Kathy had died on a Tuesday, and we had the funeral two days later. My mom and Jake were like zombies walking around, barely speaking to anyone. I felt bad for them, but I couldn't take it anymore and actually had chosen to come to my dad's house. I mean, I missed her too, but goodness, she was finally free from that rotting body. They should be happy for her. I certainly was.

I walked out to the lake with my towel and magazine, hoping to soak up some of the hot North Carolina sun. I didn't know why I bothered. My skin was so fair, I needed SPF 50+ just to keep from burning. I had given up trying to tan a long time ago. As I approached, I saw Grant lounging on one of the chairs with a book in his hand. His shirt was sitting next to him, and I felt a tingle go from the top of my head to the bottom of my toes as I watched his muscular chest gleam in the sunlight. I stood there frozen knowing I should retreat back to the house and avoid him. My body didn't seem to agree, and I was suddenly walking past him to the adjacent chair.

I set down my things and then made a point to remove my swimsuit cover in front of him, exposing my red bikini. He didn't move and his sunglasses covered his eyes, but I could see the muscles in his neck strain a little. I smiled internally. It was about time he noticed me. Every other man in the state had, but Grant had always somehow managed to stay casually aloof.

I settled myself into the chair, finding the most flattering position I could and pulled out my magazine. I had already read this one and didn't really care for any of the new fall fashion it showed. Orange seemed to be the up and coming color, and I hated orange. My guess was the fad would last maybe two months…if that.

I set down my magazine and whined, "I'm bored."

Grant didn't move, but I saw one of his eyebrows lift under his glasses.

"You wanna go out on the boat?" I asked, turning to him. My internal voice was screaming at me, but I didn't care. I needed interaction with people, and he was all that was available. End of story.

"You're asking me to go on the boat with you?" Grant asked incredulously, finally turning to look at me full on.

"Yeah, why not?"

"I don't know, maybe because we've barely

spoken in five years," he answered, his honey voice still able to bring butterflies to my stomach.

"Semantics. You coming or not?" I asked in a bored tone, masking my face of any emotion.

"I'd say no, but I'm a little too curious," he admitted with a sly smile.

I leaned into him, placing my elbows on my knees while I used my most seductive tone. "Well, you know what they say?"

"What's that?"

"Curiosity killed the cat." I was flirting shamelessly at this point. I knew I should stop, but it was actually working on him. I guess years of perfecting my talent were finally paying off.

Grant sat up and leaned toward me, leaving very little room between us. He had a full on smile at this point and answered in the same seductive tone I gave him. "Good thing I'm not a cat."

We stared at each other through our sunglasses, and I felt my body flush with a scorching heat that had nothing to do with the sun. Grant was the first to break the spell and stood up, offering me his hand. His touch sent more sparks through my body, further reminding me why I avoided it at all cost.

I grabbed my cover up and sunblock and then followed him down the pier to the boat. My dad always left his keys in there, and Grant kept the gas tank full, so minutes later we were slicing through the blue water and feeling the wind on our skin. I stood at the rail and lifted my hair to dry the sweat starting to bead on my neck. Slowly releasing the black strands, I let the wind blow them around until I felt the ends tickle the small of my back. As I turned to lean my back on the rail, I noticed Grant's eyes boring through me. I shot him a coy smile, enjoying how aware of me he was, and walked towards him.

"I want to ski," I announced as I approached. He slowed the boat down and anchored us as we pulled out the equipment. His muscles were tense as he moved. I placed my hand on his back as I reached down to grab a life vest, making him stiffen even more.

"One or two?" he asked curtly as he pulled out the skis.

"Two for now. I'll drop one if I want to." I had become an accomplished skier since my dad had moved out here. Mostly because there wasn't much else to do when I was forced to visit.

Grant moved away from my touch and threw the skis in the water. He then tied the rope and threw it out there as well. I zipped up my vest and jumped off the back of the boat and into the water. It was chilly, but comfortable enough to swim. I put the skis on, got positioned and waved at Grant. The boat bolted forward, and I was immediately out of the water and flying across the surface. Adrenalin surged through my body, and I squealed with delight as the boat raced forward. I tried all of my old tricks and even threw off the other ski. Once I felt my arms start to burn, I let go of the rope and slid in the water. Grant circled around, picked up my abandoned ski and then came back to where I floated in the water.

I climbed back in the boat and began wringing out my hair. "Wow, I forgot how much fun that is," I exclaimed, smiling.

Grant didn't say a word, just stood there staring at me.

"What?" I asked, confused.

He shook his head and turned. "Nothing, just thought I saw someone I used to know," he answered sadly.

I shrugged it off and pulled out the wakeboard, shaking it mischievously in front of him. "Come on, Grant, you know you want to."

He grinned and then grabbed the board out of my hand. "There are places for women like you, Issy."

"Really? And where is that?" I asked flirtatiously, placing a hand on my hip as I met his eyes.

"Somewhere with fire, where there is weeping and gnashing of teeth," he retorted as he threw the board in the water, following quickly behind it.

I laughed out loud, feeling it echo through my body. "I'll take that as a compliment," I yelled back at him in the water.

I pushed the boat along as soon as I saw Grant's hand go up. He was incredibly athletic and did flips and turns like he had been wake boarding his whole life. Seeing Grant on the water, so full of energy and life, made me almost forget that he spent most of his time stuck in an office doing my dad's bidding. I wondered why he still did it. He had graduated from college this past May, yet had stayed working as my dad's assistant. It didn't make sense to me. I'd so be out of there.

I watched Grant drop into the water and turned the boat around to pick him up. He was smiling ear to ear when he got back in the boat and shook out his hair, pelting me with little water droplets.

"Do you have any idea how long it's been since I've done that?" he beamed as he toweled off.

I slowly pulled my eyes from his perfect abdominal muscles and brought them back up to eye level. He grinned at me as he put his shirt back on.

"What now?" he asked as though spending the day together was a normal thing for us to do.

"Sandbar?"

He nodded in agreement and took over the driver's seat. The sandbar was on the other side of the lake and was one of the more secluded spots because the lake level dropped to only three feet. Ben and I had been out there for more than a few lake parties, and it was a known make out spot for teenagers who lived on the lake. Lucky for us, the area was empty when we anchored the boat and swam out there.

As soon as I could touch, I felt Grant lift me off my feet and dunk me into the water. Water surged around my face as I barely shut my mouth before going under.

"Oh, you are so dead!" I screamed after getting to my feet again. I tried repeatedly to get him under the water, even climbing on his back at one point, but it was no use. My five foot four frame was no match for his. Secretly, I liked his strong arms around me, even if it meant I became waterlogged. I finally surrendered, and he beat his chest like a Neanderthal. I laughed as I splashed him one more time.

Collapsing on the dry beach, I felt utterly exhausted, but happier than I had in a long time. I was even sober and feeling this way, which *never* happened. Sand stuck to my bare back and slid in my bikini bottoms as I lay there, but it didn't matter. It would wash off the minute I got back in the water. I watched as Grant sat down next to me and I leaned up on my elbows to look at him.

"You have a talent, Issy," he stated matter-of-factly.

"What's that?"

"You make people forget just for a moment that they're all grown up. Hanging out with you brings me back to my childhood."

"I'm no child, Grant."

Grant just sighed and nodded. "Trust me, I've noticed. That's not what I'm saying. It was meant to be a compliment."

"Thanks then, I guess."

We sat in silence for a while until Grant finally spoke again. "I'm sorry about your aunt."

I was surprised he knew, but then again, not. My dad probably had him send the flowers. "Its fine," I muttered. After a few more seconds I continued,

"Don't take this the wrong way, but I'm kind of glad for her. Does that make me a bad person? I mean…she's free."

I sat up and crossed my legs, keeping my eyes locked on the water in front of me. Grant slowly took my hand in his and rubbed his thumb over my palm. I closed my eyes, feeling lost in his simple touch until his voice broke through the silence.

"Is that how life feels to you, Issy? Like a prison?" he asked carefully. I finally turned to look at him, not sure how to react to such an honest question. His eyes held all the compassion I remembered growing up, and I felt my stomach turn as emotion I hadn't felt in years started to churn.

I stood up abruptly, pulling my hand from his. "We should probably get back. Sun's starting to set," I said dryly. The walls around my heart had stopped trembling, and I felt in control again.

Grant stood up too and brushed off the sand. Before I could react, I felt my head being crushed against his solid chest as he embraced me. His arms were firm and deliberate, holding me in such a way that for one moment, I almost felt safe. It only lasted for a second before reality slipped in, and I quickly struggled out of his hold and bolted to the water.

"Come on, slowpoke," I yelled playfully as I swam to the boat. I needed to seriously diffuse the situation. Too much emotion…too much hurt.

I climbed into the boat. It was getting colder, and I threw my cover over me to stop the shivering. The boat was rocking in the water, creating an idyllic scene as the sun settled down over the horizon. I turned, enjoying the view, keeping my eyes far away from Grant as he climbed in the boat.

I could feel him approach me as if my body was magnetized to his. He stood behind me and placed his hands on the rail, caging me between them. My heart was fluttering as I felt his breath on my neck. "You don't have to run away from me."

I turned around to look up at him, trying to steady my breathing. His caramel eyes locked with mine, and I could see his chest was moving as erratically as mine was. I glanced at his lips, slightly parted and so soft that I couldn't stop my body from moving forward. I leaned into him and lightly put my lips to his.

He wrapped his arms around me, cradling my head and kissed me fully and completely. It was a kiss that made me forget any other I had ever felt. I had spent years dreaming of this kiss and it was beyond even my overactive imagination.

When he finally released me, his hand was immediately on my neck, his thumb running softly over my flushed cheek. "You have no idea how long I've wanted to do that," he admitted.

"How long?" I asked in the same labored voice.

"Way longer than was legal," he stated with a grin.

I smiled back at him, the knowledge of that sending shivers down my spine. "That's not really an answer. How long?" I pressed. I needed to know.

Grant still held my neck, but used his other hand to move a small piece of hair from my face. "Since I saw you wobbling around on those ridiculous high heels."

The memory made us both chuckle a little and I reached up to slap his shoulder. "I walked perfectly in those, thank you very much," I scoffed, but then watched him closely. "Why didn't you say anything?"

Grant let out a heavy sigh and dropped his hands from my face. "You were thirteen, Issy, and I worked for your father. He gave me one rule when I came to live here...just one. You were off limits. Period."

I reached out to grab his waist and pulled him back to me. "So why now? You still work for my father."

Grant put his hands on the rail behind me again and leaned in until I was completely trapped by his large frame. I felt heat surge through my body as I stared into his intense eyes. "I don't care anymore. All I've ever wanted is you, and I'm done trying to fight it." His words were soft, but held a promise. I pulled him towards me and kissed him again, giving more of myself than ever before.

Grant's arms stayed wrapped around me as we turned and watched the sun set.

When I look back on my life, there are very few things worth remembering. But this day, my most perfect day, certainly was.

Present Day…

I woke up with a smile, my lips still burning with the memory of Grant's mouth to mine. No kiss had ever come close to replacing his, no matter how many times I'd wish it would. I sat up in bed sadly as I remembered what happened the day after. I had woken up in a panic, knowing all too well that Grant brought out feelings in me that were dangerous. I remembered my mother's lifeless eyes at the loss of her first love and bolted out of my dad's house before anyone saw me.

Grant had texted me later that day.

Grant: Where did you go? I was hoping to see you.

Me: Why?

Grant: Are you serious?

I shivered as I remembered how cold I had been to him.

Me: Listen Grant, unless you have something important to tell me from my dad, you really shouldn't be texting this number.

Grant: Unbelievable!

That was the last conversation we had until a month later when I was at my dad's again, and we went back to existing without interacting.

5. THE BOMB

My release papers were finally signed, and I was getting out of here. The last two days had just about killed me, and I wondered how I would have survived without the chatty nurses on my floor. I had tried to keep the sleeping to a minimum because my dreams came every time I closed my eyes. They were always dreams of one person...the one person I had spent years trying to forget.

I had wanted Jake to come pick me up, but my dad refused, saying he had something important to discuss with me. I cringed at the thought. His "discussions" never meant anything good for me. I sat in the lobby, clicking my fingertips on the chair, noting that my father was thirty minutes late already. Seriously? I could have been halfway to school by now.

I finally saw his large frame as the entrance doors swung open, and tried to hide my annoyance when he pulled me into a bear hug.

"You ready?" he asked cheerfully.

"Yeah, for like an hour now. You're late." My dad shot me a look—the one that took me back to when I was seven years old and got a little mouthy. I ignored it and picked up my bag in a huff, walking briskly to the car. Four hours…that's all I had left with this insufferable man. I took a deep breath. I could do this.

The first hour of the drive was uneventful. I sat in the front texting my friends as we planned my coming home party. My dad conducted business as usual using the hands free device he liked so much. I was almost starting to relax until I noticed that my dad had missed the turn off for Winsor and we were going in the wrong direction.

"Dad," I said loud enough to interrupt his phone conversation. "You missed our turn. We can't get to school this way."

"Hold on a minute," he said into the phone before glancing my direction. "We're not going back to school." The look on my face must have warned him, because he quickly got off the phone with whoever he was speaking to before addressing me.

"Listen, I know you don't realize this, but you are out of control right now. I think the best thing for you is to stay with me for a little while. I've already talked to the Dean at Winsor, and he is fully supportive. It will all be waiting for you in the fall. Meanwhile, I have a friend at Western Carolina who pulled some strings. You're going to take your classes there this semester and live at the lake. It will be a good change for you."

I was speechless, no, I think medical shock was probably a more accurate assessment. Finally, the world stopped spinning, and I found my voice again.

"Have you lost your mind?" I screamed at him. It was more like a shrill as I saw him flinch from the sound. "There is no way I am going to Western Carolina and living in that house with you and that whore. You should have just left me to die in my room."

I watched as my father's knuckles turned white from gripping the steering wheel, and I actually thought for one second that he might finally hit me. Then I realized he didn't need to, his words and actions always did far more damage.

"Kaitlyn, you will not speak to me like that!" he yelled back, the vein in his neck moving with each word.

"Don't call me Kaitlyn!" I screamed back at him, matching his volume level.

We were both out of control, so angry that neither one of us could say a word, just shake and look out the window. My father pulled the car over when he spotted a rest spot and bolted from the car, slamming the door behind him. I watched him walk over to the picnic tables on the far end of the grass and put his hands on his head. I knew I should stay in the car, but with each mile, we were closing in on my prison and moving further and further away from the school I loved. I took a deep breath and made sure I was under control before following my dad.

"You can't make me go," I said sternly to his back. "I'm an adult now and you can't force me or use my mom to manipulate me this time. I won't live there."

He turned to face me. He was still tense, but the fury was no longer present in his voice. "I can...and I will, Issy. You may be an adult in the legal sense, but you are still completely dependent on *me*. I pay for your school, your housing, your food, your lifestyle and your car."

"Fine, cut me off for all I care. Mom makes plenty of money to take care of my school."

"Your mother and I have already discussed this, and she is in agreement with me. She will not fund one cent of your lifestyle if you choose to go back to Winsor." His voice was becoming eerily calm. Just like a businessman, he knew when he had the upper hand, when he had his opponent so cornered that they would have to destroy themselves to get out.

"Then I'll live with Mom and work. I am *not* going to Western Carolina." My voice was hardened, but I could feel it quiver. I was starting to panic and even though I had spent years training my face to stay void, my dad was picking up on my subtle weakness.

"That too, will not be an option. It's my way or you're on your own."

And there it was. I was trapped, and my mother had betrayed me. No wonder she wouldn't answer my phone calls. I wondered what my dad had threatened her with to abandon me, but it didn't matter. The damage was done. He was in control, and I was left a puppet in his world...again.

"I hate you," I seethed through my teeth.

"That may be the case, Issy, but you are still

spending the next eight months at my house. And *if*, which is entirely up to you, *if* you can show me you've learned how to behave like a functional adult in that time, you can go back to Winsor in the fall, and this will all be a memory."

I didn't say another word, just spun on my heel and went back to the car. The next couple of hours were so tense that my stomach almost hurt when we finally pulled in the driveway. My dad had attempted conversation, but I refused to speak. It was the one thing I could control, and despite how childish my silence made me look, I still ignored him completely.

I opened the car door before my father even had the gear shift fully in park and ran up to the front door, trying to escape as quickly as I could.

My father's voice boomed across the steps. "Kaitlyn, dinner is at seven sharp. You will be there," he said authoritatively, using my real name as a way to provoke me.

I wouldn't give him the satisfaction and just gritted my teeth as my fingernails cut into my palms. Getting under control, I started back towards the door just as Grant opened it and stood waiting in the frame. I felt the heat surge into my cheeks the minute I looked in his direction. Those dreams had ruined all my control around him, and I felt as vulnerable and weak as I did seven years ago when he first walked into my life.

I kept my head lowered and attempted to move past him when he grabbed my wrist, forcing me to spin around and face him.

"Are you ok?" he asked calmly.

I glanced up at him, surprised by the surge of emotions his touch and voice forced through me. I knew I was struggling to keep the wall up and searched my head for some snarky comment I could make to stop the ticking time bomb in my heart. But the look in his eyes stopped me. It wasn't concern or irritation, which was what I was used to seeing from him. No, his face showed a completely new emotion…fear. He looked afraid.

"Yeah, I'm fine," I replied gently, as I pulled my hand from his and ran up the stairs to my room. I barely got there before the tears came. They were the first tears I had shed in years, and I immediately felt angry and disgusted by them. I would not give this to him. He may control where I live right now, but I would *not* let him get to me. I was too strong for that.

The tears dried as my anger surged, and I made my way to the armoire that sat across from my bed. Inside was a 51" television and every other electronic device a person could want, but that wasn't what I was looking for. Tucked deep in the back was a hidden cubby that no one would ever notice unless they had looked for it. I felt my whole body relax when I reached back and felt the cold bottleneck of the Vodka I had put there months ago.

I pulled it out and took two quick swigs before placing it back in its hiding place. The cool liquid burned in my throat as I felt it roll down to my stomach, numbing every surface in the process. I was already feeling better as I opened the door to the balcony and gazed down at the lake. I didn't turn to look when I heard a knock on my door, or when it opened. I wanted this world to disappear. Footsteps moved across my wood floors, and I tensed knowing it was either my father or Grant, and neither was welcome.

"You want to talk about it?" It was Grant, and my stomach flipped over, making me realize that my father would have been a better option.

"No," I replied curtly, keeping my eyes steady on the lake.

"Well, I do. What were you thinking, Issy? You could have died." Grant's voice was tense, the honey sweetness almost completely gone from it. "Do you have any idea how panicked everyone was? Your mother could hardly get the words out when she called me."

I started laughing. "My mother? Yeah, I'm sure she was devastated." Sarcasm was dripping from my voice as I felt her betrayal all over again. We had always unified against my father. It was the one thing that kept us steady. Now that was gone too. My father had successfully removed my very last ally.

I felt heavy hands on my arms as Grant jerked me around to face him. "Are you laughing?" he asked exasperated. "Do you not realize how serious this is?"

I struggled out of his grasp, but he was too strong to budge. "Leave me alone, Grant. If I felt like getting lectured and judged, I'd go find my father."

Grant let me go and turned as if he was going to leave, letting a heavy sigh hang in the air after him. Then I was in his arms, my head pressed against his hard chest as he held me tight.

"Do you have any idea what my world would look like without you in it? I haven't been able to breathe thinking I might lose you," he whispered softly.

I wanted to push him away, to get my bearing once again, but his arms felt so strong and safe, and it had been so long since someone had just held me that I stood frozen against him. His hand moved from my back to my neck, caressing my arm on his way. I felt his soft thumb on my cheek and then my head being tilted up. He was looking at me with an intensity that only comes with the kind of chemistry that Grant and I shared.

I shivered under his touch and watched as his eyes searched mine for some kind of response. I didn't give one...couldn't give one. I was standing on the edge of the cliff and any movement would send me over where I would have no hope of recovering.

Grant shook his head sadly. "After all this time, you're still running away from me. Why?" I stared at him blankly, pulling every memory of my father's infidelity and my mom's lifeless body to the surface in order to stay cold and distant from him.

"I'm not running, Grant, and you can't lose something you never had to begin with," I answered, coolly, easing my way out of his arms. "But, in case you haven't been informed, I'm sentenced here for the next eight months, when I will dutifully be released provided I show I can behave as the robot my father has trained me to be. Playing nice with you, however, was not part of the stipulation, so I'd appreciate it if you don't try to corner me again."

He stepped back as if I had slapped him and stared at me for a second before bringing his lips back to my ear. "Just so you know...I don't believe you. You may be able to hide from everyone else, Issy, but I see right through you."

It was my turn to be shocked as I watched him storm out of my room. My whole body was trembling, and I barely made it to my bed before collapsing. I had felt more emotion in the last three days than I had in the last three years, and the feeling was consuming me. I felt weak and insecure as I laid there staring up at the ceiling.

I had redecorated my room on my sixteenth birthday and now the recessed circle in the ceiling was pitch black, as were the walls, upholstery and bedding. It was a visual reminder of what my heart looked like. Somehow looking around the room made me feel better. It reminded me of my promise to myself. It reminded me who I was and how important it was to stay guarded in this place. My father could sniff out weakness, and destroy a person before they ever knew what was happening. He had done it with my mother and would no doubt do it with Anna whenever he got tired of her. Well, he'd made one critical error when he thought bringing me here would break me—he had already turned me to stone.

I looked at the large silver wall clock that hung over my corner fireplace. It was 6:30, leaving me thirty minutes to get ready. I swung my feet over the bed and headed towards the armoire with a purpose. Thirty minutes was plenty of time.

By the time I bounced down the stairs for dinner, I had a nice buzz going. Everyone was already seated when I came in the dining room and placed a small peck on my father's cheek.

"Hi, Daddy," I said sweetly as I took my seat. Then I nodded in the witch's direction. "Anna."

I saw a small smile start to move on my father's face before he caught it and scolded me. "You're late, Issy."

I looked up at the wall clock that showed I was exactly three minutes tardy. Good grief. "My mistake, I'm still on college time, I guess," I continued sweetly as I loaded up my plate. The one saving grace in this prison was Rosa's cooking. She had perfected the art of a family dinner.

My father cleared his throat and then began asking Anna and her illegitimate child about their day. I stopped listening the moment she opened her mouth and concentrated instead on the food in front of me. I went to reach for my glass when it dawned on me that they hadn't served wine with dinner. We ALWAYS had wine with dinner.

When Rosa returned to fill our glasses, I asked her

to bring me a glass of Merlot. She looked up at my father, and he informed me that we wouldn't be having wine with dinner for a while. I just shrugged my shoulders and continued eating in oblivion until my stomach was full.

I was starting to believe I would get through this dinner unscathed until I heard my father's voice turn to me.

"So Issy, classes at Carolina start next week. I spoke to an advisor at Winsor and registered you for some basic courses you seem to be missing. They should transfer back easily."

"Basic courses for what degree, Dad?" I asked sarcastically.

"Business, of course. What else would you take? It's nothing difficult, college algebra and Intro to Business will likely be the hardest ones on your schedule."

"I don't want to major in business."

"Ok, what do you want to major in then?" he asked calmly. I didn't have an answer and just stared at him, silently challenging his control. "Exactly what I thought," he continued. "This is a good course load no matter what you want to do."

The discussion was over, a fact left very clear by his body language. I realized sitting there that this was my father's best-case scenario. I had screwed up enough for him to take absolute control of my life, and no one would stop him because they believed as he did—that I was incapable of managing my own life. I felt the anger surge in me again as I fought for control.

"Can I please be excused?" I asked through gritted teeth.

My father saw my expression and nodded. I guess his tolerance for my outbursts was done for the day. I was moderately grateful and stormed through the door and out to the lake. The cold breeze from the water chilled me to the bone, but I liked it. I needed to feel numb.

6. WESTERN CAROLINA UNIVERSITY

After almost a week in captivity, I actually felt a little grateful for the escape that school brought, even though I had no intention of doing any more than was necessary to stay enrolled. My father had finally brought my car down from Winsor, so I at least had transportation again.

I stood looking in the mirror before leaving for school and smiled. My hair was a beautiful purple color, and I put back in my nose ring that I only wore when I wanted to tick off my father. My ensemble of tight black jeans, knee-high black boots and a tight black long-sleeved sweater adorned with multiple layers of silver chains and bracelets, just magnified my hair. It was exactly the first impression I wanted to make, and I smiled before taking two swigs of Vodka. I would need a replacement bottle very soon I realized as I swirled the last of the liquid around in a circle.

I intentionally swung by my father's office to say goodbye, and he looked up at me with a scowl. He was getting more and more agitated as the week went on. His need to "babysit" me had kept him in town far longer than I had ever seen. I secretly enjoyed the fact that Anna grated on his nerves almost as much as she did mine, which became more and more apparent the longer he had to spend with her.

"I'm off," I announced, walking into his office. Grant was sitting opposite of my father, with his back to me, but turned when he heard my voice. Seeing him after a week of avoiding all contact left me almost breathless. We locked eyes for a second, and he grinned, appraising my look. I grinned back and winked at him, knowing my father would catch the gesture and be even more annoyed.

"You look...interesting," was all my dad said before returning to whatever he was doing when I walked in.

"Thanks, Daddy, that was exactly what I was going for. See you tonight...seven sharp," I continued sarcastically. Grant was trying to hold in his laughter as this point, and while my father just waved his hand at me, I saw his ears get a very weird shade of red.

Mission accomplished, I thought as I started my car. There was no way my dad would make it another week in this house, and I was so ready for him to leave.

The drive to school only took ten minutes. While I had never been a student here, I was relatively familiar with the campus, or at least the main buildings. College bars were often the best for underage drinking, and Ben and I had spent many weekends here enjoying that perk.

I parked the car and headed to my first class,

Intro to Business, garnering second glances from most of the boys I passed by. I let them stare, moving my hips provocatively as I passed.

The class was about twice the size as Winsor's, easily two hundred chairs in a theater type setup. I stood at the bottom and looked around. Where I sat would be critical, and I needed to find someone immediately who would get me into a decent party scene.

Before I could settle on a location, I heard a whistle behind me as a dark haired hottie with two women perched on his arm walked by me. His hair was shaggy, falling over one eye casually and his ice blue eyes burned into mine as he passed. Most women would swoon from such a look, but it actually made me nauseous. Guys like that were the worst. They were totally aware of how cute they were and used it shamelessly to degrade and manipulate women. I rolled my eyes and kept scrolling through the crowd to find the perfect seat. It took only a minute for him to deposit his harem before finding his way back to me.

"You must be new here, because I have no doubt I would have noticed you before today," he said seductively as he stood in front of me, blocking my view. His arms were crossed, and I saw multiple tattoos climbing up his chiseled arms until they slid up under the sleeves of his black t-shirt.

"Not interested," I said flatly before moving around him. I was going to have to make this decision quicker than I wanted to. I found a row of empty seats that still had a good view of the class and sat next to the isle. The dark haired stalker followed me. I sighed, knowing I was trapped. Men like that were so sure every woman wanted them that they took dismissal as foreplay, making them pursue even harder.

He squatted down by my chair. "At least give me a name to go with those piercing green eyes, or I'm afraid I'll spend the whole class distracted and not learn a thing." He was staring up at me through long eyelashes, just waiting for me to cave.

"Listen," I said, annoyed. "I'm sure there are about a hundred girls in here just waiting for your charm and abuse, but I'm not one of them. Please go away." The chairs were quickly filling up and the longer he stayed next to me, the less likely my chances were at finding a real prospect for fun.

"A thousand girls would be a sad substitute for you, green eyes. Come on, just a name, what's the harm in that?"

It was becoming more than obvious that he was not going to leave, and I was about to give up when I finally spotted my savior. He was easily as tall as my dad with dark skin and a body that screamed football player. He had his cap pulled down over his eyes and his arms crossed as if he was catching a last minute nap.

"Excuse me," I snapped as I slid from the desk and made my way to the seat next to the sleeping giant. I set my stuff down and leaned into his ear whispering, "Make this idiot go away, and I swear I'll owe you." He didn't say a word, but I saw his eyebrow arch.

The dark haired stalker slid into the seat next to me and grinned. "Good choice. The view up here is much better…on many accounts." He started to lean into me, placing his forearm on my desk as he spoke.

The sleeping giant sat up in his chair and pulled his cap up off his face. He was even more intimidating than I previously thought. "I think you've got the wrong chair, Casanova, the lady's with me." His voice was steady and calm, but there was no room for argument. I took the hint and wrapped my small hands around his bulging bicep, feigning a hug.

The dark haired boy looked shocked, but finally left to rejoin his awaiting fan club. What possessed a woman to share her man was beyond me.

"Thank you," I said sighing as I released the giant's arm. "I'm Issy, and you are officially my knight in shining armor." I shot him my most charming smile and flipped my bright hair off my shoulder.

He wasn't impressed and just pulled his cap back down and went back to his hunched position. "Reggie," he said flatly, closing his eyes once more.

I decided right then that I liked Reggie. He didn't know it yet, but he was going to be my new partner in crime. I needed a Jake substitute, and he was the perfect fit. Handsome, intimidating, and totally not interested in me that way.

The class was as boring as the name implied it would be, and I spent most of it texting my friends from Winsor. I texted Jake, telling him my dad trapped me in a business class. His only response was to ask if I had heard from Avery today. I immediately tensed. Avery and I had talked every day since I got to my dad's, but I hadn't heard from her since Saturday. I knew she was still spending too much time with Jake, but she assured me nothing was going on.

Me: No. Why?

Jake: No reason. I'll call you later.

I sat up a little, knowing without question that something bad was happening.

Me: What's going on?

There was no response this time. I, in turn, texted Avery a question mark. No response either. I felt anger burn in my stomach. I hated this! I was completely out of the loop.

Class finally ended and Reggie woke back up. "I miss anything?" he asked sleepily.

"Nope. Guy figures we can't read and spent the hour going over the syllabus."

Reggie actually smiled, a row of white teeth visible against his dark lips. It made his brown eyes light up and made him appear much less intimidating, almost friendly.

I followed him out of the class and kept in step with him as he walked briskly across campus.

"So Reggie, how long have you been at Western?" I asked, practically running.

He slowed down so I could keep up and shot up his eyebrow again. "Sophomore, why?"

"Just making conversation. I'm new here, and you looked like my new best friend," I explained sweetly.

He laughed out loud and stopped to stare at me. "Who are you?"

I was amusing him which was perfect. "Issy. It's actually a very long, sad story that neither of us want to relive, so let's just say that I love to party and have fun, and you look like a guy who's got a few connections...and the ability to keep ego maniacs off of me."

"And what makes you think I have connections?"

Just then, two equally large men walked up to Reggie and did some kind of hand slap hello before settling appreciative eyes on me. I looked up at him and smiled smugly before introducing myself to his friends.

The shortest one with blond hair and blue eyes took the most interest in me, asking me all sorts of questions about school. I flirted back and before the conversation was over, had a personal invitation to a back to school party the football team was putting on. They had apparently rented out the alumni clubhouse for the night and promised a great time.

Before I could agree, Reggie's arm was around my shoulder, pulling me along with him. "Come on, Tink," he said shaking his head. "It's a good thing I have little sisters."

"Tink?" I questioned.

"Yeah, like Tinkerbell, the tiny, green fairy that wouldn't go away," he explained with a smirk.

I thought about it for a second and decided I liked it. Tinkerbell never grew up and could fly. Could there be a better nickname? "Works for me," I agreed as I curled my arm around his.

Reggie deposited me off at my next class and reluctantly agreed to meet me for lunch at the student union. This class was much smaller and more intense as most math classes often were. It had been two years since I looked at math and secretly wished Avery was still in the room next to me. She could do this stuff in her sleep. Oh well, I could buy old tests on line and at least pull a passing grade without much effort.

I exchanged numbers with a shy, smart girl named Kari, who took more notes in this one class than I had in all two years I was in college. Yep, she would be a good resource.

I quickly realized that Western Carolina was much like Winsor except everything was larger. The classrooms, the buildings and even the student union was double what I was used to. I perched myself on a bench outside and tried once again to text Jake and Avery while I waited for Reggie to show up. Still no answer. Something was definitely going on.

I looked up when I heard Reggie clear his throat and saw him standing hand in hand with one of the most beautiful women I'd ever seen. She was tall on her own, but her three-inch heels put her almost eye to eye with Reggie. Her skin was a light brown color that was so flawless I almost wanted to reach out and touch it. I watched as her full lips turned up to smile warmly at me and I returned the gesture, noticing the sparkle in her large brown eyes.

Reggie looked a little bored, but made the introductions. "Tink, this is Candace, my girlfriend." This was the best-case scenario for a girlfriend because there was no way she'd feel threatened by me.

"It's Issy, actually," I replied reaching out my hand. "But, since Reggie has been my savior today, I let him call me whatever he wants to. It's very nice to meet you."

Candace shook my hand politely and then let go of Reggie's hand so she could walk with me into the building. As we approached the food court, Candace filled me in on all the gossip regarding the people who would likely sit with us.

"The blond one you met today," she continued. "Don't ever take a drink from him or get in a room alone with him. He's not a good guy."

"Good to know," I said nodding.

"The rest of the guys are pretty harmless, but most of their girlfriends are territorial. Don't worry, though, you're with Reggie and me, so they'll be nice to you...despite how gorgeous you are," she said with a wink. "The only one really worth dating is Rusty. He's a genuinely good guy. Girls try and throw themselves at him all the time, and he never pays them any attention. He prefers the good girls."

I started to laugh. "Well, that certainly puts me out of the running," I admitted. "Doesn't matter anyway, I'm not the dating type. Too much restriction."

"Whatever you say, but maybe you should wait until you see him first." Her lips curled into a breathtaking smile and I knew right then she and I would be great friends. It made me almost want to thank the dark haired hottie who forced me into the seat next to Reggie. I had certainly hit the jackpot.

The table was almost full by the time we joined the group. The blonde from earlier waved at me, but I heeded Candace's warning and blew him off. He realized I had been warned and removed himself from the table in a huff. Candace was right about Rusty...he truly was one of the most handsome men I'd ever seen. Worse, he got better looking the more you got to know him because he was such a gentleman. It didn't matter, though, he was definitely not my type and truth be told, there were only one pair of eyes that could make me swoon and it wasn't Rusty's,

"Where are you headed to next?" Rusty asked when he saw me starting to pack up.

"I have English 282 in Ericson Hall," I answered, staring a little too long into his soft brown eyes.

"I'm heading that way too. Want to walk together?"

"Sure," I answered with a smile. He may not be a

guy I'd normally hang out with, but he certainly was eye candy and would keep me from getting lost as I searched for my building.

Rusty was definitely a gentleman, opening every door for me and taking me directly to my classroom. His large frame dwarfed mine, magnified by the cowboy boots he wore.

"So are you going to this party tonight?" I asked as we stood outside the door to my class.

"I hadn't planned to, but I may reconsider. Are you going to be there?" he asked with a shy smile.

"Of course! I'll look for you, maybe even save you a dance," I answered flirtatiously before waving at him and bouncing away into the class. I watched as he put his hands in his pockets and walked away. I finally realized why I liked him so much. He reminded me of Danny, the sweet boy from my apartment building. We hung out for a few weeks until he ruined it by declaring his love for me. I shook my head as I remembered the drama. I thought of Rusty's demeanor and realized I'd crush him in two weeks. Nope, I'd need to steer clear of that one.

I got myself settled and glanced down at the syllabus I had grabbed on my way in. My dad had all the books ready for me when I got home, so I hadn't actually looked at any of them. To my chagrin, I discovered this was a Shakespeare class. Even worse, the dark haired stalker from my business class walked in ten minutes after me and took the seat right behind me. He made a point to ignore me, but I was pretty sure it was just another tactic to get my attention. I slouched in my chair as the TA went on and on about the class. Our first assignment was an oral presentation of one of Shakespeare's monologues. Good grief. I was going to *kill* my dad!

7. PARTY CENTRAL

"Really Dad, Shakespeare? Are you trying to torture me?" I yelled as I stormed into his office.

He looked up from his computer and grinned. "What? Shakespeare's great, honey. It's full of complex comedies and heart-breaking tragedies. It should be right up your alley."

I ignored the obvious meaning behind his words and slumped down into the chair across from my dad, pouting. "I want to go see Mom for a while tonight," I announced. Truth was I had no intention of speaking to my mother, who had tried to call me at least three times a day since I got here, but I needed an alibi for the party tonight.

"That would be good; she's been worried about you."

"How would you know?" I asked rudely. My father and mother hardly ever spoke.

"Issy, your mother and I have talked every day since your accident. You should be happy. You always did want us to get along."

I felt rage crush my chest. "Whatever you are doing, you need to *stop* it," I ordered. "She is no match for you, and you know it! Just leave her alone and let her get on with her life."

84

My father looked at me like a five year old having a temper tantrum. "Really Issy, you are being overdramatic. Your mother and I have been friends for years."

I got up from the chair and stormed out without a word. So that's how he did it. He seduced her, made her believe she could trust him again. I felt the bile in my throat as I thought of my mom sitting on the phone, talking with my dad, hanging on his every word. She had never gotten over him. Eight months from now when she was no longer useful, it would end, and she would be heartbroken all over again. I wanted to hate her, but I just pitied her. Stupid woman.

Five hours later, I was ready to go. I had washed the purple out of my hair and just let my thick raven locks lay naturally down my back. I also settled on a pair of jeans, heels, and hid my red strapless bustier top with a fitted black jacket. My father would never suspect a night out in this outfit.

I had called my mom and somehow got through enough of her whining to tell her I had a study group tonight and wouldn't be able to make it. My father wouldn't be any wiser until tomorrow.

Grant was the only one home when I went to say my goodbyes. He took one look at me and stood up. "Wow, you look amazing."

My stomach betrayed me again, doing somersaults

as his voice penetrated my ears. "Where's my dad?" I asked looking bored. I didn't want to give my father any reason to call my mom looking for me.

"He's out with Anna tonight. Some gallery opening in town." Grant was speaking matter-of-factly, but never once took his eyes off me. I looked around the room, annoyed, until I noticed he was right in front of me, running his fingers through my hair. "Seriously, Issy, I haven't seen your hair this color in so long I forgot what it looked like."

I took his hand off my head, but he held on to it, and wrapped his other hand around my back, trapping me next to him. I started to feel lightheaded as his breath neared my ear. "Tell me you don't feel it," he whispered, sending waves of adrenaline down my body.

He pulled back enough to look me in my eyes which I knew for certain were clouded over with desire. "It doesn't matter, it's never going to happen," I answered softly, while my body language said something completely different.

He put his forehead to mine and let out a heavy sigh. "You haunt me, Issy. Your eyes, your smile, the way you look at me when you think I'm not paying attention, that perfect day…it all haunts me. Just tell me you don't feel it, please, so I can finally let you go." His voice felt desperate and so full of pain that I couldn't be mean to him, even though I knew I needed to be.

I reached up to touch his soft cheek. "I'm never

going to be what you need or deserve. I'm unfixable, Grant, even by you."

"I don't want to fix you, Issy. I just want to complete you…the way you complete me."

I felt the tears spring to my eyes and knew I had to get out of there, fast. His words were too perfect, too enticing. I wanted things with him that defied every promise I ever made to myself. But my body denied my request to flee and instead leaned up to kiss him unashamedly.

He responded, but not with the passionate fury that he had last time. This time it was pure intimacy, so soft and deliberate that my knees went weak. He took his time as if he was memorizing every contour of my mouth, and I let him, even though I felt the walls around my frozen heart crack a little.

When we finally parted, his eyes were all I could see, and I knew they reflected the same level of love that mine did. I wasn't even attempting to hide it this time.

"Stay here with me," he begged as he caressed my cheek, and I wanted to. I wanted to so badly that my feet felt frozen to the floor. But one night would turn into two and before we knew it, I would hurt him or he would hurt me. It was inevitable. Love was for the weak hearted, like my mother, not for me.

I found my composure and stiffened under his touch. He let go of me almost immediately and shook his head. "You're not even out the door yet, and you're already running," he accused, his caramel eyes darkening with frustration. "I'm not going to hurt you."

"Of course you're not," I said curtly. "Tell my dad to call if he needs anything." I turned and fled to my car. He didn't come after me or even text me this time. He just let me go and part of me wished he hadn't—the part I had every intention of re-burying the minute I got to this party.

The party was all it had been promised to be, and the mass of people made me even more grateful I had parked at Candace's house and rode with her and Reggie. They had freshman carding us at the door. I found the most nervous one and seductively placed my hand on his chest, leaning in to him.

"You wouldn't want to scar this soft hand with that red stamp, would you?" I purred as I watched him take a big gulp. "I don't have a wristband, so no one will serve me anyway."

He nodded shyly, letting me go through without the dreaded "under 21" stamp. I kept his eyes locked with mine until I had tucked one of the wristbands into my pocket. I rolled my eyes as I put on the band of freedom. This was getting almost too easy.

I waved at Candace who was already on the dance floor and pointed to the bar, before heading in that direction.

"What can I get for you," the bartender asked while I was digging in my small purse for some cash.

"Long Island Iced Tea," I ordered without looking up. When I finally did, I looked right into the ice blue eyes of my stalker from class who was grinning with pleasure.

"Do you believe in fate, green eyes?" he asked as he leaned his forearms on the bar.

I matched his stance, bringing our faces close together. "If I say yes, is this one on the house?"

"Baby, you say yes, and everything you want is on the house."

I leaned in a little closer before I popped the twenty-dollar bill right between our faces.

He snatched it out of my hand and raised his pierced eyebrow. "Tease," he said with a grin and started making my drink. Before handing me back my change and my drink, he looked sternly at me. "Don't take a drink from any of these guys here, you hear me? Only me, you got it?"

I nodded at his unspoken warning, thinking maybe he wasn't as bad as I originally thought, and headed to the dance floor to join Candace. Reggie was sitting at a table looking as bored as he usually did, and I smiled thinking Candace must have had to drag him to this thing. She already had a glimmer of perspiration on her face when I joined her. In minutes, I had finished my drink and just let the music take me. I had been a dancer at one point, even had a few trophies to show for it, but it all stopped when my heart went dead. On the dance floor, though, I started to feel a little alive. The extra shot my bartender had slipped in my drink wasn't hurting things either.

Several songs later, Candace grabbed my hand saying she needed a break. We giggled as we maneuvered through the crowd to Reggie's table. Rusty must have joined him at some point because he stood when we approached and gave me a shy, "hi."

I noticed him concentrating very hard on keeping eye contact with me while avoiding looking at the cleavage I knew my bustier created. Candace fell down exhausted on the chair next to Reggie and I excused myself for a moment, not really offering where I was off to. I headed straight to my dark haired bartender, who had my refill waiting for me when I approached.

"What's your name?" I asked loudly when he waved off my cash.

"Jason," he yelled back over the music. "Yours?"

I answered with a smile and a wink, leaving him to chuckle and shake his head. I found my way back to the table where Rusty stood up again when I approached. There was such a thing as being too nice, I decided.

We sat around getting to know each other as I sipped on my drink. Everyone else at the table had water or a coke, and I started to feel grateful I picked a drink that could be concealed. I watched all of them as we chatted. I had never had sober friends before and was surprised how much fun they were having just hanging out and dancing.

Rusty was especially funny and Candace was right about how the girls reacted to him. I lost count of how many came up to our table with the sole purpose of flirting with him. He was always nice to them, but would ease away when they would drape an arm over him or try and sit in his lap. I also noticed he never stood for any of them, a fact that both intrigued and concerned me a little.

"You've got quite a fan club," I teased after he brushed another girl off of him.

"Sorry about that. It seems the longer I stay single, the more determined they are to get my attention. It's gotten a little out of hand," he explained apologetically.

"So what's driving you to remain solo?" I was curious because he seemed more like the type to be serially monogamous.

"Just haven't met the right girl yet," he admitted.

"Really? Cause it seems you make that assessment pretty quickly."

He smiled at me, warm and genuine, and shrugged. "Maybe. But most of these girls here I've known for a while. Ever heard of football groupies?"

I laughed and nodded in understanding. He laughed too, exposing his dimples which made him even more handsome, if that was possible.

"I like your hair, by the way," he said nonchalantly. "Not that I didn't like the purple, or anything."

"Thanks," I answered with a grin. "You'll

probably see me sporting a whole lot more colors before the end of the semester. I never stick to any one thing very long." I was hoping he'd get the hint and realize that we were a less than suitable match, but as the night went on, I could tell his interest wasn't waning.

I finished my second drink, and while I was definitely feeling buzzed, I wanted more. I zigzagged back to Jason who once again had my drink ready for me. Before he handed it off, though, he leaned in to whisper in my ear. "That guy's got two point four kids and a white picket fence written all over him."

"Are you spying on me?"

"Call it observing," he answered with a grin before locking his eyes with mine. They were stunning eyes, so light blue that they almost looked silver. I prayed for butterflies, anything that would make me forget Grant, but there was nothing...as usual. "He doesn't seem much like your type."

"You don't know my type," I replied flatly as I reached for my glass. "In fact, you don't know me at all."

"A fact I'd like to remedy," he continued, refusing to let go of my drink, all while keeping my eyes captive. "Maybe we could start with a name?"

I shrugged and shot him my most playful smile which successfully convinced him to finally let me have the glass we were both holding. "Issy," I yelled over my shoulder as I walked away. I watched him grab his heart like he was having an attack and fall backwards. I laughed all the way back to the table and asked Candace if she was ready to hit the dance floor again. Thankfully, she was, because all I could see now when I looked at Rusty was a white picket fence which was starting to look very much like a prison.

Reggie ended our evening at one, declaring we had class in the morning. This was probably a good thing because I was completely drunk by that time. Jason had kept me refilled all night, and Rusty's constant attention had kept me drinking. I used all the available concentration I could to walk in a straight line out to the car, accepting Rusty's arm when he offered it. I cringed internally when I saw him smile and wondered why of all the women around him that he would choose me. Thankfully, he didn't try and kiss me. I would have to be very careful how I played this one. Reggie and Candace were too valuable to lose because I blew off their friend.

We were halfway back to Candace's house before they finally realized that I had been drinking. The world was going dark as I got comfortable in the back seat, laying my head down on the soft upholstery. I felt my stomach turn a little, but willed it back vowing I would not get sick in their car.

"Regg, I think Issy's drunk." I heard Candace say in a hushed tone.

"What?" he asked annoyed, and I heard his chair shift as if he was turning to look at me. "I knew I should have steered clear that first class, but no, I just had to butt in."

"Reggie, remember what Harry is always telling us. God puts people in our lives for a reason. I think there's a lot more demons in her than we realize. We are probably exactly what she needs right now. I wonder if she's ever even been around Christians before."

I heard Reggie sigh and tell Candace he loved her. Now I definitely knew I was going to get sick.

"Issy?" I heard Candace say as we pulled into a driveway. "I'm going to get your car and take you home. I need your address and your keys."

I handed her my purse and slurred the address to her before shutting my eyes for the final time. I didn't want to hear them talking about me like I was some pet project. I had been around Christians before. Parker was always talking about God to both Avery and me. And like him, they could try to save someone else. I had no interest in it.

Seconds later, I awoke to a door opening and Reggie's voice apologizing and explaining he had no idea I was drinking. Grant's honey sweet voice assured him I was a master at this type of thing and not to feel guilty at all. Ugh, they all needed to stop talking about me!

"Come here, Issy," Grant said sweetly as he pulled me out of the car. I did my best to move, but was of little help. Next thing I knew, I was weightless and held tight against Grant's strong chest. I heard him shut the front door softly and adjust my weight in his arms.

"Don't you get tired of this?" I slurred, louder than I intended.

"Hush Issy, you'll wake your father and he does not need to see you in this condition," Grant said sharply as we approached the stairs. I dramatically slapped my hand over my mouth and giggled, garnering another dirty look from him.

He managed to get me to my room without a scene and shut my door before laying me down on the bed. I felt the covers pull back and my shoes come off before my head rested on my soft pillow.

"Grant?" I said quietly, grabbing his hand as he was about to leave. He came back to me, kneeling close to the bed and touching my face with his soft caress. "I'm haunted too," I admitted before closing my eyes.

"I know, baby. I know. I'll wait for you. No matter how long it takes." He kissed my forehead and turned off my light, leaving me to the first dreamless night I'd had in over a week.

The morning light in my room was blinding even despite my dark walls. Grant had failed to pull the curtains shut last night, a gesture I'm sure was intentional. I turned my head over on my pillow and ran my hand along the floor, searching for my purse. I couldn't find it and opened one eye to spot it on my nightstand. I pulled it under the covers with me, the darkness finally allowing me to open my eyes fully. I closed them again as soon as my phone lit up and slowly texted Rosa to bring me up a green smoothie. The pain in my head was excruciating, worse than anything I'd ever remembered. My stomach turned, and I shot out of bed to the bathroom where I released the rest of the alcohol that had been sitting in my stomach. I hated it when I threw up, and rarely ever did. I felt a little better when I stood up, but the room was still spinning a little. Was I still drunk? Great, that should make conversation with my dad very interesting this morning.

I turned on the shower and stepped in thinking it would make me feel better. It did at first, but then the heat of the water and the steam started turning my stomach again, and before I knew it, I was releasing more alcohol down the drain. I sat on the tile floor, just letting the water stream over my body and tried to stop shaking. What was wrong with me? I never reacted like this to alcohol. Had New Year's changed my body that much?

I heard a knock at the door and assumed it was Rosa. "Come in," I yelled as loud as I could manage without bursting my ears. The glass door was foggy from the steam, but I could still see that it wasn't Rosa who came in carrying my drink…it was Grant.

I pulled my knees up to my chest, attempting to cover the important things and yelled, "Grant, what are you doing? Get out." My voice was not nearly as stern or loud as I intended. In fact, the faint rasp sounded pretty pathetic.

He set the drink down on the vanity and then folded his arms. "You have five minutes to get out and then we are going to talk about last night. At minute six, I'm coming in and will pull you out myself." His voice was *not* honey sweet this morning. It was demanding and direct, so much like my father that I wanted to throw my shampoo bottle at him.

"Your time starts now," he stated before walking back through the door.

Since I didn't feel like giving Grant a peep show, I turned off the water and put on my robe. I didn't bother brushing through the rat's nest that was now my hair and just sat on my vanity chair sipping my drink. It would be a cold day in hell before I took orders from Grant. If he wanted to talk to me, he could come get me, just like he threatened.

I stared at him defiantly when I saw my bathroom door burst open. He didn't say a word, just picked me up and carried me to the sitting area in my room. I felt myself being tossed into one of the chairs and almost spilled the drink I was carrying. I started to yell at him, but stopped because I could tell that was what he wanted, to invoke some kind of emotion from me. Instead, I just sat there, coolly drinking my smoothie with a stone cold look on my face.

"You are the most exasperating woman I've ever known," he accused running his hand through his light brown hair while pacing in front of me. I didn't respond, and Grant finally sat down next to me so his eyes could look closely at mine.

"You almost died of alcohol poisoning not two weeks ago, and you get wasted the first night out of this house? Are you trying to kill yourself?" he asked, looking almost as desperate as his voice sounded. I didn't respond. "Just so you know, your dad is on a tirade this morning, Issy. He knows you didn't go to your mom's, and I got the third degree all morning about what time you came in and where you were. I'm trying to protect you, but you are making it really hard for me."

"So don't protect me," I replied emotionless. "I never asked you to come to my rescue."

He stared at me in stunned silence before shaking his head. "He expects you down for breakfast which starts in fifteen minutes. You may not care, but I do, so can you please try and be there…and attempt to look somewhat presentable?" he asked looking me up and down. I had no idea what I looked like and honestly didn't care.

Grant put both arms on my chair and leaned into me, his voice turning noticeably softer. "I know you feel trapped, ok, and you think this is the only thing that helps. I've been there, Issy. I've been lost and felt hopeless, but I found an answer that is so much better than alcohol. Your father can be stifling, but can you even imagine what he's going to do if he finds out you were drinking last night? What if he takes you from here too?" I continued to stare at him with a stony look until he stood up defeated and walked out of my room.

I looked at the clock and decided it was better to face the firing squad on my terms. The smoothie was starting to work, and I was able to throw on some pajamas and brush out my hair. I dabbed a little make up under my eyes until it looked like I had just woken from a very restful night's sleep.

I made it to the dining table with two minutes to spare and shot my dad my sweetest smile as I put my napkin on my lap. "Morning, Daddy."

His entire body was rigid, and I turned to look at Anna who actually looked worried. Junior was oblivious as usual, just sitting there with a sweet look on his face. Darn that kid for being so adorable.

"Did you have a good time at your mother's?" my dad asked trying to get his voice to stay calm.

"What, you two didn't have your daily chat yet?" I replied looking surprised and slightly satisfied when I saw Anna's head jerk in my dad's direction. "There was a last minute study session I got invited to. Seems I got signed up for some really hard classes this semester, so I need all the help I can get. I told Mom last night that we'd reschedule. I'm surprised she didn't call you considering how close you too have become." I forced myself to take a bite of the toast on my plate, all the while my stomach was revolting against the food.

I watched as the hand curled around his fork went white with pressure as he glared in my direction. I continued to look up at him with the most innocent expression I could find.

Two deliberate bites later, my father had controlled himself enough to speak. "Kaitlyn, in the future, I expect a phone call if your plans are going to change." I had to give it to my dad, he was really good at keeping his temper in check around the little brat—a fact I would certainly use to my advantage in the future.

"No problem, Daddy. Now, may I be excused? I have to get ready for class."

He nodded in response, and I left the table, barely making it back to my room before the nausea hit again. I had no intention of going to class, but I doubted my father would even notice. I checked my phone for signs that Jake or Avery had answered the hundreds of texts I sent yesterday. Neither had. My gut told me something was very wrong, but I had no ability to deal with it right then. I slowly pulled the shades closed so that the room went completely dark and crawled back to bed. Sleep....I needed sleep.

8. ROAD TRIP

I spent most of Tuesday in my bed, only coming down for the mandatory dinner hour. My father asked me how my classes went, and I lied saying they were fine before changing the subject back to his day. Truth was I didn't even know what classes he had scheduled me for on Tuesdays and Thursdays. It didn't matter. All I had to do was pull a C in whatever it was.

I couldn't skip two days in a row, though, so I drug myself out of bed to get ready for the day. I felt too lazy to change my hair color again, so I just left it dark, comforted only by the fact that very few people had seen it that color. I was slightly concerned about seeing Reggie in class today. The details were hazy, but part of me remembered him not being so happy about me drinking. Why did everyone have such an opinion on how I lived my life? I threw on some tight jeans and a green silk blouse before grabbing a scarf out of my closet. I may be tired, but that was no excuse for not looking good for school.

I managed to avoid seeing anyone on my way out the door and slipped into the driver's side of my new BMW to find a note and a lily sitting on my seat. The flower had made the whole car smell, and the fragrance put a smile on my face. The note was from Grant thanking me for smoothing things over with my dad, noting that he knew I didn't have to. He also asked if I would meet him on the pier tonight. I smiled to myself before leaving and wondered how he knew lilies were my favorite flower.

The drive and Grant's note eased a little of my tension, but I felt nervous again as I entered my business class and was grateful I had gotten there early. I found the same seat I sat in on Monday and pushed down any anxiety. If Reggie was upset, I'd make him forgive me, simple as that.

I had just finally gotten myself calm when I saw Jason stroll into class. He was alone this time and immediately started looking around. I noticed he had cut his hair, making the once shaggy mop look more artistically messy. It looked good on him and made him look even cuter than before. He caught my eye, and his face lit up way more than was common after knowing a person for only two days. My stomach turned. Not him too. Well, at least there wouldn't be collateral damage with this one…and…he was a bartender. I smiled back. Maybe this admiration wouldn't be so bad after all.

"Hey beautiful," he said as he slid in the seat next to me, moving far in on my personal space.

"Can I help you?" I asked leaning away from him.

"Come on, I thought you and I were on a first name basis now." He knew I was playing with him, making his blue eyes sparkle in anticipation.

"That was when you were handing out free drinks," I stated, feigning interest in my fingernails. "In the light of day, I don't know, it's not so appealing."

He put his head down in frustration and then looked up grinning again. "You know you're breaking my heart, don't you?"

Before I could respond, I caught a glimpse of Reggie heading our way. "I recommend you take your broken heart somewhere else. Reggie doesn't look happy," I advised remaining as aloof as I had been through the whole conversation.

Jason took my advice and stood up, grabbing his backpack in the process. I lightly touched his hand, giving just a hint of a smile before whispering, "I like your hair." It was all he needed to know I was still interested, and he winked at me before finding another seat.

Reggie's eyes followed him before sitting down next to me. "I thought you didn't like that guy?" he asked in a gruff voice.

I just shrugged. "He's not so bad."

I was hoping that would be the end of our exchange, but Reggie continued. "Tink, about the other night…"

"I know, I'm sorry," I interrupted.

"No you don't know, so you need to listen. I don't appreciate being put in that situation. In the future, if you are going to drink when I'm responsible for you, I'd like to know and not be blindsided. Got it? We really like you, Issy, and want to hang out with you, but we're not into that scene. Judging from Monday night, you shouldn't be either."

My first reaction was to lash back at him. I'd never had a friend scold me before, and I didn't like it. Even Jake got an earful when he attempted to tell me what to do. Something in Reggie's face stopped me, though. It wasn't judgment, but genuine concern, and I felt slightly touched by it.

"That's fair. I won't drink when I'm out with you," I promised, closing the subject. He nodded, and we turned our attention to the fashionably challenged professor who was carefully explaining business terms I had been aware of since I was five years old.

The day continued much the same as it had on Monday, with the one difference being Rusty's obvious fascination with me. I don't think Reggie told him how the night ended, because Rusty still seemed to think I was "good" enough for him. Somehow, I managed to get through lunch without hurting his feelings. When he asked to walk me to class again, I declined, saying I needed to make an important phone call on the way, but next time. I excused myself from the group and found an obscure bench far away from prying eyes where I could check my text messages. There was still nothing from Jake who had been uncharacteristically absent since Monday. I scrolled down the list and noticed one from Avery asking me to call her.

I immediately dialed her cell, and she picked up on the second ring.

"Hey," she said, sounding slightly mellow. "Thanks so much for calling me back."

"Are you kidding? I've been trying to get in touch with you for days. What's going on?" I scolded, not hiding the irritation in my voice.

"Have you talked to Jake?" she asked, her voice sounding even sadder.

My stomach fluttered, and I sat up straight on the bench. "No, he's not answering my calls. What's going on?"

Avery hesitated for a second and then continued, "He's just having a hard time, Issy. Things between us, well, I ended it, and he's not taking it well." She hesitated again, and I jumped in.

"How hard of a time, Avery?" I asked, my voice exposing my concern.

"Hard enough that I had to stay at Parker's last night. You were right. I was fooling myself to think that we could be friends." I heard her sigh and then her voice sounded almost pleading. "He just needs somebody right now. I don't know what else to do. I know you are in class this week and all, but if there is any way you can get up here, I think you should."

Avery didn't need to say more. I knew Jake well enough to know that it was serious. I had watched him lose it two other times in our lives, when his mom died, and when we road tripped to Atlanta to find his dad—a fact he still doesn't know I'm aware of. If New Year's was any indication of his emotional stability, I needed to get up there...NOW.

I grabbed my backpack and headed straight to the parking lot, only concerned with one thing. I knew I was skipping yet another class, but I didn't care. I shouldn't be here anyway.

To my chagrin, my father was still home when I stormed in the house and up the stairs to pack. He stopped me on my way out the door, looking directly at the overnight bag in my hand.

"I'm going to Winsor tonight. I'll be back for class tomorrow," I stated without any room for argument.

"No," was his only response.

I attempted to pull my arm away from his grip with no avail. "Listen to me, I have done everything you asked of me, down to taking classes at a school I hate. I'm going to Winsor tonight, even if I have to sneak out while you are sleeping. Jake needs me."

My father rolled his eyes and snorted. He never understood my loyalty to Jake, and why would he? He had never been loyal to a soul in his life. "You're not going alone," he finally said, letting go of my arm.

"Dad, I'm almost twenty years old. I can handle a twenty-four hour road trip."

"Two weeks ago, your twenty year old self lay dying in a hospital bed. I don't want to hear it. You aren't going alone," he commanded.

"Fine. Who would you like to go with me?" I pouted, folding my arms in front of me.

"I've got some paperwork I need Steve to sign anyway. Grant can take it up there and keep his eye on you in the meantime," my dad said thinking out loud. Steve was one of Daddy's business partners. His son, Branson, also went to Winsor, so he spent a good deal of time up there. Our parents had tried unsuccessfully to set the two of us up on multiple occasions. Branson was a sweet guy, but that's a far as it went. My father finally stopped pushing it when I reminded him that breaking Branson's heart would not be good for his business relationship.

"I expect you at the breakfast table in the morning...and you better not be hung over this time." I jerked my head up to look at him, but he just raised his eyebrow at me.

"Fine," I groaned, grabbing my bag again. "I want to leave *now*, so tell Grant to hurry."

I sat on the steps waiting for only a few minutes before I saw Grant's car pull around to the front. I opened the back door and slid in behind him. He responded by turning off the engine.

"What are you doing?" I yelled, my temper already at a boiling point.

"I'm not going anywhere until you get in the front seat."

"Hey, I'm not the one who orchestrated this babysitting trip," I replied folding my arms in protest.

"Suit yourself. Just remember you're the one who's so eager to get there. I really don't even care if we go at all." He reclined his seat as if he was ready to settle in for a nap.

"UGH!" I screamed as I tore out of the back and into the passenger seat next to him. "Satisfied?"

"Very," he answered with a smirk and moved his seat back up. He started the car again and pulled out of the driveway. My nerves were fried. I had tried to text and call Jake three more times with no luck.

"Just hurry, ok?" I pleaded, looking at my phone again. Thoughts of my mother in the tub shot to my mind, but I pushed them out. Jake wouldn't do anything so stupid, would he? I really didn't know. He'd never been in love before.

"Do you want to talk about it?" Grant asked softly.

"Simple story really. Boy meets girl, boy breaks girl's heart, boy realizes he's an idiot, girl won't take him back. What can I say? Love sucks."

"That's a pretty bitter mindset, Issy," Grant lectured, glancing my way.

I turned to look him in the eye, making sure he saw I was being very serious. "It's the *only* mindset, Grant."

"Not every relationship ends like your parent's did." His voice was gentle, carefully treading on territory he knew I didn't want to discuss.

I felt my stomach burn. "Really? Name two couples you know who are still together? Just two. How about your parents? They still happily in love?" I challenged.

Grant scowled at me, and I sat back satisfied.

"Why do you still do this stuff anyway? I mean, you're a college graduate, yet you still do my dad's bidding. Besides, I thought your dad was some business guru himself. Why not work for him?"

He smirked at me before answering. "Not every task is so bad. I kind of enjoy some of them."

I rolled my eyes and he continued, "Honestly, I hadn't planned to still be working for your dad. My father had already promised me a senior position in his company as soon as I graduated. I told your dad that I'd be leaving in July and relocating to New York to work for my father. He was really happy for me and even promised to give a glowing reference for the time I spent with him."

"So what happened?" I asked, bothered by how much it unnerved me to think of Grant moving so far away.

"A few weeks before I was going to leave, rumors started flying that my father engaged in some illegal business deals. He promised everyone that he was innocent, but it didn't matter. The company's stock value started to drop dramatically and the Board of Directors suggested my father resign as CEO. Even though he was the primary shareholder, he agreed for the sole purpose of saving the company he loved so much."

I watched as Grant's face became solemn as he turned to look at me briefly before turning back to the road. "Your father really came to our aid, Issy. He bought my father's shares from him, promising to sell them back once he got back on his feet. Your father also hired him on as a senior executive in one of his companies. He even let me stay on despite the fact he had already hired my replacement."

I listened to his words with skepticism knowing my father had to have some ulterior motive.

"Grant, isn't there something else you could do, though? I mean, I'm sure you've had other offers. You can be so much more than just my dad's assistant." I wasn't sure why I was pushing this. Maybe knowing he had been so close to being free.

Grant stiffened at my words, apparently offended by them. "It may seem like a little job to you, but your dad is a very powerful man in the business world. I get to sit in on meetings and participate in business transactions that I never could as some junior associate in one of his companies. You may see it as just being his assistant, but after seven years of loyalty and service, your dad trusts me, and I know it will all pay off in the end."

"Whatever you say, Grant. But, let me fill you in on a little secret about my dad. He never does anything that doesn't first benefit himself, and he will abandon you and your seven plus years of loyalty the minute he sees fit to," I warned.

"Gees Issy, when did you get so cynical?" he asked, shaking his head.

I started laughing. "About two minutes after I was born. You don't grow up a Summers without a heavy dose of reality...and some very thick skin. I am sorry about your dad, though. I'm sure you were disappointed."

Grant smiled warmly at me and squeezed my hand. "It was a pretty dark time in my life, but I know now that I wouldn't be where I am today if I hadn't gone through it. I'm called to be content in all situations, and I'm learning how to do that with this one. God is in control, right?"

I didn't respond, mostly because I didn't want to discuss God or what Grant thought about Him. We continued to drive in silence until he started talking again. "You wanna know my best memory of you?" he asked smiling.

"Enlighten me," I responded sarcastically trying not to be affected by the way the sunlight was framing his perfect features.

"You were sixteen years old and had come to your dad's for the weekend. Not long after getting there, you found out that he was going to be gone all weekend, but still wanted you to stay and spend some quality time with your brother. He threatened to take away your car if you left. I went outside to sit on the pier because I was so angry at him that I worried I would say something if I didn't leave the room. The sun was just starting to set, and you walked out to the lake, never noticing me sitting there. I could tell you were crying, and I was shocked because I hadn't seen you cry since the night we met. Then, just when I was ready to go and try to comfort you, you started dancing. I couldn't pull my eyes away. You were wearing a white sundress and the sun behind you displayed your silhouette as you moved with such grace and strength that it took my breath away. In that moment, gravity didn't exist and you were as free as a bird. To this day, it's still the most beautiful thing I've ever seen. I broke up with my girlfriend the very next day because I knew I couldn't be with her when I felt what I did for you."

He smiled at me when he finished, his eyes showing total adoration. I felt his words linger in the air, chipping away at my defenses, threatening the resolve I was already struggling to maintain. I remembered that day as if it had been yesterday, but never knew he had seen me. My heart swelled and the feeling sent a surge of fear and anger through my body.

"What's your worst?" I asked, trying to stop the way my hands were trembling.

"What do you mean?"

"Our best memories of a person are often destroyed by our worst ones. So what is it? I know you have plenty to choose from." My voice was demanding as I looked expectantly at him.

"Why are you doing this? Why are you so intent on trying to make me hate you?" he asked, frustration seeping from his mouth.

"Because Grant, ever since my accident, you have somehow rewritten all the history between us and now have this idealized version of our relationship—which doesn't actually exist, may I remind you. I wont let you make me out to be something I'm not just so you can bang the boss's daughter." He gasped at my words, but I didn't relent. "What is your worst?"

"Besides right now?" he asked in a disgusted tone. I just raised my eyebrow and waited. "Ok fine, my worst was in July, the first time I saw you after we kissed."

"Why was that your worst?" I pried, unwilling to let him downplay the memory.

He let out another heavy sigh, something he always did when frustrated with me. "Everything was happening with my dad, and I just needed some kind of comfort. I had been anticipating seeing you all day, and when you walked through the door, you looked at me like I was a stranger. I wanted to hold you so bad my arms were shaking, and you acted as if you didn't even know me. That was my worst. Thanksgiving wasn't exactly fun for me either."

I watched as his face hardened, and I nodded, knowing I had made my point. "That feeling you've got right now in the pit of your stomach...remember it. That's all I have to offer you, Grant...heartache and disappointment."

Tension hung in the air between us like a blanket while the slight roar of the car engine was the only relief from the silence. Finally Grant spoke up, his tone back to the sweet honey sound that set my senses on fire. "I guess that's the difference between me and you, Issy. I'd take a hundred of your worst moments if it meant I could have just one of your best. You forget, I've already seen the person you try to hide from everyone else, and she is all I want. And it hasn't just been since your accident that I've felt this way…your accident just made me realize I may not have all the time in the world to act on it."

I wondered if it was possible to love and hate someone in equal measure, because that was exactly how I felt after Grant's words penetrated the thick walls around my heart.

9. WHAT A MESS

I leapt out of the car as soon as we got to my apartment, ready to be free of the heaviness still hanging in the air.

"I'm going to run this paperwork by Steve's house. Will thirty minutes be enough time?" Grant asked through the open window.

I just nodded and turned to run up the stairs. I couldn't wait to get home even if it was just for a few minutes. I put my key in the lock, but it didn't work. I tried one more time before the door suddenly swung open and Parker stood there with a tense look on his face. He immediately relaxed into a smile once he realized it was me.

"Expecting someone else?" I asked with an arched eyebrow.

Parker simply moved out of my way so I could come into the apartment. "Not really. Avery said you were coming by and asked me to meet you here. She had to work this afternoon and was running a little late."

I looked down at the useless key still sitting in my hand and took a defensive stance. "Do you want to tell me why my key doesn't work?" I didn't like feeling like a stranger in my own apartment at all and tried to keep my irritation in check. I knew Grant had set me on edge, and Parker didn't need me flying off the handle on him.

Parker walked over to the bar and picked up another set of keys. His whole body was rigid, and I realized for the first time that Parker was tenser than I'd ever seen him. "Before I give these to you, I need to know you are not going to give one of them to Jake."

I eyed him defiantly. He obviously hadn't been informed that I don't like being told what to do, a feeling that was unquestionably magnified after two weeks with my father. I watched his face soften a little, and he reached out to hand me the keys. "Issy, I know you and Jake are extremely close, and you would do anything for him. I actually really respect that. But, I'm asking, for Avery's sake and for mine, that you not give him a set of keys while you aren't living here." I watched as he ran his hand over his stiff neck and let out a sigh. "I won't be able to sleep at night knowing he can come in here whenever he wants to, whether invited or not."

I took the keys out of his hand and shot him a smile that I hoped would relieve a little of the tension in the room. "Wow Parker, I never pegged you for the possessive type," I accused playfully.

He just shook his head. "I wish that were it. Jake's been…in a word…relentless."

I waited for details, but they never came so I just

sighed and headed to my room, leaving Parker to wonder what I was going to do. After I felt he had suffered enough, I came back out of my room and leaned against the doorframe with my arms folded. "Ok, I won't give him the keys. But, I'll be back in the fall, and I will give him a set then."

"Thanks Issy, I appreciate it," he said looking visibly relieved. "Avery just texted that she is on her way. Do you mind if I stick around and wait for her?"

"Suit yourself," I called out before storming through my room, packing all my favorite outfits and any bottles of liquor that weren't empty. But as much as I searched, I could not find the one thing I was specifically looking for. At Christmas, Avery had given me a small silver flask with my name on it. It was one of my most favorite possessions, and I wasn't leaving here without it.

Finally after tearing apart the room, I found it under my bed, still filled with some very fermented liquid. I rushed to the kitchen sink and cleaned it out before it made me sick. Then I closed it up with soapy water still in there, hoping to kill whatever had been growing in the small bottle. Parker was watching SportsCenter on the couch and the nostalgia almost brought tears to my eyes. Jake had been doing the same thing for years, and now everything was different.

Before I had time for a pity party, Avery came tearing through the door, out of breath. "Did I miss her?" she asked frantically to Parker.

"I'm in here," I called, leaning over the bar.

She rushed to me and practically knocked me over with her hug. "I'm so happy to see you!" she cried with tears in her eyes. Stepping back, Avery looked me over with a smile. "You look so good; all your color is back. Goodness Issy, last time I saw you…" she had to stop herself as tears started to roll down her cheeks. I couldn't help but chuckle. Avery was the worst at hiding any type of emotion, but I sort of loved that about her.

She noticed the flask in my hand and scowled. "I hate that thing. I should have thrown it in the trash with the rest of your bedding."

"No way! I love my flask."

"That flask almost killed you, Issy." Then she looked up at me with a horrified expression. "Please tell me you've quit drinking."

"Let's go talk," I offered, my eyes motioning to Parker. She seemed to understand my need for privacy and followed me to my room. After I shut my door, Avery looked nervous. She sat on my bare mattress and was fidgeting with her hands before looking up at me.

"I don't think I can ever be in this room without thinking of that night," she admitted quietly. "I've never been more afraid in my entire life."

"Well as you can see, I'm fine. I've been drinking for years, Avery, without any problems. I just over did it one night."

She looked at me incredulously and shook her

head. "I know I can't tell you what to do, but can you promise me to at least try and cut back?"

"You know I don't make promises, I don't intend to keep," I answered honestly. Avery just nodded, and I felt a twinge of guilt. "Ok, enough about me. Tell me what's going on with Jake." I put the precious container in my purse and then set the rest of my bags by the door before turning back to her.

She looked up at me with her eyes wide. "He's out of control, Issy. When I left his apartment on Monday, I thought that was it. He was angry, but he walked away. But then that night, it was like he was watching me, because the minute Parker left, he came storming in the apartment demanding to talk to me. He said he refused to let me go and that I was confused."

I watched as she relived the scene in her head and saw her shiver as she quit talking. "What did he do, Avery?"

She shook her head and fidgeted some more. "He just got rough, but I know he wasn't in the right frame of mind. He was so drunk, Issy. I've never seen him like that. I don't even know how he got up the stairs. I finally just conceded and held him until he passed out. Then I left and went to Parker's."

I glanced nervously at the door. "You didn't tell him, did you?"

"Of course I did. We don't keep secrets anymore. I learned my lesson the hard way on that one."

I immediately understood why Parker was so tense when I walked in the door. "Did Parker confront him?"

"No, but only because I begged him not to. Call me crazy, but I actually think that's what Jake wants, someone to turn all of his fury toward." She shivered again. "No, Jake and Parker need to stay far away from one another. But, that's kind of why I called you. I didn't come back home until this morning when the locksmith met me here to change the locks. Jake was gone, but...he sort of trashed the place, especially my room. He tried to call me several times, but I haven't picked up. I'm sorry, I just cant be the one he turns to anymore. It's not healthy for either of us."

I closed my eyes and rubbed my temples. This was so much worse than I imagined. Jake had done the same thing when Aunt Kathy died. My mom and I just watched in horror as he ripped apart his bedroom in a fit of rage before completely collapsing in tears. Fear gripped my stomach again as I realized he was all alone. I had to get to him. "Don't apologize, Avery. You were absolutely right to call me. I'm just sorry about your room."

She shrugged and then stood up from the bed. "It's fine. He really only ruined one thing. Odd thing is, he destroyed his favorite picture in the room...the bridge."

A knock on my door stopped the conversation as I heard Grant ask if I was ready to go. I pulled open the door and pointed to my bags.

"Hey Avery," Grant said cheerfully as he grabbed the two duffels. "It's nice to see you again."

"You too," she replied skeptically and then turned to me after he left. "What's Grant doing with you? I thought you hated him."

"I do," I retorted with a shrug.

She slanted her eyes at me and then smiled. "You're totally lying. You like him, don't you?"

I was shocked she could read me that easily and immediately voided my eyes. "Need I remind you of a certain brown haired boy from the third floor? Don't go there."

She lifted her arms in surrender and walked into the living room. Avery had been the one to push me on Danny despite my warnings. She got to see first hand that I wasn't kidding when I told her I didn't do relationships.

I glanced around my room one more time before leaving. The emptiness made me sad and regretful. For the first time since New Year's, I wished I had done things differently. It seemed unfair that one stupid moment could rob me of so much. I pushed the thought out of my head and pulled myself together. I was here tonight, and right now being with Jake was all that mattered.

Grant was still at the door talking to Avery and Parker as I locked my room back up. I joined the group and gave them both one last hug before leaving. "I'm glad you're happy," I said to Avery as I released her, and I really was. She looked more at peace than I had ever seen her.

"I am, and I want to tell you all about it sometime." She hesitated and then looked determined. "I want to tell you about what Christ did for me, ok?"

I rolled my eyes, but said, "Ok." I guess Parker had finally gotten to her too. She hugged me one more time before I bolted down the stairs, attempting to hide how sad I was to leave.

Grant was already loading my bags in the car when I joined him and he shot me a disapproving look when he heard the bottles clang in one of the bags. "Did five days in the hospital not teach you anything?" he lectured as he shut the trunk.

"Save it, Grant. You're my ride, not my conscience. Now let's go!" He slammed the door and started the car, still sporting his "unhappy" face. I turned to examine him and asked, "Seriously, do you ever just have fun? I mean really, really let loose?"

"Issy, not every one needs to drink to have fun."

I nodded, feeling a challenge coming on and knowing I had my flask nicely secured in my purse. "Ok then, you are going to come out with Jake and I tonight, and I want you to show me that you can have fun…without alcohol."

"You're inviting me out with you?"

"Only if you aren't going to be the stiff old guy in the bar, and you change out of those ridiculous khaki's," I challenged, eyeing his perfect form.

A slow, seductive smile crept across his face. "You're on."

I sat back and grinned, my mind scolding me a little for wanting to spend time with him. It was just too big an opportunity to miss. We were away from my father, free of the roles we had played for years, and I couldn't help it. I wanted to see what Grant looked like in my world.

We pulled up to Jake's, and I felt my stomach turn. Now that I was here, I kind of wanted to run away. I plastered on my most easy going smile and grabbed my bag. "Varsity Club, ten o'clock," I reminded him playfully.

He just grabbed my hand and looked right through me. "You ok? I can come with you if you want."

I scowled back at him. "Stop doing that. I don't need you to protect me."

He pulled his hand back sadly and watched as I walked up to Jake's door. He didn't drive away until I was safely inside and had shut the door.

"Go away!" I heard Jake call from his bed in a drunken stupor. I felt relief flood though me. I could handle drunken Jake.

"Well, I would, but I keep getting complaints of the stench coming from your apartment. It smells much like a pathetic idiot who had the misfortune of falling in love." I jumped out of the way as Jake's shoe came flying over the rail and almost caught my leg. The soles of my shoes were crunching broken glass as I walked around the small space, observing the mess. I leaned down and found two frames that were irreparable. One held a black-and-white picture of a zip line and black glove. I carefully removed it from the glass and turned it around.

For when you need to remember her.
Avery

I set it down carefully, understanding why Jake had thrown it across the room. The other frame held a close up picture of Avery that was breathtaking. Jake must have taken it when she wasn't aware because the photo was a shot of her looking at something in the distance with a soft smile. Her wavy hair looked like spun gold being blown away from her face and her silvery blue eyes were sparkling. She looked genuinely happy. I let out a heavy sigh.

"Hey Jake, since you obviously don't want these pictures anymore, I'm going to toss them with the glass, ok?" I yelled up to him.

"Issy," Jake warned, not moving.

I pulled out the broom and started sweeping. "If you want them, you're going to need to come and get them. Otherwise, they're going in the trash."

I heard Jake's bed creak and then him take the stairs two at a time before pulling the pictures violently out of my hands. I watched as he very carefully set them in-between the pages of a book so they wouldn't get damaged in any way.

"You look terrible," I announced walking up to him. "And you don't smell all that great either."

Jake looked at me with disgust and then turned away to head back up to his bed, grabbing a half empty bottle of Jack Daniels on his way up. "What are you doing here anyway? I thought you had a one-way ticket to soberland. As you can see," he continued, showing me the bottle. "We are doing just fine."

"Jake, I have no problem with you drinking, but at least if you are going to do it, have some fun with it. Don't just hole yourself up in sweaty sheets and pout. Let's go out. I'm only here for one night."

I heard the bottle hit the floor as Jake fell back on his bed. "Of course you are, because everyone always leaves. My dad, my mom, you, Avery. Liars. That's what all of you are. She said she would always be there for me. Told me she loved me. Instead, she changed her locks. Can you believe that?" He was laughing at this point—a scary kind of laugh that usually came right before a breakdown. Then there was silence. I walked upstairs, and he was asleep, sprawled facedown on his bed. I took the bottle out of his hand and threw some covers over him. I'd let him sleep it off for a few hours before waking him up.

I finished cleaning up his mess and then poured myself a drink, savoring the dark liquid as it burned my throat, numbing me. But the longer I sat alone listening to him snore, the more irritated I became, and finally I stormed back up to his bed to take a picture of his sorry butt, so he would never forget what an idiot he was for letting his defenses down. After making sure I got a good one of him drooling, I kicked him with my foot.

"Alright, the self pity party is over now. Get up."

He responded by slapping my foot away and turned over. I stormed back down the stairs and filled a pitcher full of ice-cold water, which I poured all over him minutes later.

He leapt out of bed and stared at me in disbelief. "What's wrong with you?" His voice was full of fury and disorientation.

"What's wrong with me? Look at yourself. You and I had a pact, Jake, for this very reason. Is this really who you want to be? Some slobbering jerk who's pining for a girl that doesn't want him?" I felt my voice rise uncontrollably as all the fear I'd felt since Avery's call fueled my rage. "You are as bad as my mother!"

He stared at me blankly, his head drenched from the water I had poured on him, and then just hung his shoulders and started crying. I rushed to him and held him tight, feeling the fury leave me as I allowed him to cry without any shame.

"Just make it stop hurting, please Issy. I just want it to stop."

"I wish I could, Jake," I whispered as I rubbed his back. "If I knew the secret to doing that, I'd have a much different life right now. You've got to just block her out and move on."

"But I don't want to. Being with her was the only time I felt alive."

Jake was slowly getting himself under control and we sat on his bed side by side, my arm still around him. "Jake, you didn't feel that way because of her. She just gave you the freedom to pursue it. If you want to feel alive, then go live. Party, break a few hearts, skydive, do whatever you have to do to feel something. Just don't be this person."

He chuckled and then held me tight. "I could give you the same advice."

"Jake, I live with my father. Talk to me when I'm out of survival mode. Speaking of which, I only get one night of freedom, so you have to pull yourself out of this slump and go out with me."

He smiled at me before kissing the top of my head. "I'm so glad you're here."

"Good. But you really do need to go shower." I urged pushing him away. "I mean, seriously…you stink."

"Fine. But not before I do this…" And next thing I knew, Jake had poured the remaining water from the pitcher over my head before running down the stairs. I chased him, and we engaged in a water fight until both of us were laughing uncontrollably and drenched from head to toe.

When a truce was finally called, Jake threw me a towel and stuck out his hand. "Pact reinstated?" he asked with renewed determination.

"You tell me." Our matching green eyes locked and he nodded. I shook his hand, and dismissed the picture of Grant that shot in my head when I did so.

10. VARSITY CLUB

My heart was heavy with anticipation as Jake parked the car. I told myself it was because I hadn't been here in a while, but deep down I knew it was because Grant was coming out with me for the first time ever. I had taken great care to make sure I looked irresistible tonight wearing tight, blue marbled leather pants and an army style t-shirt with multiple holes in it. I kept my hair dark at the roots and put silvery streaks in at the tips. Jake confirmed I was stunning and reminded me that I shouldn't ever dress like that when he wasn't around to look after me.

Jake had sobered up enough to drive, but I had a nice buzz already going and fingered my flask tucked deep in my purse. Grant would surely be watching me like a hawk, and I knew the bottle held just enough to keep me sated for the night.

The music boomed when we walked in, and I saw Jake's face tighten just a little as I was sure memories flooded his mind of Avery and their first night out together.

"You ok?" I asked over the music.

"Yep," he answered with a smile that looked forced. "Time to make new memories, right?" Just then a leggy blond walked by and gave Jake a very inviting stare and smile. He followed her with his eyes and then looked back at me.

"What are you waiting for?" I asked with a laugh. He winked and bounced off in her direction. I looked up to see who all was here from school and immediately locked eyes with Grant who was waiting at the bar. He stood up to come over, and I felt my knees start to tremble. I'd never seen him look so devastatingly handsome. He had changed out of his normal work attire and into some stylish jeans that looked like they had come right off the runway. The crew-necked black shirt he wore fit him like a glove and magnified his broad chest.

My eyes never strayed from his until he reached me and wrapped his arm around my waist, pulling me up against him. "You never fail to take my breath away," he whispered in my ear before kissing me softly on the cheek. It was right then that I knew I didn't want any barriers with him tonight. I'd go back to being numb tomorrow, but tonight, I was going to take some of my own advice and live a little.

I shot him a mischievous smile and pulled him on the dance floor, moving against him as if we were the only two people in the room. He responded, but used his strong arms to dictate our movement, keeping it controlled and noticeably PG rated. I wrapped my arms around his neck and pulled him close to me, leaning in to kiss him.

He moved his lips past mine and whispered in my ear. "I'm not going to kiss you like this."

"Why not?" I asked pulling back in confusion.

"Because I feel like I'm on display in here, and I'm not going to let you cheapen us to some one night stand."

Insulted, I turned and stalked off the dance floor. I hadn't gotten too far before I felt him grab my waist and spin me back around. "Issy, stop it. I *want* to be here with you. You're the most gorgeous woman I know and believe me, I want nothing more than to kiss you. But not when you're just going through the motions. Can't you just let yourself go?"

"That's what I'm doing!" I yelled, exasperated.

"Not your body, Issy. I want all of you. I want the girl I saw on the sand."

I stared into his pleading eyes and let him pull me back out to the dance floor. I followed his lead and just let the music fill me up, allowing my mind to shut off and let my body take over. Grant moved with me as if he had been designed to fit perfectly. His fingertips burned every surface of my skin, and I allowed mine to move along his chest and arms freely. I was so absorbed with him that I barely noticed when an hour had passed without so much as a sip from my flask.

Grant and I moved to the couches to catch our breath and drink some water. He looked genuinely happy as he pulled me next to him, keeping his arm wrapped tightly around my shoulders. I liked seeing him look that way. His eyes had a sparkle to them that was so often absent when we were at my dad's.

Jake wasn't too far from us, making out with the blond he had followed when we first arrived. He pulled away when he saw us sitting down and walked over.

"Grant," Jake said putting his hand out to him. "Issy didn't mention you were here."

Grant reciprocated the handshake and then settled back next to me. I watched how Jake's eyes appraised how close we were sitting and the way Grant possessively held me. Jake stiffened, and I knew exactly why. He and Grant had never gotten along. Jake was one to hold a grudge and had never forgotten how Grant scolded me the day they first met.

"Grant's my babysitter for the evening," I explained giving Jake the stare that screamed for him to butt out. "Having fun over there?"

"I could ask you the same question." Jake didn't release my eyes as he spoke. "Need I remind you of a little pact we made?"

"I'm not the one who broke it the first time," I answered back in the same cold tone.

Grant looked between us, a silent battle obviously occurring. "Care to fill me in?"

"No," we said in unison, and Jake finally turned away.

"Fine. As long as you know what you're doing," Jake scoffed, dismissing the conversation. "Grant, can you make sure she get's back to my apartment in one piece? I've got an invite that I don't plan to turn down." And with that Jake was leaving with the blond.

Grant shook his head in disgust. "I guess Jake's over the girl you mentioned."

"Not really, but he'll be one step closer after tonight." Grant's head snapped around to stare at me. "What?" I asked when I noticed he was angry.

"Do you even hear yourself, Issy?"

"She didn't want him. What's he supposed to do?" I asked defensively.

"You know life isn't always about self preservation. Sometimes people come into your life for a short period of time, but it's always for a purpose. You don't just dismiss them because they disappoint you or are no longer useful."

I stood up angrily and crossed my arms. "You know, for a moment there, I actually thought you and I could have some fun. But here you go again, trying to change who I am. Listen, I'm *glad* Jake isn't alone tonight, ok? I'm glad I'm not going to find him wasted in his bed again, heartbroken. I happen to appreciate self preservation."

Grant wasn't backing off and stood up to face off with me. "Call it whatever you want to, Issy, but in the cold morning light it's all the same thing…denial. The sad thing is that you've been living in it for so long now that you don't even recognize it."

I felt my stomach start to knot as he stared at me. It was so infuriating how easily he could get to me with just a simple statement. "I'm going to the ladies room," I snapped, grabbing my purse.

Grant caught my arm before I could storm off. "Don't you dare leave this place without me." I was ready to blow off his comment and walk away, but something in his eyes stopped me. There was a silent warning there that I found both intimidating and irresistible.

When he saw I understood, he let go of my arm. I practically fled to the bathroom, my hands shaking as I pulled out the flask in my purse. I had the equivalent of three shots before I finally calmed down and had my barriers firmly back in place. I fixed my hair and touched up my makeup before examining myself in the mirror. My emerald eyes were cold and distant. I smiled, exposing the poised lady I was taught to be, and headed back out to find Grant.

He sat stiffly on the couch, keeping his eyes peeled to the door. I watched how the women around him were noticing him and felt a twinge of something I hadn't felt since I was thirteen years old. I pushed it down, reminding myself that I didn't care and bounced over to him as if the conversation never happened.

"You ready to dance?" I asked sweetly when he stood to face me. I could tell he was prepared for another battle and seemed genuinely surprised by my change in attitude. That surprise turned to frustration as I stared blankly at him.

"No, you go ahead. I'm not at all interested in this person," he said curtly.

I let his words deflect off me and shrugged. "Suit yourself." Then I was gone. I spotted a group of people I knew from school and joined them on the dance floor. They all welcomed me in with open arms and told me how much they had missed me. I felt the last few weeks fade into a distant memory as I absorbed myself back into my old world. A world where there was no judgment and no one was waiting around, trying to save me.

Two hours later, I had emptied my flask and exhausted myself on the dance floor, floating between so many partners that I had lost count. I was ready to go and went to search out Grant. He was still seated on the couch where I had left him, but was now engaged in conversation with a beautiful brunette whose legs were crossed towards him and whose hand flirtatiously touched his arm whenever she could. I studied him, waiting to see how he reacted to her, and smiled when I saw his face. He looked antsy and slightly annoyed until he looked up and saw me standing there. Without a second thought, he stood up and walked towards me. Before I could say a word, I felt his hand on my neck as he pulled me in to kiss him. It was hard and deliberate, almost angry, and I could taste the alcohol in his mouth. So much for him not drinking.

The kiss ended as abruptly as it had begun, and he put his forehead to mine. "Can we leave yet, or are you planning to torture me all night?"

I didn't say a word, just headed to the door with Grant in tow behind me. Neither one of us were in any condition to drive, so I hailed a taxi that had us back to Jake's within minutes. Grant was stumbling to the door and it felt odd to see him in that condition. He was always so controlled and calm. The minute I opened the door, he fell straight on Jake's couch and moaned.

I shut it behind us and got Grant some water and aspirin, feeling very much like I was stuck in opposite day. He sat up to swallow the pills and water, and then put his head in his hands. "I never drink like that."

"Well there's a first time for everything," I said as I kicked off my shoes and set my purse on the chair. "Don't worry, I won't tell my father."

"I don't want us to be like this." He glanced up at me, and his face looked pained.

I walked over to him and kneeled down, taking his face in my hands and looking him right in the eye so there was no confusion. "Grant, there is no US. If tonight showed anything, it's that we are totally incompatible."

He started laughing and pushed my hands off his face. "You are such a liar, Issy. I don't even think you recognize the truth anymore. We're so compatible that it terrifies you because I won't put up with your crap." His voice had lost all humor at this point and he grabbed my arms trapping me in front of him. "I saw you dance with every single one of them. I saw the way you manipulated them. You and I both know that's not what you want."

"You're drunk, Grant. Go to bed." I was struggling to get out of his grip, but he wouldn't let go, his eyes begging me to give him some kind of validation.

"Well, I have to hand it to you. You exceeded your worst tonight," he finally said, completely defeated. I felt his hands drop from my arms as he fell back against the couch, closing his eyes in the process.

Tears stung my eyes as I watched him sleep, resisting every urge to caress his hair and tell him I was sorry. I had hurt him on purpose. I just didn't realize how much seeing it would hurt me too. As much as I tried, as much as I fought it every day, it was no use. I genuinely cared about him.

I lost count of how many minutes I sat watching him sleep, but it was long enough to memorize every part of his face. I noticed a small scar under his chin and wondered where he got it. I also noticed that his eyebrows were just slightly darker than his hair and that he would periodically smile in his sleep. I let my fingertips slowly explore his face, running the tips over every section I had just examined. When he shifted under my touch, I quickly pulled back, not wanting to wake him.

It was 3:00 a.m. when Jake finally came through the door, and I hushed him so he wouldn't wake up

Grant.

"You still up?" he whispered, looking shocked. "And sober too?" He then noticed Grant laid out on the couch, fully clothed, and arched an eyebrow.

I pointed for Jake to follow me up the stairs. He grabbed us some waters and then pulled an extra blanket and pillow out of the closet. I was sitting with my legs crossed leaning up against his headboard when he finally joined me, taking a seat right next to me.

"Did you have a good time tonight?" I asked once he was settled.

He just shrugged and handed me the water bottle. "It was fine."

"Not as therapeutic as you had hoped, huh?"

Jake just sighed and leaned his head back against the headboard. "I think it's going to take a lot more than a one night stand to get over her." He looked back at me, noticing the pain in my face. "You want to tell me what happened?"

"I happened. What else?" I admitted with a sarcastic laugh.

"You care about him, don't you?"

"I think I always have, Jake. It's been seven years now, and fighting the attraction doesn't seem to get any easier."

"Well, it's obvious he feels the same way. You ready for all that entails?" Jake asked cutting right to the heart of my fear.

"No, of course not."

"Then I'd walk away now…while you still can."

I threw my hands up in exasperation. "I've tried. I've been cold, cruel, direct and even tried to seduce him so we'd just get it out of our system. It doesn't seem to phase him."

Jake started laughing and shook his head. "Yeah, that's what happens to men when they are in love. I knew the first time I kissed Avery that she was different. I should have stayed away…I just couldn't."

"Do you think if maybe if you hadn't tried to fight it so hard, things would have turned out differently?"

"At first I did. Lost a lot of sleep over that idea. But I realize now that it really wouldn't have mattered. I was going to destroy her either way. There's just too many demons in here for any sort of stable relationship. Part of me is happy she has Parker."

I gave him a look that told him clearly I did not believe him.

"Ok, it's a very small part of me. The other part still wants to beat his face in."

I chuckled and rested my head on his shoulder. "So where do we go from here?"

Jake put his head down on mine and sighed. "I don't know, kiddo. I honestly don't know."

139

11. BUSINESS MARKETING

The soft chime from Grant's phone woke me up before he could move to silence it, and I stretched across Jake's bed not wanting to move. It felt as though only minutes had passed since Jake and I finished our long conversation last night, but the lack of sleep was worth it. We hadn't been that open and honest with each other since my aunt Kathy died, and it felt good to have our friendship back, even if just for a night.

I tip toed down the stairs when I heard Grant shut the bathroom door and tried to stop the anxiety that hit when I saw his black shirt lying over the side of the couch. Last night had been horrible, and I just wanted to pretend it never happened. I heard the shower turn on and started rummaging through Jake's kitchen for the ingredients to go in my hangover juice. Maybe Grant would take it as a peace offering.

While Jake was normally good about keeping my green leafs on hand, his refrigerator definitely showed signs that he had been alone for the past couple of weeks. Oh well, there was enough in there for me to throw something together that might at least take the edge off the headache I knew Grant would have.

Once his drink was tucked safely in the fridge, I

busied myself by getting as ready as I could without a bathroom. I propped my portable vanity mirror up on the bar and tried to make my face look as fresh and well rested as possible. We had to be at breakfast in two hours, and I knew my father would be looking for any excuse to pull me from Winsor permanently. My father didn't agree to let me go on this little road trip because he cared; it was a test, and we both knew it. I braided my hair loosely so I wouldn't have to deal with the tangles and quickly threw on some comfy jeans and a t-shirt before Grant finished up.

By the time he emerged from the bathroom, letting the steam from the shower escape into the hall, I was completely ready to go and had my bag waiting by the door. He seemed hesitant as he approached me and refused to make eye contact.

"I made you some hangover juice," I offered, setting the drink on the counter. "It's not full strength, thanks to Jake's bare kitchen, but it's enough to take the edge off. I doubt my father will even notice."

Grant just nodded and continued to stuff his old clothes into the duffle bag he brought. He was back in work mode, complete with the stiff khaki's and button up shirt I'd come to expect on him. His tie lay around his neck untied and his feet were bare, but other than that, it was as if the person from last night never existed.

I felt like we had gone backwards, existing again without interacting, and my body screamed at me to fight it. I knew I should say something significant to him, but I couldn't find the words, so I just lightly stepped across the space between us and reached around his neck to grab the tie. His body stiffened under my touch, but he didn't stop me as I quietly lifted his collar and tied a perfect knot in the silk material. I moved it in place and then ran my fingers along his neck as I lowered the collar back down.

I hesitantly looked up at him through my eyelashes. We stared at each other without speaking, mine a look of expectation, his a look of confusion, but at least it was a connection. With an apologetic smile, I backed away and took my turn in the bathroom, hoping the entire time that Grant and I could somehow find some middle ground with each other. I knew I couldn't give him everything he wanted, but I also knew I wanted us to have something. I just didn't know what that looked like.

Grant was gone when I finished in the bathroom, no doubt to pick up his car from the Varsity parking lot, and I took the opportunity to run upstairs and say goodbye to Jake. He was passed out cold on the floor next to the bed, and I wondered where he got the ability to sleep in any position.

"Jake," I whispered gently in his ear. "I've got to go."

His response was a soft grunt.

I chuckled and then whispered at him again. "Don't forget to live."

His response this time was a thumbs up and I

kissed his cheek before heading back downstairs and out the door. Grant had just pulled up with the car and stopped in front of me, lining the car up to where I was facing the back seat. That maneuver said it all, but I sat in the front seat anyway. He glanced my way when I shut the door and shook his head as if to say he couldn't figure me out.

Finally after ten excruciating minutes, Grant let out his signature sigh and started talking. "I want to apologize for last night. There is no excuse for how I acted."

I waved off his apology. "Grant, you weren't that bad."

"Yes, I was. I got angry and then just started making one poor choice after another. I'm supposed to set an example—look different from the rest of the world. Instead, I fell right into old patterns as if my life hadn't been completely changed." The silence lingered again until Grant continued, "Issy, I think I've had this idea of us in my head for so long now that I started to believe I could want it enough for both of us. What last night showed me is that you're simply not ready, at least not ready to give me the only version of yourself I'm willing to accept. I don't know, you may never be ready, and I guess I'll just have to come to terms with that."

I didn't realize I wasn't breathing until Grant quit talking, and I absorbed how defeated he sounded. I wanted to tell him he was right and I was terrified, but instead I just nodded silently.

"You know, before you decided to hate me, we were actually pretty good friends. Do you think maybe we could find our way back to that point and get past all this awkwardness?"

I turned to face him, offering my most genuine smile. I even truly meant it when I said, "Yes, I'd really like that."

Our talk did a lot to diffuse the tension between us, and I even noticed Grant relaxing as he teased me about how disgusting my green smoothie was.

"I told you it was a modified version," I yelled, feigning hurt. "People come from miles around for that concoction, and you got it without even asking. You should feel honored."

He shot me a smile that sent waves of excitement through my body. "I do, Issy. And you don't tie a bad knot either." I felt myself blush and couldn't believe it. It was like I was thirteen all over again.

My dad seemed completely surprised when I was already seated at the breakfast table when he walked in the room. He didn't say a word, but nodded in recognition.

"Anna and Junior are out this morning, so it will just be you and me," he said as Rosa came by to fill our coffee cups. I tried not to feel nervous, but I was sure my dad would try and trap me into saying something incriminating about the trip.

"She's gone a lot lately. Trouble in paradise?" I

asked sweetly, trying to keep the conversation off of me.

My dad scowled at me and began cutting his omelet. "So, don't you have a business marketing class today?" he asked between bites.

"Um, yes?" I answered, completely unsure because I had skipped the class on Tuesday.

"You didn't go to class on Tuesday, did you?" His voice was getting the commanding tone he used when talking on the phone to his employees.

"It was just the first day. All they go over is the syllabus the first week anyway. It's not a big deal," I said defensively.

"It is a big deal because that is an important class. Probably the most important one you have this semester." He set down his fork as he spoke and took a second to really look at me, his eyes getting wide when he noticed my outfit. "Please tell me you are not going in that. You look like you're twelve."

I smirked up at him. "Seriously Daddy, when have you ever seen me leave this house without looking fabulous?"

He grinned back and continued eating again. I couldn't figure out why he all of the sudden cared so much about my school. He'd never before taken any interest except to bug me periodically about choosing a major. Another control thing, I realized. Now that I was in business classes, he cared…figured.

I finished eating and then excused myself to get ready. The silver in my hair washed out in the shower, but I liked the look so much, I recreated it. I found a wide-necked sweater dress that fell just off the shoulder, and paired it with some leggings and ankle boots. The addition of my wide rhinestone belt placed right at the hip made me look magazine worthy, and I smiled at the final product. I certainly did not look twelve in this outfit.

I could hear my father and Grant in a heated discussion when I walked down the stairs, and despite my need to get to class, I couldn't help but stand by the door and listen.

"Grant, I know I told you I'd give you your shot, but it's just not the right timing now. All our focus is on the merger," I heard my father say dismissively.

"Sir, I understand that, but we can work this outside of the merger. What I designed is brand new technology; I just need the startup funds to test run it for our clients. I promise you it will revolutionize the software division. If we wait too long, the market is going to catch up." I could hear the pleading tone in Grant's voice and felt my stomach knot a little for him.

"We are not discussing this further. Robert Marsh and Stone Electric are all I want you to think about. It is our only priority."

I quickly moved away from the door and slipped out of the house. I knew the conversation was over the minute I heard the tone in my father's voice. I felt my heart ache a little for Grant. He'd waited seven years for this shot, and my dad dismissed it without a second thought. Anyone else, I would have felt a little satisfaction in being right, but with Grant, I wished I hadn't been.

I pushed the thoughts away as I drove. I was getting too soft with him, and it was irritating me. I found the female power anthems on my playlist and sang the rest of the way to school. It did its job because I almost felt invincible when I walked into my marketing classroom. I stood at the door like I normally did and glanced around for a safe spot. The chairs were all organized into sections of eight and I noticed students conversing and moving around as if seating had already been assigned. The professor was standing at the white board writing out instructions, so I quickly approached him to find out where I was supposed to sit.

"Sir?" I asked to get his attention. He turned his irritated eyes toward me and waited. "I'm Issy Summers. I wasn't feeling well on Tuesday and didn't make it to class."

The middle-aged professor set down his marker and folded his arms as he continued to glare at me through round glasses. "Ms. Summers, groups have already been decided and work has already begun. I'm not going to force one of these teams to let you in on all their work. You will just have to do the assignment solo."

I couldn't believe he was being so rude. Seriously, how much work could be done in two days? But just when I was ready to make my argument, I heard a sultry voice behind me tell the professor I could join his group.

"Very well, but you will need to resubmit the group form with the change," the professor snapped and turned back to finish writing on the board, completely dismissing me.

I glanced over my shoulder to see who my savior was, noticing immediately that he came from money. I had seen his outfit on display the last time I went to Neiman Marcus and knew the Rolex watch he was wearing was valued in the five digits.

"I'm Robbie. You're more than welcome to join us. We've got a pretty descent group."

"I'm Issy," I replied appreciatively. "I think you are officially my savior."

Robbie cocked a half smile and pointed the way to our section, allowing me to move in front of him as he guided us there. Most of the group was already seated and seemed fine with me joining them. One of the girls seemed irritated by it, but I also noticed the way she looked at Robbie and figured it really had nothing to do with me.

Robbie pulled out the seat next to him and offered it to me with a grin. I took it gladly and made a point to cross my legs toward him. There were definitely sparks between the two of us, and I enjoyed the feeling after such an intense week.

The group work for the day consisted of choosing what product our marketing firm was going to represent. Each sheet held a list of constraints from the client along with public response, popularity, etc. Normally, I wouldn't say anything because I really didn't care, but for some reason, one of the products really jumped out at me. The group had almost unanimously gone with a new Pepsi product when I spoke up.

"I know the Pepsi one seems like the easiest because it's so well known, but I actually think we should consider the Mansfield product."

The girl who didn't like me to begin with made a dramatic sigh and whined, "Taking an unknown product like that will be way too much work. Pepsi is easy money and an easy grade."

The others seemed to agree with her, but I didn't relent. "But since we're really not making money, we have to look at it practically. I really think he put this in there just to trap us. If you compare them, the Pepsi one has twenty-five constraints. That means we will basically have no flexibility throughout the entire project. The Mansfield one only has three. That allows us to do the branding and marketing any way we want to. To me, that would be way easier, because we could be creative. Not to mention, the public response to Mansfield was the best of all the products."

I noticed that the group suddenly started looking at the Mansfield product differently and discussing it, but it was Robbie who sealed the deal.

"I think Issy's right. We should do the Mansfield one," he stated as if he was the president of our little company.

Everyone else agreed, and we completed the required form, leaving us a good fifteen minutes to spare before the end of class. I pulled out my phone and started texting Candace to see what she was doing tonight. I was itching to go do something that wasn't wrought with intensity and drama like the last two days had been. Not to mention, I really liked Candace. We would laugh non-stop when we were together, and she was becoming one of my favorite texting buddies.

I felt Robbie move close to me and whisper in my ear. "So, you're smart and beautiful." It was a statement as if he already knew me, and I had surprised him.

I turned to look closely at him, examining every line in his face to try and remember if we had met before. Nothing came to me, and I was sure I would have remembered him if we'd met. His face was too distinct to forget. It was wide with a defined chin, free of any afternoon stubble. His eyes were hazel and set wide apart giving him a very distinguished and aristocratic appearance.

I responded as I usually did when men took notice of me and flashed him the smile that was casually aloof, but still inviting. "You seem surprised?"

"I guess I'm just used to a certain type of woman," he offered leaning into me.

"And what type is that?"

"Let's just say that none have quite caught my attention like you have." He smiled at me the way I was sure had women eating out of his hand on a regular basis.

I turned away, feigning boredom. "Well, I don't know, I may not want that kind of attention from you. I'm very picky."

Robbie started laughing, and I realized I liked the sound. It was full of a humor and confidence that very few men our age had. "I have no doubt you are."

The professor started talking, ending our bantering, but I felt Robbie's eyes stay on me even when I had turned away from him. When class was over, I grabbed my bag and started for the door, only getting a few feet down the sidewalk before I noticed Robbie running after me.

"So," he said panting a little. "I'm done for the day, what about you?"

"Maybe. Why are you asking?"

"Well, I thought we could grab a bite to eat," he offered. "My car is just right over there."

"Robbie, I make it a practice not to get into cars alone with boys I've known for only an hour or two."

He smiled and then draped his arm over my shoulder. I didn't pull away. "Well, we are in luck then, because my driver makes the perfect chaperone. Come on, one lunch…how bad could it be?"

I eyed him, trying to decide if I wanted to go. He was definitely charming, but I had known many guys just like him in high school, and they bored me within a few minutes. Problem was, I really didn't have anything else to do. The move to Western had definitely taken a hit to my social life.

"Fine, but I'm choosing," I agreed, and he responded by squeezing my arm.

"You got it."

His car was literally parked at the end of the sidewalk, and I teased him a little for needing to be driven to class.

"Commuter parking is a bear. Why bother when I can have door to door service?"

"Spoken like every other spoiled rich guy I know. Come on, Robbie, I thought you were trying to impress me." I was definitely flirting at this point and liked how I saw his eyes sparkle a little when I did so.

Robbie opened the back door of the car for me. "Your chariot, my lady."

"Ah, at least he's a gentleman," I kidded running my finger softly along his hand as I climbed in the car.

Robbie climbed in right behind me and asked, "Where to?"

I gave him the name of my favorite sandwich shop that I knew was close to campus. His driver didn't say a word or join us when we parked. It made me think of Grant and how he always tried to irritate me when we were in the car together. Robbie opened the door for me again at the restaurant, and I scolded myself internally for thinking about Grant once again when I was out with another guy.

We found a table in the back and ordered. Robbie

sat across from me at the table, and rarely looked away while we talked.

"So Issy can't really be your first name," he stated after we got our drinks.

"No. It's short for my middle name, Isadora."

"Isadora. I like that. Does anyone ever call you that?"

"Just my mom. She hates Issy…says its unsophisticated or something," I explained with a shrug.

"Does it bother you?"

I wasn't sure why the third degree on my name, but I answered anyway. "No, Isadora is fine. The only name I hate is my first name, and nobody ever calls me that except for my dad when he's trying to get under my skin."

Robbie laughed and nodded. "Noted."

"What made you chose Western?" I asked after eating a few bites of our meal.

"My dad's an alumni, so it was just always where I would go. Not much of a story."

I watched his mannerisms as he spoke and was surprised that I didn't see any bitterness in that statement. It intrigued me so I pried a little more. "So most of the 'spoiled rich guys' I know, no offense, are one of two types. Either they do whatever their daddy says and secretly hate it, or they become completely rebellious and add nothing but disgrace to the family name. I have a feeling you fall into that first category."

Robbie laughed again and shook his head. "Nope, I'm afraid I don't fall into either. I've known from early on what my role was to be, and it became very clear that if I played my part well, I got whatever I wanted. While friends of mine are worried about finding a job, I have one waiting for me in my father's company as soon as I graduate in May. Can't see why I'd be bitter about that."

"You're a senior?" I asked, completely dismissing the other things he mentioned.

"Yeah, aren't you?"

"Nope, just a sophomore, thank God. I'd be freaking out if I was a senior already."

"Huh, that's surprising."

"Why?"

"Because that Marketing class fills up the first week of registration, mostly by seniors."

"Well, I have a dad who likes to pull strings," I explained flatly.

"And you don't like it when he does that?"

"Let's just say that his strings usually complicate my life."

Robbie leaned across the table and smiled. "Ah, Daddy issues, just like every other spoiled rich girl I know. Come on, Isadora, I thought you were trying to impress me." Robbie's eyes were unreadable, but there was no doubt he had seen right through me.

"Touché," I said arching an eyebrow at him, ignoring the fact that he had called me Isadora. It didn't bother me, but definitely confirmed that this guy had no problem being bold. Everything Robbie did was deliberate, the way he spoke, walked and even his laugh felt managed and controlled in a way that exuded confidence and authority, so I knew his use of my middle name was intentional.

We finished up and walked back out to his car, the driver getting our door the minute we approached.

"Where should we go to next?" he asked as we got settled.

"Oh, you think I enjoyed our lunch enough to spend more time with you?" I asked sarcastically, sending a coy smile his way.

Robbie watched me intensely, his eyes darkening just a little. "We can do whatever you want. Name it and I'll make it happen."

I felt a little lost for words. There was something very intriguing about Robbie, but I also felt my stomach flip nervously when he looked at me like that. For the first time ever, I felt as if I'd met my match. However, I was unwilling to relent in the standoff he had started, so I matched his stare, letting my green eyes penetrate his. "I want to fly."

I saw Robbie's mouth move into a smile that showed he was pleased with my response, and then pulled out his cell phone without ever taking his eyes off me. Fifteen minutes later we were pulling into a large field where I saw a small plane and hang glider waiting.

"Are you serious?" I screamed as we got out of

the car.

"I said I would make it happen. Have you ever been hang gliding before?"

I was practically jumping up and down squealing with excitement and noticed how Robbie just hung back and watched me, his face showing complete satisfaction at my joy. I ran back to him and grabbed his hand, pulling him with me towards the plane.

"Come on!" I squealed. He came willingly, and I realized he looked genuinely happy, the controlled armor lowered for just a moment.

The next several minutes were a blur. The pilot instructed me on what was going to happen, put a helmet on me and then got us both strapped in the glider. The harness was a full body one, and Robbie was at the bottom. I was strapped above his back. My adrenaline was surging at this point in anticipation when they asked if I was ready.

"Yes," I screamed pumping my fist in the air. "Let's go."

I heard Robbie laugh again, but my focus was suddenly lost when the plane took off with us in tow. The wind ripped at my face as we accelerated, and my stomach dropped the minute we were airborne. For a moment, the world came to a standstill, and the screaming in my head went silent. I was flying, and it was the most exhilarating experience of my life. I put out my arms, mimicking an airplane, and felt nothing but peace. I could hear Robbie trying to show me things, but I wasn't listening. I didn't want to think about him or remember I was on a glider. I just wanted to soar like a bird, free to make my own choices and decisions, free from the tyrannical control of my father, and free from the unexplainable draw I had to the only man who could break my heart.

I felt the glider drop suddenly when the cord connecting us to the plane detached, and I opened my eyes just to make sure we were ok. I didn't feel fear, but if I was going to die, I didn't want it to be a surprise. Robbie was in complete control, guiding us through the air with precision and grace. The ground below looked so small and insignificant that I wondered if I too was just dust in the wind. I had yet to do anything remarkable with my life, and the idea of that felt a little disappointing. I shook it off, reminding myself that I didn't care, and just watched the ground slowly approach us as Robbie brought us in for a perfect landing.

As soon as we were stripped out of our harnesses, I pulled off my helmet and shook my hair free, delight covering my face. "That was the most amazing experience I've ever had. Thank you." I flew into his arms with such force that I almost knocked him over.

Our hug suddenly became a kiss as Robbie's hand settled on the back of my neck. It was everything a first kiss should be, soft and careful, warm and exciting, and Robbie certainly knew what he was doing. I kissed him back whole heartedly, satisfied in the fact that his kiss sent no butterflies to my stomach or stirred up emotion that made my knees go weak.

There was no fiery passion that I had to bury or tears I had to keep at bay. No, this was a kiss I could control.

Robbie slowly released me and smiled. "You are an extraordinary woman, even more so than I imagined you would be."

"So you've been imagining me? For what, the fifteen minutes we spent in class?" I teased, trying to understand his comment.

"Something like that," Robbie admitted, his eyes completely unreadable. He kept his arm around my shoulder and guided me to his car. Time had flown by so fast today that I hardly noticed it was pushing five o'clock. Robbie opened the door for me, and I slid in, but he shut the door, leaving to discuss something with his driver. I took the opportunity to check my phone and see who had texted me. Candace had replied that she was watching her brother tonight, so she couldn't hang out. She did invite me to her church again, which I politely declined. Between Avery and Candace, the subject of God was coming up constantly and honestly starting to annoy me a little.

The only other text I cared about was from Jake who sent me a picture of himself holding keys. The caption read: **Living a little…finally agreed to move in with a work buddy. It's the ultimate bachelor pad. What about you?**

Me: I went flying today…top that one! Oh, I better get a set of those keys. What does your new

roommate look like anyway?

Jake: Don't even think about it.

I started to laugh and was so engaged in texting him back that I hardly noticed Robbie get back into the car. He cleared his throat, bringing me out of my bantering session with Jake. I threw my phone back into my purse and smiled up at him. His face was unreadable, but that intense look that made me nervous was back. "Everything ok?" he asked in a calm tone.

"Absolutely." I was trying to stay lighthearted and ease some of the tension that was suddenly between us. "I was bragging to my cousin, Jake, that I went flying."

Robbie's face immediately relaxed, giving him back his charming demeanor. "Ah, Jake's your cousin." It was a statement, not a question, and seemed to close the discussion somehow. "So, I'm not quite ready to call it a day yet. Any way our adventure kept you interested enough to join me for dinner? Our estate is not far from here, and I already made arrangements for someone to go get your car if you want to come."

I studied him for a minute, trying to decide if I trusted him or not. He had been a complete gentleman all day, but periodically I would get the nagging sense that there was something else going on in his head. "Robbie, I appreciate the offer, but I really don't know you well enough to go to your house alone or give you my car keys."

"I have a house full of employees, one who has raised me since I was a baby. I promise you, Isadora, we will never be alone. Dinner on the veranda, out by the pool, watching the sun set. Come on, you can't turn that one down," he urged.

"You assume I'm a romantic, Robbie. I'm not." I made sure to keep eye contact when I said it so there was no confusion. I had decided after Ben that I would never again tie myself to one person, and I was starting to get that vibe from Robbie.

"I would never dare to assume anything about you," he promised, taking my hand in his. "Just have dinner with me."

I considered my other option, dinner with my father and Anna, and decided that dinner with Robbie was actually the least offensive of the two.

"Well, you did take me flying, and really that alone should get you another meal with my extraordinary company," I said dramatically, flipping my hair back and intentionally using the same term he did earlier.

He cocked another side grin and then told the driver where to go.

12. ROBBIE

Estate was the absolute right word to describe Robbie's house. We had to navigate through two separate security gates to enter the property, and then the house alone was large enough to be one of our campus buildings. Rarely was I affected by wealth or extravagant living, but even I had to admit his home was remarkable. It captured all the grandeur and beauty one would expect from a North Carolina mansion, complete with an oversized water fountain sitting just adjacent to the driveway.

The driver opened our door, and Robbie took my hand to lead me to his house.

"Wait, I want to make a wish," I announced, changing our direction back to the fountain.

Robbie gave me a confused stare, but followed along anyway. I pulled two pennies out of my purse and was shocked when I saw the pristine bottom of the fountain pool. "Don't you ever use this thing?"

Robbie just continued to slant his eyes at me as if he was trying to figure me out. I shook my head and handed him a penny. "Close your eyes and make a wish."

His side grin reappeared as he did what I asked.

We stood there quietly until I said to throw it in. I wished for the same thing I had since I was a little girl—a different life. It was always my hope that one day I would wake up in a completely different world and be told this was all a dream. When I finally opened my eyes, Robbie was watching me again, his eyes back to the dark intensity that gave me chills.

"What did you wish for?" I asked playfully, trying to get that look to go away.

Robbie grabbed my hand and pulled me towards him. "I already got my wish," he admitted right before kissing me again, this time with much more force than the first one. I responded again, but was starting to get a little concerned about where this was going.

When I pulled back I made sure there was some distance between us. "Robbie, I like you, but I want to be honest right away. I don't do the relationship thing...at all. I just don't want there to be any confusion after today. I mean, we can hang out and have fun, but that's really all I'm capable of." Something told me Robbie was not easily manipulated, so I needed to be straight with him, or I had a feeling I'd end up at girlfriend status before I ever knew what hit me.

He smiled with such confidence and assurance that I wondered if he even heard what I said until he pulled me back to him and whispered in my ear, "There is no confusion, Isadora. I know *exactly* where I stand."

I eased away from him, satisfied with his response, but still concerned with his body language. He wrapped his arm around me again and guided us back to his house. The inside was no less grand than the outside. The style was similar to my father's, although less tacky and more expensive. It still felt cold and overdone, much like a museum full of priceless artifacts that were to be seen and not touched.

"So did you do all of this yourself?" I asked teasingly, trying to gauge if this was his style too or if he was subject to his parents like I was.

"No, this is definitely my mom's doing. But I do appreciate fine things. Every piece in this house is rare and often a one-of-a-kind. Some pieces took years to negotiate and procure." He watched my reaction when he spoke, and I sensed a double meaning in it. His mood then switched abruptly as he led me out to the back of the house.

It was breathtaking and much more my style. A stone walkway led us out to the grounds where the space was divided into three separate areas. The main area was filled with a large rectangular pool that appeared to have no boundary on the far end, leaving the water to simply cascade off the side. On the left, a large fireplace was surrounded by plush chairs and tables. Nearby sat a stone hot tub with steps that also descended into the pool. To my right was a covered veranda, complete with a dining table and chairs. Large white draperies were tied to each pillar giving it a whimsical look. The view consisted of plush gardens with flowers of every color and style.

I watched as Robbie snapped off a fresh daisy and tucked it into my hair with a smile. "Now this is my domain, and you look as beautiful in it as I thought you would." I let him guide me through the gardens, explaining the different plants to me. I realized that while I enjoyed his company, being with him suddenly made me feel ten years older. He was intelligent and knowledgeable, but every move was so precise that I wondered if he planned each step out in his head before taking it. I resisted the urge to just start tickling him, if anything just to see what it would do to his controlled movement.

When I couldn't take it anymore, I yelled, "Stop. I feel like I'm on a tour. This is no way to enjoy a yard." I started to tug on his arm a little, giving him a mischievous grin before taking off in a sprint towards the only open grassy area, my body language urging him to chase me. I watched him hang back a little before taking off after me. He caught me by the waist, and I pushed him over, sending both of us to the ground with a soft thud. I was laughing uncontrollably at this point and started tickling him until he finally pinned me to the ground with his body covering mine.

"Are you always this wild?" he asked breathless after the laughter stopped. His eyes were sparkling, and I got to see a hint of a boy in there.

I grinned up at him. "Oh I'm just getting started. I

haven't even had a drink today."

A second later his mouth was over mine, hungrier and more persistent than either time before. I eagerly kissed him back, rolling him over until I was on top and in control again. I felt his hand start to move up my leg and under my dress, but I didn't stop him. I wanted to be lost in the moment, free to do whatever felt good. However, a persistent buzzing from my phone ended the kiss, and I finally jumped off of him to answer it. "What?" I scoffed into the phone when I saw it was Grant.

"Where are you? It's past seven, and your dad is about to lose it." I looked down at my watch and cringed. I had completely forgotten about the seven sharp rule in the house.

"I'm with a friend. Tell my dad I'm not going to make dinner tonight."

I could hear Grant let out a sigh as his voice tensed up. "Tell him yourself," he said and seconds later I heard my father's stern voice.

"Kaitlyn, you know I expect you at this dinner table by seven. Where are you?"

I rolled my eyes and winked at Robbie who had pulled himself back into the controlled gentleman. "I'm with a friend I met in class today. Trust me, Daddy, you would blissfully approve."

"Your marketing class?" he asked as his voice took on a pleased tone.

"Yep. I'm going to have dinner with him and then I'll be home, ok?"

My father cheerfully agreed which struck me as odd, but I chalked it up to the fact that he realized my friend was a business major.

"Unbelievable," I said after hanging up. "My dad waits until I'm almost twenty years old to try and be fatherly. Go figure."

Robbie smiled and pulled me up off the ground. "Maybe he just sees that you're a woman now and wants the best for you."

"Robbie, I'll let you in on a little secret. Defending my father is the quickest way possible to put me in a terrible mood."

"I'll keep that in mind," he replied as he led us back to the veranda, where a full meal complete with a bottle of red wine awaited us. Robbie pulled out my seat, and pushed it in once I was settled, before taking the one right next to me. I watched him as he moved like royalty at the dinner table. I felt as if I needed to draw on all of the training my mother had imparted on me just to get through the dinner. I mimicked her, eating delicate bites while quietly making conversation. I couldn't figure out why I actually cared to play along with the charade, but it just seemed fitting in this environment, next to Robbie's mannerisms.

"So I get the feeling Western wasn't your first choice," Robbie stated as he filled my glass.

"Not at all. No offense," I answered. Robbie arched an eyebrow, but didn't say anything. "I've actually been at Winsor, up by Asheville, since I graduated."

"I'm familiar," he stated with a nod.

"Well, on New Year's, I had a little too much to drink, and Walla, I was whisked away to my father's house and put in his protective custody. My sentence is up in August."

"What happens in August?"

"I go back to Winsor, of course. Western is just to appease my dad. But don't go telling our group that," I teased with a smile. "I don't want them to know that I could really care less about our little project."

"You seemed to care today," he reminded me, taking another perfect bite of his dinner.

"That's only because the Mansfield product was awesome. It reminded me of me...lots of popularity with very little constraint." I was laughing a little as I spoke, trying to get Robbie to relax again. He was always so stiff.

"I can see that. Where as I am much more like the Pepsi product...guaranteed success, but straddled with a multitude of constraints."

I watched his face again. They were empty words, spoken with no emotion to tell me whether or not he was bothered by them. "It doesn't have to be that way, you know," I offered.

"Ah, you forget, I like being able to get whatever I want. In fact, I am every bit the spoiled kid you said I was." The intensity was back in his eyes, sending a shiver down my spine.

"See, I knew it," I responded throwing my arms

in the air as if disappointed. The relaxed Robbie returned, and we finished dinner without any more intense moments.

When the meal was over, Robbie led me out to the fireplace, where someone had already started the blaze for us. He sat me down and pulled me next to him snuggly so we were watching the fire like a couple who had been doing it for years. The intimacy of the moment made me uncomfortable, and I shifted away from him stating that I should probably head home.

"I'd like to see you again," he stated, moving me back towards him.

I didn't know how to respond. Robbie had somehow managed to turn a lunch date into an all day event and now seemed to want to do the same thing again. He wasn't the kind of guy who took the brush off easily, so I just smiled and said, "I guess you could call me."

He took his phone out and handed it to me, carefully watching my every move. I put my number in there, making sure to label it Issy just to make a point. I stood after I handed it back to him, indicating I was ready to go now. He didn't try and stop me, just took my hand and led me back out front where my car waited with the keys inside.

We were at the driver's door when I felt him lean up against me, trapping me between the car door and his body. "What was your wish?" he asked in a sultry voice, never taking his eyes off mine.

I glared back at him, keeping my eyes as void as his were. "It doesn't matter. It will never come true." He responded by giving me a soft kiss and then opened my door for me. I felt relief when I turned the key and drove away from his house. That confined feeling I always got around guys came flooding in with more intensity than usual tonight and didn't leave until I was a good ten miles away from Robbie's property.

Grant and my father were still working when I got home. My father exuded jubilance while Grant looked completely miserable.

"Did you have a nice time tonight?" my father asked when I approached the office.

"It was fine," I responded with a shrug. "Why the midnight oil?"

"Nothing for you to worry your pretty little head about, Issy," my father answered dismissing me. "Its all paperwork and contracts at this point."

I didn't argue and tried to push away the guilt that suddenly sprung up when Grant looked in my direction. I went upstairs to change, and filled my flask with the stash I had in the armoire. My trip back to Winsor had replenished me nicely.

I could hear my father and Grant still talking when I tip toed down the stairs and out to the lake. The wind was blowing now, and I felt it rip right through my silk pajamas as I walked along the water. The liquid in my flask warmed me from the inside until the combination of the two succeeded in numbing every part of me. I rolled up my pant legs and started to wade a little in the water before I heard Grant's voice behind me.

"I'm not coming in after you this time," he joked as he approached me.

"Ah come on, I thought you loved saving me," I kidded back with a mischievous smile.

Grant took the flask out of my hand and sniffed the contents, handing it back to me with scowl. "Can't leave home without it, huh?"

"But I am home," I stated absently, looking back over the water.

Grant rolled up his pants and stood next to me, not saying a word. It was one of the things I most appreciated about him. He never pressed me to talk. Finally after minutes of silence, Grant chuckled and said, "Are we going to stand here forever, because I really can't feel my toes anymore."

I turned to look at him, forgetting that we had been standing in freezing water and walked backward to take a seat on the dry part of the sand. He joined me and I offered him a drink of my flask, but he declined.

"I overheard you this morning," I admitted after taking another drink. "I'm sorry my dad is stonewalling you."

"You heard us?" he asked, surprised. "I must have been more agitated than I thought. Probably the regret I've been fighting all day."

I just raised my eyebrow at him and didn't say a

word.

"I had hoped to present an idea at your father's board meeting tomorrow. He had promised me last month that he would give me fifteen minutes. Now, he wants all the focus on this stupid merger that is practically a done deal."

"My father is going to New York tomorrow?" I asked, completely forgetting that the other information was what he cared about.

"Yep, leaving first thing in the morning. I don't expect him back until after the weekend."

"Oh, that is the best news I've ever heard," I yelled, throwing myself back on the sand. "A whole weekend without seven o'clock dinners and curfew."

"I wouldn't get too excited. He's leaving me here to babysit you."

"Grant, we both know you are a terrible babysitter," I said, pinching his side a little to make him laugh. He finally did and laid back next to me. The stars were covering the sky, and our shoulders were touching just enough to send fire racing down that side of my body.

"So tell me about your new friend," he finally said after the silence lingered between us.

"Nothing to tell really."

Grant moved to his side so he could look at me. "You spent the whole day with him."

"How do you know it's a him?" I asked, not moving from my position.

Grant laid back down and shook his head. "You

are impossible."

Seconds later, he was on top of me, tickling me so hard that I thought I would die of laughter. I wiggled out of his grip and took off down the beach, but he easily caught me, lifting me up so fast that my breath caught. He was moving towards the water with determination, and held me so tightly, I had no hope of escape.

"Tell me about him, or so help me, you will be drenched in ice cold water."

"Grant, put me down," I screamed, starting to believe he would really drop me.

"Tell me."

"Fine, he's handsome and rich, and he took me flying today. He's so captivated by me that he probably has our children's names picked out already. You happy?"

Grant stopped and set me down on the dry sand, looking far too smug. "Yes, very."

"How does that make you happy?"

"Because you don't like him. I just wanted to make sure." He was slapping his hands together to get off the sand that came from my pajamas.

I put my hands on my hips. "How do you know I don't like him? I may be completely in love," I yelled back defiantly.

"Ok, let me ask you this, how would you describe me?"

Before I could calculate a response, I blurted out, "Infuriating, exhausting and very close to getting pelted by a handful of sand."

He walked towards me and put his hands on my arms. "Exactly. All emotions, Issy. With him, it was just facts."

I glared at him, suddenly angry. He just smiled and let go. "All emotions," was all he said before taking off back to the house.

13. TOO MUCH AFFECTION

I had never been so thrilled to wake up on a Friday before. I knew my father had left early this morning and wouldn't be back for days. The feeling of freedom descended on me like a blanket and I jumped out of bed, ready to plan my weekend.

I heard my phone buzz and grabbed it as I took off toward the bathroom.

Avery: Good morning, Issy! I wanted you to know I'm praying for you today.

I scowled, but texted back anyway.

Me: Thanks. Any big plans for the weekend?

Avery: Not really. Just hanging out with Parker. What about you?

I hesitated for a minute, not wanting to get a lecture, but finally wrote back.

Me: Not yet, but should by the end of the day

Avery: Please be careful

Me: Always am

Avery: ☹ You know what I mean

Me: Stop worrying. Got to get ready for school. Will text later.

Despite the gnawing conscious Avery gave me, I was feeling especially edgy today so I put long blue streaks around my face and left the back completely black. I chose a pair of silver and black, stripped capris that shimmered in the light and paired it with a silk black tank top and leather jacket. My black stilettos completed the look that screamed high-class party girl, and I was ready.

Candace and Reggie, I was learning, were not the partying types, but the group at the lunch table was usually talking about some wild party after another. I'd just have to make it known that as much as I liked Reggie and Candace, we definitely did not share the same moral compass.

Jason was already in class when I showed, and I noted he was once again seated next to my chair. I approached him with a smile, liking the outfit he was wearing. Torn up jeans, with a tight ribbed sweater and two choker chains around his neck. It was sexy in a bad boy kind of way.

"You skipped class," he stated when I sat down. He looked slightly irritated.

"I had a family emergency. I'm sure I didn't miss anything important."

"Well, considering I waited all day to see you without your bodyguard, it was a pretty big blow to my ego. Lucky for you, I was still nice enough to get you a decent monologue." His cheerful demeanor was back as was his need to enter into my personal space.

"What are you talking about?" I asked moving away from him. I had to admit he smelled really good, though. It was a spicy scent that definitely wasn't as expensive as Robbie's woody smell, but still not cheap.

"We got assigned our monologues for class. I will be doing Romeo, of course," he explained with a wink. "I did my best to get you Juliet, but two other girls wanted that one. I still got you Hamlet and one of the most famous speeches of all time." He sat back satisfied, waiting for me to thank him properly.

"I would thank you, but you seem to be doing a pretty good job of that yourself," I teased, but still gave him a look that showed I really did appreciate him looking out for me.

"Well, it's time to make my exit," Jason said as Reggie approached. "You going to be in class today?"

"Maybe."

He shook his head and sighed. "You're killing me, green eyes." Then he was gone.

The class drug on forever, and I saw Reggie dosing off more than once. I've decided that the University used the words "Intro to" as a synonym for boring and pointless.

When class finally ended, Reggie lifted his chin at me. "See you at lunch?"

"I'll be there," I replied as I packed up my bag. It seemed pointless to do so since I hadn't taken one sentence of notes. I walked down the steps and out the door, but stopped the minute I saw Robbie standing about ten feet away, engaged in conversation with someone.

"Hey," Jason said, coming from nowhere and slipping his arm around my shoulder. "In case you decide to skip class again. I wanted to let you know I am working tonight at Macy's off Broadway. If you come by, the bouncers won't card you."

I turned my head to look at him, but didn't move his arm. I found his easy mannerisms charming even though I wasn't letting him know that yet. "You think I'm the type of girl to sit on a bar stool all night drooling over a guy?"

"No, I think you're the type of girl who likes free drinks and might just be attracted to a certain bartender who gets off at eleven."

Out of the corner of my eye, I could see Robbie approaching us, so I slipped out of his arm and told him I'd see him in class. He took the hint and left just in time for me to turn and smile at Robbie.

"Hey, what are you doing here?" I asked sweetly as he approached, trying not to show how stalkerish I thought it was.

"I've got class here in a few minutes," he answered casually, but I could tell there was some irritation to it. "Who was that?"

"Just a friend. Speaking of class, though, I have to get to Algebra. See you later?" I started to move around him, but he caught my arm and pulled me back.

"I want to see you tonight," he stated, getting the dark look in his eyes again.

"I've got plans, but you can call me tomorrow." I was trying to be as friendly as I could while attempting to free my hand from his tightening grip.

He was making me nervous until he suddenly let go and smiled, his eyes no longer showing any kind of emotion. "Tomorrow then."

I shot him a little wave and then walked away, moving much faster than I normally would. I was starting to question if I ever should have gotten in that car with Robbie. I didn't see him going away very easily.

Algebra went smoothly except that we were assigned homework, which I found pretty ridiculous for a college class. I couldn't remember the last time I did homework. I scheduled a meet up with Kari to go over it on Tuesday. Thank goodness for kind, smart girls.

I was eager to get to lunch. I wanted to see where the group was going tonight and needed to get settled before Candace's crew got there. Unfortunately, I wasn't so lucky, and sure enough Rusty was standing and offering me a seat when I got there. I took it with a smile, still trying not to offend my new friends.

"Hey Issy," Rusty said casually as I sat down. His eyes lit up when he saw me, and my stomach dropped a little.

I watched as the others got to the table and started discussing their evening plans. I stood and headed that way, unwilling to miss the opportunity. "Um, I'll be right back," I said to Rusty as he watched me leave.

I perched next to one of the girls whose name was Rachel I think. Despite how cold they were on the first day, most had warmed up to me, especially since they saw I was not the type to flirt with their boyfriends. I abhorred cheaters and would never go after someone's boyfriend.

"Hey guys, any big plans this weekend?" I asked casually.

"We're still debating it. You have any ideas?" Rachel asked, scooting over a little to give me more room. That gesture made me immediately like her.

"I have an in with a bartender at Macy's, but I've never been there before," I offered.

Rachel's boyfriend perked up at the idea. "I love that place. It's this hole in the wall bar, but they play the best music, all blues and jazz. They also have a lot of live music and pool tables."

"But is there a dance floor?" Rachel asked, still unconvinced.

"Of course. I wouldn't dare to suggest it otherwise," he responded, giving her a kiss.

"Great," I stated, ready to get away from the lovebirds. "I'll see you guys there around ten then?"

They all agreed, and I headed back to the other side of the table where my calmer friends were. I felt a little guilty for not including them, but if they came, I knew I would have to be on my best behavior, and I didn't want to be tonight.

"Hey Candace," I said smiling when I sat back down.

"Hey Issy," she said cheerfully. "We were just making plans for the weekend. Wanna catch a movie with us?"

"Well, I sort of have plans already. Next time?" I offered.

Candace looked over at the group down on the other end of the table and raised her eyebrow at me. Thankfully, she didn't say anything.

The rest of lunch was fun. Rusty and Candace kept me laughing, and I was actually disappointed when I had to leave to get to Shakespeare. Rusty came with me, without asking this time, I noted. He seemed more shy than usual, and I realized that I was going to have to give my speech…yet again.

"Issy, I was wondering if you maybe wanted to go get dinner some time," he started once we reached my building. I knew it was coming, so I had prepared most of the walk for it.

I let out a sigh and then put my hand on his arm, giving him a look that showed I really did regret having to do this. "Rusty, I'm not what you want. I can promise you that. All those girls you dismiss because they aren't right for you, well, I'm exactly like them."

"Issy, you are nothing like those girls. They have one layer. You get past it and there is nothing else there. You, well you have probably a hundred layers. I'm not talking about a relationship here. I just want to get to know you better. You intrigue me." Rusty didn't sound desperate or insecure. He just sounded factual, and I smiled thinking it was really a sweet thing to say.

"You are a great guy, but I just don't do the dating thing. I'm sorry. I'm only at Western for a few months, and then I'm back to my old life. But, I'd really like to be friends, if that is something you are willing to do."

Rusty matched my regretful smile, but still accepted my offer. "I can live with that."

I waved goodbye and slid in my chair, feeling very much like I had dodged a bullet. Jason came in minutes later and moved into the seat behind me.

"Here's your monologue," he offered with a grin as he handed me the paper. "Luckily it's only the first ten lines. That speech is forever long."

"Great. I get to pretend to be a tragic hero. How poetic."

Jason missed my double meaning. "So, are we on for tonight, green eyes?" he asked as he leaned the whole desk forward to reach my ear.

I turned slightly and caught his playful look. Jason would be fun tonight; I had no doubt of that. "I've got a few friends coming with me," I offered, waiting to see his response since I didn't specify what gender my friends were.

"Perfect, I'll let the bouncers know you are all friends of mine. That is…if *you* are going to be a personal friend of mine tonight." His words were full of meaning, and there was no question in his eyes that he saw tonight as a date.

I glanced up at him through my eyelashes and sent a look that did not need interpreting. When I turned around. I heard Jason mumble, "That woman's going to be the end of me."

I sat back smugly and thought, *he has no idea.*

Everyone was gone when I got home, and the silence actually felt refreshing. I was not usually one to be alone, but the constant surveillance I had in my father's house made isolation almost feel appealing. I took the boat out, enjoying the way the wind whipped through my hair. I got to the center of the lake, and then anchored myself before pulling out my phone to call Jake.

He answered right away, and I could hear giggling in the background. "Hey sweetie, what's up?" he asked in a tone that said he had already started drinking for the evening.

"I'm sitting in the middle of the lake all alone and actually enjoying it," I admitted.

"I'm sorry, I thought I was talking to my cousin, Issy. Could you please go find her and get her on the phone?"

"Ha ha," I joked, wondering what his partner must be thinking as he ignored her to talk to me. "So, you going out tonight?"

"Not sure yet. Staying in is looking pretty promising at this point. Who knows, maybe I'll do both," Jake answered with a chuckle.

"Ew, gross Jake, spare me your sordid details. Although, I have my own hottie I'm going to abuse tonight as well."

"Just be careful, Issy. Men are dogs."

"I know. I'm talking to one right now," I accused with very little judgment in my voice. After all, it had been me who pushed him in this direction. I just hoped it didn't get out of control.

Jake laughed and then I heard the giggle in the background again. "Hey, I've got to run, but listen, you need to call your mom, Issy. She's worried about you."

"Tell her I'll call her when she bails me out of jail. Until then, she's on my list."

"Issy, don't be a brat. You know your mom's been through hell and back this year," Jake scolded, taking her side as usual.

"Save it, Jake. I'm not discussing this with you. Go back to whatever naughty thing you are doing, and I'll talk to you later." I ended the call before he could say more. I hated when Jake lectured me about my mom. I felt rage start to form in the pit of my stomach again and took the boat back to the shore. There was only one cure when I felt like this, and it wasn't fresh air.

By the time nine thirty hit, I was calm and happy, and more than ready to go. I was dressed to kill in my favorite black skirt, knee-high socks and high heeled combat boots. My shirt was open at each shoulder and hung just low enough at the neckline to keep men guessing. I added more blue streaks to the back of my hair and straightened it until it hung like a board down to my waist.

I found Rosa before I left asking if she had seen Grant. I felt I should at least let him know I would be out tonight, so he wouldn't come looking for me.

"Mr. Grant left earlier. He was very handsome. I think he actually have date tonight," she offered with a smile. Rosa loved Grant.

I got that feeling again, the one that started in my gut and moved up until there was a full knot in my throat. I pushed it down, furious at myself that he could still make me jealous. I voided my eyes. I had no intention of Grant getting a play by play of me losing it.

"Could you please tell him I'm going out tonight, and not to wait up?"

"Mr. Grant will not be happy about that, Issy. Your father either." Rosa got that motherly look on her face that made her look so soft and loveable that I couldn't help but give her a big hug. She seemed surprised when I did, but just smiled and squeezed me back. I left without another word and bounced out to my car. There were tears in my eyes. Why, why were there tears? I wiped them in disgust and skidded out of the driveway. I couldn't get to Macy's fast enough.

I was fully in control by the time I parked my car at the bar. I checked my reflection in the rearview mirror. My eyes were empty, and my smile so perfected that even I wanted to believe I was happy.

As promised, the bouncer let me in as soon as I gave him my name. I watched as he appraised me and whistled appreciatively.

"Jason's one lucky guy," I heard him mutter under his breath as I walked past him into the bar. It wasn't what I expected. The walls were all painted a dark blue and the entire room wasn't much bigger than the large square bar situated at the center. Coasters from all over the world were placed on the ceiling and liquor bottles lined the back wall. Jason was in the middle, moving with grace and efficiency as he made drinks for everyone. I watched as he laughed and worked. He was completely carefree and truly seemed to enjoy people being around him. I could hear a band in the distance and noticed that the bar continued around the corner.

His eyes suddenly caught mine, and his whole face lit up as if I were a present on Christmas morning. I waited for some physical reaction, but there was nothing, just an echoing emptiness that consumed me. I moved slowly towards the bar and found a seat, making sure to cross my legs as seductively as I could before leaning up to talk to him.

"Wow. That's all I'm going to say," he stated as he came towards me, leaving only a few inches between our faces. "What are you in the mood for tonight?"

"Shots. Lots and lots of shots," I answered, not taking my eyes from his.

"You got it." He was off, pulling out a bottle and

two shot glasses before coming back to me. I watched as he poured us each a drink and then lifted his glass. "Only with me, ok?" he asked, making it clear once again that we were together tonight.

"I hope you're not a light weight," I answered as I reached for my drink. I tapped his glass and we slammed it back together, never really taking our eyes off one another.

"Your friends are already back there with the band," he offered, taking my hand in his and sliding his fingers between mine. "I'll join you soon."

I nodded and slid off the stool, sending him one last glance before turning the corner. He was openly watching me, and I realized I was glad. I actually really did like Jason. He was fun, easy and never once asked me to be something I wasn't. Yes, it was settled, Jason would be my perfect mind eraser for the night.

The band was outstanding, better than any I'd heard before. It was sultry music, the kind that made you just want to sway and listen as it filled your soul. And sway, I did, with Jason next to me the entire night. He was the perfect partner, dancing when I wanted to, drinking when I wanted to, and never once crossed any physical boundary without my initiation. I initiated a lot.

We closed down the place, staying far later than any of my friends, until finally Jason whispered in my ear, "They're going to kick us out of here soon, green eyes. Where do you want me to take you?" There was no questioning the meaning in his voice or the way he looked at me when he said it.

My eyes were heavy from the alcohol, but I still knew what I was doing. "Your place," I answered as I leaned up to kiss his neck. He stiffened under me and then pushed me out the door to a waiting cab. His apartment wasn't far, but I took the opportunity in the cab to show him just how interested I was. His lips were warm and hungry, ready to accept all I had to offer him. I felt a twinge of guilt, knowing I felt nothing for him, but I pushed it away, and kissed him harder. His touch was making me numb and the screaming in my head had settled several shots ago.

We barely made it into the apartment before I went after him again. He kept trying to get me to slow down, said he didn't want to rush it, but I didn't want to hear him. I didn't want to hear anything or feel anything, and it worked because minutes later, my world went black.

14. JUST FRIENDS

I felt like I was being smothered as I woke up. I could feel Jason's bare chest up against me, and his arms were wrapped so tightly, I could hardly breathe. I slowly detangled our legs and moved carefully so I wouldn't wake him. I didn't remember anything from last night, but the fact that I was stripped down to my purple lace bra and panties left little to be imagined.

I squinted my eyes as the light in the room which sent a shooting pain through my head, and began looking around for my clothes and my phone. I found them all in a pile on the floor, and cringed when I saw that Grant had called fourteen times last night. There was a missed call every half an hour until finally a text message came in at 8:00 a.m. that said if he didn't hear from me in two hours, he was calling the police and my father.

I glanced at the time. It was nine fifteen, I let out a sigh of relief. I slowly pressed the buttons to text him back, barely able to move my head it hurt so bad.

Me: I'm fine. I'll be home in thirty minutes.

My phone immediately rang, and I answered it hesitantly, knowing it was going to be ugly.

"Where are you?" was all he said. His voice was

shaking.

"I'm fine. I just need to get my car."

"I have your car, Issy. I found it when I searched all over town for you last night. Give me an address." Grant was angry, super angry, and the last thing I was going to do was let him walk in here and see me like this.

"I'll get a ride."

I heard him sigh and then his tone was so stern I got chills. "In thirty minutes, I'm calling your father." I hung up on him. I couldn't deal with that right now.

I felt Jason's arm snake around my waist and pull me back into bed.

"You think I'm going to let you sneak out of here like that?" he asked as he leaned over me, moving the hair away from my face.

"Kind of hard to sneak out without a car," I conceded, staring up into his blue eyes. I really wished I could remember what had happened. "So, did we?"

"No, we didn't," he answered with a grin. "Not for your lack of trying, you little minx, but I'd prefer you actually be able to remember it when we do sleep together."

I felt relieved and touched his face in appreciation. "You're a good guy, Jason."

His face changed a little, getting more intense than I'd seen him. "No, I'm not, which is why last night is more confusing than I care to admit. But don't be mistaken, Issy. If you put me in that position again, I can't promise I'll be such a gentleman."

I nodded. "I understand."

I started to move him off of me, but before I could, he leaned down and ran his lips over mine. "By the way, you're the most beautiful thing I've ever woken up next to." Then he kissed me. It was the kiss of a man who didn't want me to leave his bed…ever, and I immediately felt my stomach turn. For some reason, in the morning light, being with him felt wrong. When he finally let me go, I stood up and started to get dressed. He watched as I moved, making me feel even more uncomfortable. I sat down to put on my shoes and felt him move closer to me.

"Listen Jason, I don't…" I started before I felt Jason's fingers on my lips.

"Save the speech, Issy. I've got it memorized, I've used it so much. You don't have to make me any promises. I'll take whatever I can get."

I laughed and then raised my eyebrow at him. "Apparently not."

He shook his head and then stood up to get dressed as well. "Ok, I'll take what I can get and still be able to look at myself in the mirror. Come on, let's get you home. From what I heard, we've only got twenty more minutes until your father gets called."

The ride home was horrible. Jason's motorcycle swayed in such a way that I wondered how I would ever keep from throwing up. Once we got to my house, I had to sit there for a second with my forehead on his back, just to settle my stomach. When the nausea finally passed, I stood up, ready to avoid goodbyes and simply walk towards the house. I could see Grant standing in the door frame waiting on me. Jason got off his bike before I could leave and grabbed each of the lapels on my jacket before bringing me close to him.

"I put my number in your phone last night. You call it any time, ok?" he offered before giving me a good-bye kiss. Once he was back on the bike, I looked back towards the door. Grant was gone.

Nerves consumed me as I took the walk of shame up the front steps. I had no idea what to expect. Part of me was angry with him for making me feel this way when I had made it more than clear we were not together. But part of me thought of how I would feel if I saw a girl leave his room the morning after, and once again felt guilty.

When I finally shut the front door, Grant was in the foyer pacing with a phone in his hand. I watched him as he walked back and forth multiple times without saying a word. When he appeared to have calmed down, he turned to me, his eyes enlarged with fury. "Do you have any idea what you put me through last night? I didn't know where you were, or if you were dead in an alley somewhere. Seriously Issy, do you ever think about anyone besides yourself?"

I felt my body stiffen in defense, and my eyes go cold. "I told you not to wait up."

I watched as he backed away from me and put his hands in the air. "I can't be near you right now." He turned and stalked away, slamming his bedroom door so loud that I jumped in response.

I felt the tears burn my eyes, but pushed them back, unwilling to accept I had done anything wrong. I slowly walked to the kitchen and thankfully Rosa was already working on my green smoothie. She didn't say a word, but I could tell from her stance and facial expressions that she was just as disappointed with me as Grant was.

I took the hangover juice and three aspirins before heading up the stairs to my room. The tears were uncontrollable now, and I just sat on the floor by my door and cried.

Several hours of sleep and a hot shower later, I felt almost human again. I glanced at my phone and saw three missed calls from Robbie. Knowing I had kind of promised him a date, I called him back.

"Hey, it's Issy," I said after he answered the phone.

"You really know how to make a guy sweat it, don't you?" His voice sounded calm and cheerful, but I still had this eerie feeling he was mad at me.

"I'm sorry. I really don't feel good today. May I take a rain check?"

There was silence on the other line until Robbie finally spoke, once again perfectly controlled. "Sure. I hope you feel better soon. Did you have fun last night?"

"It was ok. What about you? Did you do

anything?" I asked, trying to stay on the phone the appropriate amount of time before getting off.

"Nothing big, just went by this little place called Macy's. Ever been there?"

I felt a chill go down my spine. If he had been there, he'd seen me with Jason and the two of us had given PDA a whole new meaning.

"Anyway," Robbie continued before I spoke again. "I'll check in on you later. Have a good night, Isadora."

"Thanks Robbie, you too." I hung up the phone and noticed I was shaking. Then I realized what it was…Robbie scared me. There was something that wasn't right, something I was missing. I just couldn't figure out what it was.

I let out a breath, and walked over to my balcony. I could see Grant standing on the pier with his arms leaning on the rail. I knew he did that when he was upset and needed to calm down. The guilt came tumbling back on me again, and I finally conceded that I was going to have to break down and apologize or suffer with it the rest of the night.

I knew he heard me approach him, but he didn't move when I took a spot next to him on the rail. "I'm sorry about last night. I should have called." I was sincere in my apology and really hoped it was enough to make him stop being angry.

Grant continued to stare into the unknown, before turning to me with haunted eyes. "You know, Issy, I almost think it would be easier for me if you felt something for these guys versus knowing that you are only with them because you want to feel nothing."

I went to speak, but as usual Grant continued on his long soliloquy, looking off into oblivion once again. "When I found out that your dad was bringing you here, I was thrilled. I actually believed that maybe you could find some healing in this place. But now I realize how naïve I was. Instead of being a part of your healing, I've got a front row seat as you self destruct, and there is nothing I can do about it."

I put my hand on his arm so he would stop talking. "Grant, you can't heal in the same place that broke you to begin with. I'm sorry I keep disappointing you, but you expect too much from me. I just want to do my time and get out of here."

Grant leaned over and put his head on his hands, shaking it back and forth. "You have no idea how hard it is for me knowing that you spent the night with that guy. Every time I think of it, I get nauseous."

"Not that I owe you this, but I didn't have sex with him," I offered, hoping to ease some of the pain.

Grant stood up again, but didn't look any less miserable. "I guess that's good, but I don't feel any better. He still got to hold you and kiss you and wake up with you in his arms. He has no right to that kind of intimacy with you."

"Grant, you wouldn't have wanted the person I was last night. You've made that very clear." I stared at him apologetically and watched as he slowly relaxed, pulling me in for a hug.

We just stood there, holding on to one another until he finally pulled away and lifted my face to look at him. "I need you to promise that you will never do that to me again."

I nodded and then buried my head back in his chest. "I promise."

I heard Grant chuckle. "I don't know how Jake managed to keep you alive as long as he did. I have a whole new respect for the guy."

I pulled away and laughed, letting him in on our little secret. "Jake had our phones synced to where he could locate me anywhere. I got mad at him once and turned it off. After a night similar to yours, he changed all my passwords, and now even I can't mess with my phone. When I got tired of getting humiliated by him, I just started going home every night."

Grant shook his head. "The man's a genius. I totally should have thought of that."

We made our way back to the house, still wrapped up in each other, and watched a movie together. I even cuddled with him on the couch. The movie turned into several card games of Speed where I was declared the ultimate champion. By eight o'clock we were starving and made a floor picnic in front of my fireplace.

"Ok, so tell me all about this software project my dad is too stupid to invest in," I stated as we ate our food.

"Well, the technical stuff is probably a little over your head, but basically it connects all of the financial software in each company we support and funnels it through one system. This will allow our customer support center to fix bugs instantly instead of having to learn each unique system." I could see the excitement in Grant's eyes when he talked about it.

"Sounds brilliant," I agreed. "Does it only run with my dad's software?"

"No, it would work with any of them. I'd just have to make a few adjustments," he explained.

"And does it compete with something my dad already has on the market?"

"No, it's brand new. Why?"

"So forget my dad, go get your own investors. Branch out," I suggested, trying to figure out why he was putting all his faith in my father.

"Your dad is a very powerful man, Issy. It's not smart to cross him." Grant's voice was defeated and resigned to the fate my father had given him.

"That's just what he wants you to think so you won't leave him. But goodness, Grant, you have a perfect opportunity here. You know all his contacts and all his competitors. Get investors quietly and then market it to the competition. My dad won't know what hit him." I was starting to get excited at the prospect of Grant getting out from under my dad's thumb and jumped up on my knees as I spoke.

He saw my eagerness and laughed. "How exactly am I supposed to quietly get investors?"

"Well, I will teach you," I offered, pulling him up off the floor. "There are several tactics that can be used when selling a person an idea."

"You mean manipulating them," Grant interrupted.

"Not manipulation. Remember, this is a great thing for them and for you. It's win win." I stood face to face with him and squared my shoulders. "Ok, so your first tactic is the assumption tactic. Most people will automatically assume my dad supports you simply because you work for him. For example, you go to this investor and tell them you have a great new software product, and as a personal favor, you want them to be the first ones to get a chance to invest in it. They in turn say to you, 'well, Andrew Summers is a shrewd businessman.' You kindly agree that he is. They assume that my dad is an investor as well and next thing you know, there is a check in your hand."

"Issy, I don't know whether to be impressed or terrified by how good you are at this," Grant stated looking at me in awe.

"Oh, I'm just getting started. The second tactic that is critical to master is the avoidance tactic. This is especially helpful when you have inquisitive businessmen. You once again present your software idea as if you are doing them a favor. But this time they ask you, 'what is Andrew Summers take on this product?' You smile and say, 'we both know Andrew Summers never makes a business move without first knowing it's going to be a success.' Once again they assume my dad is an investor. You will have money in your pocket in fifteen minutes, and never once did you distort the truth."

Grant walked toward me and put both his arms around my waist and grinned. "Better be careful, Issy, you might just grow up to be a shrewd business woman yourself."

I felt the butterflies start in my stomach as Grant's voice tickled my ears. My hands were resting on his chest, and I could feel his muscles underneath the thin material. "I'm only good at this when I believe in the product," I explained softly, unable to pull my eyes from his.

"And do you believe in my product, Issy?" Grant asked, moving closer to me.

"I believe in you." The words came out a whisper, but I knew Grant heard them.

He brought his head to mine, and I closed my eyes, anticipating his kiss. It never came. Instead I felt his breath next to my ear, sending even greater waves of desire through me. His voice was soft, but unmistakably clear. "I made a promise to myself that the next time I kissed you, it would be because you had given me all of you. I want to know when I kiss you that I will be the last person to ever do it." He leaned back up and searched my eyes. I knew I couldn't give him what he wanted, so I backed away, offering a regretful smile.

We sat back down and finished our meal, as I continued to give him "manipulation" lessons as he called it. When we finally called it a night, I felt a wave of peace that warmed me to the core. I found myself wanting to trust him, wanting to believe I could safely love him. The screaming in my head was noticeably quieter when I went to bed that night.

15. ROBERT MARSH

My dad came back early on Sunday and was irritable the minute he walked in the door. I noticed how all the staff shied away from him and even Grant seemed edgy. I decided I needed to get out of the house before I got my head chewed off. I almost made it out the door before I heard my father call me into his office.

"Yes, Daddy?" I asked sweetly as I hung by the door. "Is everything ok? You seem tense." I was trying not to sound patronizing, but I thought his attitude was ridiculous.

My father scowled at me and made a noise that sounded a lot like a bark. I started laughing, bringing an even deeper line to his forehead. "Do you have any idea how difficult you are making things?" he asked me, giving me a stare that came from a place of pure exasperation.

"What did I do?" I asked defensively. "You haven't even seen me in two days."

"I don't have to be here to know what you are up to. A bartender, Kaitlyn, really? I'm surprised you didn't make the front page of the society section with the way you carried on."

I stared at him in stunned silence. "Are you

spying on me?" I finally yelled, ready to go to battle.

I watched as my dad rubbed his temples, the stress covering his face. "I don't have time to argue with you right now. I have a merger that's hanging by a thread here."

"I thought it was all paperwork and contracts at this point," I reminded him sarcastically, using his exact terminology.

"It was," he said flatly. He waved his hand at me, letting me know we were done, but I heard him yell one more time before I even left the doorway. "I want you home by four."

"Fine, but don't think this conversation is over. Spying on me is over the top, even for you." I was shaking when I left the house, not even sure where I was going to go. I decided on the mall, knowing retail therapy always helped. Several hundred dollars later, I felt better and headed back home well before the four o'clock deadline.

My father's door was shut when I walked in, but I heard muffled voices from the kitchen. I walked towards the noise, but stopped outside the door when I heard Grant and Rosa talking.

"I don't know how to reach her," he said sadly. "Every time I even bring up the subject of faith, she shuts down. I'm scared if I push too hard, I'll lose her. She's already so close to the edge."

"You may not be the one meant to reach her," Rosa stated, patting his back.

"I won't accept that. I see her. Behind all the walls

and self-destructive behavior, I see that warm, caring girl who's just lost and hurt. I won't give up on her."

I heard Rosa sigh. "Neither will I. Keep praying, honey. God is in control."

I sucked in a breath, not wanting to hear any more, and headed straight to my room. I started putting away my new clothes when I saw a stunning black dress hanging from the handles of my armoire. It had an asymmetrical neckline that cut across the torso diagonally and draped in the back, exposing just enough skin to be sexy without being tacky. It still had tags on it and cost well over $1000. I was admiring the material when I heard my father clear his throat in the doorway.

"What is this for?" I asked, turning to face him.

"There's a dinner I need you at tonight. I'm willing to overlook your complete lack of judgment this weekend, as long as you come tonight and behave the way I know your mother taught you to." His voice was stern and authoritative as if I was one of his employees. I bit down on the side of my cheek to hold back the expletives I was dying to throw at him.

"Isn't this Anna's role? You've never wanted me at one of these before."

"Anna is still in New York. We had plans, but since I had to come back here to do damage control, she stayed. Now, this is a VERY important dinner with Robert Marsh tonight. Having a female presence tends to keep the tension down in the room," my father explained.

"What kind of damage control?" I asked, glaring at him. I still wanted to know how he heard about Jason.

"Pictures, Issy. Very disturbing pictures of you being groped by some tattooed waste of space in a bar. You forget where you are. You don't have the anonymity here to behave the way you did at Winsor," my father finally explained once again rubbing his temples.

"Jason is not a waste of space. And besides, what does any of this have to do with Robert Marsh and the merger?"

"Nothing," my father growled. "It's just too much for me to deal with in a span of twenty-four hours."

I looked closely at my father, who seemed more vulnerable than I'd ever remembered. "If this merger means that much to you, Daddy, I'll go, but not because I feel guilty about Friday night, which I don't. I'll go because you asked me to and because I can't wait to wear this dress."

I actually saw my father smile. He came over and gave me one of his signature bear hugs that practically crushed my chest. "That's my girl."

I was almost completely ready to go when I heard a knock at my door. I opened it up to find Grant whose smile suddenly became full admiration.

"Wow, where are you going in that?" he asked, looking me up and down. I pushed away thoughts of his conversation with Rosa and just let myself enjoy his attention. It really was a beautiful dress, and I wore my hair wavy and black just the way I knew Grant loved it. The ensemble was sophisticated and classy, and I couldn't help but notice I looked just like my mother had at this age.

"You like?" I asked spinning around a little. "My father is taking me to a business dinner with none other than the infamous Robert Marsh. I don't know what he is thinking, I always do something to tick him off." I was joking around, but stopped when I saw Grant slump down on one of my chairs looking completely bewildered.

"Why would he bring you to dinner with Robert Marsh? That doesn't make any sense." Grant was talking to himself at this point.

"He said having a female there keeps things more social or something like that," I offered, walking up to put my hand on his shoulder. "What's the matter?"

"Nothing. I just don't get it. He has explicitly refused to bring Anna to anything related to this merger. It just doesn't make sense why he suddenly wants you there, especially now that things are rocky again."

"Are you comparing me to Anna?" I snapped. I had noticed she didn't get under my skin quite as much as she used to, but I still didn't want anyone thinking we were anything alike.

"I wasn't trying to insult you, Issy. I'm just surprised," Grant said standing up. He then changed his tone and smiled at me again. "You do look absolutely breathtaking. I can't say I blame your dad for wanting to show you off."

I smiled back at him and spun around once more before meeting my father downstairs. His eyes brightened the minute he saw me and did a little bow before taking my hand. I beamed up at him, feeling more special than I had in years. It was the first date we'd had since I was twelve years old.

The restaurant he took me to was definitely worthy of my dress as it was tucked away inside an exclusive five star hotel. Every table was full, but we were guided to the back and through a private door where our table sat right next to a beautiful fireplace. The back wall was entirely glass and overlooked the perfectly manicured grounds outside the hotel.

Our dinner guests were seated with their backs to us, and I gave my father a confused look when I noticed there were two of them. My father just smiled and led us around the table where both men stood to greet us.

I knew my eyes gave away my shock the minute I saw Robbie stand and button his suit coat before introductions were made. He looked equally as stunned, but then pleasantly surprised. I was not so much. I should have guessed my father had an ulterior motive by bringing me here.

"Robert, this is my daughter, Kaitlyn," my father said proudly as he introduced me. "Kaitlyn, this is Robert Marsh and his son, Robbie." I reached my hand out to greet the two men with all the grace of a princess. Years of ballet and rigorous etiquette training from my mother had adequately prepared me for this exact moment.

"It's very nice to meet you, Mr. Marsh. Robbie, good to see you again." My voice was pure honey and my eyes completely void, giving no indication that I felt an eerie, tingling sensation when Robbie touched my hand.

"You two know each other?" my father asked as soon as he realized there was familiarity there.

Robbie cocked his side grin and turned back to my dad. "We have business marketing together. Isadora is the newest member of our group. Oh, I'm sorry, do you go by Kaitlyn?" Robbie asked, turning to me.

I felt grateful to him as I knew he did that only to spare me from being called Kaitlyn all night. "No, Isadora is fine. I actually prefer it," I said, giving my father a glance that only the two of us would recognize.

Once the small talk was over and our meals were brought out, Mr. Marsh and my father began negotiation on their deal that I presumed was heading south. I felt Robbie lean into me and whisper, "And here I thought I'd be spending a miserable evening with Kaitlyn Summers. I only agreed to come because my dad practically dangled a trip to Cancun in front of my eyes."

Robbie was considerably more charming in this setting, and I quickly remembered why I had found him attractive before he started to get all creepy on me. "I can't quite figure you out," I admitted, looking up to make sure my dad wasn't listening. "One minute, you're this charismatic, confident guy and the next you're, well, something much less charming." I left out the words scary and intense, but they floated to my mind as well.

"I admit, I came on a little too strong. It's just been a while since a girl wasn't completely smitten by my money that I didn't quite know what to do. I've played the part for so long now that sometimes I don't even realize when I'm doing it. Do you think you could give me another chance? Get to know the real me this time?"

I looked in his eyes, expecting to see the emotionless void that always seemed to be there. But this time, they sparkled with vulnerability and honesty. I could hear the soft music of the band and noticed a few couples were even dancing to the old fashioned music. I knew I was probably out of my mind, but I had promised my dad I would be the picture of perfection at dinner tonight, so I relented.

"Do you want to dance?" I asked him, setting down my fork.

He stood in response and put out his hand, leading me by the small of my back to the dance floor. I felt him gently pull me into him, placing his right arm around my waist as he held up his left arm for me. I delicately placed my hand in his, while my left hand gripped his shoulder. Seconds later, we were spinning around the dance floor as if we'd been dancing together for years. It was obvious that his parents had trained him just as impeccably as mine had trained me, and for the first time since I met Robbie, I felt like I understood him. He was trapped in the same world I was. A world of unending expectation and pretension. A world that required absolute control at all times or you would be devastated by those around you.

We finished our dance and immediately heard the other guests start to clap. Robbie backed away while I curtsied in response and then led me back to the table. "Mesmerizing in any setting," he stated with a proud smile on his face.

"I wasn't the only one out there, Robbie. You were practically Fred Astaire," I teased as he pulled out my chair for me. He just chuckled and took his seat.

Our fathers were notably examining the two of us, practically drooling at the mouth. I resisted every urge to roll my eyes as I saw a repeat of the Branson saga happening all over again.

Dinner ended with my father and Mr. Marsh coming to some kind of agreement as the mood shifted to a much more social one. The men ordered a round of drinks, and I glanced at my father who smiled in approval as I sipped my wine. It was truly remarkable what a hypocrite he was. Mr. Marsh told embarrassing stories on Robbie, who gracefully laughed and nodded, letting his dad have fun at his expense. My father considered chiming in, but one look from me kept him in check. I had been the perfect companion tonight, and he knew my patience was starting to wane. It was almost midnight and several rounds later before they finally called it quits.

My dad was swaying a little as he walked, but was practically beaming as he slapped Mr. Marsh's back and shook his hand. "Looks like everything's back on track, wouldn't you say?" Mr. Marsh nodded in agreement and then made eye contact with his son.

"I guess that's my cue," Robbie whispered to me as we watched them interact. "I had a really good time tonight."

I smiled up at him. "I did too. I like this version of you," I admitted.

"I'll keep that in mind," he said with a wink before kissing the top of my hand. "See ya Tuesday."

My father was in no condition to drive, so we taxied it back to the house.

"I seriously need to consider getting a driver," he said as he stepped out of the cab and straightened out his jacket. I watched the white car drive away and saw my dad sniffing his clothes as if he now smelled middle class.

"You're such a snob," I teased, pushing him towards the door. "It's good for you to see how the rest of the world lives. It keeps you grounded."

"Sweetheart, after this merger goes through, you are going to experience wealth like you never have before."

"Thanks, but no thanks, Daddy. I've had about all

I can take."

He looked at me and shook his head in disbelief before placing his heavy arm around my shoulder. He was a mammoth of a man, and I practically fell over as he used me to stabilize himself on the steps.

"I'm going to bed, sweetheart," my father said once we made it into the house. "See you in the morning, seven sharp." I saluted him with my lip curled in a snarl once I knew his back was to me, and headed up the stairs. I was starting to hate those words.

I turned on my light and practically jumped out of my shoes when I saw Grant slouched over in the sitting area of my room.

"He's got a son," Grant said flatly, his head still buried in his hands.

"So I discovered," I answered, wondering why he seemed so stricken. I took off my shoes, feeling my calves relax as my bare feet hit the ground. "You ok?"

He looked up at me and gave a weary smile. "Yeah, just had that moment of recognition today when someone that once sat high on a pedestal came crashing down."

"If you are talking about my father, well, I'm surprised it took this long," I muttered, crossing my arms and throwing him a look that said I told you so.

"You don't seem that upset about it."

"Grant, there isn't much my father can do at this point to surprise me. Trying to set me up with the rich son of a potential business partner is right up his alley. If you recall, he spent years trying to do it with Branson."

"Issy, Branson's father had nothing on Mr. Marsh. I also highly doubt his son is anything like Branson. I don't know. It just seems like everything is working against me."

Grant stood and looked at me, his eyes showing all the longing that I knew was there for both of us, and seemed to get more powerful each day we stayed "just friends." I wanted to revolt against his no kiss declaration, so I turned my back to him and glanced over my shoulder. "Do you mind?" I asked eyeing my zipper.

I felt his fingertips move to my neck before pushing my hair to the side. Every nerve ending in my body was ablaze, and I closed my eyes as his touch seared my skin. I felt the zipper give and then his fingers follow it down my back, leaving a trail of fire in its path. I didn't want to move, only wanted more of his touch. I felt him move closer to my back, leaning down to run his lips softly over my neck.

"Did you like him?" he asked gently, his voice slowly bringing me back to reality.

I moved away from him before I lost myself completely, my arm across my chest being the only thing to keep the dress from falling at my ankles. "I actually already knew him. Small world, huh?"

I saw Grant's eye move into a slant. "How well do you know him?"

"Not that well," I answered with a laugh, only

slightly offended by his question. "We have business marketing together. He's not a bad guy. In fact, I think he has as many Daddy issues as I do."

"Wow, that's a nightmare waiting to happen," Grant teased, his body starting to relax a little.

I threw my shoe at him and he jumped out of the way just in time. "On that note, I'm getting out of here before you permanently hurt me. See you tomorrow, Issy."

"Night Grant," I said as he shut the door, and to my delight, the warm feeling swept over me once more.

16. POWER COUPLE

I was relieved when I didn't see Robbie outside of my class on Monday, especially since Jason was being overly affectionate. He had been waiting for me in the seat next to mine and didn't move, even when Reggie sat down on the other side of me. I kept feeling his hand move to my leg and tickle under my kneecap while the professor droned on about the basics of business.

"Jason, stop it," I hissed after he had done it a third time. He just grinned, but kept his hands to himself, no doubt satisfied that I finally acknowledged his existence for the first time today. I had hoped that Jason meant what he had said and would back off, but that didn't seem to be the case. I silently cursed to myself. I had picked Jason for two reasons. One, he was hot. Two, he was a ladies man. There wasn't supposed to be any attachment. I glanced back at him, noting how his icy blue eyes locked onto mine, and slouched back in my chair. This was going to get ugly.

Even more confusing was Reggie's response to me. He barely offered me more than a nod this morning and left class without saying a word. I didn't know Reggie well, but I'd seen his mannerisms enough to know he was upset with me.

When lunch arrived, the confusion that had clouded me all morning finally disappeared when Rachel grabbed my hand and pulled me into the seat next to her.

"Oh my, Issy. How do you do it? You are officially my new mentor. You broke Rusty's heart, just when all of us were starting to question if he even liked girls. Then Friday night you had the hot bartender eating out of your hand and now this? Unbelievable."

The "this" she was referring to was a close up picture on the front of the society section that showed Robbie leaning down to kiss the top of my hand. I looked smitten and charmed by the affection, although I never remembered feeling either of those things when he had kissed me. They must have had a ton of pictures to pick from and just got lucky with this one. The headline read: **POWER COUPLE**, but the caption below was even more nauseating.

"Watch out, ladies. It looks like Kaitlyn Summers, daughter of Computer Tycoon, Andrew Summers, has landed North Carolina's most eligible bachelor. Have the two most powerful families in North Carolina finally merged? Neither party would comment, but sources close to the couple say they have been seen together on multiple occasions."

I felt my ears begin to ring a little as the words "Damage Control" slipped in my head. No doubt my father had staged these pictures just to replace the ones of me and Jason.

"Rachel, who all have you shown this to?" I asked, interrupting her battery of questions.

"Everyone. Are you kidding...you're famous!"

I felt my stomach turn a little as I glanced down at the other end of the table. I excused myself from Rachel and sat down next to Candace who had made very little eye contact with me. Rusty stood up slowly and muttered something about needing to get to class. Reggie left with him, and neither acknowledged me.

I put my head in my hands and shook it. This was exactly what I didn't want to happen.

"You had quite a weekend, I hear," Candace said quietly.

I turned my head to look up at her through my hands. "At least one of you is still talking to me," I blurted, feeling a frustration I couldn't explain. Truth was, I really did like these guys. They reminded me of Avery, and were the kind of people that cared about others more than themselves.

"Don't mind them. Rusty's ego is bruised, and Reggie is his friend. Although, tip for next time. If you tell a guy you're not into dating, don't kiss someone else in front of his friends and then show up on the cover of a newspaper with the words power couple. It tends to send the wrong message."

I couldn't help but laugh at the irony of it all, and

Candace soon joined me, until we were wiping tears out of our eyes.

"Issy, I know we haven't known each other that long, but I feel a kinship with you. So I'm going to tell you this and I want you to hear it." Candace was being serious now and facing off with me to ensure I was listening. "I'm worried about you, but I'm not going to lecture you. If you ever need me and I mean ever, I'm here. No questions asked. You got that?"

She was so sincere and seemed so confident in what she was saying. I put my head back in my hands and sighed. "No one's ever truly there for you, Candace, not really. But thanks."

"Well, maybe not for you, not yet. But I know someone who is there for me whenever I need Him. He has never let me down."

I chuckled at her serious tone. "What's Reggie think of your affection for this guy?"

Candace just smiled. "Don't worry, Reggie knows Him well. I'd love to introduce Him to you some time, too."

I knew she was talking figuratively, because she had made it no secret that she was a Christian. Not wanting to have this conversation, I threw my hands up in protest. "No way, I'm steering clear of men for a long time."

Candace started laughing again and then followed me out of the Student Union. "When you're ready to meet Him, you'll know." Then she was off with a wave.

I dreaded going to Shakespeare, but skipping again was not a good idea. The class was too small for me to go unnoticed, and participation was probably all I had to save my grade.

I hadn't really eaten lunch, so I was thirty minutes early to class. I straddled the concrete wall outside my building while I waited and checked my phone. It was disturbingly sparse. Avery had checked in on me, of course, but my other friends from Winsor were forgetting me. Jake also seemed lost in another world. His internship had turned into a full-fledged job he loved. I got a knot in the pit of my stomach that told me everything was changing, and I didn't want it to.

I was still looking down at my phone when I saw Jason's torn up jeans straddle the wall in front of me. I closed my eyes in protest, having no energy for this right now.

"I know we're not a power couple, green eyes, but I did figure you would at least talk to me." Jason's voice was mild, but there was no question he seemed hurt.

I looked up at him and felt mildly guilty. He'd been nothing outside of perfect to me, letting me have complete control of our relationship, if you would even call it that.

"I'm sorry, Jason. Today's been kind of a bad day," I explained, not really telling him anything.

He scooted up closer to me and placed his hand on my thigh. "What do you need from me?" he asked sincerely, looking deep into my eyes, searching. There was nothing to find; I had deadened them the minute we started talking.

I straightened up, and then sent him a smile that said all was right in the world. "I need you to forget Friday happened and go back to bantering with me just like before, a man on a mission to get that first kiss."

"I am on a mission, Issy," he promised and stood up to help me off the wall. "All charm and no drama. I can do that."

"Thanks," I replied, relieved to have the conversation over with.

But it wasn't over with because Jason pulled me around the corner to a secluded alcove in the building and backed me up against the wall. I felt his hands on my face as his icy eyes penetrated mine. "But before I can erase it from my memory completely, I need to know it wasn't a dream." Then Jason's lips consumed me, hungry and desperate. I allowed him the moment, giving him what he needed to let go. But I felt a little more of myself die inside. The numbness was getting easier to recreate…even without the alcohol.

I slammed the repulsive picture of me and Robbie on my father's desk, not even bothering to knock.

"What is this?" I demanded with my arms folded.

My father chuckled before picking up the paper and leaned back in his chair. "Sweetheart, this is not my doing. Although, this little article did send our stocks soaring today. Trust me, if I was responsible, I'd take credit for it."

I threw myself down in the chair. Now who was I going to yell at?

"Speaking of Robert Marsh, though, we've been invited to their house for dinner tonight."

"No way. I'm still trying to recover from the last dinner you made me go to."

My dad stood up, no doubt to intimidate me, and pressed his fingers together. "That wasn't a request. But, since I don't want you doing anything to embarrass me tonight, I'll give you a carrot. You can have a weekend pass to Winsor, assuming tonight goes well."

I felt anger rock my stomach. "You are bribing me now? What happened to protecting me at all cost, so much so you had to send a chaperone with me last time? Don't get any ideas, Daddy. I am NOT Robbie Marsh, and I will NOT 'play my role' just to get what I want." I stood to face him defiantly, but my stature compared to his was pretty pathetic.

I watched as the vein in my father's neck started to pulsate. "You will go to that dinner tonight, Kaitlyn, or so help me, I will make a call and release that empty, over-priced room back to the University."

I gasped in horror. My apartment, the only place that ever felt like home. It represented my independence, my freedom. I took one look at his face and knew he wasn't bluffing. This merger was consuming him, changing him more and more into a man I hated.

I stormed out of his office without a word and ran to my room. There was another dress hanging from the armoire, sending a fire of fury down my spine. I threw open my balcony door and screamed at the top of my lungs before collapsing on the deck. I could almost see the shackles on my feet as I wondered if I would ever again be free.

I descended the stairs intentionally five minutes later than my dad requested and found all of them hovering by the door. My dad had classed Anna up tonight, I noted. Her blond hair was swept back into a French twist, and for the first time in years, I didn't see her panty line through her dress. Junior was there as well, dressed in a suit to match my father's. I saw his six-year-old eyes look up at my dad as if he was superman.

That was when it hit me. It was the moment it all made sense. My father marrying Anna had nothing to do with my mother or me or even Anna. It had everything to do with Junior. He was given a son, his legacy that he could mold in to a man worthy of his name. I watched as Junior's little hand reached up to hold my father's, and I realized that for the first time in seven years, I didn't hate that little boy. I felt sad for him. He would never be his own man, and just like me, would be forever owned by our father.

My father finally noticed me and scowled. "You're late."

"I'm here. Just be thankful for that," I answered back in disgust.

My father led us out the door like one happy family, and I wanted to hurl. His new driver held the door of the limo open for us, and I watched as Junior and Anna got in the car, leaving my father and I alone for a second.

"Nice driver, Daddy. It didn't take you long," I noted sarcastically.

"I was losing too much time in the commute," my dad replied dismissively. I started to get in the car, and felt his hand grip my arm. "Kaitlyn, you will not embarrass me tonight. Do you understand?"

I stiffened under his grasp and pulled at my arm unsuccessfully. "I understand that if you call me Kaitlyn one more time, you will be praying for me to simply embarrass you." It wasn't an idle threat. I was dangerously close to the edge, and I could tell my father saw it in my eyes. He let go and didn't once call me Kaitlyn the entire way to Robbie's estate.

Robbie was waiting for us outside and greeted my father and Anna appropriately before showing them to the front door. When he got to me, he smiled and gave me a kiss on the cheek. It felt like a natural hello, so I didn't take offense to it.

"I brought these for you," he said lightly as he opened his palm to show two shiny pennies. His eyes were sparkling again, full of life and vibrancy. I was drawn to it, knowing mine held nothing that matched. I touched the penny and felt the tears sting my eyes. I couldn't stop it. I turned away from him, fighting to find the shield that was failing me.

"Hey, you ok?" Robbie asked softly, his hand rubbing my back. He walked around to face me, lifting my chin. "Listen, I know that article was a nightmare today. I got it from all sides too. You're not in this alone, ok? Let's just get though this dinner and the merger, so maybe one day you and I can have a cup of coffee or something without all this pressure." With two thumbs he wiped the tears that had spilled over my eyes. He was only the second man I had ever cried in front of. I should have felt terrified, but I didn't. I felt like he understood.

He held my hand and led me to the fountain that was lit up beautifully against the night sky. I noticed our previous pennies still marred the pristine surface and smiled up at him. "You left them there?" I asked not masking the surprise in my voice.

"Of course, they aren't moving until you finally get your wish." He flashed me a genuine smile and then closed his eyes to make the wish. Who was this person? He was the complete opposite of the stiff, possessive guy who had tried unsuccessfully to seduce me with his wealth. Was it possible that I had actually met someone who had as many layers as I did?

I threw my penny in the water with a small splash. The wish was the same, as was the reality that it would never happen. I needed to pull myself together.

The day was wearing on me and I cursed myself a little for not packing my little silver flask.

I didn't realize I was staring off into space until Robbie touched my arm to get my attention. "Isadora? You still with me?"

I gave him a weak smile and nodded. He led me back up to the house and into the massive dining room where his and my family were waiting. Robbie brought me over to his mother for introductions. I had my mask firmly in place and performed to such a measure that even my mother would have been proud. Mrs. Marsh was not much more than a robot herself. She was still beautiful despite showing signs of aging, and looked as if she had some surgical help in that respect, but she was like a dead woman walking, hardly smiling or interacting. She looked more like a quiet accessory to Robbie's father than an actual person. Watching her, I didn't know whether to feel sorry for her or for Robbie, who had to live with two people who had the personality of a limp noodle. My dad certainly had his faults, but at least he was still full of life.

I felt my chest starting to constrict as the conversation waned on, and we had only made it through two courses. My father and Mr. Marsh were in deep discussion about some computer hardware, and Anna was giving Mrs. Marsh a detailed explanation of the charity work she was involved in. I watched Junior. He seemed lost in his own little world, no doubt fully detached from the environment.

I must have looked as miserable as I felt because Robbie leaned over and whispered, "I'm not really hungry if you want to get out of here."

I looked at him as though he offered me the world. He stood in response and walked over to his mother to whisper in her ear. She nodded and smiled. Then Robbie addressed my father. "Sir, would you mine if I steal Isadora away for a while?"

My father didn't even try to hide his elation at the idea of Robbie and I spending more time together. "Sure, you kids go have fun."

I was practically running out of the house as we found our way to the back yard. I didn't say a word, just took off my shoes, sat on the edge and dipped my feet into the pool. The cold water made me gasp, but internally, I loved it. I had lost my edge tonight, unable to numb myself to my life. The water would help...it always helped.

Robbie sat down beside me, careful to stay far enough from the pool edge not to get any water on his clothes. I thought of Grant and how he put his feet in the water too, just to try and understand what I was feeling. Robbie did not.

"On a scale of one to ten, I'd say that was a twelve for one of the most boring dinner parties ever," Robbie offered after an uncomfortable stretch of silence.

I turned to him, my chest still constricting from the walls that had continued to close in on me since I first read the words, "Power Couple." I was practically pleading when I spoke. "Robbie, I need to get out of here and just do something crazy. Anything. I can't handle another minute."

Robbie stood and put out his hand. I took it and he pulled me up. My bare feet were on the pool deck, but I couldn't feel anything as I followed him. He stopped by the outdoor bar and pulled out a bottle of tequila and guided me to a walkway that led us away from the house. With each step, I felt the walls start to recede, and just knowing I could have a drink soon eased my panic.

It was dark where he was leading me, so I moved up to hold on to his whole arm as we walked, not wanting to stumble around on my feet that were just starting to get some feeling back in them. Just as I thought it couldn't get any darker, there was suddenly a faint light in front of us. We were out by the stables, and I could smell the horses as we approached.

"You may want to put your shoes on now," Robbie suggested as he opened the door. "Its not really a barefoot place."

I did as he suggested thinking my high heels weren't really that appropriate either, but oh well. The horses greeted us as he pulled open the large doors. I watched as he patted a few of them, talking as if they were long time friends. I held back. This wasn't really a setting I was used to, and hadn't really ever been around animals.

Robbie noticed my hesitation and laughed. "Did I

actually find something you're afraid of?"

I shot him a look at went right up to the horse and patted its head as it nodded up and down. "I'm not afraid of anything," I answered after brushing my hands off.

Robbie smirked and continued to move deeper into the barn. In a room away from the horses, he finally stopped and sat down on a block of hay, patting the area next to him for me to take a seat. I moved without hesitation and took the bottle out of his hand as I sat. I screwed off the top and drank down the clear liquid as if I was parched in the desert. It immediately soothed me, burning off any emotion as it scorched my throat. When I was done, I handed it back to Robbie who also took a long swig.

"You ever shoot a bow?" he asked after closing the bottle again.

"No, why, do you have one?"

Robbie stood up and flipped on a switch, lighting up the back wall and two large archery targets.

"May I put my dad's face on one of those?" I asked standing. Robbie kept surprising me. I had truly never been so baffled by another person.

He laughed and then opened a chest to pull out a large bow and several arrows. "I don't really keep pictures of your dad around, but it is great for blowing off steam." I watched as Robbie held the bow with precision and then perfectly shot the arrow into the bullseye of the target.

I arched my eyebrow at him. "Impressive. Care to

make it interesting?" I asked shaking the bottle in front of him.

"What did you have in mind?"

"Every time I hit the target at all, you have to take a drink. Every time you hit the bullseye, I have to take a drink. If we miss, it goes back to the other person."

"You're going to be taking a lot of drinks," he warned me.

"Isn't that the point?"

"Ok, but at least let me give you a little lesson." I felt Robbie put his hand on my waist and move me in front of the target. He showed me how to hold the bow, pull the string and even how to use my breathing to help stabilize it. I couldn't help but notice how close he was standing as he guided me through the motions.

I pulled back the bow, ready to take my aim when I heard him whisper in my ear, "You have to become completely in tune with your target before you strike." There was something in his tone that sent a shiver down my spine and made my stomach flutter a little. I was still trying to decide if they were nervous flutters or something else when I heard him say, "now let go."

The arrow went soaring through the air and completely missed the target. I scowled and demanded to do it again. He gave me another arrow, and I made sure to concentrate this time. I released. It wasn't pretty, but it did hit the outside of the target.

"Drink up," I demanded, feeling a little smug.

Robbie took the bottle and put it to his lips for a drink. His intensity was back and didn't once take his eyes off me while he drank. I felt the butterflies again. It was the look in his eyes…the calm assurance that he could get anything he wanted, and I suddenly felt like the target.

He put down the bottle and took the bow and arrow. Seconds later, the arrow was in the bullseye, and it was my turn. The liquid didn't burn as bad this time, my throat still numb from the last drink, but I was secretly wishing for some limes.

We went back and forth like that through six more rounds. Robbie never faltered, hitting the bulleye every time he picked up the bow. I was not so lucky and hit the target only two more times. I set down the bottle from my last shot and started to walk towards the bow again. The room shifted, and I reached out, feeling like I was about to fall.

I felt Robbie's arms grab me to keep me steady. "You ok?" he asked in a voice that seemed concerned, but also showed signs that he was affected by how close we were now standing.

The room was still spinning, and I could feel my stomach lurch a little. "I think I just need to sit for second," I whispered, relying solely on Robbie for balance at that point.

He walked us over to the block of hay, and I immediately put my head in my hands after we sat. I couldn't get the room to stop and the more it spun, the more my stomach turned. I just needed to lay down for a minute and I'd be ok. I felt Robbie's shirt next to my cheek and closed my eyes. Then the world went black…again.

17. THE BLACKOUT

Satin and silk surrounded me at every angle as I tried to pry my eyes open. A rich smell of flowers penetrated my senses and almost made my stomach turn as it combined with the fresh linen smell of the sheets covering me. I couldn't seem to focus and was still trying to figure out where I was. The barn...that was all I remembered. Robbie. Every one of my senses went on alert as I realized I had been with him when I blacked out. My stomach turned as I felt around the bed, but there was no sign of anyone. Relief brought tears to my eyes, but it still didn't explain where I was, or how I got there. Where was my father?

When my eyes were finally able to focus, I pulled back the covers to try and stand. Immediately, I noticed that my clothes were gone, including all of my under garments, and I was wearing a long white silk nightgown. The fear that always seemed to accompany Robbie started to work down my spine as I searched for anything I recognized in the room. There was nothing, no clothes, no shoes, and most importantly, no phone.

The room itself also held no familiarity. While

beautiful with antique white furniture and soft silk drapes that covered the large windows, it looked more like a high-end hotel room than something anyone would live in. I walked over to the mirror that sat above an ornate white fireplace and examined myself. My hair was perfectly brushed and my makeup was gone, making me look younger and fresher than I ever did when I woke up the morning after I drank too much. It was obvious that someone not only undressed me, but also took great care to make sure I looked beautiful before I went to bed. I smelled my skin and realized that I had been bathed.

Just when I was about to start panicking, I heard a small rap at the door followed by one of Robbie's housekeepers coming into the room.

"Ms. Summers, you're awake. Very good. Mr. Marsh is waiting for you at the breakfast table," she explained as she immediately started to tidy up the bed.

"Um, could you tell me where my stuff is?" I asked, trying to keep my voice from shaking.

"I'm sorry, miss, we got rid of your clothes. Mr. Marsh said they were ruined," she explained looking a little worried.

I stood there trying to decide if I was more shocked or angry at the idea that Robbie would have the gall to get rid of my things. But since this poor girl was obviously not the one to blame, I gritted my teeth and tried to remain calm. "What about my purse?"

"I'm not sure, miss. I'll check right away." She

then walked over to the large double doors on the opposite side of the room and opened them for me. "There are lots of beautiful clothes in here, miss. Please use whatever you need."

I didn't want to wear someone else's clothes, I wanted my own. I also didn't like the idea that I was put in a room that appeared to be the holding cell for Robbie's conquests. I folded my arms across my chest and stared at the closet full of female clothes and shoes. "Does Robbie have women over here a lot?"

The housekeeper looked horrified and quickly shook her head. "Oh no, ma'am, you are the only girl I've ever seen here. Mr. Marsh is not like that."

"Then who are all these clothes for?" I knew I was being nosey, but things were just getting weirder by the moment, and my patience was wearing thin.

"For you, miss," she explained as if she didn't understand why I would even ask that question. "Please, Mr. Marsh is waiting. There should be everything you need in the bathroom and I will check on your purse." With those words, she practically ran out of the room. She must have sensed my frustration, which was exasperated by the pounding headache that had moved in once the shock wore off.

I stalked over to the closet and found it full of outfits already put together, all with the tags still on. Everything was sized perfectly to fit me and I noticed my hands shaking as I examined each one.

Since I wasn't about to approach Robbie in the see through nightgown, I resigned myself to wear one of them, even though they were far more conservative than anything I'd normally buy. I found a new set of bra and panties in the lingerie drawer and put them on. Again, my exact size.

I slid on the cropped black Armani pants, buttoned up the white asymmetric jacket that was paired with it, and tried not to think about how creepy all of this was. In the bathroom I found an array of lotions, perfumes and makeup, all of which had never been used. I opened what I needed and finished getting ready before really examining myself in the mirror. It was me, but a completely different version. I put my hands on the vanity and tried to catch my breath. The walls were closing in, and I looked in the mirror again, staring face to face with a woman who looked just like my mother. It was a woman I swore I'd never be. I didn't want this life. I didn't want Robbie and his billions of dollars. Yet, here I was, wearing clothes that weren't mine, staring into a face that was completely different than the one I stared at when I was still at Winsor.

Tears were dangerously close to the surface, but I managed to keep them at bay. Once controlled, I pulled out a pair of red heels and left the room. The hall was vast and went on in each direction so far that I had no idea which way to go. I turned to the right and hoped I would run into anything that looked familiar. Luckily, I found the stairs and slowly descended, clutching the rail for dear life. My headache was excruciating now and the dizziness was still coming in waves. The rail stabilized me until I reached the bottom and found my way to the dining area where we ate last night.

Robbie was already seated, reading through a stack of papers as he sipped his coffee. He matched the setting, looking just as extravagant in his layered sweater and blazer that probably cost more than most people's monthly salaries. Nerves hit my stomach again, and I grabbed onto the door frame trying to maintain my balance. I searched my mind, attempting to remember anything about the night before. There was nothing…only the fear that Robbie and I may have taken our relationship to a level I certainly didn't want.

He finally looked up and saw me there. His face lit up as a smile appeared. "You're awake." He stood and walked over to me, wrapped one arm around my waist and put the other on my face. Before I could protest, he pulled me in for a long, lingering kiss. I didn't respond in any way, but Robbie either didn't notice or didn't care. Neither option set well with me.

"You look amazing. How are you feeling?" he asked when he finally pulled away.

"Like I'm going to throw up," I answered honestly with a scowl, leaving out the part that he had more to do with that fact than the leftover tequila.

"You do look pale. Come and sit." He guided me over to the chair next to his and before I was fully seated, one of his housekeepers had a green smoothie and three aspirins placed in front of me. I immediately took the aspirin and began to drink my smoothie while Robbie settled back in his chair.

It took me a few minutes, but finally it registered. "Wait. How did you know about my smoothies?" I asked.

Robbie looked back up from his paper and smiled at me, picking up the hand closest to him. He kissed my fingers before glancing back at me. "I've made it a point to learn all I can about you, Isadora."

My stomach turned as I slowly pulled my hand away. I had to get out of here. "Do you know where my purse is? Or what happened with my father?"

Robbie didn't seem the least bit affected by my mood. "Your father left last night, and your purse is on the chair where you left it."

My eyes darted to the chair I had sat in last night and sure enough, the purse was right where I left it. I stood up immediately to go get it and checked my phone before I sat back down. I didn't want Robbie reading my messages over my shoulder. There was nothing from my father, but Grant had texted me twice. The first was to find out if I was ok. He noticed I hadn't come home with my father. The second was two hours later and made the butterflies in my stomach start to move with extreme agitation.

Grant: I'm done.

I slowly put my phone in my purse and took my seat again.

"Everything ok?" Robbie asked with a smile, but his eyes had darkened again, and his voice had a new tension in it.

"What happened last night?" I asked hesitantly. Part of me didn't want to know.

Robbie looked almost amused, borderline sinister. "You don't remember?"

"No."

He stood up and moved behind me, setting his hands on my shoulders, massaging them a little. I felt his breath on my neck before his lips moved against it. "You were exquisite," he whispered, continuing to move his lips up my jawline and to my ear.

"What's that mean, Robbie?" I asked, my voice getting high and shaky. "What exactly happened?" My entire body was shaking from both repulsion and fear. If it were anyone else, I would have stood up and given him a piece of my mind. But this was Mr. Marsh's son, and if there was one rule in our house, the only real unbreakable rule, it was that I was to behave a certain way around Daddy's business associates.

Robbie's grip got tighter as I felt him move closer to me. "It was intimate in a way that went beyond anything physical. You may not remember, Isadora, but I certainly do." He let go of my shoulders and sat back down, his emotionless smile returning.

I still didn't know what he meant. "So, we didn't sleep together?" I asked, needing a verbal confirmation from him.

He raised an eyebrow. "No. We did not."

I put my head in my hands, so relieved I wanted

to cry. "Did my father even check on me?" I still couldn't wrap my mind around the fact that he had just left me there. Did he not know how dangerous that was? Did he even care?

"I called his assistant and told him you would be staying with me, and that I would take you to class today," he explained while he continued to look at his paper.

My head immediately jerked up. "You called Grant? What did you say?"

Robbie noticed my reaction, and I saw his eyes darken again. "I didn't mention you were drunk. I just said you decided to spend the night here and to let your dad know. He asked to speak to you, but I told him you were in the bath and couldn't talk." Everything Robbie said was factual, as if he was relaying a message with no feeling. I felt my palms start to sweat as I thought of Grant's words. He thought I stayed intentionally and had Robbie call to tell him. Surely he knew better. I would never be so cruel.

"Robbie, I need to get home," I said standing up, my balance wavering as soon as I did.

He was immediately at my side, stabilizing me. "We have class in thirty minutes. It won't look good if you skip again, especially after being a late add on to our group." There was no negotiation in Robbie's voice. It was a tone I recognized from my father. The discussion was over.

He led me to the front door, keeping his arm

firmly locked around my shoulder. He was a lot stronger than I had ever realized. Before getting in the back of his car, he pulled me in again for a long intense kiss, which I once again did not respond to. Robbie was living in his own world this morning, and I was a fixture trapped inside of it. I could feel my heart racing as the car drove away. I just had to get through this class and get home. Then I would make it clear to my father that merger or not, I was never seeing Robbie Marsh again.

Robbie continued to kiss my neck and rub my leg the entire drive despite my protests. It was as if he wasn't hearing anything I had to say.

"Robbie, seriously, you need to stop," I urged pushing him off of me again.

"I'm sorry. You just look so gorgeous in that outfit and smell so amazing this morning," he explained moving back but still not taking his hand off me.

I was wearing the perfume that was in the bathroom and made a mental note that I would never buy a similar fragrance. The last thing I wanted was to be more attractive to Robbie. "Yeah, about the outfit. I'll have it cleaned and will get it back to you."

"Nonsense," he said, dismissing my words. "It belongs to you now."

I started to protest, but realized it would do no good, so I just held my tongue and looked out the window until I saw the campus approach. It was the first time I actually felt relieved to be at school.

The driver stopped and then got out to open our door. Robbie went first and then offered his hand to help me out. I took it, but immediately regretted doing so, because he pulled me into a crushing embrace the minute I was out of the car and kissed me in front of a mass of people. I stared at him in shock when he released me, but he only smiled and began walking us towards our class, my hand still held captive by his. I tried to pull it away, but his grip tightened, almost cutting off my circulation.

Fury consumed me, and I stopped in my tracks, refusing to go any further. Robbie leaned into me with a fake smile plastered on his face. "What are you doing?" he whispered.

I stared him fully in the eye, my green eyes penetrating his so there was no confusion. "If you don't stop touching me, I will forget everything my father has taught me about social etiquette." It was not an idle threat as I was two seconds away from screaming at the top of my lungs.

Robbie let go of my hand and smirked. "My you are testy in the mornings. I'll have to remember that."

My hand itched to slap his face, but I kept it locked beside me as I stormed towards class not caring that I had left him standing there. I was already seated when he joined the group, his charm and charisma garnering admiring glances from the ladies around us. He sat next to me and wrapped his arm around the back of my chair, careful not to touch me in the process. To anyone else, it looked natural and intimate, but to me, it was a clear gesture of possessiveness. He wanted everyone in class to know we were together, and I just wanted to scream that we weren't.

I didn't say a word this time in the group, only nodded in agreement to whatever they wanted to do. It felt as if time was moving backwards, leaving me stuck in there for what seemed like hours. We finished our classroom assignment and waited as the professor gave final instructions before releasing us. I stood quickly and grabbed my purse. Maybe Jason or Candace was on campus and could give me a ride home. I wasn't getting back in that car with Robbie.

I was just starting to text them when I felt Robbie behind me, once again closer than necessary. "Put that away. I'll take you home." It was not a request.

"No thanks. I'll find my own way," I snapped, moving away from him again.

I felt my arm being grasped and then I was spun around to face him. He took the phone out of my hand and leaned into me again. "I'll take you home. Your father entrusted you with me, and I'm not handing you off to someone else," he demanded sternly.

"Fine," I said through gritted teeth.

He handed back my phone, which I quickly put out of sight in my purse, and gestured toward the car. I walked ahead of him and climbed in as the driver held it open. Robbie was right behind me and looked as angry as I felt. The tension was palpable and seemed to grow thicker as we drove.

Then, as if he flipped a switch, Robbie's face relaxed into a smile. "I guess I'll have to get used to that fiery temper of yours," he conceded with a chuckle.

It was official. This guy was delusional. "Robbie, this is the last time we will be hanging out, so you don't have to worry about getting used to anything," I replied sharply.

"We'll see how you feel after you calm down," he said dismissively. "Things always look differently after a little sleep, and I'm sure you're exhausted after last night."

I didn't argue. I didn't want to think about last night. I just wanted out of this car and out of these clothes, which I strongly considered burning as soon as I got home.

The sight of my house almost brought tears of joy knowing that I would soon be free of the metal prison I was sitting in. The driver parked the car and I opened the door before he could get out of his seat. I was almost free when I felt my hand being tugged and Robbie's moist lips on my fingers again.

"Get some sleep. I'll see you tomorrow," he said smoothly.

I jerked my hand away and took off in a sprint up the stairs to my house. I slammed the door just for good measure and put my back to it, feeling adrenaline surge through my entire body. My chest was heaving up and down as my palms ran over the detailing in the wood door. I could feel myself getting out of control; the fear, anger and regret pouring through me in waves.

I didn't look up until I heard footsteps and saw Grant stepping out of my father's office. He stared at me for a long time, standing there frozen to the door, and just shook his head before walking away towards his room. The emotion I had just started to get under control came rushing back as I watched him retreat, and I felt my body catapult forward after him.

"Hey, don't you judge me and walk away," I screamed, taking out all my fury on him. "So you're done with me, huh? Fine, I never asked you for anything to begin with."

I had followed him into his room where he was throwing some clothes in a duffle bag. My breath caught as I looked around. It was completely bare, except for a small bible on his nightstand. His posters, personal affects, everything else had disappeared. "What happened to all your stuff?" I asked suddenly, forgetting we were in the middle of an argument.

He didn't turn to me or react in any way. Just calmly explained, "Issy, I've had my own apartment for over a year now. I just stay here when I have to."

I couldn't believe it. I had been so focused on my life since coming here, I failed to even notice that Grant had moved out. The thought hit me harder than I cared to admit. I wanted him here. He was my rock, my one source of stability in a world that felt completely chaotic.

"Why didn't you tell me?" I asked, still in shock over knowing he had his own life outside of this house.

Grant finally turned to me, his eyes cold and hard. He only looked at me like that when I hurt him, but for some reason, it held no satisfaction today. "Frankly, Issy, it's none of your business where I live. Although, I'm sure you've got a case of whiplash from the leap you took from 'the help' to a billionaire's son. I bet your daddy is licking his chops," he spit out, sarcasm dripping from his lips. He looked me up and down in disgust and turned away. "You're even starting to look like one of them."

Anxiety took over my stomach again as I thought of waking up with nothing but a nightgown on. I hadn't asked Robbie for details on exactly what "intimate" meant and the idea that his hands were on me last night made me want to burn off all of my flesh. I pushed it out of my mind, choosing to focus on Grant instead. I didn't want him mad at me, and I certainly didn't want him leaving. "Grant, please don't be like this," I pleaded walking over to him and putting my hand on his arm.

He tensed under me and turned to look at me again. His eyes still cold. "You promised," was all he said before he resumed shoving clothes in his bag.

"Promised what? Why are you so mad at me?"

He spun around in shock and stared at me, my face showing all the confusion that I felt inside. "After motorcycle guy, you promised me you wouldn't do that to me again. Leave me with images of you and someone else together all night long. Then I get a phone call from lover boy who treats me like some insignificant idiot, while he tells me that you and him are going to make a night of it. It's like you dream up new ways each day to rip my heart out. I can't do it anymore."

"So you're mad at me because Robbie made you feel insignificant?"

"No, I'm mad at you because you did!" he yelled, his eyes betraying all he was feeling.

He wasn't insignificant. In fact, he was the most significant person in my life right now. I had to make him see that. "Grant, I didn't want to be there. I drank too much and blacked out. I woke up in some strange room with a strange nightgown on. My purse and clothes were gone, and my father was nowhere to be found. I don't want Robbie Marsh! Everything about him makes me sick." My voice was shaking and I knew I had tears in my eyes. I tried to pull them back, but I couldn't. There was too much emotion surging through me.

Grant looked like a statue as I spoke, taking in all I just threw at him. "What do you mean you blacked out?" he finally asked.

"We were drinking tequila and messing around with some archery stuff while my father finished his business dinner. That is the last thing I remember until this morning."

I watched as Grant ran his hands through his hair,

anger starting to turn into concern. "Is this the first time you've blacked out?"

"No, I did that night with Jason too, but it wasn't as drastic," I answered honestly feeling somewhat relieved to tell someone about it.

Grant turned to me, his face unreadable. "Do you have any idea how dangerous that is, Issy. You've blacked out twice in less than a week, both times with men who you've only known for a few weeks. They could do anything to you and you wouldn't even know it."

"They didn't. I asked both of them and they didn't," I explained, my voice still shaking with fear.

"So they say," he yelled exasperated. "You really don't know. Guys like Robbie Marsh are used to getting whatever they want. How does this not terrify you?"

"It does, but I went there with my father, Grant. I never imagined he'd just leave me," I screamed, tears spilling over now. I turned to flee, but I felt Grant's arms around me, holding me tightly from behind.

"You have to stop drinking, Issy. It's out of control, and one of these days, your luck is going to run out and you are either going to kill yourself or find yourself in a position with devastating results." His voice was honey sweet again, the harshness gone and I turned into him, holding on for dear life. He caressed my hair and told me it would be ok. I wanted to believe him, wanted so badly to finally let myself go. But then he said it, and everything came into focus once again.

"Baby, I love you too much to watch you destroy yourself."

I'm not even sure he knew he said it out loud, but it didn't matter. He said it. I stiffened under him and pulled away, my mind and body fully back in control. "I need a shower," I said, excusing myself.

Grant's face grew stern again. "Why does my loving you scare you so much, Issy? Stop running from me. I'm not going to disappoint you. Don't you see that you can count on me?"

"Love is for the weak, Grant, and I am not weak. I'm not a broken girl that needs to be fixed or a project that you can take to church to make better," I replied bitterly.

"That's where you're wrong, Issy. Loving and being vulnerable is hard. It takes courage to feel, courage to hurt. This shell you've created to keep everyone out—that's weakness, Issy."

"I am who I am, and if you don't like it, then go away." Despite my anger, I felt my heart constrict with each word I spoke.

Grant just shook his head and resumed packing before dismissing me with his hand. "Whatever, Issy, I've been in love with a ghost for years now. What's one more disappearing act?"

I turned to leave before my heart took over and pulled me back to him.

"Issy," I heard over my shoulder. I didn't turn around. "I won't wait for you forever."

I didn't acknowledge him, just took off running up the stairs.

18. THE NEW JAKE

The morning didn't offer me any relief from my agony. My father had left for New York, so I still hadn't been able to confront him about leaving me at Robbie's. Worse, I was having a terrible reaction to my blackout this time. I woke up in a sweat at least three times last night after dreaming of Robbie taking advantage of me. In every dream, I was trapped in some room, unable to move or escape. I would call for help from my father, but he would just smile and walk away, leaving me alone and vulnerable to whatever Robbie wanted to do. Just as he would begin touching me, I would wake up shaking and terrified.

I finally gave up on sleep and got ready for school. I didn't have to be at breakfast this morning, but even that fact didn't ease the tension I felt all around me. I went to the armoire and found my stash. I had promised myself I would cut back on the drinking after yesterday, but this morning was not the time to start my new resolve. My hands were shaking uncontrollably and my heart wouldn't stop racing as I took the first drink. The burn immediately made me feel better, but it took two more before the shaking stopped.

I looked in the mirror and still saw the stripped, controlled version of myself that Robbie loved and immediately hated my reflection. I tore through my closet until I found the wildest punk outfit I owned and put it on. The gray, faded jeans were torn to shreds at the kneecaps and my long-sleeved *Wild Cats* t-shirt was also torn up at the torso, but I wore a strawberry red tank top underneath it. I put the same color red streaks in my hair to where the black was only visible underneath. The final touch was to add my nose ring and multiple chains and bracelets. It was the first time I had seen the true Issy in days and immediately felt a surge of confidence and adrenaline. This was *my* life, and I wasn't going to let anyone tell me how to live it anymore. I was not and would never be my mother, and if my father or Robbie Marsh thought they'd turn me into her, they were sadly mistaken.

I took one more drink of my liquid courage and bounced down the stairs. My father's office door was open and I detoured to peak in. Grant was sitting at his desk working on the computer when I came in and jumped on the chair in front of the desk.

"Hey! Whatcha doing?" I asked playfully, feeling more and more like myself.

Grant glanced up at me for a second and then back down at the computer. He looked tense and irritated, and I couldn't tell if he was happy to see me or not. "I'm once again stuck here to babysit you, Issy, while your dad is off doing the final negotiations on the merger. Since you've gotten home, I've been left out of every meeting and have had limited view of the contracts. Somehow my college degree and years of experience has earned me 'nanny' status." His voice was as cold as his posture, and I quickly realized that he was still mad at me.

"That's not my fault, Grant. Maybe my dad is threatened that you are getting too good and may want to do something else. He's tricky like that, you know," I offered, still trying to keep the mood light.

Grant looked back up at me and his eyes held no affection. "Of course it's your dad's fault, because it couldn't be yours, right Issy?"

"What's that supposed to mean?" I yelled standing up.

"How much have you had to drink today? I mean it's nine in the morning, surely you've touched your flask by now." I stared at him with my mouth ajar, but he didn't relent. "Your dad is terrified you are going to kill yourself, and based on that outfit, I'm sure you are already well on your way today. So yes, Issy, I'm left here, hopelessly in charge of making sure you survive until your dad returns tomorrow night."

I couldn't move or speak, just felt the rage turn inside me with such intensity that I truly felt steam coming out of my ears. This was the same guy who had just judged me for looking like one of them yesterday.

"Thanks for not disappointing me," I hissed through gritted teeth and tore out of the office. Grant was siding with my father now, too. Was there anyone left who was on my side?

I got my answer really quickly when Jason didn't show for class, and Reggie opted to take a seat on a different row. Just when I thought it couldn't get worse, Kari was upset at me also because I forgot to show for our study session yesterday. I had completely forgotten. I tried to apologize, and she accepted, but couldn't seem to fit another meeting in her schedule.

In the interest of self-preservation, I didn't even go to lunch for fear that the cold shoulder would be unbearable with Rusty and Reggie at the same table. By the time I got into Shakespeare, my nerves were so tense that the "fight or flight" feeling was consuming me.

When Jason walked into class and settled behind me, I almost hugged him. "Hey," I said, turning around to face him. "You weren't in class today."

He glanced up at me, his eyes full of hurt and anger that seemed misplaced if they were meant for me. I thought we were good.

"You made the headlines again," he said flatly as he handed me this morning's society section. My hands were shaking when I took it, not wanting to see anything that would have him this upset.

It was another picture of me and Robbie, only this time, we were locked in a kiss that looked far more passionate that anything I'd ever felt with him. They must have gotten it yesterday when he trapped me after getting out of his car.

The headline read: **ITS GETTING SERIOUS**. The caption below was even more exaggerated.

"Robbie Marsh and Kaitlyn 'Isadora' Summers are now sharing rides to school, and some sources even say they've been sharing overnight accommodations. Neither side would give an official comment, but Mr. Marsh's public relations rep did confirm that Robbie was happier than she'd ever seen him. Will a 'Save the Date' announcement be coming soon? I think so..."

My stomach turned as the bile sat just on the back of my tongue. "You shouldn't believe everything you read," I replied sharply, handing the paper back to him.

"Well, a picture says a thousand words, *Isadora*," he retorted sarcastically, adding extra emphasis on the name they had used in the paper.

"Don't call me that," I spatted before turning back around in my chair. If I hadn't been so angry, I knew the tears would have come, but I was seeing red. I listened as the TA reminded us that our monologues were due on Friday, and that no make-ups would be given. I made it through the first thirty minutes of class, but then finally excused myself, telling the TA that I wasn't feeling well and would see her on Friday. I hadn't even looked at that monologue, but I didn't care. I just wanted out of that room, out of the building and off of this horrible campus.

I got in my car and started driving, not really caring where I was going. Fifteen minutes later, I was on the highway heading towards Winsor. I didn't care what the backlash would be. I just had to get out of there. My phone rang, and I saw Robbie's name light up. I pressed "ignore" and accelerated. It didn't seem to matter how fast or far I drove, the chains kept following me.

When I finally got to Jake's apartment, I sighed in relief, knowing that at least one person I saw today wouldn't hate me. I went to let myself in when I realized the key didn't work. Crud! I forgot he moved. I grabbed my phone and called him. Voicemail. I texted him next telling him I was in town and needed directions to his apartment. A few minutes later, the text came, and I jumped with joy.

His apartment was actually a condo in the most upscale part of Asheville. I had to punch in a gate code just to enter the area and found his door just around the corner. The complex was notably high-class and obviously not your typical "campus" housing. I questioned how Jake could afford to live here, but pushed it out of my mind. It was none of my business anyway.

He opened the door on my first knock and pulled me in for a big hug. I just held on to him, the tears finally making their way to my eyes.

"Hey sweetie! What are you doing here?" he asked

as he held me.

I willed the tears away and then put on my most cheery face before letting him go. "I felt like playing with my cousin tonight. You game?" I asked with a smile while I took him in. He looked totally different. He was wearing a fitted gray suit and tie that hung loose around his neck. His shirt was untucked and was still partially unbuttoned. I looked around him and saw why. She was putting on her shoes and was meticulously dressed in a fitted suit. Her hair was a polished blond and styled in a bob to her shoulders.

I raised my eyebrow at him and he just gave me a devilish smile before pulling me into the condo. The blond walked by him and kissed his cheek before grabbing her keys. He barely acknowledged her exit, and instead turned to ask me what I thought of the place.

"I'm not sure, Jake, I'm still trying to process you in a suit," I admitted, not mentioning that I had never seen him treat a girl so disrespectfully before. This behavior was not what I had in mind when I told him to live a little.

He finished buttoning his shirt and straightened his tie. "I'm a working guy now, Issy. My new job is amazing."

Jake went on to tell me how all of this happened so fast. He had been interning at this stock company for months when right after New Year's, his boss came in and offered him a full time position with a signing bonus and commission. He took it immediately and readjusted his entire schedule to work around it. One the guys in his office told him about the three-bedroom condo he owned, and asked if Jake was interested in splitting the rent. Jake had originally turned him down because of Avery. He hadn't wanted to give up the privacy his apartment gave them.

He continued to fill me in, taking a seat on the stiff black sofa in the living room. "So after you left last week, my first course of action was to call and take the space. That apartment held nothing but bad juju for me anyways,"

I watched him as he sat there, looking like an arrogant yuppie with his legs crossed and his arms stretched out across the back of the couch which held no cushions, and felt my stomach drop a little.

"Please tell me this version of you is for the people you work with, and my Jake will reappear sometime during the night." My voice was sharper than I intended as I sat down opposite him on one of the black club chairs that looked like the back had been sliced off at the arm rests. Don't get me wrong, I love modern décor, but this room was all black and white with no color or personality. Jake was a jock who loved the outdoors and comfy, leather couches. He'd always dressed nicely, but never cared what country his shoes came from before. This new Jake could probably quote me the type of leather he was wearing.

"Sorry Issy, this is the new me," he confirmed

standing. "I'm blissfully happy and completely over my poor lapse in judgment."

I slanted my eyes at him. "You're lying."

Jake then turned things around on me. "Well, I was going to take you by the office, but I can't take you anywhere looking like that, Issy. What got into you this morning?" he asked appraising my look.

"I don't know, maybe a personality, or maybe I'm finally taking a stand that I am not Kaitlyn Summers, Daddy's robot princess. What about you, Jake? Should we go back to your apartment and get your personality, because your eyes look about as colorful as this over-priced yuppie condo."

Jake smiled and there was a hint of a sparkle that disappeared almost as quickly as it came. He pulled me into another hug and promised to go change. "I need you to tone down your look just a little, though. I'm taking you out tonight, and we'll definitely be seeing people I work with."

I let out a dramatic sigh and rolled my eyes. "I'd love to help you out, Jake, but I kind of came spontaneously. No bags, sorry."

Jake smiled mischievously and wrapped his arm around me as he led me into his room. "Well, it turns out that you left a small wardrobe of clothes at my old place, and I was kind enough to have them cleaned and waiting here for you. They've actually been a great resource for me when the women get to clingy."

"I seriously almost threw up in my mouth, Jake," I said, my lip turning up in disgust. "I don't want to hear anything about your late night escapades."

Jake laughed a genuine, hardy laugh and squeezed me tighter. "I love you being here," he admitted.

Jake's bed was still in disarray from earlier and I gasped when I saw the black satin sheets that adorned his platform bed. He had officially met every stereotype of a man whore. The room was a carbon copy of the living room, and felt just as cold and empty.

"Was this place already furnished?" I asked in horror.

"Of course not. I picked all this out myself, what do you think?" he asked proudly as he tidied up the bed.

"I think you need some color in your life, Jake."

"You're all the color I need, Issy," he replied with a sarcastic smile. I punched his arm and then started looking through his closet that was full of every type of suit possible. My clothes were all the way to the left and had dry cleaning bags over them. I pulled out one of my favorite dresses and went to the bathroom to change. Jake had a few of my shoes as well, which was good considering I only brought my combat boots. The dress was a dark sage green and had a corset type top with a billowy skirt hitting just below the knees. My accessories and hair dressed it down a little and kind of made me look like a walking contradiction. I liked the look and touched up my makeup with the stash in my purse.

Jake had changed by the time I got out of the

bathroom, wearing just a different version of the same look he had earlier. His shirt was less formal, but still button up and his jacket was a sports coat versus a suit, but still more stiff than I'd ever seen him.

He glanced at me and smiled. "That's more like it. Now I'm going to have to threaten all my coworkers to stay away from you."

I shivered at the thought of one of Jake's yuppie coworkers hitting on me. I had no interest in men right now. I just wanted a nice evening out with Jake where I could get the thought of Robbie, Jason and most importantly Grant out of my head. "No need," I confirmed. "I have sworn off men for an indefinite period of time."

"Grant's still getting under your skin, isn't he?" he asked with a smirk.

"Shut up. I don't want to talk about Grant or my father or my stupid life. Let's just go get a drink and pretend it's still last year, and you and I are happy and healthy, ok?"

Jake laughed. "Got news for you, Issy, we've never been happy or healthy. But, I have to admit, it does sound good to pretend we are for at least one night."

"Good," I said nodding as I threaded my arm through his. "Let's go dazzle your new friends."

Jake kissed my head and led me out to his new car, a black Mercedes sports car that looked brand new. I whistled as he opened the door for me, and

Jake just grinned. I had never known him to be so into wealth and status before. It was kind of shocking. I wondered what he'd say if he knew I had a billionaire stalking me. I didn't tell him, but noticed how my hands started to shake when I pictured Robbie in my head. I pushed it out and turned to Jake. "So where are we going?"

"There is this new Martini bar downtown. It's the 'hot' spot for young career types. No dance floor, so you'll probably hate it."

"Who needs a dance floor when you have tables?" I asked sweetly, batting my eyes.

"Don't you dare, Issy. I have to work with these people." Jake looked genuinely concerned, and I laughed.

"Calm down. You and I both know I have been trained extensively for these types of people. You should see the show my dad has had me putting on lately. He's even been providing the proper clothing. Can you believe?" I asked shaking my head, trying to hide how much it really did bother me.

"Can I believe that your dad is an obsessive, control freak who thinks he owns you? Yes, I can believe that. Just be careful, ok? You play the role too well, and your father just may get some ideas."

"What do you mean by that?" I asked, feeling butterflies in my stomach.

"Nothing specific. I just have seen what some people do when it comes to money, Issy. It's scary. Thinking about it now, it's actually pretty incredible that you turned out as normal as you did."

"Normal, huh? I don't think I've ever been called that one before," I replied with an arched eyebrow. I didn't want to be normal.

Jake laughed and pinched my arm. "Not that kind of normal, Issy. More that you have heart...even if I'm the only one who sees it."

"Sorry to disappoint you. My heart is dead, Jake. Has been for a long time."

"Whatever you say," Jake conceded as he pulled up to the valet waiting on our car.

The valet opened our doors and Jake took the ticket, not even bothering to thank them. Even his walk had changed as did his mannerisms the minute we walked in the door. There was no doubt that we turned heads and Jake seemed to relish in that fact. He put his arm around my waist and led me over to a table full of men wearing similar suits. The bar had high tables spaced throughout and modern black couches along the walls. They had replaced a few of the bulbs with colored lighting giving the entire space a blue hue. The bar was sleek and bare, with only glasses visible to the customers. The bartender wore a button up black shirt and slacks and had his hair perfectly styled. It made me think of Jason and his casual look and movement as he worked. I felt my stomach turn as I thought of his angry eyes when he looked at me this morning. If I was honest with myself, I really did deserve it. I never once considered his feelings in all of this. I had dismissed him as a heartless gigolo because he had that bad boy look, when truthfully he had been more of a gentleman and friend than polished and refined Robbie ever was.

Before we reached his table of friends, I looked up at Jake and excused myself to the bathroom. Once alone, I pulled out my phone and sent two texts. The first was to Jason.

Me: I'm sorry. Would rather make headlines with you than that pompous, overdressed jerk any day. Forgive me?

Jason: Nothing to forgive. You've been honest with me from the start. I was a jerk. I'm not used to this jealous thing, green eyes. You seem to bring out the worst in me.

I smiled sadly and texted back.

Me: I tend to do that. See ya Friday.

I switched over to Grant, feeling a little better. At least Jason didn't hate me. I erased my text several times, not knowing what to say to him.

Me: I'm relieving you of your babysitting duties tonight. I'm with Jake and will be back tomorrow before my father gets home. I'll send his contact info in a second.

After I texted the contact info, Grant sent a short reply.

Grant: Thanks for letting me know.

That was it. No pleasantries, no anger. My heart fluttered a little as I heard his words in my head. He wouldn't wait forever...and why should he? I had given him nothing but frustration and pain. I glared at myself in the mirror and cursed. For a heart that was supposed to be dead, it sure was hurting a lot right now. I took out my flask and drank down the rest of the warm liquid. It didn't make the pain go away, but at least it made it disappear from my face.

I made sure I was the picture of perfection one more time before I left and joined Jake and his friends. They all stood when I approached and stared in a way that made me feel as if I was walking up to them naked.

Jake walked over and put a protective arm around me before introducing me to his friends. I gave them all a charming smile and played my role perfectly. It seemed crazy to me that I came to see Jake just so I could escape this world, and ended up right back in it. How had he become this person?

The only one in the group that didn't get on my nerves was Jake's roommate, David, who at first seemed as average as his name. But as the night wore on, I found him more and more charming. His blue eyes would crinkle a little when he laughed and his relaxed, genuine demeanor was refreshing next to the other guys who either name dropped or priced dropped everything throughout our conversation. Even worse, they each cornered me at one point to ask for my number and touch me in some inappropriate way. I was sure by the end of the evening that they had some bet going on to see who could get me to go home with him first.

Jake was oblivious to all of it as he was targeting his own take home gal. David was the only one who seemed to notice how ridiculous his friends were acting and asked if I wanted a ride when he was saying his goodbyes. I jumped at the opportunity, realizing that Jake was more interested in picking up women then spending time with me.

I grabbed my purse and walked with David over to tell Jake I was leaving. He had his hand on some girl's leg as he was leaning in to whisper in her ear. She looked a lot like the girl from earlier, but had brown hair this time, which she kept tossing over her shoulder. I felt my stomach turn. No wonder he couldn't get over Avery; not one of the girls I had seen him with had a fraction of the beauty or class that Avery did.

Jake pulled back when I walked up, and the girl sent me a challenging stare as she looked me up and down. I almost rolled my eyes. First off, gross. Second, if I did want Jake, there would be no competition. Hands down, I would win. I completely dismissed her and turned to Jake. "I'm going to catch a ride with David, ok?"

"You're leaving? Why? It's still early." He looked genuinely sad to see me go even though he had practically ignored me all night.

"I'll just catch you back at your place." I glanced her direction and leaned into Jake so she couldn't hear me. "Don't you dare bring that trash home with you," I whispered.

Jake just smirked at me and kissed my cheek before saying goodbye. I shook my head and followed

David out of the bar; his friends were staring in awe as we left.

"I think you won the bet," I teased when he had started driving away. Like Jake, his car was very expensive, but much more practical and a lot less flashy. It seemed to match his personality.

"You picked up on that, huh? Sorry, we can't bring those guys anywhere."

"It's fine. Guys like that are easy to read and easy to avoid. I just can't believe you and Jake choose to hang out with them," I noted as I took off my shoes and sat with my legs crossed in the seat.

"We work with them. That's the extent of it." David paused for a second and then had a confused look on his face. "I have to say, you are not at all what I expected."

"And why's that?" I asked playfully. I didn't think David was hitting on me, so it was easy to relax next to him.

"I don't know. Just the way Jake described you. He said you were beautiful, which I must admit, he certainly didn't exaggerate. But I guess I just pictured you acting younger."

I started laughing and turned to face him. "David, you are an incredibly perceptive person. It feels like everyone I know has been trying to make me grow up these last few weeks. I guess they were more successful than I realized."

He pushed my arm playfully and then smiled. "Ah, growing up isn't so bad as long as you can still channel your inner kid every once and while. At least you get to make your own choices."

I started laughing again and shook my head. "Oh, if only that were true."

David didn't understand, and I didn't feel like telling him my dysfunctional history. We changed the subject to much lighter topics until we were finally at their new condo. David showed me how to work the TV and where to find all their movies. He then said good night and headed to his room.

"David," I called before he shut the door. "It was really nice to meet you. I'm really glad that Jake has you for a roommate." David just smiled and said goodnight. Jake needed someone stable right now, because it was far too obvious that he was going off the deep end.

I searched through Jake's closet again and found a pair of my yoga pants and a fitted t-shirt. I was more than grateful to get off this dress that constricted my chest. Sometimes fashion really was uncomfortable. Jake's shower felt amazing and I decided there was one thing I did like about his new place…his bathroom. It was spacious and sleek, and the shower had two showerheads that hit all the right places. I finished washing out all the color that had been my rebellion for the day and got dressed. I began looking through Jake's cabinets to find the bag of toiletries I always kept as his place. It wasn't under the sink, so I pulled back the mirror to see if he had put my things in there.

The sight I saw was terrifying. There were at least ten prescription bottles of pills all stacked next to each other. I looked at each of the labels. Five of them were painkillers and had my mother's name on them. The other five were Jake's. Three were prescription sleeping pills while the other two were pills for anxiety and depression. My hands were shaking as I looked at the date on them. They were both dated January 3rd and were almost empty. I noted that he had several refills available for each. It also didn't escape my mind that he had started taking them right after my accident.

I closed the cabinet, not knowing how I was going to approach this with Jake. We had never really talked about that night I almost died. Maybe we needed to. I found my bag after looking in two other drawers and finished getting ready for bed. I stared at myself for a long time in the mirror. I looked young and could probably pass for seventeen since my hair was loose around my face and I wasn't wearing any makeup. I didn't feel young, though. I felt like I was trapped in someone else's life while my youth slipped away from me. Worse, I couldn't see a way out. The longer I stayed with my father, the more sure I was that I would never be free.

I settled in on the couch and turned on a movie while I waited for Jake to get home. His apartment felt cold and lonely, and I wondered how he could live here like this. I itched to call Grant, just to hear his voice, but instead looked through all our text messages. I scrolled to the one that said: **I'm done**, and my stomach knotted.

Jake walked in just in time to save me from my madness. Leaving me alone with my thoughts was dangerous. He didn't bring the girl home with him, but it was obvious that he had gone home with her. His coat was draped over his arm and his shirt was untucked and wrinkled. Jake tossed his jacket onto one of the chairs and fell on the couch next to me. He was holding a business card that had a number written on the back of it.

"Lucky number ten," he said with a grin while he looked at the card. "I may even call this one."

"Just ten Jake? I would have thought you'd have a much higher number than that," I teased, not really wanting to know.

Jake raised an eyebrow at me and smirked. "That's just post Avery. You don't want to know the actual number."

I stared at him in disbelief. "It's only been a week, Jake!"

"What can I say, I've been busy."

I put my head in my hands and shook it. "What has happened to you? You're even worse than you were in the frat house," I accused, staring at him. "You use women as if they are nothing, and your cabinet is so full of pills, I don't know whether to slap you or commit you."

Jake's face got real harsh and immediately defensive. "How dare you lecture me on using substances or people, Issy. You are the master at that game. I bet there are no less than five guys right now that would fall on a sword for you, and you couldn't care less about any of them."

I drew back from him like he had slapped me and stood over him. "Ok fine, maybe I do drink too much or use people, but at least I treat them with some dignity. Do you honestly think this is how you are going to get over Avery? By sleeping your way through women who couldn't hold a candle to her? Is that why you take the pills, Jake, to erase the fact that you have lowered your standards so dramatically? It's pathetic, and you know it!" I knew I was being cruel and hurtful, but I didn't care. Jake needed a slap in the face.

"You think I'm pathetic," he said shaking his head. His eyes were starting to get that cloudy look again that only happened when he was trying to escape his reality. "You want to hear pathetic. Try sitting on the same bench every day, just so you can get a glimpse of her as she tosses her hair and chews on her pen. Watching just long enough to see him show up and hold the only woman I've ever loved. So yeah, Issy, I'm pathetic. Sue me for trying to forget." Jake practically spit out the words as he spoke.

I covered my mouth with my hand. "Why are you doing that to yourself?"

Jake rubbed his temples. "Because for those few minutes, I have hope. Hope that one day he won't show up, and I'll get a second chance."

I couldn't believe it. Jake had turned into a stalker. I thought of Robbie and felt rage explode within me. "Jake, you have to stop this! She doesn't want you. Just leave her alone and get on with your life."

Jake jumped off the couch and grabbed my arm. "Don't you minimize my pain, Issy. You have no idea what I'm going through. But you will. Just wait, one day you are going to watch as Grant looks at someone else the way he used to look at you, and you are going to know just like I do that you missed your chance. One day he's going to offer all of himself to you and you are going to run away, and when you come back it will be too late. When that happens, Issy, then come talk to me. Until then, butt out." Jake threw down my arm and stormed off to his room, slamming the door in response.

19. DECLARATIONS

The nightmare that came that night was worse than any I had previously experienced. I was back in the room, trapped on all four sides, but this time one of the walls were made up of glass I could see through. I banged and banged, but no one was there to help me. Suddenly, Grant appeared outside the glass and looked devastatingly handsome in a tuxedo. He looked happy, almost giddy. I watched as he looked up towards me and his face showed all the love and adoration that made my heart swoon. I smiled back at him and called out his name. He didn't see me. Instead, there was someone else there, walking up to him in a long white dress. Her back was to me, so I couldn't see who it was, but it didn't matter...it wasn't me.

His eyes followed her, never losing the look of love in them. I started screaming and banging on the window. It was supposed to be me. Didn't he know I was in here? I banged and screamed until my throat went hoarse, but it was no use. I watched them walk away together, never once hearing my cries. Suddenly I wasn't alone in the room, and I felt fear shoot through me as Robbie cornered me by the window. "Now you are all mine," he said as he touched my face. I tried to scream and to move away from his grip, but I couldn't. I was stuck there, totally vulnerable to him.

Next thing I knew, Jake was shaking me awake. "Hey, it's ok," he said softly when I sat up. I was violently shaking and panting as if I had just been running. My throat felt hoarse and dry. I looked around the room, making sure I knew where I was and saw the morning light through the windows.

I turned my frightened eyes to Jake and just threw myself into his arms. It was just a dream. I was safe.

"Issy, what is going on?" he asked, his voice full of concern. "You were screaming at the top of your lungs for someone to help you."

I shook my head in his chest. "It was just a dream," I stated, still trying to convince myself it was. But what if it wasn't? What if it was a glimpse into my future? I heard Grant's words echo through my head again, *I won't wait for you forever.* I pulled back from Jake and looked at him, knowing exactly what I had to do.

"I'm sorry, Jake, I can't keep our pact anymore," I stated with resolve. It was as if the light had finally come on, and I knew without question that I loved Grant, and I couldn't lose him.

Jake just smiled and nodded. "Go get him, tiger. It's about time you heard what I've been saying."

I jumped out of the guest bed I had been sleeping in and bolted to the bathroom, only taking the time to brush out my hair and brush my teeth. Minutes later, I was throwing my ball of clothes in the back of my car and racing home at speeds that could get me arrested. The hour trip felt like a lifetime as I drove, feeling more and more panicked that it was going to be too late.

Relief flooded me when I pulled in the drive and saw his car parked in his spot around the corner of the house. I threw my car in park and ran up the front steps, taking them two at a time. I rushed to his office first. The light was on, as was his computer. His phone sat on top of several stacks of papers, but he was nowhere to be found. I checked my dad's office next, but it was locked. I tried his room...empty. The panic was getting stronger. I had to find him...I had to tell him. I ran to the back door, and almost started crying when I saw him standing at the end of the pier by my father's boat.

I didn't hesitate and ran until I was standing right next to him. "I want you to kiss me," I declared, still panting from all the adrenaline surging through me.

Grant looked startled and completely confused. "Issy, when did you get--"

I didn't let him finish. "I want you to kiss me. I know what that means. I remember the promise you made, but I don't care. I want you to be the only one who ever kisses me again."

My words finally registered in his mind and he didn't wait even a second before pulling me gently into his arms. He held my face and looked into my eyes. I stripped myself of every barrier I'd ever had and looked at him with all the love I felt exploding out of my heart. His lips were gentle and warm, sending shivers through me that felt euphoric. I wrapped my arms around him and poured myself into him, memorizing every part of his perfect mouth.

He pulled away from me and just stared in shock. "What made you change your mind?" he asked as he caressed my cheek.

"You said you wouldn't wait forever. I didn't want to lose you," I answered honestly.

Grant smiled and put his forehead to mine. "I was lying, Issy. Truth is, you're the only girl for me. There is no acceptable substitute."

I jumped up on him and wrapped my legs around his waist so we were eye level. "I'm glad you lied," I admitted, smiling and began kissing him again. I could kiss him forever and it would never be enough. We had wasted so many years. I had no intention of missing any more.

Grant set me down on the rail and pulled back again, careful to keep his arms wrapped around me. "What happened with Jake? You're like a different person," he pressed, noting the obvious difference in my appearance as well as my demeanor.

"I just saw someone I never want to be. Someone I would undoubtedly turn into if I ever lost you," I answered as I touched his face and searched his eyes. Grant appeared taken aback by my honesty and affection. I didn't care. The walls were gone and happiness filled my soul. "So no more dates, ok?" I teased.

Grant looked surprised. "What date?"

I smiled sheepishly, not wanting to admit the jealousy I felt that night. "Friday night. Rosa said you had a date."

Grant leaned in brushed his soft lips over my cheek and then my neck. "Rosa misunderstood. I had hoped we might have a date that night, but you were gone when I got back."

Desire raged through my body as his lips sent chills down my neck and my arms. I jumped off the rail and got in the boat, pulling Grant along with me. We barely stopped kissing to let him start the engine up and back away from the pier. I stayed behind him while he drove, keeping my arms wrapped tightly around his waist. We got to the center and he anchored the boat. Soon after, he sat down and pulled me onto his lap, still kissing me and touching my face and hair as if he was assuring himself I was real.

"I keep thinking I'm dreaming," he said softly as he looked at me.

"This better not be a dream," I scoffed with a grin. "I'll be ticked!" I kissed him again and felt desire flow all through me. I wasn't going to fight it this time. I began loosening his tie and unbuttoning his shirt. "I want you so bad," I whispered, making it very clear what my intentions were.

Grant stopped my hands and stared in my eyes. "There's no rush, Issy. We have all the time in the world. As gorgeous as it is, I've never just wanted your body. I want your soul."

It was the first time his words didn't scare me. I wanted to give him everything. "Ok," I said slowly, "so how does that work?"

Grant just laughed and brushed my hair out of my face. "Well, let's start with you telling me why you've pushed me away for so long. Tell me why you are afraid."

I suddenly felt nervous and started to get off Grant's lap. "I'm not afraid of anything."

Grant's grip kept me immobile while he forced me to look at him. "Yes, you are. Tell me. Trust me," he whispered as he gently caressed my face.

"I'm scared of being broken like my mother was," I finally answered. "She loved the wrong person and he failed her."

Grant pulled me to him and embraced me while he rubbed his hand up and down my back. "People will always fail us in one way or another. Sometimes brokenness is a good thing, Issy. I would know."

I pulled back and looked at him questionably. "When have you ever been broken?"

Grant let out a long sigh and then looked a little nervous. "I've wanted to talk to you about my life for a long time now, Issy. Are you sure you're ready to hear it?"

I just scowled at him and he chuckled before beginning. "It was this summer. After everything with you and my dad, I just felt my life was a joke. Every dream I ever had was slipping away, and I was powerless to stop it. I felt bitterness and anger deeper than ever before. When you dismissed me, I went to the gym that night and beat on a punching bag until my knuckles bled, yet I still felt this rage that wouldn't go away. The next day, I was driving to your dad's house and while stopped at a light, I turned to see a church on the corner. I had seen that church a million times, but that day, the sign said something that made my gut clench. It said, 'Peace I leave with you; my peace I give you.' I stared at the sign so long that cars started beeping at me. I wanted that peace."

Grant took a break and smiled at me. I slanted my eyes and looked at him. "Did you ever find it?"

"Not right away. That Sunday I went to the church. I sat in the back so no one would notice me and just watched all the people in there. The music was amazing and so different from what I expected. The people were different too. They were really friendly and introduced themselves to me even though I tried to hide in the shadows. But what really did it for me was the sermon. The Pastor was doing a series on the fruit of the spirit, and that day he was talking about peace. I was fascinated by this idea that some supernatural being could give me peace when my life was crumbling around me. I didn't buy it at first, but I was curious, so I started going to church every Sunday and meeting with the Pastor during the week. He didn't push me, just answered my questions and told me more and more about Jesus Christ. Two months later, I finally understood, and I surrendered my life to God. It was the scariest moment of my life, and then it was the most beautiful moment, because I immediately felt the peace that was promised."

I hung on every word he said, watching his eyes as he shared with me. I knew he believed every word he spoke. I was glad for him—glad he found something that would make him happy. Religion had never bothered me; I'd always felt that it was what some people needed to get through life. I just never really believed it was real. I could tell, though, that Grant did believe it was real, so I was careful in how I responded.

"I'm glad you found that peace, Grant."

He smiled at me again and pulled me close. "You can too," he offered hesitantly.

I leaned in to kiss him and just rested my head on his shoulder. "Can we talk about other things for a while?"

He rubbed my back and sighed. "Sure."

So that's what we did. We talked and kissed for hours, sharing all the details of our lives with each other that had previously been hidden. It was an intimacy I'd never known with anyone else, and it happened without shedding one piece of clothing.

Feeling a freedom I hadn't felt in weeks, I stood by the rail and let the wind blow through my hair. Grant arms were soon around me, and I leaned back against him, feeling warmth and security.

"Can I ask you a favor?" he asked as we stared across the lake.

"Sure."

"Will you come to church with me on Sunday?"

I turned to face him, trying not to look annoyed. I was fine with him being religious, but it wasn't for me. "I don't think I belong in a place like that. It's meant for people like you and Avery. People who are genuinely good."

Grant just laughed. "Are you kidding? Church is meant for everyone, especially those that recognize they are sinners. It's a big part of my life now, Issy, and I want to share it with you. I want you to meet Pastor Boyd. I've told him a lot about you."

"What?" I yelled, pushing him away. "You talked about me to someone else?"

"Don't get mad. I went to see him after our road trip disaster and told him how I acted. I was so disgusted with myself that I had to tell someone. I felt like I'd ruined any chance of being with you," he explained.

"What did he say?" I wasn't sure I wanted to know.

"He said I shouldn't be in a relationship with an unbeliever."

My jaw dropped as I stared at him. Grant just laughed and winked at me. "Don't worry. I told him it was too late for that. My life was already intertwined with yours, and I was completely in love with you."

I couldn't help but smile at his admission. "I bet he didn't like that answer."

"He's a good man, Issy. He was just worried about me." Then Grant laughed as he remembered something. "He said not to marry you or get too physical with you. I thought he was crazy, but now I can see why he warned me. You're completely irresistible." Grant leaned in to kiss me again, but I pushed him away.

"Now I'm definitely not stepping one foot into that church!" I was pouting, which seemed to amuse Grant even more.

"Awe come on, since when do you care what someone else thinks? Besides, he also gave me the best advice I'd ever been given. He said to pray for you and not to give up on you. He reminded me that God was in control and only He had the power to change your heart. I already see Him doing it, Issy. Every day, you get more and more beautiful because I see your heart softening."

I wanted to be mad at him, but the way he was staring into my eyes melted any resolve that might have been there. I leaned up and kissed him, letting my heart and soul pour into his. I would have stayed on that boat forever with him, locked away from the reality of life, but my stomach betrayed me. It let out an obnoxious growl, alerting both of us to fact that it was well past lunchtime.

Grant laughed and teased, "I guess I should feed you, huh?" I lightly hit his arm and then started to move around him. He kept me trapped in his arms, his eyes suddenly getting very serious. "You realize now that I've got you, I'm never letting go. Don't wake up tomorrow and think you're going to run away from me again."

I smiled warmly at him, my stomach fluttering from the intensity in his eyes. "I never want you to let me go." My admission brought a smile to Grant's lips and surprised me too. It was true, though. I had loved him for as long as I could remember, and knew I always would.

Grant drove us back to the pier and carefully docked the boat. I made my way to the edge and smiled mischievously at him. "Loser makes lunch," I yelled as I took off running down the pier. I was laughing so hard I almost couldn't run and had to look at my feet just to stabilize them. I finally looked up and almost ran smack into Robbie and my dad who were standing right in front of me. The beauty of the day immediately disappeared as my stomach knotted at the sight of both of them.

Seconds later, I felt Grant try to stop himself as he plowed into me, holding me tight to prevent our fall. He got his bearing and immediately stiffened as he looked at my father whose face showed nothing but fury.

"Mr. Summers. I didn't expect you until tonight," Grant stammered.

My father crossed his arms and glared at the two of us. "So I see," he responded, his voice sharp and accusatory. "I've been trying to contact you for hours. Seems that you were too distracted to remember your phone."

I watched as Grant's hand immediately went to

the pocket where he usually kept the phone, realizing with horror that it wasn't there. "I'm so sorry, sir. I must have set it down."

My dad's voice did not relent, and I was starting to get angry at the way he was talking to him. "Well, I'm not about to repeat my instructions. There is a long voicemail I suggest you go listen to."

Grant nodded and then squeezed my elbow before heading back into the house. It was an intimate gesture that wasn't lost on either my father or Robbie. I folded my arms and stared at them, ready to receive the same tongue lashing Grant got.

Robbie's eyes were dark, sending chills down my spine. He kissed my cheek and gave an emotionless smile. "You missed class. I was worried you weren't feeling well, but I guess you're all right." He put his arm around me possessively and addressed me while looking directly at my father. "We couldn't have you missing the party tonight, now could we?"

I wiggled out of his hold. His touch was dangerously close to making me scream. "What party?"

My father finally spoke up, his eyes still challenging mine with fury. "We're announcing the merger to our senior leadership tonight. A party tends to keep the mood light and gives us the opportunity to dispel any concerns that layoffs might occur."

"Well Robbie, thanks for the invite, but I'm afraid I won't make it tonight," I said sweetly, leaving no room for negotiation in my tone.

Robbie shot my father a look and then turned to me. "Well, if you do decide to come, I'll be sure to save you a dance." He kissed my hand before I had the opportunity to pull it away and said his goodbyes.

My father and I continued to stand there in a silent battle while waiting for the other one to speak. I finally broke the silence. "It's nice to see you, Daddy. How long has it been? Oh yeah, since Monday night when you abandoned me," I accused, my eyes slanting in hatred.

My father didn't say a word, but the vein in his neck was pulsating with exaggerated intensity. He turned and stalked into the house, and I followed him yelling that I wasn't done talking about it. He found my car keys on the foyer table and picked them up.

"These are now mine. Since you can't be trusted to stay in town when I'm gone, you will no longer have the means to leave," he declared, ice dripping from his words.

I stared at him in shock. How did he know? The only person who knew I had even left was Grant, and I knew he didn't tell him. "Are you still spying on me?" I screamed, and my father put up his hand to dismiss me. I was not letting this go. "Where were your spies Monday night, huh Daddy? When Robbie undressed me and bathed me and then did God knows what else while I lay unconscious? Where were they then, or better yet, where were you?" I screamed, tears starting to sting my eyes.

My father was shaking with fury, but I didn't stop.

Years of pent up aggression flowed out of me in that moment. "You can't even see it. You are so blinded by their money that you can't even see how far your head is stuck up their a--" The slap across my face sent me to the floor. I grabbed my cheek, stunned that he had finally done it.

"You will not speak to me like that," he hissed before storming off into his office and slamming the door.

20. DADDY, WHAT HAVE YOU DONE?

I stayed on the floor, my cheek throbbing from the impact and just started laughing. Anyone watching would have thought I was crazy, but I had done it. I had finally broken through his armor and touched a nerve deep inside him. He didn't have the words to fight me, only his hand, and that was a victory. I pulled myself off the floor and ran up the stairs, still reeling in my accomplishment.

I threw open my bedroom door and stopped abruptly as yet another dress hung from my armoire, this time with a note attached to it. I stepped toward it and read the note.

I saw this dress and knew you would look beautiful in it. See you tonight.

--- Robbie

I growled and tore up the note until it lay in tiny little pieces on the floor. I then grabbed the dress and threw it into the hall before slamming my door shut. I was NOT going to that party tonight. I went to the bathroom and took off the clothes I had been in since last night and stepped into the shower. My cheek still throbbed when I touched it, and I wondered how bad the bruise was going to be. I'd like to see how Daddy was going to explain that one tomorrow.

I dried off and wrapped my hair tightly in a towel before putting on my robe. I wondered if Grant was ok, or if my dad was still tormenting him over forgetting the phone. I went back to my bedroom to grab my phone and text him, but stopped when I saw the dress laid carefully across my bed with another note attached. My hand shook as I grabbed the offensive paper, but felt my body relax when I saw my father's handwriting.

You will attend the party tonight. Non-negotiable.

Over my dead body, I vowed as a grabbed the dress once again and stormed to my father's room, banging on the door. I heard him yell to come in and I did, stalking right up to him and throwing down the dress so he wouldn't miss my point. He was standing in front of his large tri-fold mirror that captured his entire frame, and continued to put his cuff links into his tuxedo shirt. He looked at me through the mirror and raised his eyebrows. He was in complete control again, and even smiled at me.

"I'm not going," I stated, folding my arms. "Threaten me all you want. Take away my car, my apartment, my school. I. DON'T. CARE. I am not going." I felt like this was my last stand and if I lost this battle, I would inevitably lose the war.

My father didn't say anything at first, just finished his sleeves before moving to his bow tie. Finally he spoke. "You still haven't talked to your mother, have you?" he asked, his face unreadable.

"What's your point?"

"She's not doing well. In fact, I haven't seen her this bad since...when was that? Oh yeah, your thirteenth birthday."

I gasped as visions of my mother's lifeless eyes filled my head. My father noted my reaction and continued, "It's a funny thing, Kaitlyn. When your mom and I divorced, I bought out her half of the house. She claimed she didn't want it—too many bad memories, I guess. You threw such a fit that she finally conceded and stayed, insisting on paying rent for it. A few months ago, I finally convinced her to stop, which was a good thing since financially, she really couldn't afford it."

"What are you talking about? Mom has plenty of money."

"Does she?" he asked rhetorically. "Seems that after your Aunt Kathy died, your mom developed a little habit that takes a lot of funds to sustain." He stopped talking, letting the information sink in. I thought of the multiple bottles of painkillers I found in Jake's cabinet and brought my hand to my mouth. When he saw I understood, he began talking again. "My real estate agent says the market is finally at a point where we could get a great price on that little piece of property. I've been hesitant, knowing it would leave your mother with nothing, but I don't know. You tell me. What should I do?"

I stared at him through the mirror, seeing only the monster he had become, and picked up the dress off the floor.

My father smiled, and I turned to leave before he could see the tears start to fall. "Be in the foyer at six sharp," he announced before I slammed his door.

I was shaking when I picked up my phone to call my mom. She finally answered after two attempts, but her voice sounded strange.

"Hey baby," she slurred. "How are you?"

"I'm good Mom. How are you? Daddy says you aren't feeling well," I said gently, the tears rolling down my cheeks with force now.

"Oh, he worries too much. I'm fine. Just tired, baby. I'm going to sleep, but I'll call you later, ok?" She didn't wait for me to respond, and I sat there with the phone to my ear, refusing to accept the silence I got when she disconnected.

Functioning on autopilot, I got myself ready for the party and met my father by the door. I didn't acknowledge him, nor did we speak in the ride over to Robbie's house. I watched as the car navigated through both security gates and felt as if they were prison doors shutting behind me.

Robbie met us at the front door and looked at me in awe when I stepped out of the car. The emerald dress he had picked out was empire cut and strapless. The gown was fancy enough to be seen on the red carpet and even had under garments sewn into it so there were no lines. It was once again a perfect fit, a chilling reminder of the closet full of clothes he had stashed away. I knew the dress brought out my eyes in a way that made them almost seem unnatural, but they exposed only the empty shell I was tonight.

He pulled me towards him and attempted to kiss me. I turned away before he was successful, and he settled for my cheek, pretending it was his intention. "You look stunning, Isadora. I've never seen anyone so beautiful."

He offered me his elbow. I had no intention of taking it until I heard my father clear his throat. I conceded and allowed Robbie to guide me into the ballroom that was full of people. I hadn't seen this side of Robbie's house before, and the vast space was grand enough to be in the movies. Large chandeliers hung from the ceiling, and the walls were covered in various designs, all carved out of wood and painted to match the walls.

Robbie led me directly to the dance floor and pulled me close to him. I allowed him to lead me around, still not saying a word. He leaned into me while we danced and commented on my lack of personality. "You're not yourself tonight."

"That's because I'm here under duress," I answered icily, staring at him with all the disgust I felt for him.

"Ah," he said nodding, tightening his grip on me. "Let's get you a drink then. It always seems to lighten your mood."

He led us off the dance floor and excused himself to the bar to get our drinks. I wanted the alcohol, could almost taste it in my mouth, but I didn't trust myself, and I certainly couldn't trust Robbie or my father. I moved to the corner hoping Robbie would lose sight of me and checked my phone. Jason had texted me a reminder that our monologue was tomorrow. I chuckled when I read the word "slacker" next to it.

Grant also had texted me.

Grant: I'm finally done with my list. Where are you?

Before I could reply, I felt someone staring at me. I glanced up to find Robbie in front of me holding my drink. He handed it to me and took my phone out of my hand. I watched in stunned silence as he scrolled through my texts.

"Jason?" he asked, looking up.

"A friend," I replied sternly, holding out my hand to get my phone back.

Robbie just nodded and looked down at it again. "Grant?"

I felt my stomach drop a little, but kept my face unreadable. "Another friend. Now can I have my phone back, please?"

Robbie eyes darkened a little as he handed back my phone. "Somehow, I doubt that one," he said calmly, and then put his hand on my elbow to lead me through the room.

I stopped when I saw we were at the ballroom doors, refusing to go any further.

"I have something I want to show you," Robbie explained trying to move me forward.

"I'm not going anywhere alone with you."

"Trust me, you will want to see what your father's been up to. It's just my office, Isadora."

I hesitated a minute, but the need to know trumped my survival instinct, and I followed Robbie to his office. He shut the door behind him after we stepped inside, and I heard a loud click that put my nerves immediately on alert.

Robbie walked past me to the large window overlooking his garden and began talking. "You know, Isadora, it's a good thing I'm an only child, because I have never been very good at sharing something that I believe to be mine." Robbie turned to look at me, his eyes terrifyingly calm.

I decided it was a bad idea to have come with him and backed up to the door to turn the handle. It didn't budge. I felt around the handle for a lock but there was nothing.

"It's fingerprint activated," Robbie explained with a smile. "Incredible technology."

I could feel myself shaking as I watched Robbie walk over to his large mahogany desk. "Come here," he directed, holding out his hand. "I promised you information."

I slowly walked over to him and looked down at his desk. The first thing I immediately saw was my framed picture sitting there. It was my father's, and I recognized it immediately because I had given it to him for his birthday last year. The frame was purchased at an antique store in Asheville and I knew it was a one of a kind. "Where did you get this?" I asked, shock registering on my face.

"Your father gave it to me," he answered as if surprised I didn't already know that. He picked it up and looked at it. "It's truly a masterpiece, Isadora," he mused before setting it back down and walking back towards the window.

"I'm still kind of surprised you don't remember me," he continued, turning to face the garden again. "It bothered me at first, especially considering I couldn't get you out of my head. But then I realized it was actually to my advantage that you didn't."

"Robbie, what are you talking about?" I demanded, my voice betraying my fear and rising anger. "Why would I remember you, and when did you get this picture? My father only keeps it at his office in New York."

"Your getting emotional, Isadora, and its clouding your usual intuition. Look around. You're missing a vital piece."

I looked around the room, exasperated, and then looked back down at Robbie's desk. My eyes immediately spotted a piece of paper that had my name on it. It was my schedule for Western and had been signed by my father at the bottom. "So he gave you my schedule. How does that answer my questions?" I asked, irritation present in my voice.

"Look closer, Isadora. You're still missing it."

I looked at the paper again and finally saw what he was referring to. I felt the entire room shift, and I clutched the edge of his chair to steady myself. My father's signature was dated November 10th, two months prior to New Year's and my unfortunate brush with death. I looked back up at Robbie, my eyes wide with horror.

He smiled at me, knowing I had seen what he wanted me to. I pulled over the chair and sat down, sure I was going to fall if I stood any longer. Robbie seemed pleased with my response and started talking again.

"You know when I met your father, it was because my dad wanted me to witness their exchange. Your father had approached us with the merger idea last summer and was still waiting to hear what we were going to do. My father decided it wasn't worth the time and effort it would take, when the profit margin on our side was so small. On your father's side, now that was another story. So I went with him, willing to learn all I could before I graduated. Your father was very gracious, bringing us into his office, showing us all around the room while he pitched how great the merger would be. I allowed him to go on, feigning interest while I examined the contents of his office. That's when I saw your picture, and suddenly I realized that there was something worth far more than money that I might gain from this little merger."

My ears were ringing as Robbie's words tore at my heart. I refused to hear what he was telling me. Refused to believe that my father would use me as leverage in a business deal. "But why me?" I whispered, my voice unable to work properly.

Robbie came over to me and handed me the last envelope on his desk. Inside were hundreds of pictures of me, starting as early as October. Me and Avery dancing, Danny and I kissing outside our apartment complex, Jason and I up against the wall making out in the bar, Grant and I arguing on the beach. The pictures went on and on until the final one was of me last night sitting at the table with Jake's friends.

"It was you," I whispered, finally understanding how my father always seemed one step ahead of me.

"I've been watching you for a long time, Isadora. Studying you, learning you. I must say, you have been my most challenging acquisition yet."

"But why me?" I asked again, my voice getting louder. "You didn't even know me."

He stood behind me, rubbing my bare shoulders as he spoke. "Winsor truly is a beautiful campus. I can see why you love it there so much. I hadn't ever made it up there until last August when a friend of mine begged me to visit before classes started. He insisted we go to this club on campus and watch a local band playing there. *Wild Cats*, I think they were called."

My heart started fluttering as recognition flooded my memory. I had been there with Jake that night. I searched for anything that would remind me of Robbie, but there was nothing.

Robbie continued to explain. "We were hanging by the bar, talking, when all the sudden, the lead singer of the band reached down and pulled a girl up on stage. I watched you with fascination, as did every other man around me. Your vibrancy was intoxicating as you bounced around the stage singing with the band. I had never been so struck by anyone in my life. I watched as you danced your way up to the bar and got yourself a drink. I approached you, unable to stay away from the inexplicable draw I had to you, and you turned and smiled at me. Your eyes were riveting, as unique and striking as the rest of you."

Robbie leaned down and starting rubbing his lips on my exposed neck and shoulders. "We danced and flirted until, I assume now it was Jake, came and pulled you away from me. It happened so fast, I didn't even get your name. I was hooked, addicted to you like a drug I could never get enough of. I went back the next night to find you, but you didn't show. I learned from the bouncers that your name was Issy, but as you well know, it's kind of impossible to find someone who goes by a name that isn't really her name. When I saw your picture that day, I knew you were meant to be mine."

I felt like I was going to throw up. I stood up and walked away from him, my whole body shaking with rage and hurt. "So it was all a lie?" I yelled, glaring at him. "My father, you…it was all staged so what, I would somehow fall for you?" I couldn't even believe the words myself. Then I thought of Monday night, and my heart started to pound. "Did you lie to me about the other night too? Did you…did you…rape me?" I could hardly form the words, and part of me didn't want to know.

Robbie stared back at me, his eyes so intense that fear gripped my heart. "Is it really rape when the person belongs to you?" he asked flatly, waiting to see my response. I stood paralyzed, my mind refusing to process what he was telling me. Before I could scream, Robbie continued, "Regardless, I did not touch you that night. Your father had made that a stipulation in the contract, something about getting the milk for free before the deal was final."

"And when is that supposed to be?" I demanded, my voice shaking uncontrollably now.

"Why Isadora, next week…on your birthday." He walked towards me and rubbed his hand over my cheek. "And how I have been dreaming of that night. I may not have touched you the other day, but I did view the merchandise, and like I said before, exquisite."

I pushed Robbie away from me with every bit of strength I had and ran towards the door. I knew it was locked, but I tugged on it anyway, banging my hand on it so someone could hear me. Suddenly, I was trapped against the door, my cheek pressed into the wood so much that I could smell the paint.

"You see, Isadora, I own you. Bought and paid

for, and I even have the contracts to prove it," he purred as he kissed the back of my neck. I struggled against him, but it was no use. He grossly overpowered me. I couldn't stop the tears that were racing down my cheeks. "You are my most prized possession. A one of a kind gem that every man wants, but no one can truly have…until now. A wild spirit only I get to tame." His words and touch were nauseating, and I began to believe I would faint if I couldn't get him to stop crushing my lungs.

Robbie turned me around, careful to keep me pinned as he did so and pressed his mouth to mine. I turned my head back and forth to resist, causing him to crush me even harder. I felt his hand start to move up my leg as he lifted my dress. I tried to scream, but his mouth was fully consuming mine. I fought with everything in me, finally getting my mouth closed when he moved to my neck. "What is it you want, Isadora?" He asked as his hand reached the top of my thigh, terrifyingly close to my panty line.

"I want out of this room," I cried, my tears choking me now.

"Then play your role." With those words, he began kissing me again, and I knew exactly what he was telling me to do. I kissed him back, imagining Grant the entire time. I had promised Grant I would never kiss anyone else, and in my mind I didn't. I had somehow completely detached from my body, but I knew deep down, the heart that just started to beat again, had died once more. Robbie honored my response by moving his hand and straightening my dress. After more time, he slowly backed away from me, allowing the kiss to be over.

I stared at him with hatred as he took his two thumbs and wiped the tears off my face. "I knew you would learn quickly," he said, smiling in satisfaction.

He ran his thumb under the handle, and I heard the click once again. Seconds later, the door opened, and Robbie led me back to the ballroom as if nothing had happened. As if he hadn't just crushed my entire world.

21. TO BE

I was still trying to get the shaking under control as we entered the ballroom. Apparently the merger announcement had been made while we were in Robbie's office because people were milling around looking much more stressed and agitated than before. I fit right in with all of them. I knew exactly what it felt like to fear the future and know your fate is out of your hands.

I felt Robbie's breath on my neck again and cringed. "I need you to be the picture of grace for fifteen more minutes, and then I'll have your father take you home."

I seriously considered walking away and doing everything I could to embarrass both Robbie and my father. But the reality that I had no way home and Robbie's house was fortified by two large security gates kept me well behaved.

Robbie made me dance with him one more time. He introduced me to several of his colleagues and friends as his girlfriend and then had us pose for a myriad of pictures, one of which would undoubtedly show up on the society page in the morning. The screaming in my head was nothing less than a constant shrill by the time he approached my father.

"Isadora's had a lot of information thrown at her tonight, Andrew. I think it's best if you get her home so she can get a good night's rest," Robbie explained as we approached.

I didn't look at him, but assumed he agreed because we were quickly on our way out the front door. The limo was waiting when we got there, and my father got in first, leaving me alone with Robbie. I questioned how much longer I could keep it together. The façade was tumbling and Robbie's shear proximity to me sent ripples of fear through my body.

Robbie turned my chin so I would look at him. "Since you no longer have your car, I'll be happy to take you to class in the morning."

"That won't be necessary," I replied coolly.

"It's no trouble. I'll see you at breakfast…seven sharp."

I had a visceral reaction to his words and jerked my head away to get in the limo. I sat opposite my father and gripped the seat as I settled my racing heartbeat. My eyes peered out the window, praying for an escape, but none seemed possible. When I had finally calmed enough to speak, I glared at my father who was calmly checking emails on his phone.

"If you think I'm going to play along with your little game, you are sadly mistaken. I will not be at breakfast tomorrow morning, nor will I EVER belong to Robbie Marsh."

"I would think you'd be flattered. There are very few things the Marsh's don't have and are willing to do anything to get."

"Flattered?" I yelled, stunned that he would even dare to use such a word. "That you prostituted me out to the highest bidder?"

My father rolled his eyes at me. "You're being overdramatic, Kaitlyn. Think of it more as an arranged marriage. Many cultures all over the world do it. You could do worse. Robbie Marsh will provide you a life that others would kill for."

I was sure I heard him incorrectly and shook my head to try and get the words out of my mind. "And how exactly did you think you were going to get me down that aisle?"

"Well, I had hoped you would go willingly. I went through a lot of trouble to set up a chance meeting, but Robbie blew that one out of the water. I told him you can't charm a charmer, but he wanted to do it his way. You blowing him off for the bartender sent him over the edge...almost killed the deal, in fact," he explained, his eyes actually having the nerve to toss judgment at me.

"That's why you set up the dinner," I mused to myself. It was all making sense now.

"Robbie did much better that night. I told him he had to be the one thing you needed, and I must say, he is a master at playing his part."

"And what exactly is it you think I need?" I spatted, hating how calmly my father was behaving. It was like he already knew he would win.

"An ally, of course."

I turned my head and looked out the window, remembering how I had started to believe that Robbie was a victim just like me and could be trusted. The tears were too powerful to hold back and I felt them roll down my cheeks. I hadn't cried in front of my father since I was thirteen and the fact I was now made me feel even more defeated than the conversation did.

"I won't marry Robbie," I whispered, still not facing my dad.

My father's voice got really sharp and he leaned up on his knees to direct them at me. "Kaitlyn, this deal is everything to me. If you mess it up, I will slowly take away everything you cherish. Then I will do the same thing to every person you love, until all of you are left with nothing."

I turned to face my father, my tone matching his. "Then I guess it's a good thing I don't love anyone but myself, because I'd rather have nothing than Robbie Marsh."

My father smiled, and sat back in victory. "Now now, Kaitlyn, we both know you love Jake and even your mother if you're really honest with yourself. Funny how quickly Jake got that job, isn't it? One day an intern, the next a paid stock broker with a signing bonus and commission. Seems almost too good to be true, don't you think?" I didn't respond, just glared at my father. "I should call Steve again and see how Jake's doing. After all, it was my insistence that got him the job in the first place."

I sat back and looked out the window again. My father had orchestrated it all so perfectly. With two very strategic moves, he now owned both my mother and Jake. They were pawns, leverage to keep me in line. He honestly believed I would sacrifice myself for them.

The rest of the drive was done in silence, a silence so deafening that my ears actually throbbed when we pulled up to the house. I fled from the limo and went straight to my room, ripping off my dress as soon as I crossed the threshold. I then showered, trying to scrub off Robbie's touch that felt seared into me. I hadn't even noticed I was sobbing until suddenly, the world stood still and clarity descended from the sky. I knew what to do. The decision immediately calmed me. The tears stopped and the shell that had been shattered earlier was back in place. I was once again in control.

I dried off and calmly put on my pajamas before filling my flask to the top. There would be no need to stop drinking now. I descended my stairs gracefully and walked out to the lake. I stood watching the water, enjoying the cold night air on my skin when I felt Grant's arms wrap around me and his lips kiss my neck.

"I missed you so much tonight," he whispered, holding me tight. I leaned back into him, enjoying the way his arms felt around me.

We watched the lake together until I finally spoke. "How much money is my dad making on this merger?"

Grant let out a heavy sigh. "1.4 Billion dollars"

I nodded. At least I wasn't cheap. I squeezed Grant's arms. "I get it now. I didn't for the longest time and was so angry with her for what she did, but I now understand why. That was the day he broke her."

Grant turned me around and stared into my empty eyes, his face showing nothing but concerned confusion. "Hey, what happened? Who are you talking about?"

I looked at his face, memorizing every line, every perfect feature and put my hand on his cheek before gripping his shirt. "Grant, I want you to promise me something, ok?"

He nodded. "Anything."

"Promise me you will get away from here. From my father and his control. Promise me you will take your idea and run free. I need you to promise me that," I pleaded, pulling on his shirt.

Grant reached up and held my face. "I'll promise, but only if you come with me." I watched the hope in his eyes. He saw a future for us. He had no idea that my father had already sold me to another man.

I smiled at him. "I'll always be with you."

He pulled me towards him and held me tight. I held on for dear life, knowing it would be the last time I'd ever feel his arms around me. Tomorrow everything would change.

I woke up early and quietly went through the steps of getting ready for the day. I made sure to pick an outfit Robbie would appreciate and left my hair dark and wavy. I examined my eyes as I applied my makeup. They were completely void and my face the picture of an ice queen. I practiced my smile and once I had it perfected, I descended the long staircase and walked towards the dining room. Robbie was already seated next to my father, as was Anna and Junior who I hadn't seen in days. I quietly took the seat that Robbie had pulled out when I approached.

He leaned in and kissed me hello. "You look beautiful as always," he stated with a smile.

"Thank you, Robbie," I replied, using my mother's melodic tone.

Breakfast consisted of business conversation until Anna dared to address me. It had been the first time we'd spoken since Thanksgiving, and I assumed she only had the nerve because Robbie was sitting there.

"There's a beautiful picture of you and Robbie in the paper this morning," she offered, handing the paper to me. I accepted it with a smile and glanced at the couple that graced the cover. We were the picture of wealth and class, and even looked truly happy together. The paper went on to talk about my dress and who the designer was and how much it had cost. I almost laughed when I thought of the ripped $5000 garment that was now stuffed in my trashcan.

I felt Robbie move the hair off my shoulder and squeeze my neck affectionately. "It was certainly a night to remember," he agreed, sending me a look that held a double meaning.

I put my hand on his leg and gave him my most charming smile. "I know I won't be forgetting it any time soon."

Robbie was practically beaming as he ushered me out to his waiting driver. We passed Grant in the foyer. He was leaning up against his office door with his arms folded. I could see confusion and anger in his eyes when we passed. Robbie must have seen it too, because he made a point to kiss my neck before opening the front door. I didn't turn to see Grant's reaction. I knew facing him would make me question my choice…and nothing was going to make me change my mind.

Robbie was up to his usual antics in the back of the car, rubbing my leg and pulling me in to kiss him. I played my role perfectly and had Robbie so crazy that he had to wait a few minutes before we could get out of the car. He proudly walked me to my building, keeping my hand possessively in his, and drew me in for a long kiss when Jason approached the building. I continued to play my part until he finally pulled away to say goodbye.

"Robbie," I called, pulling him back to me. "I want something."

"Anything," he answered, his eyes dark and intense.

"On this paper are two people I care about. I want them each to have a bank account set up in their name only. I want $10,000 put in each of them," I explained. I knew that amount of money was nothing for Robbie's family and would be enough to get Jake and my mother back on their feet if my dad followed through with his threat.

"That's a pretty big request, Isadora," Robbie stated, putting his arms around my waist.

I leaned in and seductively kissed his neck. "I thought playing my part got me whatever I wanted. Did I misunderstand?" I asked batting my eyes.

"I'll text you the account numbers when I'm finished," he agreed, his breath labored again. "I'll be waiting when you finish today, and I will expect a proper thank you."

I nodded, and turned to head into class. I didn't bother with my old seat, and immediately sought out Jason. He looked miserable and defeated as he slumped down in his chair. I scooted next to him and smiled. "You're taking me out tonight."

Jason looked stunned and then a grin slowly appeared on his lips. "You got it, green eyes. Where to?"

"Somewhere well out of town, where no one will find us, and I can drink without issue."

Jason nodded and squeezed my leg under the desk. "I know just the place."

Unlike usual, my classes went by as if on fast forward. Even algebra was tolerable, although I didn't bother turning in the assignment. Maybe knowing that it was my last day in school made me appreciate it just a little more.

Even lunch was enjoyable. Rachel went on and on about my dress in the paper, but other than that, I made sure to just sit back and enjoy each person I saw. Candace was as warm as always, and we laughed and joked as we ate. Even Rusty and Reggie were somewhat cordial.

I excused myself after getting Robbie's text and forwarded it on to Jake telling him not to ask, unless he needed to.

Jake: Everything ok?

Me: Couldn't be better. Just keep info for a rainy day.

Jake: Ok, I will

I hesitated for a second, but then sent the last text anyway.

Me: I love you.

Jake: You sure you're alright?

Me: Promise

By the time I reached Shakespeare, I was surer than ever that I had made the right decision. Grant had texted me four times trying to find out what was going on. I finally texted him back.

Me: Remember your promise.

Grant: Remember yours.

I turned off my phone, knowing in an hour it would be flooded with messages I had no intention of taking. I was the last one in class, which got me the honor of being picked first to do my monologue. I smiled and walked to the front of the room. It was the one assignment I was looking forward to. Turns out that Hamlet was much more like me than I realized.

I sat in the chair facing the class and took a deep breath. Suddenly, the room was empty and I could see the lake out in front of me as I began to quote William Shakespeare.

"To be, or not to be: that is the question:
Whether 'tis nobler in the mind to suffer
The slings and arrows of outrageous fortune,
Or to take arms against a sea of troubles
And by opposing end them?"

I could feel my hands shaking as I remembered the very moment I decided I would follow in my mother's footsteps. She had known it was the only way...as did I.

"To die: to sleep;
No more; and by a sleep to say we end
The heart-ache and the thousand natural shocks
That flesh is heir to, 'tis a consummation
Devoutly to be wish'd. To die, to sleep;
To sleep: perchance to dream:"

I could feel myself whisper the last words as my eyes filled with tears. The lake slowly disappeared and I was back in class staring out into faces that were frozen in awe. I stood up and slowly made my way back to my seat.

I felt Jason lean into me. "You were chilling," he said in awe.

The TA stood in front of the class and cleared her throat. That seemed to wake everyone up and the class erupted with applause.

"Issy, that was exactly what I was looking for. Outstanding job," she praised.

Person after person went up to do their monologues after me. Some did great, other's totally bombed. I enjoyed Jason's the most as he truly seemed to become Romeo. I also noted he didn't take his eyes off of me the whole time he spoke.

As the class came to a close, I started to get antsy as I watched the time. I knew we'd get out early today, but the window was getting dangerously close to closing. Robbie would be waiting, and I needed to leave before he noticed anything was wrong. As soon as we were dismissed, I grabbed Jason's arm and pulled him out the back door, practically pushing him along.

"What's the hurry, green eyes?" he asked as he watched me.

"Jason, either we move it, or you will get to watch Robbie kiss me again. Your choice."

Jason didn't need to hear that twice and quickly led us to his motorcycle. We were off campus before my normal class period even ended, and I just held on to Jason and let the wind blow across my face. So soon…I would be free.

We stopped at Jason's apartment first, and I went right to his liquor cabinet and poured a drink while he changed. He came out of his room, looking as sexy as ever when he joined me. I handed him a glass and he reached up to move hair off my face.

"Is this a date, green eyes?" he asked, his eyes penetrating mine.

"If I say no, will you still take me out?"

"Of course. I told you I'll take whatever I can get," he answered, his eyes still searching mine.

"Then let it just be whatever it is and not force me to define it."

Jason nodded and then grabbed my free hand, placing his fingers between mine. I took another drink and moved closer to him. "Just make me a promise." He nodded. "No matter what happens tonight, you don't take me anywhere but here. When I pass out, I want it to be with you." Jason easily agreed, having no idea what I was really saying. Only I knew that if Avery and Parker had just left me alone that night, the last few weeks would never have happened. Only I knew that when Jason laid me in bed tonight, I would never wake up.

I poured myself another drink and drank it down quickly as Jason watched with awe. "Why do I feel like every time I'm with you, you are on a mission to kill yourself?"

"Because I am," I answered flatly, my eyes as void as my heart.

Jason just shook his head and finished his drink.

"I will never understand you."

The night went on in a blur. The amount of alcohol I consumed was pushing dangerous levels and I could feel the affects when I danced. I held on tighter to Jason, trying to avoid falling. The room was spinning and I was having a hard time focusing on anything around me.

I leaned into Jason. "I need another drink."

"Babe, I really think you've had enough. I've never seen anyone drink like you have tonight."

I answered him by running my hands up his chest and pulling him in for a long, provocative kiss. He responded immediately, not wanting to let go when I pulled away.

"One more," I whispered. "And we'll go home."

Jason walked me over to a chair and went to get me another drink. Even sitting, I was having a hard time keeping my body from swaying with the room. I felt my stomach turn, but I willed it away. Throwing up would counteract everything I was trying to do. I had to pass out first. I gripped the chair, trying to steady myself, and suddenly started hallucinating because Grant's face was right in front of mine.

"Issy?" he said softly, putting his hands on my face. I tried to get my eyes to focus, but they wouldn't. "Baby, how much have you had to drink tonight?" His words were floating through my head, but I couldn't process any of them. I just stared into the face I had hoped would be in my final dream and closed my eyes.

22. THE ILLUSION OF HOPE

My warm dream suddenly turned into a nightmare. It was cold, so cold, and wet. I felt water pelting me from all sides, and I lifted my arms to try and stop the flow. I felt something hard against my cheek and it made me jerk away.

"Wake up, Issy, you cant sleep," I heard in the distance.

But I wanted to sleep. That was the point. The water continued relentlessly and I felt the other side of my face being lightly slapped. I sent my arms flailing, trying to stop whatever was attacking me. My eyes slowly became light enough to open, and I looked around the tile prison that surrounded me. I turned my face away from the stream of water that was coming out of the showerhead as I realized I was sitting in a tub I had never seen before. The quick motion sent my stomach in a whirl, and I barely crawled out of the tub fast enough to make the toilet.

I felt someone grab my hair and rub my back. "That's it. Get that poison out of you."

When I was sure there was nothing left in my stomach to get rid of, I slid down to the floor. My whole face was flushed and the cold tile felt amazing against my cheek. The heaving had brought tears to my eyes that seemed to flow without control as my soaked body lay shivering on the floor.

I felt a blanket being wrapped around me as the sad, honey sweet words hit my ears. "This can't be what you turn into, Issy, it's too…tragic."

His words only made the tears come harder and sobs started choking me. The dam was broken and every tear I'd ever withheld came pouring out of me with no chance of stopping it. Grant lifted me onto his lap and rocked me while I cried. "Just let it out, sweetheart, it only gets easier from here."

I wanted to believe him, but he didn't know. He didn't know what my father had done, how far he had fallen. "He sold me," I cried, my words barely audible through the sobs. "To Robbie Marsh…for 1.4 Billion dollars."

I heard Grant gasp, which just made it all seem more hopeless. "You should have let me die. I wanted to die." I cried, pushing away from him.

His arms where immovable and I finally stopped fighting and just sat there and cried.

"I told you, I'm not letting you go, even if that means I protect you from yourself," he whispered, rubbing his hand over my hair to console me.

I cried until I had no more tears, which seemed like hours. When I finally calmed, Grant stood me up and gave me some dry clothes to change into. I looked into his eyes, and the compassion overwhelmed me, making me turn away from him.

His clothes practically swallowed me, but I didn't care. They made me feel safe, and since I knew the feeling was fleeting, I just wanted to keep the dream as long as I could.

Grant was pacing when I shut the bathroom door and walked toward his bed. "Why didn't you tell me?" he asked sharply, his eyes catching mine.

"I knew you wouldn't let me do it, and my disappearing was the only answer," I admitted. Grant took a deep breath and pulled me into his arms. I pushed him away and wiped the stray tears that fell from my eyes again. "My father will stop at nothing to make this merger happen."

Grant took my hands in his and looked at me intently in the eyes. "God is bigger than your father, Issy. You only feel this way because you haven't allowed Christ to infiltrate your life. I get it. I felt the same way this summer, completely lost, but God changed all that. He gave me hope, perspective, and a purpose, Issy." Grant was pleading with me. I could see it in his eyes.

I felt my anger stir as I pulled my hands from his. "Hope? Are you kidding me? There is no hope for me, Grant. I'm selfish and cruel. I use people all the time. Even last night, I knew what I was doing to Jason, and I didn't care. I needed him and to hell with the collateral damage. Your God doesn't want me," I yelled, the retched tears returning to my eyes.

"Issy," Grant replied softly, his tone exposing how much he hurt for me. He gathered me in his arms despite my protest. "There is no sin too great for God. He even died for you, knowing you would be exactly who you are. All you have to do is accept His love…it's unconditional."

"My own father sold me to the devil in a business deal. I have no concept of that kind of love," I said flatly.

Grant's eyes glossed over a little as he tucked a piece of hair behind my ear. He knew I was done talking. "I wish I could take away your pain," he whispered.

I felt the tears stream down my face as I looked into his loving eyes. "Me too."

Grant sat on the bed and pulled me to him. "Let's just get some sleep. We'll figure out what to do in the morning. I'm sure it's not as bad as it seems."

I gave him a ghost of a smile and allowed him to believe everything would be ok. I even started to believe it myself, because as I laid on his chest, his arms wrapped tightly around me, I felt myself wondering about a father who actually loved his children more than himself. I even started to wonder if that same father could save me from mine.

The shuffling of papers woke me up. The room was still dark indicating the sun hadn't risen yet, and Grant sat stiffly at a small desk as he read through pages of information. The small desk lamp was just enough to frame his profile and made me want to jump out of bed and kiss him.

"Hey," I said softly to get his attention.

Grant looked up and his face was rigid, anger so heavy in his eyes that I was sure he was shaking. "How did I miss it? It's right here, clear as day, and I just missed it."

"Grant, what are you talking about?" I asked, getting off the bed so I could go to the bathroom.

"You're KIS. It's all over this, Issy." Grant stood up holding one of the documents and began reading. "Upon the signing of this contract by both parties, KIS shall be immediately relocated to 500 West Manor Road and shall be guaranteed the following: a proper namesake with all the rights and privileges afforded by such, lavish accommodations and attire, and proper compensation should the undersign determine to terminate the arrangement."

"Grant," I said, walking up to him. He pulled away from my touch, unable to look at me.

"No, it gets worse," he stated as he continued to read. "It is not required that KIS be afforded any contact with previous affiliations and may be confined if necessary." Grant was pacing the room now. "He can't get away with this. It's human trafficking, Issy. I'm calling the police, today."

I let out a sigh. "Grant, who is going to believe us? Robbie and I have made the paper multiple times, always looking like a couple in love...mutually. KIS could mean anything, and I have no doubt my father has a backup plan just in case. We can't beat him,

Grant."

Grant threw the paper back on his desk and pulled me into his arms. "Then we'll run. We'll disappear until this whole thing dies down. Baby, I'm so sorry. I should have seen it; I should have protected you."

"There was a reason my father kept you out of those meetings, Grant," I reminded him, trying to ease some of his guilt. "This isn't your fault. Robbie had hinted numerous times as well, and I never caught any of it. I ignored my instincts and just made this whole thing a lot easier for them."

"Listen, I will stall your father. I'll tell him I found you and set up a meeting place. You take my car and go home and pack up just what you need to survive. I'll meet you at Nation's bank in one hour. I have enough savings to keep us hidden for a while."

"Grant, it will never work. Robbie's had someone following me since October. I'm surprised my father isn't already here."

"Trust me, Issy. They were frantic last night. They had no idea where you were."

"Then how did you find me?" I asked, pulling away from him.

Grant grinned as he looked at me. "You told me your secret, remember? I called Jake."

I sighed and walked toward the bathroom. "I guess it's worth a try, but I'm telling you. My father always wins."

"He's smart, Issy, but so are you. You got away

once, remember, you can do it again."

I simply nodded and shut the door. I found myself looking around the bathroom that had somehow brought me back to life, and wondered if he was right. Maybe we could win. Maybe it would just work.

I heard Grant on the phone when I stepped back into the room. He put his finger to his mouth to indicate I needed to be silent.

"Yes sir, she was at Winsor. I found her at one of the clubs she took me to last time we were there." Grant was silent as he listened and then continued, "Well, she's still passed out. I can wake her and bring her home, or wait until you come. Whatever works for you." Grant then nodded and smiled. He glanced at the Marriot confirmation code on his computer. "Yes, the Marriot in Asheville, room 215. I'll see you and Mr. Marsh in an hour. Yes sir, I understand. I won't let her out of my sight."

Grant ended the call, and ran over to kiss me. "Time starts now, baby. We've only got an hour, so you have to hurry."

Minutes later I was in his car driving to the lake house. When I pulled up, I looked around for my father's car, but it was missing, giving me a rush of hope that maybe Grant was right. I parked around back so no one could see the car and slipped in through the back door and up the stairs.

My room was just as I left it when I entered and I tore through the closet, throwing as many clothes in my duffle bag as would fit. I ran to my armoire and grabbed multiple sets of underwear and was just about to stuff them in the bag when I looked up and saw him standing there.

He was leaning against my balcony with his arms crossed. When he saw I noticed him, he slowly walked forward and shut the doors behind him. "Don't mind me. By all means, continue," he said calmly as I stood frozen in fear. My father had always been an intimidating man, but never in my life had I feared him...until that moment. I started moving again, forcing my eyes to go void, hiding the fact that he affected me at all.

"I decided my mother and Jake would survive," I said flatly as I zipped up my bag and lifted it off my bed.

"Yes, I got that message loud and clear last night when you disappeared," my father said calmly as he walked around the bed and placed two photos in front of me. They were pictures of me and Grant on the pier the day I came home from Jake's. The first was us looking in each other's eyes, the intimacy clear to anyone who looked at it. The other was of us kissing.

My father made a ticking sound with his mouth and shook his head. "Turns out that Grant has been up to some very sneaky things the last several years. Embezzlement...that's a felony, isn't it? He had the nerve to shave off ten percent from each business transaction and put it into an off shore account.

Looks like the apple doesn't fall too far from the tree. Such a shame. I was just about to call the authorities when I heard of your disappearance." My father descended into one of the chairs in my sitting area and put his elbows on his knees. "I wonder how far you'll get before the cops pick him up?"

"You're bluffing. Grant is squeaky clean, and you know it."

"That he is, but he is also very trusting, and when I directed him to open an off shore account and put away money for your trust fund, he did so faithfully...every time. Those accounts don't have names attached to them...just numbers, and somehow, I can't seem to remember that conversation now."

I closed my eyes, knowing full well it was checkmate. How I didn't see it before, I'll never know. My father owned Grant too. He always had. I set down my bag and walked over to my father. I had one other choice left, and knew it was worth it. I had let others sacrifice for me my whole life, but now it was my turn. I would do this for him...set him free.

"I want my own contract. If I follow through with this merger, you will send no less than ten letters of recommendation to your top investors lauding Grant's performance and his integrity. I also want a written statement that you directed Grant to open that account and transfer money to it."

"Now why would I do that when you could turn around and run off with him?"

"I know it doesn't mean a whole lot to you, but you have my word. I will not run off with Grant. His freedom for my cooperation. Or do I walk out right now?" I asked sternly with my arms crossed.

"Tell you what, our press conference is in two hours. After our announcement, Robbie is going to get down on one knee and put a really large diamond on your finger. You say yes, and I'll send out three letters. Each day you behave, although after last night I doubt Robbie will let you out of his sight, I'll send two more. The day we sign the merger, I will hand you the letter exonerating Grant. That's my counter offer, Kaitlyn. Take it or leave it."

"I want the letter in my hand before you sign, or I will make a public scene and expose all you are doing. I will not give myself to Robbie without that letter...and it better be notarized."

My father chuckled. "Why Kaitlyn, it seems you have picked up something in those business classes after all. It's a deal," he said standing, his face betraying his arrogance. I felt his hands on my shoulders and I turned my head away in disgust. "Let this be a lesson to you. Love makes you weak. In time you'll see, Robbie is a much smarter choice."

Then he walked out of my room, but not before reminding me what time I was to meet him in the foyer. I walked over to my bed and pulled the covers back. I laid there, wrapped in the lingering smell of Grant that was embedded in his clothes, and cried until my phone chimed indicating my hour was up.

Grant had set it so I wouldn't get distracted.

I wiped my eyes and vowed they would be the last tears I ever shed again, and started typing out a message to him.

Me: I've changed my mind. Hope is an illusion and so is love.

Grant: Don't do this, Issy. Don't let him win.

I punched out the next text knowing every word was a lie.

Me: I don't want what you are offering me. I don't want to be on the run, pretending to be someone I'm not. I will only disappoint you and make myself miserable in the meantime.

Grant: I DON'T BELIEVE YOU.

I sent the last one and then blocked his number from my phone.

Me: There is a reason you called her a ghost. She doesn't exist. You are in love with a fairytale. I'm sorry.

I took off his clothes and placed them high in my closet before dawning my robe and walking out to the balcony. I could feel the wall rebuilding over my heart. It was fortified this time, as I was more aware than ever what kind of pain comes when you let your guard down.

A light knock on the door brought me from my thoughts and I walked over to open it. Before stood a middle aged lady I didn't recognize who was holding a garment bag and rolling a small suitcase behind her. She seemed frazzled and stressed and started talking a mile a minute.

"You must be Isadora! Wow, what a wonderful canvas to work with. I'm Suzzy, Robbie's stylist. I'm so sorry I'm late. I just got the call that you were back. Now lets get to work. Oh my, we only have 35 minutes to pull this off."

I moved out of her way and she rushed through the room barking orders at me. I complied with everything she said and let her turn me into Robbie's idea of what the perfect woman looked like. I stared at the reflection of a girl I didn't recognize. My hair had been swept up in a stylish and complex twist high on my head, making me look much older and more sophisticated than I was. The makeup was kept light everywhere except the eyes, which were so dramatically emphasized that it was hard not to stare into them. The dress was an ivory color and had a whimsical feel to it. It had a straight neckline and small spaghetti straps that sparkled in the light. The dress emphasized my bodice and small waist before flowing in all directions finally ending with an asymmetrical hemline at my shins.

Suzzy stood behind me and sighed, wiping a tear out her eyes. "You look breathtaking. Robbie will be beside himself."

She gathered up her things, and I smiled at her, graciously thanking her. She beamed and left the room, never once realizing she was looking into the eyes of a dead woman.

I grabbed my things, to include the purse I was given to match my dress. I didn't bother to pack my phone. It held nothing for me now.

My father, along with Anna and Junior were standing at the bottom of the stairs when I approached. Anna let out a gasp and my father smiled and nodded. I followed them without a word to the waiting limo and took my seat gracefully.

"Issy, you look incredible," Anna gushed. "That dress had to cost a fortune."

I just smiled at her before correcting her. "It's Isadora now, Anna, but thank you."

Robbie was waiting when we arrived. I watched him out the window, his face showing all the tension and anger he must have felt over the last twenty-four hours when I was missing. I closed my eyes. Even the numbing I had done to my body couldn't hide the fear and repulsion that shot down my spine. I truly hated him with such measure that I feared what I would do if we were ever out in the barn again next to his archery set.

The door of the limo opened and Robbie reached in for my hand. His grip was tight and hostile as I felt practically jerked from the car. In my heels, I was only a few inches shorter than him and was immediately staring into his dark hazel eyes. For a second, they looked wild and dangerous, but then I watched his eyes relax as he examined me, moving from the top of my head, down to the shoes he had no doubt approved for the day.

"You may just be stunning enough to make me forgive what you put me through yesterday," he said with a sadistic smile before he grabbed my waist and pulled me towards him. His smell made my stomach turn with nausea, and I had to fight every instinct not to push him away. I felt his breath on my exposed neck as his words sent chills rippling through my body. "Forgive...but not forget."

Robbie turned to address my father. "I assume we have the last hurdle taken care of?"

My father shot me a look and then went back to Robbie. "I'm working it. Rest assured, though, it will no longer affect the deal."

I knew they were talking about Grant, and my stomach knotted as I looked at my father, my eyes threatening as I silently ensured he would keep his end of the deal. He simply nodded in my direction and began to lead Anna and Junior into the large hotel where the press conference was to be held.

I started to follow them, but felt Robbie's grip tighten, leaving me trapped next to him. He turned me around and slammed his mouth over mine. It wasn't a kiss of passion or caring, but a kiss of ownership and anger. It didn't require a response. Robbie was simply making a point that he was in control.

When he was finished, he allowed us to walk in the hotel together, his mask firmly in place as we posed for various photographers. As promised, after the merger announcement was made and various questions answered, Robbie approached the microphone.

"There's one more announcement that needs to be made today. Actually, its more of a question," he said with a wink, making the different press agents start moving around in excitement, grabbing their tape recorders and ensuring the cameras were set. Robbie came and took my hand, pulling me up from the chair I had been assigned to sit in. He led me to the middle of the room where there would be nothing blocking our view from the hundreds of flashes that had already started. I did my best to look confused and excited, playing the part fully.

He dropped to one knee. "Isadora Summers, you have swept me off my feet and ensured that if I lived a thousand years, I would never get enough of you. Marry me. Make me the luckiest man in the world." His eyes held complete sincerity and I actually believed he meant it. In his sick, twisted, selfish brain, Robbie truly believed he loved me.

I put my hand to my mouth, making a grand gesture of shock and excitement, before saying, "Yes." The diamond really was obnoxiously large, princess cut and at least three carets with a row of smaller diamonds surrounding it. The stone was so large that the band consisted of two small rows of diamonds that came together to form a single row at the back. It fit me perfectly, but felt misplaced on my small finger.

Robbie stood and picked me up, spinning me around before kissing me in front of the cameras. I responded as was appropriate and we heard the room erupt in applause. When all the interviews and pictures were complete, I was ushered into Robbie's car, even though we were all going back to my father's house.

"Isadora," Robbie began, his voice holding all the authority of a businessman. "Eric is going to be your driver until next week when you move to my estate. He'll take you everywhere you need to go and will also serve as a bodyguard when needed."

I wanted to correct him that the term was prison guard, but instead simply answered, "Thank you, Robbie. That was very thoughtful of you."

Robbie sat back and lifted my finger, examining how the ring looked on it and smiled. He had won, and he knew it. My entire body was tense in the confided space as I waited for Robbie to start touching and kissing me like he always did. Surprisingly, he was hands off—a fact I was extremely grateful for until Robbie explained.

"I let you cloud my judgment once. I won't make the same mistake twice, Isadora." He glared into my eyes as he ran his finger down my arm. "Time is short, and all good things are worth waiting for."

Nausea filled my stomach again, and I turned to look out the window, away from his penetrating eyes. My gesture wasn't acceptable to him because he took my chin in his hand and turned my face back to him. "I own you, and I will not share," he said coolly, his eyes wild and dangerous again.

"I understand," I simply stated and Robbie

released my face. The screaming in my head went to new octaves, but my shell was impenetrable. There were no tears, no shaking or labored breathing. I had accepted my fate.

When we reached the house and entered, I excused myself to go change into something more appropriate for lunch. Robbie conceded with a light kiss on the inside of my wrist and told me not to take too long.

I sat down in the black chair near my fireplace and began removing the strappy shoes that were killing my feet. Just when I got the second one off, Grant came storming into the room demanding, "Take it off!"

I stood to face him, shock and relief registering all over my face. The sight of him sent a whirl of emotion spinning through my insides and threatened all the resolve I had managed that day. He was shaking with fury and desperation. "Take his ring off your finger, Issy!" he yelled as he grabbed my hand to pull the offensive metal off of me. He didn't stop shaking until the ring was lying on the floor next to us. He took me into his arms and held me. He had tears in his eyes, and I clung to him as if he were my lifeline. I had never seen him cry before, but understood, because I felt the same desperation.

"You can't do this. You can't let him win. You have to fight. It just takes faith, Issy, please," he pleaded as he searched my eyes.

I didn't even get a chance to respond before my

father and Robbie's driver were on him, pulling him away from me. It took both of them to hold him back as he fought them pleading, "Don't be this person, Issy. I know you're still in there." His eyes caught mine and held them captive, silently pleading with me, until Robbie rushed in and stood next to me.

I watched in horror as Grant fought himself out of their grip and lunged at Robbie, taking him to the floor. He got one solid punch in before my father and Eric had him back under their hold. "I'll kill you," Grant screamed towards Robbie. "If you lay so much as a finger on her, I swear, I will kill you!" He didn't get a chance to say anything more as the men pulled him out of the room and down the hallway.

My body was trembling while my head screamed at me to go after him…to fight just as he told me too. But I didn't have the faith Grant had. Robbie and my father were too powerful, and I knew if I fought them, Grant would suffer. At least this way, one of us would be free.

Robbie stood up and straightened his suit jacket before rubbing his jaw, which was already starting to bruise a little. He didn't seem the least bit affected by the scene that had just taken place. Instead, he slowly reached down and picked up the ring that lay on my floor.

"Now that was an unfortunate display of drama, wouldn't you say?" he asked, his voice thick with sarcasm as he put the ring back on my finger. "Lunch is waiting. Don't take too much longer," he directed before leaving my room.

It was three hours later before Robbie finally departed for the evening. He placed a soft peck on my cheek before promising to see me in the morning. While grateful that his advances were limited, part of me feared what to expect when he no longer felt the need to hold back. A shiver went through my body as I realized that fateful day was only four days away.

I walked by Grant's office that had already been cleared out of anything that reminded me of him. After seven years of him practically living in that office, it seemed unimaginable he would never again be in there. My eyes darted to his bedroom and soon my feet followed as I opened the door. The space was as empty as my life felt, except for the small bible sitting on his nightstand. I picked it up, wanting to have something of his. I noticed several pages were marked and highlighted, and wondered why he thought the words were so important. I held the small book to my chest and shut the door.

My phone was ringing as I entered my room and I smiled, feeling really happy it was Jake on the other end.

"Hey," I answered softly, trying to keep the shell firmly still in place. Jake would never understand what I was doing.

"What's going on?" Jake demanded without even a hello. "Grant's here, and he's out of his mind. Says you're engaged?"

"Grant's there?" I asked, shock registering in my voice. I heard Grant tell Jake to give him the phone, and I quickly countered. "Jake, if you give him the phone, I'll hang up."

"Hold on," I heard him whisper into the phone and then shuffling and a door closing before he got back on. "I'm alone. Now what's going on?"

I closed my eyes and hardened my heart. "I'm engaged!" I announced playfully through the phone. "Surprise. Daddy set me up with a handsome, rich billionaire, and what can say, I'm hooked."

"Give me a break, Issy. You've never cared about that stuff."

"Well neither have you, Jake. I guess we've both changed," I retorted.

"Grant said you're being forced, that your dad threated me and your mom and that's why you're doing it."

I let out a long exasperated sigh. "Grant's delusional. He was fun at first, but then tried to get me to run off with him, living on love, so to say. Sorry Jake, I'm just not that girl. "

"I'm not buying it, Issy. I know how you feel about him," he said sternly.

I didn't want to say the next words as I knew they would be a knife in his back, but I had no choice. "Listen Jake, Grant's living in fairyland. I lost interest the minute I had him. You know how I work. I'm his 'Avery,' and like you, he just needs to get over it. I want someone else."

Jake was quiet for a second before his emotionless voice stated, "I guess you were right about that heart of yours." Then he hung up.

His words shook my shell a little, but I felt comfort knowing the two men I loved were together. Maybe they could both help each other to move on. My head was suddenly filled with the image of Grant in yuppie clothes hitting on various women in the blue bar, and I almost lost my lunch. I pushed away the thought. I had no right to him anymore. He was free. So why did I feel more lost than ever before? I stared at the armoire, knowing a few drinks could numb the hurt. I also knew from experience the pain would only return in the morning. I stared at Grant's bible and wondered how this little book changed him so much—how it offered him such unending hope.

I sat on my bed and pulled open the worn pages. Yellow highlights stood out against the white pages and seemed to capture a message of peace, hope and God being in control. My eyes scanned the words, feeling more connected to Grant with each one I read.

Before I realized it, I had read the entire book of John, understanding for the first time who Grant was always talking about. Was this Jesus person real? Did He really die on a cross? And why? Why would he do that for me?

I searched more pages for those answers and found one page that Grant had folded. I turned up the edge and noticed he had my name scribbled on the side of the page. Tears stung at my eyes as I read the precious words,

"The Spirit of the Lord is on me, because he has anointed me to preach good news to the poor. He has sent me to proclaim freedom for the prisoners and recovery of sight for the blind, to release the oppressed,"

Grant had always seen my oppression. He always knew I saw life as a prison. He truly believed Jesus could set me free. My hands shook, and I picked up my phone, dialing the one person who I knew could explain this to me.

"Issy?" Avery asked in a sleepy voice. "Is everything ok?"

My voice was shaking as I spoke. "How do I find freedom, Avery? Real freedom?"

There was silence on the other line before I heard Avery moving around. "You have to believe in Christ, Issy. You have to recognize that you are a sinner and allow Him to forgive you. Then you have to follow him. That's real freedom, Issy. Everything else is just an illusion."

Tears were streaming down my face and my heart was racing. I'd never felt so lost and desperate in all my life. "Can you help me?" I whispered.

Avery started crying on the other line. "Of course," she said and then started praying. It was all starting to make sense, every word Grant, Avery or even Candace had spoken. Peace rippled through my body as I cried with Avery on the phone. I prayed for forgiveness and hope. I prayed for strength and discernment, and finally, I just prayed for Jesus to change my life completely.

When I got off the phone with Avery, I just numbly looked around my room. The silence was almost deafening, because for the first time since I was thirteen, the screaming in my head had stopped.

23. THE LETTER

Time was my biggest enemy, passing so quickly that suddenly I woke up the day before my birthday and realized I only had one day left before I officially and completely belonged to Robbie Marsh. My father had kept his end of the deal and handed me copies of all seven letters that had gone out on Grant's behalf. The last three were to go out today and the final letter, the only one that really mattered because it exonerated Grant, was to be put in my hands tomorrow on our way to the office where all the merger paperwork would be signed.

I heard my phone buzz and reached out to grab it. Avery had sent me a text with the bible verse for the day. I smiled as I thought of her. Our friendship had grown exponentially the last few days. I didn't tell her much about my situation, because I felt the less she knew the better, but we talked a lot about the bible. We were both reading so much and didn't always understand what it meant. Luckily, Parker was usually around to explain it to her, so she would pass it on to me.

She tried once to ask me about Grant, but I skirted the topic by just admitting I cared about him, but the timing was wrong. As always, she respected my privacy and didn't push for more information.

I stretched out in the soft, luxurious sheets, wondering what I was going to do today. I had convinced my father to withdraw me from Western, making him realize that my new profession was to be the stunning wife of billionaire businessman, Robbie Marsh, and nothing else. Going back to Western and seeing everyone free to live their life would just be a reminder of how much I had lost. As it was, I found myself falling into despair pretty regularly. I attempted to read the bible and pray when it happened, but sometimes still allowed myself to drink until I felt numb again. Old habits are hard to break, and I was realizing how much I had relied on alcohol to bury my problems.

The sun was now penetrating even my dark curtains, and I knew it was going to be a beautiful day. I silently prayed for an escape, just as I had every day since I prayed on the phone with Avery. As always, the answer was silence and I just sighed. This faith thing was way harder than it sounded.

I walked to my balcony and glanced out over the lake. It was perfectly serene, not even a ripple in the water. I noticed movement in the sand and watched as Junior sat building a sandcastle while Rosa lounged next to him.

I ran to my closet and threw on some airy capris and striped long sleeve shirt before heading out to the beach. I approached Junior and saw Rosa sit up with a concerned look on her face. I gestured that it was ok and sat down next to Junior on the sand and started helping him build the sand castle. He turned his little eyes to me skeptically and pushed up his round eyeglasses before handing me my own bucket to use.

When we had completed the grandest sandcastle of all time, we both just sat back and admired our work. Junior had directed me how and where to put all the sand, and I was impressed at the eye for detail that little kid had.

"I think you might be an architect in the making," I said affectionately, rubbing his brown hair a little. It dawned on me that those were the first words I had ever actually spoken to him.

He just shook his head. "Nope. Daddy says I'll run his company one day. I want to be just like him," he answered, looking as resolved as a six year old could.

"Well, that sounds like a good plan. Just remember you can change your mind one day if you want to."

Junior nodded and then turned to examine me again. "Where did Grant go?"

I felt my heart constrict for just a moment before I answered him. "Grant decided he wanted to do something on his own. He has this great software idea he needed to pursue. Don't worry, he is going to be just fine."

"I miss him," Junior said sadly. "He would play

Frisbee with me on days like this."

I stood up and brushed off my pants. "Well, I'm not much of a substitute, but I'll play if you'd like."

Junior hurriedly got to his feet and ran to get the Frisbee. When he got back, he took my hand in his and smiled up at me. I smiled back and felt the tears fill my eyes. I was powerless against them.

"Issy?" he asked, surprising me by using a name I hadn't heard in days. "You wont be sad forever. Rosa taught me to pray…and I've been praying for you and Grant every day."

The tears were running down my cheeks now as I squeezed his little hand. "Thanks Junior. I hope you're right."

We played Frisbee together until Anna stood on the pier and called for Junior to come in the house. He ran up to me and gave me a big hug before running through the back door. I walked towards the house myself, but stopped when Anna stood in front of me. There were tears in her eyes and she just reached out and embraced me whispering, "I'm sorry," before running off to the house. I didn't know which one she was apologizing for…what she did to my mother or for what my father had become. It didn't matter. It was done. You can't change the past…no matter how hard you try to.

I glanced back one more time at the sandcastle that Junior and I made, and smiled. Grant would be proud of me. I nodded in satisfaction and turned to go into the house. Just when I was about to put my foot on the stairs, I heard the doorbell ring. Normally Rosa would get it, but I was right there, so I turned and opened the door. It was a postal worker complete with a hat and funny looking shorts, and he was holding a thin package.

"I have a certified letter for Mr. Andrew Summers," he stated, but not before getting that look in his eyes that most men do when they see me.

My stomach flipped as I knew exactly what was in that package. "I can sign for him," I offered in my most charming voice all while moving my body to display the best angles. "I'm his daughter."

"I'm sorry, ma'am, but I can only allow Mr. Summers to sign," he apologized while never taking his eyes off my chest. I smiled internally thinking this was going to be easy. But before I could even begin to move towards him and work my magic, Rosa came storming out of the door.

"You late! Mr. Summers expect letter here two hours ago." She then grabbed the letter out of his hand and scribbled on his notepad. "Shame on you. She just a girl!"

The man jumped back, horrified. He apologized profusely, never once mentioning the letter Rosa took from his hand. Rosa pushed me in the house and then slammed the door. I starred at her in disbelief as she handed me the envelope.

"You have two hours," she whispered.

"My father will fire you when he finds out, Rosa. I can't let you do this." As much as I wanted that letter, there was no way I was letting Rosa take the fall for me. She was the only real stable person Junior and I had left in this house.

She made a ticking sound and waved her hand. "God in control. What can man do to me?" She walked off with a smile, and I watched her in amazement. I guess that's the faith everyone has been talking about.

For the first time in days, hope started to infiltrate my heart again. I ran up the stairs as fast as I could and then sat in my closet with the light on. The envelope was sealed at the top, so I used a razor blade to cut a straight line at the bottom seam to open it. Minutes later, I was able to slide out the notarized letter exonerating Grant. My heart was pounding as I tried to figure out an escape route that would work. Robbie's driver stayed perched in front of my house 24-7, so there would be no leaving by car. I'd have to go on foot and would never make it out in broad daylight. Just as I started to feel the hope slip away, I noticed another small paper sticking out of the envelope. It was a handwritten note to my father on a yellow legal pad.

Mr. Summers,

As requested, the attached letter has been notarized according to your specifications. I have checked with our legal team and this letter would in no way be admissible in court if Mr. Forrester was to go to trial on charges of theft and embezzlement.

John

My anger burned red hot inside of me. He was going to give me a fake just in case I figured a way to run. With the anger came clarity and soon I had a plan that I knew would be my only chance for escape.

I ran down to Grant's office and made a quick copy of the letter and note before heading back to my closet with super glue. I slid the original letter back in to the envelop and sealed back the bottom. After inspection, it looked untouched. I hid the copy of the letter and both copies of the forgery proof in my lingerie drawer, knowing my dad would never go in there. Minutes later, the envelop was sitting on my father's desk as if it had been there the whole time.

I looked down at my watch and realized I still had an hour before my dad came home. I busied myself with the other arrangements, moving with such confidence and speed that for a moment, I felt like my old self. I caught a glimpse of myself in the mirror as I passed, and even saw a little spark in my sad eyes.

The front door slammed, making me jump, and cold shivers rippled down my spine as I quickly hid any evidence of what I was planning. My father was home earlier than expected. I cracked open the door and tiptoed to the stairwell. There was a place Junior would hide where no one could see him, but at the same time gave full access to see the foyer and more importantly, the entrance to my father's office. I crouched there now, my heart racing in fear and anticipation. If my father realized the letter had been tampered with, my last chance to escape would slip between my fingers.

"Rosa!" I heard my father call out in fury. I couldn't see his face, just the opening of his office as Rosa quickly approached it. I felt afraid for her, knowing the risk she took helping me.

"Where do you get off signing for my mail?" he continued once she stood in the doorway. His voice hadn't softened any.

"You no want the letter?" She asked innocently.

I heard my father let out a sigh. Rosa could make anyone go soft. "That's not the point, Rosa. The letter was certified."

"Yes sir, but Grant gone now, and no one here to sign for letter. Next time, I let him leave, ok?" Rosa's voice was remarkable. She actually made my father sound ridiculous.

I heard him sigh again and then he must have waved her off, because she turned around to leave. I watched as she sent a quick wink up to me and then scurried off to the kitchen. I covered my mouth so I wouldn't giggle and tiptoed back to my room.

Minutes later there was a knock at my door. I had

expected him, but still felt my hands start to shake. I said another little prayer and stood, making sure my mask was firmly in place. "Come in."

My father strode in taking large steps and seemed more confident and self assured than ever. It was the march of a victor, and as I watched him, I had to bite the inside of my lip just so I wouldn't say anything to give away the information I held.

"I have your last three letters," he announced, offering them to me.

I glared at him and took them out of his hand with a nod. I had hoped that would be it, and he would stroll right back out of my room. Instead, he lowered himself into one of my chairs and smiled. "So, tomorrow is the big day."

I turned to stare at him, my lip practically bleeding from biting it so hard. "Why are you still here?" I asked through my teeth.

"Come. Sit. This may be the last time we get to talk for a while," my father said patting the open chair next to him.

"No thank you," I answered, walking over to put the new letters with the other ones on my desk.

"Kaitlyn, Sit."

I closed my eyes and got my beating heartbeat under control before walking over to him and dropping in the chair next to him like a spoiled child. "Is this where you threaten me again, Daddy, because I'm not sure how many more people you have on your list that I actually care about."

My father leaned up in his chair and placed his large hand on my knee before meeting my eyes. His blue eyes looked hard, but sincere, and mine slanted in response, knowing I had no trust left in this man.

"I know you hate me right now, but I also know this is what is best for you. For all of us. My methods may be unconventional, but deep down you know I'm doing this because I love you. I want the best life possible for you."

I shook my head and met his eyes again. "No Daddy, you did what's best for you, and you used me to get it. And I want you to remember something as you enjoy your billion-dollar prize. Every time Robbie touches me, I will hate you, and every time he kisses me, I will pray that one day you will feel as dead as you have forced me to become."

My father's armor cracked for just a second. If I hadn't been staring so intently into his eyes, I would have missed it.

He leaned back in the chair and then pulled out another piece of paper that had been tucked in his pocket. "I noticed you and Avery have been doing a lot of talking these last few days."

I couldn't read him and had no idea what he was about to do. "So what? We're friends."

"Grant's been staying at Jake's. Are you aware of that?"

"I knew he went there, but I didn't know he stayed. I lied to Jake if that's what you are asking." My mask was getting harder and harder to secure as I felt an unspoken threat with each one of my father's words.

"Seems odd, is all, that Grant is at Winsor, and suddenly you and Avery are chummy again. If you are using her to funnel information back to Grant, let me assure you, it's a stupid move."

My mouth flew open as a gaped at my father. "I would never put Avery in the middle of this. She has no idea what is going on."

My father watched me closely, trying to determine if I was lying or not. Finally he sat back a little, but still stared intently at me. "Kaitlyn, I want you to realize something. If you run, I will find you. I have unlimited resources and technology."

I felt my armor start to crumble as I said the words, *God is in control* over and over in my head. "I haven't had any contact with Grant since you dragged him out of here," I assured him, trying to appear unaffected by his comment.

"Good," he said patting his legs with is hands. He stood abruptly and strode back to the door, his demeanor as confident as it was when he walked in. "Avery's on an alumni scholarship, isn't she? Huh. Nice to know my money is going to a good cause. Anyway, dinner is at seven sharp. Your fiancé will be joining us, so you might want to dress a little nicer than that." Then the door shut, and I fell to my knees in tears. If God really was more powerful than my father, I needed His help desperately.

6:45 came quicker than I wanted it to, but I descended the stairs anyway, trying to keep my hands from shaking and my eyes as empty as they had been since the day I watched Grant getting dragged out of my room. Robbie had been the picture of control since our engagement and watched me mercilessly. Part of me wished for the return of the love struck guy he had been before. This version of him was chilling.

Robbie was already in the living room with my father when I approached. I had changed as my father requested into a casual gray and black baby doll dress that came just to my knees. Robbie's eyes lit up when he saw me and kissed me hello before whispering that I looked beautiful. It was the same greeting I had received every night this week. The only difference was this time he lingered a little longer, staring into my eyes until I finally turned away.

The dinner went just as all the others had. My father and Robbie talked business while Anna and I silently listened. Every once and a while, I would wink over at Junior, making him snicker silently as he ate. It made me smile, another thing that didn't go unnoticed by Robbie.

Dinner ended, and Robbie put his hand on my leg, indicating he wanted me to stay seated as my father and Anna excused themselves, Junior following in tow.

I watched as they left the room and felt butterflies fill my stomach again. The continuous fear I had around Robbie just felt magnified tonight knowing I was so close to escaping.

"Let's take a walk," he offered as he stood.

I nodded and put my napkin on my plate, trying to keep my eyes away from his as I scrambled to get my mask firmly back in place. He led me out the back door and down the porch to the pier. I stopped walking, not wanting to go any further. The sand and pier were mine…and Grant's. I didn't want Robbie anywhere near it.

"Can we just sit out here?" I asked, noting the seating area around us.

Robbie positioned himself to where he stood right in front of me, his body so close, I could feel his warm breath on my skin. He leaned in and ran his lips gently over my cheeks and then onto my neck. I felt his hand as it moved up my arm and settled on my neck as well. He wrapped it around me, his fingers caressing the bones in the back of my neck as he ran his thumb over my throat. I felt his lips move across my face again as he made his way to the opposite side of my neck and then to my ear.

"That spark in your eyes, Isadora, is irresistible. If I thought for one moment it was for me, I'd be putty in your hands." He quit talking just for a second so he could kiss down the side of my neck, his hand never leaving its threatening position around my neck. "But since neither one of us are stupid, maybe you'd like to tell me what's going on." Robbie pulled his head back, his eyes dangerously dark as his hand tightened around my neck.

Fear surged through me as I met his demanding stare. "I spent the day with my brother. It was the first time we've ever really spoken, and I guess I enjoyed it," I answered, hoping the partial truth would appease him.

His eyes searched mine. "And what drove this sudden shift in relationship?"

"I'm moving to your estate tomorrow, Robbie. I guess in my own way, I was saying goodbye."

Robbie's eyes brightened with the mention of tomorrow, and I noticed how his grip loosened, but I could still feel my body shaking. He slid his hand from my throat and took off his jacket to wrap it around me before pulling me close to him. It was the closest our bodies had been since the day he proposed.

"One day, Isadora, those eyes will light up for me. In time, you will learn to love me," he whispered, his voice showing its first hint of vulnerability.

I allowed my arms to respond, but just enough to rest them at his sides. Any more would be a warning sign to him. "I hope so," I replied, letting tears fill my eyes for affect.

He tipped up my chin and wiped the tears away before using his other hand to caress my cheek. His eyes were sincere as he leaned in to kiss me, giving me more of himself than he had in days. I hesitated at first, but then kissed him back for just a moment before turning my head away from him.

He smiled, satisfied at my response or lack of it, I guess, and led us back in the house. He stayed for a movie, forcing me to cuddle up next to him on the couch as we watched it. He didn't kiss me again, but certainly explored every contour of my hip and leg as we watched. Periodically, he would slip his fingers up under the hemline of my dress, but always seemed to stop himself from going any further.

My mind was constantly running, calculating every touch, every response and every look that I gave him. Tonight's performance had to be flawless.

The movie finished and he stood to leave, offering me his hand in the process. I followed him out to the foyer as he put his jacket back on to leave.

"I added a little extra security for tonight, so if you need anything, just let Eric know," he said as he pulled me towards him. I knew exactly what that meant. He was watching me. I had played my part perfect tonight, but it didn't matter. Robbie wasn't taking any chances.

I kept the disappointment from flooding my face. His eyes shifted as he embraced me. I could see the longing in there, the hunger I knew he felt and had resisted for days. "Tomorrow," he whispered before kissing me one more time. His eyes told me to respond, and I did, playing my role as precisely as I had for days. He walked out without another word, and I stood watching the front door and wondering how I ever could have thought I'd be free.

Grant's words filled my head, *Your father is smart,*

Issy, but so are you. You escaped once. You can do it again.

I glanced towards the kitchen and thought of Rosa's words, *God is in control. What can man do to me?*

Filled with resolve once more, I turned and walked up the stairs, careful not to reset the alarm before I did so.

The next five hours were the worst of my life as anticipation, fear, and excitement ripped through my stomach. I was dressed head to toe in black and put my hair up in a navy baseball cap to hide my appearance when necessary. The cap had a large white symbol on the front, which I had covered in a black sharpie earlier. It was three in the morning before I made my move, certain everyone else in the house was fast asleep. I had walked up and down the stairs five times this afternoon and knew exactly where to step to avoid any noise.

My descent was successful, but I kept my breath held as I moved towards the back door. I could see several of Robbie's men parked out front and prayed there was no one around back. I slipped out the door, and managed to shut it without a sound and moved as quickly as I could to the pier before jumping down the other side of it. No one ever used this side of our property line. It was covered in sea grass up to my waist, and I cringed a little knowing it was too dark to see any creepy crawlies that might be in there. I pulled my backpack out that I had hid under the deck earlier and slipped it on my back. I packed light, bringing only copies of the letters for Grant, the original forgery note, a change of clothes, and the break up letter for Robbie I was going to leak to the press. The actual one was much shorter and simply read, "Go To Hell!" with my ring sitting on top. My dad's letter was pretty similar except it included a copy of the note John had sent with a reminder that contracts were void when one party faulted. I smiled to myself as I thought of his face when he read my words, "Another thing I picked up in that business class of mine."

I stopped my mental pat on the back and inched toward the path I had made earlier in the day. I got on my hands and knees, wincing as I did so because this type of thing was not up my alley, and crawled through the tall grass to our neighbor's property line. When I was sure I was out of view from our house, I moved toward the sand and took off in a sprint. Unlike our other neighbors who had built a brick fortress around their property line, most of the people on our street kept the beach clear, and I easily navigated the five houses necessary to get to Ben's house.

His house was completely dark as I approached it, grateful that his parents were more likely to be out of town than home. They only really used this house in the summer. I slipped through his yard unnoticed and navigated through his security gate, so grateful that they hadn't changed the code since we dated. The taxi I had set up was waiting around the corner and I slipped in the back.

"Where to?" the man asked looking at me

through his rearview mirror. I kept my head lowered to especially hide my eyes which would make me distinguishable to anyone who questioned him, and gave him the address.

"I want to take the long way around the lake," I directed, knowing it would keep us from driving in front of my house.

"It's your dime, lady," was all he said before putting the car in drive.

Forty-five minutes later, we were pulling in front of the house number I gave him. I handed him my fare and told him not to bother waiting on me to go inside. He obliged and took off, never noticing that I had no intention of going in the house in front of me. I walked the three more blocks I needed to before getting to my final destination.

Candace lived with her parents, but had her own apartment over their garage. I walked up the steps and knocked on the door, my adrenaline being the only thing keeping me from a complete meltdown at this point.

I saw a light turn on and then the locks turn. "Issy?" she said sleepily. "What are you doing here?"

I looked up at her, unable to keep it together any longer and just let the tears flow. "I had no where else to go."

Candace pulled me in her apartment and shut the door, embracing me in the process. As promised, she didn't ask any questions, just made up the couch for me. I closed my eyes that night, but hardly slept. Only time would tell if my escape had worked, or if like everything else, it was just an illusion.

24. DESPERATION

GRANT

I woke up in another drunken haze as I had the last four mornings since Issy tore my heart out. Today was her birthday. I threw off the covers and stood, stretching the muscles that hadn't been used in days. Everything ached, my head, my back, my heart...everything. Rubbing my temples, I slowly made my way to the bathroom. Jake had let me stay in his guest room all while supplying me with an unhealthy amount of booze. I knew I shouldn't be here, behaving this way, but every time I thought of that day, the anger and bitterness hit with such force it took my breath away.

I had sat hopeful on the couch as Jake spoke to her on the phone, praying fervently for God to intervene and get her out of there. I was sure Jake would help, that between the two of us, we could beat her father and free her. He had barely closed his bedroom door when I stood and started badgering him. "What did she say?"

Jake just shook his head and tossed his phone onto the chair. "Sorry man. Issy is fickle. She always has been." I watched him walk into the kitchen and pour us each a shot of whiskey.

"Is that all?" I yelled. "Jake, her father is selling her to this man, and you are pouring a drink? What is wrong with you?" I refused to believe what he was saying. I knew Issy. She didn't want Robbie.

"Listen, I know my cousin, ok, a whole lot better than you do. She wants this, or at least she does today. Who knows, she'll probably change her mind again tomorrow."

I walked over to the kitchen and grabbed the counter, doing everything in my power to get the rage in my stomach under control. This couldn't be happening. Not again. "She's lying," I insisted.

Jake just pushed the drink towards me. "She said you wanted to run away together, that you had some hero complex when it came to her. I know you love her. You're not the first, and you certainly won't be the last man to fall under her spell. There's a trail lining Winsor."

I stared at him, and tried to ease the pain consuming me. His eyes were so much like hers that I had to turn away from him. "It's different with me," I whispered, doubt already starting to work its way into my heart. She had run away from me so many times, turned to other men for escape. Her only promise to me was heartache and disappointment.

"I'm sure she made you feel that way. I even thought she cared for a while. But the truth is, Issy doesn't fall in love. She never has, and she never will. I have no doubt she cared about you, but..." Jake quit talking and took his shot without me. I could tell he didn't want to be the one to pass her message on to me.

"But what?" I yelled. It sounded more like a growl, even to me, but I was dangerously on the edge of losing control.

"She lost interest the minute you asked her to run away with you. I'm sorry, man. Having a future with you was never the plan."

The autopilot started at that moment. I sank down on the bar stool and took the shot Jake had offered me. It was the first of many, and now I was having a hard time even looking at my face in the mirror. I splashed water on my face and stared at the broken man in front of me. What was I doing?

I stumbled back to my bed and pulled out my phone, texting Issy for the hundredth time.

Me: Happy Birthday. Please talk to me.

Issy: Message failure -- blocked by recipient.

I stared at the words, having seen them so many times I had them memorized. Instead of throwing my phone across the room as I normally did, I dialed a different number.

"Pastor Boyd's office, may I help you?" his assistant answered.

"Hi Janice. This is Grant. Is Pastor Boyd available? I really need to talk to him." She must have sensed the desperation in my voice because seconds later the phone was ringing again.

"Grant, how are you?" he answered, sounding as

cheerful as always.

I started crying before I could speak. It was ridiculous. I never cried, but guilt and shame hit with such intensity, I felt powerless. He didn't say a word, just let me pull myself together. "I've been better," I finally said.

"What's going on?" he asked softly.

I spared him the messy details and just got to the point. "I'm angry at God. I'm so angry; I can hardly stand it. In a matter of days, I lost everything that was important to me. My future is gone, and all I feel is this intense bitterness because I don't understand why. I was doing everything I was supposed to." I threw my pillow across the room as I spoke the last words, the anger starting to billow up in my stomach again.

"Grant, you are experiencing what every Christian will at some point in their life. What you are feeling is normal and even valid. But you have to make a choice here. Either you can continue to shake your fists at God and ask why, knowing full well there will never be an answer that satisfies you. Or, you can ask the more important question…Who? There is an answer for that one, and it's all over the bible. Focus on the Who, Grant, and the why will start to fade away."

I let out a heavy sigh, knowing he was right. I hadn't touched my bible in days, so it was no wonder my questions had remained unanswered. When I didn't say anything, Pastor Boyd continued, "May I pray with you?"

"Sure," I answered. "That would be good."

His prayer made me cry again, but also made me feel empowered for the first time in days. I could feel God's forgiveness flow through me as my heart recognized how sorry I was for my behavior. I thanked him and promised to come see him when I was back in town. I didn't know when that would be; there were things I needed to do first.

Jake was already dressed for the office when I emerged from my room, duffle bag in hand. It was the bag I had packed for Issy's and my escape. I pushed the thought out of my head and made my way over to the coffee.

"He lives," Jake stated with a smirk. "I don't think I've seen you upright in four days."

Embarrassment ripped through my stomach. I was probably the only Christian influence in Jake's life, and here I was acting like an idiot right in front of him. "Not my finest hours, that's for sure. I'm really sorry you had to see me like that."

"Don't worry about it, I've been there." He downed the last of his coffee and grabbed his jacket off the back of the chair. "You headed out?"

"Yeah, I've been here long enough. I'm headed to New York for a while. I've got a business prospect I need to run down."

Jake looked interested as he put on his suit coat. "No kidding. Anything I should know about? I'm always looking for new companies to invest in."

I chuckled to myself. He was just like every other stockbroker I knew. "Not yet, but if something comes of it, you'll be the first to know."

Jake was walking over to shake my hand when a pounding at his door stopped him.

"Who'd you tick off this early in the morning," I asked with a smirk. "I haven't seen any ladies here in days."

"Ha ha," Jake deadpanned as he walked towards the door. The pounding was relentless. He looked through the peephole in the door, and I watched his entire body go rigid. "What does he want?" Jake muttered, barely loud enough for me to hear.

The door swung open and in stepped Issy's father, tossing Jake to the side as he pushed his way into the condo. "Where is she?" he demanded, his face matching the fury of his words.

I froze in place, a million thoughts filling my mind. She had run. All this time, I was here, wasting away, drowning my sorrows in a worthless resource while she was fighting to escape. I cursed myself as I recognized how much I had failed her. The self-loathing tried to take over, but I stopped it. Focusing on the past would do no good. I had to find her.

"What are you talking about?" Jake demanded, slamming the door.

Issy's father didn't say a word, just started tearing though the place looking for her. I could see the rage on Jake's face as he watched her father violate his condo. Mr. Summers finally gave up searching when he saw me in the kitchen. Within seconds, I felt his hands on my shirt as he threw me up against the fridge, causing magnets and papers to crash to the ground.

"Where is she?" he screamed. His desperation made me smile. She had really gotten away this time.

"So she finally got away from you?" I asked smugly, hating the man in front of me. "It's about time." My face hid the erratic beating of my heart as I wondered the same thing. Where would she have gone?

Jake stood next to us in the kitchen, his face a mix of anger and confusion. "What is he talking about, Grant?"

I pushed Mr. Summers off of me and straightened my shirt before meeting Jake's eye. "I was telling the truth, Jake. It looks like Issy found a way to escape without our help. She never wanted that idiot." I was disgusted at myself, disgusted at Jake. We had completely failed her.

Jake's reaction was immediate and explosive. He lunged at her father, taking his massive frame to the floor. I saw the first fist fly and barely made it out of the way. Jake had completely lost control and was cursing and beating Issy's father until I was finally able to pull him off the bleeding man. Shaking uncontrollably, Jake fought my hold as Andrew Summers found his footing and stood up.

"You are both dead men if I find out you had

anything to do with her disappearance," he threatened through bloody teeth and stalked out of the apartment. I stared at him in confidence, no longer intimidated by the man. I may have failed her once, but I would never again.

I let go of Jake, but he fell right to his knees. He was struggling for air, and I quickly realized he was having some kind of anxiety attack.

"Jake," I yelled as I kneeled in front of him and gripped his shoulders to make him look at me. "This wont help her, you hear me? You have to breathe. Ok?" I showed him how to breathe, reminding him over and over that Issy needed him to be strong right now.

His eyes were wide with fear, but he nodded and slowly his breathing returned to a normal cadence. I backed away when he started to stand, and watched as he held onto the back of the couch. "You have to find her," he whispered, still trying to get his body under control. "She can't be alone. It messes with her head."

"I will, I promise." I grabbed my bag and walked towards the door. Jake still hadn't moved. I closed the door without saying another word to him. I couldn't even begin to offer him hope when fear was practically crippling me too. I didn't even know where to start. Images of her in my bathtub trying to give up penetrated my mind, but I pushed them away. I had to believe she would be strong.

I started my car and took a few calming breathes.

There was only one other person I knew at Winsor. Calling her was a long shot, but I was desperate.

I stood up as Avery approached the table and pulled out a chair for her. "Thank you so much for meeting me," I said taking a seat.

"Sure. Is everything ok? You said it was about Issy?"

I watched the concern in her blue eyes and smiled. I had always suspected that Avery was a genuine friend to Issy. Seeing them fall into a mass of giggles at Thanksgiving had touched something deep in my heart. I hadn't seen Issy laugh like that in years.

"Avery, I'm going to be very cryptic here, and you'll have to forgive me, but it's for your own good. Have you talked to Issy at all in the last few days? Has she mentioned anything about her dad or another guy maybe?"

Avery started fidgeting and nodded. "We've talked a lot actually, but never about what's going on in her life. Issy doesn't share personal things like that."

"Have you heard from her today?"

Avery just shook her head, and I couldn't help feel deflated. I put my head in my hands and tried to pull myself together. Where would she go? Thoughts of Issy trying to hurt herself again consumed me.

"Grant, are you ok?" Avery asked softly, putting her hand on my back.

I looked up at her and tried to fake a smile. "I'm just worried. She's missing, and no one knows where she is." I knew I shouldn't say more, but Avery's eyes held such compassion that it just seemed to flow out of me. "Issy's not in the best mental state right now, Avery. Last time I saw her was right after she tried to kill..." I couldn't continue. I put my head back in my hands and tried to keep the desperation from consuming me.

"Grant, I'm not sure how Issy would feel about me telling you this, but..." I jerked back up to look at her. She seemed to be battling with herself as to whether to say anything, but finally seemed to make a decision. "Issy accepted Christ on the phone with me a few days ago and has been reading your bible ever since. She didn't say much, but I know she cares for you. I don't know what's going on with her, but I do know this, she is no longer without hope. I don't think she'll hurt herself again."

Relief, amazement, and awe for a God that does the impossible surged through me. "She believes?" I whispered, still in shock.

Avery just smiled. "I know, it's hard to imagine. She's so stubborn. But she was ready, and I truly believe she meant it."

I reached out and hugged Avery so fast it startled her. "Thank you. Thank you for being there for her to turn to. I always thought it would be me, but God had different plans." I released her and let out the breath I had been holding. "You have no idea what hearing that does for me."

She was crying, but smiling. She wiped her face and apologized, acting annoyed with her tears. "Hard to believe He would use me...I'm so inadequate. But I guess that's what He specializes in, right?"

"I sure hope so," I agreed, thinking of what a disappointment I had been for the last few days. "Listen, Avery, if Issy's dad approaches you, please be careful. Tell him whatever you know; don't try and protect me or Issy. He is a dangerous man."

Avery's blue eyes got real big, but she nodded. I squeezed her hand and apologized for having to run, but she seemed to understand. There was so much I had to do. If I was going to find her before her father, I needed money and technology. I gripped my steering wheel and prayed before leaving.

"Please Lord, protect her for me. Give me wisdom and confidence, and please guide me on Your path...not my own."

25. MY SANCTUARY

ISSY

It had been seven days since I knocked on Candace's door in the middle of the night, and I was still as skittish as a kitten, practically jumping at every foreign sound and running for the bathroom when anyone approached the door. Candace was patient with me, never pushing too hard to find out what happened. I had told her I was in trouble and that no one could know I was there. I assured her I hadn't done anything illegal, and she promised to keep my secret.

She hit her final straw last night as I once again woke her up with my screams. The nightmare was always the same. I was running down the beach as fast as I could when suddenly I would be back in the room again, trapped. Seconds later Robbie would appear, his eyes dark and dangerous as he trapped me against the wall. "Oh Isadora," he would say harshly, "You've been a very bad girl." Then I would wake up dripping in sweat and shaking with fear.

The light flipped on, and I covered my eyes to adjust to it.

"Ok, that's it, Issy, I'm sorry. You have to tell me what's going on. All of it," Candace demanded as she sat on the couch next to me.

I sighed and rubbed my eyes, trying to get the shaking under control. "The less you know the better, Candace."

"See comments like that aren't going to cut it anymore. You've been here for almost a week, and I've watched as you acted like a scared child. Now something happened and since your being here is causing me to lie to every person I know, I should at least know what I'm lying for."

I put my head in my hands and nodded. "You're right. You should know." I then spent the next two hours reliving the nightmare that had transpired since New Year's, not leaving out any detail. I told her about the prayer I said on the phone with Avery and how I remembered she also believed in Christ. I even told her about my mom which was something I had never talked about with anyone...even Grant, although I was sure he knew. Remembering the events of the last few weeks reminded me once again that I had put Candace in danger by coming here. My father and Robbie would ruin her and her whole family if they knew, and I told her so.

She sat silent for a long time when I finished. "I understand if you want me to leave," I offered. "I never meant to involve you. You were just the only one I could think of that no one knew I was connected to."

I was just about to stand up to pack my bag when suddenly Candace grabbed me into a strong embrace and held on tight. "I'm so sorry," she whispered with more compassion than I'd ever known. "Stay here as long as you need."

She pulled away, and I saw her wipe her eyes before turning off the light and getting back into bed. I couldn't move, could hardly breathe. I had nothing to offer. My name had been stripped, my status, my money…everything. I brought nothing but danger into her life, and she still cared enough to let me stay. The enormity of that fact felt overwhelming as I laid my head back on the pillow and closed my eyes.

Candace was gone when I woke up again. She had class early on Wednesdays and it made me think of Jason. I wondered what he thought when I never showed back up for class after that night, and if Grant had even bothered to tell him I was leaving. I would never know, I guess.

I had left my phone in my room after deleting all the contacts that affiliated me with Candace out of my phone. I left a million more in there knowing my father would hunt down each one. I hoped it would keep him occupied enough to give me time to figure out my next move. I hadn't thought past getting out of the house, and I knew I couldn't live on Candace's couch forever. A few thousand dollars sat in my wallet that I had saved and hidden since New Year's. I had been taking cash periodically out of the ATM at a rate so insignificant my father never noticed.

Unfortunately, the money was only enough to keep me housed and fed for a few months. Not to mention, going out in public at this point was extremely dangerous.

Candace had mailed my fake breakup letter to the press from school for me and had graciously picked up a paper each day. I looked with anticipation, but it was never mentioned. I should have known Robbie's family controlled the paper. There had been one small blurb in the business section that the merger had been postponed briefly for negotiations, but that's all that had been said.

I threw down the paper in frustration. I was itching to get on the internet and find out what was going on, but having been raised in a house with a computer tycoon, I knew that hitting any site linked to them could be tracked, so I stayed away from Candace's computer.

The hours that Candace was gone were the worse. I hated the silence, hated the loneliness. I tried to use the time to study the bible and pray, hoping to ease sadness that hit every day. I was almost grateful for Candace's "No alcohol" stipulation, as I still felt tempted to drown my sorrows. Praying definitely helped, but I still missed people.

I heard Candace's lock turn and practically ran to greet her as I had every day since getting here. She walked in, and I flew to embrace her. "I'm so glad you are back," I said squeezing her tight.

When I pulled back, I noticed the apprehensive

look on her face and I backed up. "What's going on?"

"Issy, I know you didn't want me to tell anyone, but honey, I had to. I can't carry this on my own, and you need more support than I can give you."

Fear consumed me as I stared at her. "What did you do?"

I watched in horror as Candace backed towards her door and opened it so Reggie and Rusty could walk in. They hated me, hadn't even spoken to me in weeks. I immediately panicked and grabbed my bag, throwing as much in there as I could find around me.

Reggie was the first to approach and touched my arm, making me freeze. I kept my gaze away from him.

"Tink, please. Let us help you." His words were gentle and sincere. I slowly turned toward him, my eyes guarded as I assessed his intention.

"Why would you want to?" I whispered as I stared into his gentle brown eyes. The bored, annoyed Reggie was long gone and in his place was a warm, concerned man who appeared to genuinely care.

"Why wouldn't I?" was all he said in response. He tugged on my arm and took the bag out of my hand before tentatively putting his arms around me. "You can trust us." I hugged him back, feeling safer than I had in weeks.

Rusty was next and appeared sorrowful as he approached me. "I owe you an apology," he said with his hands deep in his pockets while he kicked the couch a little with his cowboy boots.

I almost laughed. "Why?"

"I was too busy licking my wounds to be what you really needed...a friend. I hope you can forgive me."

I stared at him in awe. "Rusty, there is nothing to forgive," I assured him.

He glanced up at me with a boyish smile, dimples showing slightly on each side of his mouth, and embraced me. He felt solid and safe, just as Reggie had, but held me just a touch longer.

Candace had tears in her eyes, but still managed her sarcastic wit. "Excellent. It's settled then, and thank goodness, because girl, you are high maintenance."

We all started laughing, and I knew she was right. I glanced around at my small group of friends, people who had only known me a short while, but were willing to sacrifice so much for me. It seemed like an impossible dream.

That day was the last time I spent any time alone. Between Candace, Reggie and Rusty, I had constant company in the small apartment and soon a week became a month without me even really noticing. Candace had thankfully gotten me some more clothes so I wasn't doing laundry every day. She also insisted I stopped pouring over the paper which never held any news on the merger anyway. Our little group was so different than any I'd been around before. None of them drank which was the first major difference. They also were so encouraging to each other, praying unashamedly when we ate or when they could tell I was down. Candace and I started studying the bible together, and it was so nice to have someone who could answer all of my questions.

The biggest surprise, though, was realizing how quirky and fun they all were. Rusty especially. He was like a goofy kid most of the time and kept me laughing so much that half the time my side hurt.

I thought of what Grant had told me once, that I made people forget they were all grown up. Well, Rusty did that for me. He made me forget I was in hiding and basically had no idea what my future looked like. I felt like I could just be myself with him and play and kid around like I used to with Jake all the time.

His presence made the loss of Grant and Jake seem less intense although I'd still feel a pain in my chest as I thought of the way he looked when they ripped him from me. I wondered how he was doing and if he was still angry at me. Tears threatened my eyes, but I pushed them away. I hadn't cried once since being here and I wasn't about to start now.

"You ok?" Rusty asked as we sat watching a movie. He ran his hand along my shoulder as he asked, his brown eyes full of concern.

I smiled up at him, still in awe sometimes that he had a face as beautiful as it was. Rusty was a man's man. Strong, chiseled jaw, straight nose and lips full enough to be called kissable by any woman alive. I saw his eyebrows pinch together as he watched me examine him.

"You're really a beautiful man, Rusty. Inside and out," I explained as I looked at him. Dimples formed as I watched his mouth turn into a smile.

"Ditto," he replied, taking my hand in his. He pulled me near him, and I snuggled up next to his warm body, feeling safe and secure. I leaned against his chest and I felt him kiss the top of my head. I closed my eyes and soon drifted off to sleep.

My dream that night was the worst ever. I was running and running, fear gripping my heart as I willed my legs to move faster. It was as if I was on a treadmill, because I never moved, just ran in vain. Suddenly the room was around me again, and Grant was there. He was tied to a chair and gagged with a towel. There was blood dripping down his face and I could see bruises already starting to form around his eyes. I rushed to him and freed him. He just fell from the chair into my lap. I shook him and screamed at him to wake up, but he never did. Just lay there still and cold. Then he disappeared and the room was empty again. I looked around and screamed out his name, banging the walls so fiercely that my hands started to bleed. I suddenly felt Robbie's presence all around me. It was suffocating and fear overwhelmed me as I backed into a corner and fell to the ground. Robbie was in front of me, crouched on his knees as he rubbed my face. I shook my head back and forth as the tears streamed down my cheeks. "You can't run forever, Isadora. I told you I don't share." I heard

Rusty's voice in the background, calling my name. Robbie heard it too, and looked around, his eyes more dark and dangerous that ever before. "He's next, Isadora," was all I heard before Rusty finally jerked me awake.

I was shaking and sweating and felt tears dripping off me. Rusty was holding me tight, trying to get me to focus on his face. When I finally did, he sighed in relief and embraced me even tighter. "Gees, Issy, you scared me half to death."

I sat up and wiped my eyes. "I'm sorry. It was a nightmare." My hands were still shaking, and I couldn't get the image of Grant's lifeless body out of my mind.

"Issy, that wasn't just a nightmare. You were shaking uncontrollably and screaming. I couldn't get you out of it. You are still shaking," he said noticing that I hadn't calmed down yet. He moved closer to me, but I jumped off the couch and grabbed my bag.

"I have to leave," I whispered in a panic. "I've put all of you in danger. I'm so stupid. He always wins."

Rusty rushed to me and took the bag out of my hand. "Stop it. You're not going anywhere. He's not getting past me, ok? You're not alone anymore." He captured me once again in his strong arms and didn't let go even when I resisted. "Issy, it's times like these that faith is required. God is in control. Look at all He's already orchestrated for you." I eventually stopped fighting and calmed down. When he finally let me go, I sat back on the couch.

"I need a computer," I stated frantically without an explanation. I had to know if Grant was ok.

Rusty walked over to his school bag, pulled out his iPad and handed it to me. I knew it was a risk, but I had to know. I Googled Grant's name, but nothing came up. Next I searched through all the North Carolina newspapers for his name. I knew with each site I looked at that I drew more and more attention to myself, but I didn't care. I had to know he was ok. I finally got a hit from a business article dated two days ago. Relief flooded me. There wasn't much, but it was enough to put my restless heart as ease. It confirmed rumors that Andrew Summers' former assistant, Grant Forester was now working with long time competitor, Mark Stonewall, on a new software development. I smiled to myself and erased the history from his internet browser.

"I have to reset you back to defaults, Rusty. I'm sorry," I explained as I basically wiped his iPad clean. "You can reload everything back from your computer."

"Whatever, Issy, that's fine. I barely know how to use that thing anyway."

I handed it back to him when I was finished. I hoped I'd been fast enough to stop any trace to his device. Only time would tell.

"Why do you do it?" I finally asked after Rusty had joined me again on the couch.

"Do what?"

"Take such good care of me? All of you. It

doesn't make sense to me."

Rusty turned to look at me. "We love you, Issy," he stated as if it was the most obvious answer in the world.

I shook my head. "See, that's the part I don't get. I've only loved two people in my whole life enough to sacrifice for them. One was the only family I've ever really had, and the other, well, I guess he was kind of family too. Yet, you guys have only known me for a few months. Most of that time I didn't treat you all that nicely either, and still you love me more than even my own parents ever have."

"Issy, all three of us have known a love so great that it changed our lives. All of us were broken and lost, and Christ pulled us out of that through his unconditional love. Once that kind of love has been shown to you, it kind of just shines through, you know?"

I laughed a little, thinking of the life I'd always lived. "I hope you're right, Rusty. I want to be like that, but I'm not like you guys. I'm not proud of the person I was. I used people all the time, never caring who I hurt in the process. I mean that's how I met you guys in the first place. I actually thought Reggie might be my ticket into Western's night life."

"Issy, that's the beauty of salvation. You are a new creation. The old is gone and the new has come. There is nothing about your old life that has to define your new one."

I sighed and pondered on his words for a second.

"I know you're right. Is it wrong to miss things about my old life?"

"What things?"

"I miss dancing. Not the club dancing so much, but real dancing. I used to study ballet, and then everything fell apart. I stopped dancing when I couldn't hear the music through the screams in my head. My head is silent now, and I just wonder what it would be like to do it again."

Rusty squeezed my hand and smiled at me. "No Issy, there's nothing wrong with missing dancing."

We sat in silence, and I wondered how life had brought me to this point. I closed my eyes, and prayed for Grant's protection as I remembered every line on his beautiful face. Despite the distance, we were still connected. I was realizing that we always have been.

26. THE DANCE

It had been two months since I escaped my father's house, and while Rusty was my ever present help mate, I missed Jake and Grant so much that it was hard to breathe sometimes. I just wanted to know they were ok, but seeking them out was still too risky. My friends could see me slipping further and further into a depressive state and tried everything to get me to smile.

Finally, after two more days of half smiles and one word answers, Rusty had had enough.

"We're leaving this apartment tonight," he stated when he walked in from class. I was still in my pajamas and hadn't even bothered to shower. "You can't live like this, Issy. It's not healthy."

I sighed and threw myself back on the couch. "You say that as if I have a life, Rusty. I don't."

"I will try not to be insulted by that comment considering that you and I have been inseparable for two months."

"I didn't mean it like that. You know I adore you." And I really did, but I missed life. I was starting to wonder if maybe I just traded one prison for the next, only I was now the jailer.

"Which is exactly why we are going out tonight…around people, with music."

I sat up on the couch, excitement filling my stomach. "Really?" I didn't even care at that moment if it was careless. I had to get out of this house.

"My church is having a live band tonight and there will be so many people, we will have no problem blending. Now go shower. I didn't think it was possible for you not to look beautiful, but now I'm not so sure."

I jumped off the couch and charged him, making him pay for his comment with tickles. He finally conceded and apologized. I kissed him on his cheek and whispered, "Thank you," before running off to the bathroom.

Since my wardrobe was drastically reduced, I had to settle for a pair of jeans, a long white tank top with a small belt around the waist and some heels. It wasn't quite the Issy from Winsor, but I definitely felt more like myself than I had in months. I even put a few pink streaks in my hair which felt pretty fantastic. The most notable difference, though, were my eyes. They looked alive, almost happy.

I opened the bathroom door and spun out in front of Rusty. "Ta da. What do you think? Have I been officially transformed?"

Rusty's dimples were deeper than usual when he took me in and then I was off my feet in an explosive hug. "Your stunning, but more importantly…you're happy."

He set me back down and then gently moved some hair away from my face that had shifted during the hug. I recognized the look in his eye, and stepped back from him, hoping the act would send a message.

It was earlier than I'd ever left the apartment before, and while it was still dusk and the sun was pretty much gone, it still felt weird to be outside when the stars weren't out yet.

"You ok?" Rusty asked as he took my hand.

"Yeah." I sighed a long heavy sigh and looked at him. "I'm just nervous, I guess."

He squeezed my hand, and then grinned at me. "No worries. I've got your back."

I knew he did. I knew he would die before he let anything happen to me. That was partly what made me nervous. Him being out with me tonight was equally as dangerous for him as it was for me. But it had been two months, and at some point I had to start living again. I took a resolute breath and pushed my anxiety away.

Rusty was right about the crowd. We walked into a large auditorium that easily sat three thousand people. Rusty found us a seat near the aisle, so we had quick access to the door, and ushered me in. The lights were still on, so Rusty kept his arm around me while I buried my face into his massive chest. The fact that Rusty was a good foot taller than me and about a hundred pounds heavier was a blessing since I wanted to disappear.

The lights finally went down and the band started

to play. Rusty was right, they were sensational. It felt like a genuine rock concert and after only two songs, I relaxed and started cheering and dancing with everyone else. After a pretty good set of fast songs, the lead singer came to the mike and introduced one of their latest singles. It was a ballad, and I stood fixated as I listened to the words. It was like they wrote it just for me.

I felt Rusty rub my back. "You ok?" he asked when he saw my stricken face.

"This song," I whispered. There was no need to say more. He understood.

"You wont always feel like this, Issy."

I just nodded and kept the tears at bay. I was grateful and a little sad when the song ended and they went back to the heavier music. I started to relax again and just let the sound and lights fill me up. Then out of nowhere, I heard someone calling my name.

"Hey, you're Isadora Summers! Oh my goodness, the papers have been swarming with your picture," the girl in front of us gushed.

I felt my face drain of all color and my knees suddenly went weak.

"Sorry. Her name is Lisa, but she gets that all the time. It's the eyes," Rusty said quickly, wrapping a protective arm around my waist. I was grateful, because I almost thought I would faint.

"Wow. The resemblance is remarkable," the girl continued, examining me. "The eyes, the hair, everything."

I finally found myself and put back the mask that had been gone for months. It was remarkable how quickly it came back to me. I smiled sweetly at the girl. "Thanks. I heard she's pretty. Do you know her?

"Me? Oh no. She's engaged to some billionaire…not really my class level, you know? She's been missing for months, though." She looked at me again through slanted eyes. "You sure you're not her? I mean, you could be twins."

"I'm pretty sure I'm not her," I laughed nonchalantly. "Born and raised in Georgia. I'm just visiting friends for the weekend. Its nice to meet you, though."

She took the hint and said the same before turning around to enjoy the rest of the concert. As soon as she did, I started trembling. The trembling became shaking as Robbie's face bombarded my memory. I hadn't thought of him in weeks and now it felt like he was surrounding me on all sides.

Rusty moved quickly and had us out the door and in his truck in record time. The drive back to Candace's was silent, the atmosphere a drastic shift from the one we had on the way there. I could tell that Rusty was upset because his whole body was tense and he would periodically rub his head with his right hand.

My fear and shock soon became anger as I watched him. "Did you know about the papers?" I asked through gritted teeth.

Rusty didn't answer at first and then sighed. "Yes."

I almost jumped out of my seat. "And you took me out anyway! What were you thinking? That no one would notice, that I exaggerated the danger? Why would I hide out for two months in a thousand foot apartment if it wasn't serious?"

Rusty just shook his head. "I'm sorry. I messed up."

I couldn't speak, because I knew if I did I would yell at him, and I didn't want to. Rusty wasn't like Jake or Grant. He couldn't handle seeing that side of me. So, I stayed silent until we got back to Candace's where I jumped out of the truck before he even had it in park.

Candace was home studying when I stormed in the house and grabbed my bag to pack.

"What's going on?" she asked, standing up and watching me with concern.

"I was recognized. Seems that the three of you didn't feel the need to tell me there's a search party out for me right now." I was being short and cold with Candace despite the fact it wasn't her fault.

"Issy, calm down. There is no search party. It was announced last week that the merger fell through and the papers are speculating that your disappearance had something to do with it. You've only been in there twice."

Candace was the voice of reason as always, and her words did start to make me feel less panicked. I stopped packing long enough to see that Rusty had come in and was standing near the front door. He looked devastated. "I just wanted you to smile again. I would never do anything to intentionally put you in jeopardy, Issy."

I threw down my bag and put my head in my hands. "I know Rusty. I just don't know what to do now. I can't stay here."

Candace came over and put her hands on my shoulder. "Yes you can. I wasn't with you. They still don't have any connection for the two of us." Candace looked up and Rusty. "Rusty will just have back off for a while until we make sure everything's ok. No contact for a week."

I looked over to Rusty, and he looked even worse than before. "Whatever I need to do," he agreed sadly. "I'm so sorry."

My anger and fear had finally dissipated, and I walked over to Rusty and hugged him. He responded with a hug so tight that I thought I might split in two. "Don't own this mess, Rusty. It's mine, not yours. I'm sorry I yelled at you."

He hesitantly let me go, and then kissed my cheek before leaving. I threw myself back on the couch and huffed, "Back to isolation."

Candace sat next to me and patted my leg. "I'm not happy about what happened tonight, Issy, but honestly, I'm glad I had a reason to send Rusty away. He needs some space from you."

I jerked my head to look at her. "Why do you say

that?" I had never treated Rusty poorly.

"Issy, that boy is head over heels in love with you. You're going to shatter his heart when you leave. I know it's inevitable, but maybe weaning him off of you a little at time will make it less devastating."

I crossed my arms and held myself, trying to make the chills go away. Candace was right. While I would never intentionally hurt Rusty, I knew he was falling for me and didn't say anything. "You're right. I'll back off."

Candace stood back up and walked over to her desk to resume studying. She looked my way sadly. "My week is crazy, Issy. I'm not going to be around much. Are you going to be ok?"

"I'll be fine," I lied and covered myself with the blanket. I fell asleep that night in my clothes and didn't wake up until Candace shook me awake at three in the morning because she heard me crying. The nightmares were back, only this time there was no running. I was already in the room, only now I was strapped to the chair and gagged just as Grant had been. Robbie was standing over me, but I didn't fight this time. There was just no fight left in me.

The week that followed was miserable. I spent most of my time sleeping. It seemed to make the days go by faster. The nightmares continued, but no one knew because I no longer cried or screamed. In every one, I was broken and did whatever Robbie asked of me. I kept trying to pray, but still felt so alone and afraid. The bible assured Christ was always with me, but the sadness overpowered me.

I felt a hand on my cheek as Rusty stood over me. "Hey sleeping beauty. It's time to join the land of the living again," he whispered.

I sat up and rubbed my eyes. "Is our week up?" I asked.

"Not quite, but I couldn't wait any longer, and Candace said you needed me."

I fell into his arms, hoping the feeling of defeat would go away, but it didn't. In fact, it felt even heavier, because now it held the guilt of knowing every moment I spent with Rusty was one more that could hurt him.

"You shouldn't be here, Rusty. You need to go have a life. My prison sentence shouldn't be yours too," I stated, moving away from him.

"Issy, I know you can't say the same thing. But the last two months have been the happiest in my life. No matter what happens, it's been worth it for me." Rusty took me back in his arms and I didn't stop him. I needed to be held so bad. "I have a surprise for you," he finally said.

"Rusty, I don't think I can handle anymore of your surprises."

"This one is safe, I promise. Put on some clothes you can move around in," he directed, ushering me towards the bathroom. I did as he said and put on some tight black yoga pants and a workout tank top. I slipped over my black hoodie and realized this was the same outfit I had worn the night I escaped. The joke was on me. There was no escape.

"Let's go," I said flatly, and Rusty just led me out the door. It was dark already, and I relished the feeling of the cool breeze against my face. I let it lift my hair and just stood there, with my eyes closed, taking it all in.

I felt Rusty stand in front of me and capture my face. He put his forehead to mine and then before I could say a word, I felt his lips. He felt as soft and tender as I would have expected, the love he had for me radiating through as he kissed me. I slowly moved away, not wanting to hurt him anymore than I already had.

"I think I'm falling in love with you," he whispered.

His words made my heart hurt. "Rusty, I love you too…as a friend. You have shown me more compassion and sacrifice than I deserve. I've spent my life using people, taking all I can because it filled me in some way, never caring who I hurt in the process. I'm not that person anymore, and I can't do that to you."

"Friendship can turn into more," he offered, still looking hopeful.

"Yes it can, but not when there's already someone else filling that place." My words finally registered and Rusty let me go.

He took one more heavy sigh and then ushered

me to his car. "Come on. You're still getting your surprise."

I smiled up at him, amazed by his goodness and got in the car. He drove quietly for a while and then finally asked the question I knew had been plaguing him. "So who is it?"

I sat back in my seat and smiled sadly. "When I turned thirteen, I met a boy, and ever since, his name has been permanently tattooed on my heart. I've tried everything to erase it, and I mean everything. But no matter what I do, or how much time passes, it never goes away. I can't escape him."

"He's a lucky guy," Rusty mused as he squeezed my hand.

The laughter came instantly as I shook my head. "Rusty, the fact that you think that shows how little you really know me. I've tortured that poor guy, but he's free now, and that makes me happy."

Silence hung in the car until a few minutes later when we pulled into a small strip mall. All the lights were off and every business appeared to be closed. Rusty pulled right in front of a glass door that read, "Lisa's Dance Studio."

"My sister owns this place. It's how I pulled that name out so quickly the other night. Anyway, I asked if I could use it at night, and after a myriad of questions and innuendos, she finally gave me the keys." He handed the keys to me and then smiled. "Go dance, Issy."

I didn't know what to say. Words couldn't cover

the emotions that were surging through me. He seemed to understand and reached over me to open my door. "I left a CD in there for you. It's *Tenth Avenue North*, the band we listened to the other night. The song is called *Worn*. Get going. I'm going to blow off a little steam, and I'll be back."

I squeezed his hand and then stepped out of the car. I knew I had hurt him, but I also knew it was less than it could have been. He watched me until I got the door unlocked and opened. I gave him a little wave and closed the door. I found the lights and followed the hallway until I saw a large room with mirrors covering the space. Ballet bars ran along the wall and in the corner sat a large stereo system. The CD Rusty had mentioned sat next to it. I held it gingerly, wondering if I could handle hearing that song again in my current state.

I stared at it while I removed my hoodie, and then some more while I stretched. Finally, I took a deep breath and put it in. The music filled me, and I started to move, losing myself completely in the sound of the piano and lyrics. Soon, there was no studio, no gravity, just me and the music as I moved across the space, each word ripping through my heart.

> "Let me see redemption win
> Let me know the struggle ends
> That You can mend a heart that's frail and torn

I wanna know a song can rise
From the ashes of a broken life
And all that's dead inside can be reborn
'Cause I'm worn"

The tears came without notice. I spun and danced, feeling myself fight against the defeat that had been plaguing me all week. Then out of nowhere, I heard an audible voice in my head.

He has sent me to proclaim freedom for the prisoners...

Fatigue gripped at me, but I pushed though, wanting to find that place again where I believed those words.

To release the oppressed...

If those words were true, then why did I still feel so scared. Why were my father and Robbie still winning?

I have set you free. Why are you still afraid?

The words stopped my movement, and I collapsed on the floor, letting the sobs take over my shaking body.

"God, please help me," I pleaded through my tears. "I'm so sad. I've had so little faith. Forgive me." The words were simple, but the tingle that I felt from the top of my head down to my feet wasn't...it was peace. All this time, I had been holding on to my fear, letting it consume me slowly. Not anymore. It was time to let go of the past, and let God have control.

I closed my eyes and continued to cry, letting all

the hurt I had buried pour out of me. Then through my tears I saw the shoes approach me. As my vision cleared, I expected to see Rusty's worn cowboy boots, but it wasn't. They were new and expensive, Italian leather that still creaked when he walked. I pulled myself up to see with my own eyes if it were true.

"You found me," I whispered.

27. NO MORE RUNNING

He fell on his knees next to me and pulled me in his arms. There were tears streaming down his face, and I felt every one because his cheek was pressed up against mine.

"Of course I found you. I never would have stopped looking." His honey sweet words tickled my ears and fell into my heart, making it swell.

"But I set you free," I cried, pulling away from him so I could see his beautiful caramel eyes. It felt like a dream, but it wasn't. Grant was there, holding me, touching me. He was real.

He stared in my eyes and then wiped them dry. I did the same for him. He seemed so happy and yet so sad. And why wasn't he kissing me?

We got to our feet, still staring at one other as if turning away would make the other disappear. "I can't believe you're real," he whispered, as he touched my face and hair. He pulled me into his arms again. I buried my face in his chest, absorbing every inch of his smell and touch. "I'm so mad at you," he said tensely, but never moved to release me. "Why didn't you come with me? I didn't want to be set free...not from you."

"I couldn't, Grant," I whispered against his chest.

He pulled me back to look at me, his hands gripping my arms in desperation. "Why?"

"Let her go," I heard Rusty yell from the door. He was practically running towards us, and my heart stopped when I saw the look on his face. Rusty was ready to kill Grant, and certainly had the size to do so.

"Rusty stop. It's ok. He's my..." I stopped because I didn't know what to call him. We had never even had the chance to define it. "Friend," I finally said. Rusty stopped charging, but still pulled me out of Grant's arms and into his.

In that moment, I could have sworn I'd stepped right into a bad romance film. Both men were facing off, their eyes threatening as they stared at one another.

I put my hand on Rusty's arm so he would look at me. "Rusty, this is Grant. I've known him since I was thirteen."

Rusty caught the look in my eye, and he knew what I was saying. His eyes widened as he looked between Grant and me. It was like he finally registered that both of us had been crying and not just me. I saw Rusty's jaw tighten. I knew this was hard for him, but he reacted just as I would have expected him to. "I'll wait in the truck," he stated. "Come get me if you need anything." A few seconds later, he was gone.

I turned back to face Grant, but he had turned away from me. His whole body was tense, and his hands were on his head, which I knew from experience meant he was trying to get his anger under control.

"My father was going to accuse you of embezzlement. You had opened an off shore account for me and had been putting money in it for years. It was a set up from the very beginning...a way to control you, I guess, when he needed to."

Grant turned around and stared at me in disbelief. "That's why you stayed?"

I nodded. "I couldn't let him do that to you, and I also knew you wouldn't let me if you knew the truth."

Grant gathered me in his arms again. "You negotiated the letters too, didn't you?" I just nodded into his chest. "You're unbelievable." His words were one of frustration, not adoration, so I knew he was still angry. "You know I didn't want that." He pulled me back to look at him, his face stern. "I would have rather died than leave you with him. There is nothing worse than the hell I went through that day...and every day since."

I dropped my head, feeling defeated all over again. "It was the only choice I had, and I did what I thought was best. Why are you so angry at me?" I asked, my eyes pleading for some explanation.

"Are you serious? Why am I angry?" Grant's voice rose another octave. "You didn't trust me. You didn't talk to me. You just gave up and let him win."

"No I didn't. I ran. I escaped again just like you told me to." My voice was getting louder now too and I felt my temper start to surge. I had been around

Grant less than ten minutes and already he had my emotions churning and every one of my senses alert.

"To someone else!" he yelled, gripping my arms again. "You escaped to someone else…not me." Grant practically pushed me away and walked toward one of the mirrors. I watched as he gripped the ballet bar and leaned over to put his head on his hands.

I didn't want him that far away. I never wanted him far away again, so I followed him and tentatively ran my fingers up and down his back. "I knew you would be the first place he looked, and I couldn't risk putting you and Jake in the line of fire like that." My voice was calm, and I hoped he would see my reasons.

Grant let out a heavy sigh and I couldn't help but smile. I knew a long speech was coming next and then he would forgive me. "I saw him kiss you, Issy. I've been following him for days. After all this time searching, I can't believe I found you just to lose you all over again." His voice trailed off, but there was no missing the desperation in it.

I stepped away from him, finally realizing what had been going on in his head all this time. He thought I had moved on. I pulled on his arm, forcing him to stand up and look at me. "Grant, I gave Rusty that moment because I cared about him. He is a good friend, and I never would have survived without him. But let me make this clear so there is no confusion." I put my hands on his face so he wouldn't look away. "There is no one, and I mean no one, on this earth that I love more than you. I'm barely the type of girl that falls in love once. Surely you know, it would never happen twice. You're it for me. There's no acceptable substitute. Now kiss me, already. I haven't seen you in two mon--!"

Grant's lips were on me before I had a chance to finish, and my body was rushed with a fire so intense I thought I would perish right there. He pulled back and chuckled, his lips still touching mine. "You love me, huh?" he teased. I didn't answer, just pulled him back to me and showed him how much.

I wanted to kiss Grant forever, wanted to stay wrapped up in his arms for a lifetime, but I knew Rusty was still outside. In the past it wouldn't have mattered that I hurt him, but today it did.

"I need to talk to Rusty," I explained as I pulled away. Grant watched as I grabbed my hoodie and pulled it back over me.

"I'm going with you," he stated, following me. "No more secrets, no more running. It's you and me, Issy." I could tell he expected a battle, as his posture was tense when he approached me.

Instead I just smiled at him and offered my hand. "Ok."

He took it and pulled me back to him, examining my face and my eyes. "Avery told me what you did."

"I found your bible, and saw the verse you marked for me. That's when I knew, so thank you. I wouldn't have made it these last two months if I hadn't had God's strength. Even when I doubted, I felt Him with me. And you," I admitted, absorbing the beauty of his caramel eyes.

He shook his head and chuckled, his face a mixture of shock and elation. "Will you ever stop amazing me?" he asked.

"I hope not."

After another long kissing session, we finally made it to the front door, where I saw Rusty leaning against his truck. He looked up when we opened the door and immediately glanced at our hands which were now intertwined and would probably stay that way forever if Grant had his say.

Grant stepped forward first and offered his hand to Rusty. He hesitated at first, but finally shook Grant's hand. "Thank you for taking care of her," Grant said before they released from the handshake.

Rusty put his hands deep in his pockets and kicked the ground a little. Finally he looked up at me and smiled, his dimples just faintly visible. "I'd do it again."

It was a statement of no regrets, even though I knew deep down he was hurting. Rusty was strong, though, the strongest person I'd ever known, and I knew he would be fine.

After two hours of introductions and long goodbyes, Grant and I were finally alone and sitting in the suite he had rented just outside of Western. I looked around at the grand and expensive décor and raised my eyebrow.

"This doesn't look like something you can afford on an assistant's salary," I noted. "I guess things worked out with Mark Stonewall after all?"

Grant was at the bar, pouring us each a coke and jerked his head toward me. "How did you know?"

I shrugged and pulled my feet up on couch. "I Googled you. Call it a moment of weakness."

Grant handed me my drink and kissed me on the nose before settling next to me on the couch. "Well, thank goodness for your weakness, because that was the first real lead I'd had in a month."

"Speaking of that. How did you find me?" I asked.

"It wasn't easy, Issy. I have been searching for you since you disappeared. Non stop. First, I started monitoring Google for any searches on you, me, Jake, Robbie or your father. There were several hits, and with each one we started monitoring the owner. I'd check purchases, email, facebook, etc. Nothing was really panning out until a twitter feed went out that there had been an Isadora Summers siting at a concert near Western. I checked all the computers that we had been monitoring, and sure enough Rusty had purchased Tenth Avenue North tickets online. I put a trail on him a few days ago, trading off with a private investigator I had working for me."

"Wow," I stated in disbelief, staring up at him. "I guess I knew it was possible, but it still amazes me what can be done with computers."

Grant set down his glass and turned me to face him before grabbing my hands. "The world didn't stop while you were hiding. A lot has happened since you disappeared."

I took a deep breath. Up to this point, I hadn't asked, because part of me didn't want to know if my father had indeed followed through with his threats to ruin everyone I cared about. "I realize that. What has he done?"

Grant squeezed my hand a little tighter, and then his eyes penetrated mine. "Before I tell you, I want you to understand that nothing that has happened is your fault. You hear me?" I nodded, but could already feel the tears in my eyes. There would be only one reason why Grant was being so careful. Something happened to Jake.

"After your father and Robbie's goon dragged me out of your room, they gave me something that knocked me out. I woke up in my car outside my apartment complex. Every item from my office was stuffed in a box in the back of my car. It took me another thirty minutes before my head was clear enough to drive. I went straight back to the lake house, but couldn't get past all the security. I was losing my mind at that point and knew I needed someone who could help me get to you. I tried to call Jake about a million times, but that guy never answers his phone."

I couldn't help but laugh because I knew it was so true. "You have to text him."

Grant just glared at me in jest and then continued. "Thanks. Good to know. Anyway, I finally gave up and just drove up there. He was less than happy to see me, especially since he had company, but he kicked her out the minute I told him you were in trouble, and I needed his help. I told him all about the contract and the threats your father had made. I could tell he didn't believe me, especially since he said you hadn't mentioned any of it to him, and he knew that I had been driving you crazy."

I laughed again and Grant pushed my leg. "Stop, this is important," he scolded.

"I'm sorry, really. It's just hard for me to picture you and Jake together...having a conversation. You're so different."

"Tell me about it. Well, I finally convinced him to call you so I could talk to you without your bodyguards around." Up to that point, Grant had kept the conversation light, but then it shifted, his eyes getting dark and serious. "By the way, if you ever block my phone number again, Issy, I swear I will shatter your phone into a million pieces. I'm not letting you push me away anymore." Grant looked at me, and I knew he was serious. The last two months had been hard on him, and despite his love for me, I could sense he still was angry with me for what I put him through.

"I'm sorry about that."

He nodded and then patted my leg, taking a deep breath before continuing. "Jake told me you didn't want me and that it was time I stop thinking you ever would. Believe it or not, Jake and I kind of bonded in that moment, even though it was one of the lowest points of my life."

"I'm so sorry, Grant. Please know that I only said those things in order to protect both of you."

Grant took my hand and squeezed it. "You have to understand. You'd been all over the map with me, and while I clung to that one afternoon, it made more sense what Jake was telling me. You said it yourself; I was in love with a fairytale. So…I believed him. The days to follow, I became someone I'm not at all proud of."

I felt nausea hit my stomach and looked away from him. I had no right to be jealous. I had set him free. His hand was instantly on my chin as he brought my face back to look at him.

"Nothing like that, Issy. I don't use women in that way; I never have. But I was bitter and angry. I fell into the Issy numbing cycle and drank myself into a stupor. I've loved you as long as I can remember, and I've always held to the idea that we would have a future together. When I lost that, everything just went gray. Luckily Jake let me stay with him. That guy really is at his best when he has someone to take care of."

I smiled warmly at him. "I know this first hand. I'm glad he was there for you."

"After a couple of days, I slowly pulled myself together. I called Pastor Boyd again and he helped me adjust my thinking. After a lot of repentance, I was ready to put one foot in front of the other, and try to get my life back together. Then before I even left the condo, your dad came storming in demanding to know where you were. As soon as Jake realized that you disappeared, and that I had been telling him the truth, he went after your father. I was able to pull him off, but not before Jake did a good amount of damage to your father's face."

"Am I wrong for being glad that Jake hurt him?" I asked with a smirk.

Grant didn't smile back at me, and I felt butterflies in my stomach again. "Normally, I would say yes, but your dad pressed charges. Jake was arrested for assault. He spent two nights in jail before we could get him out. That little account you set up pretty much saved the day. All this happened before I had the deal with Mark, and neither of us had the liquidity to get him out."

"He told me he would ruin anyone I loved if I messed up his merger. Of course Jake would be his first target," I whispered, nausea filling my stomach.

Grant pulled me to him and settled us next to each other on the couch. "We can finish talking about this tomorrow if you want," he offered.

"No. I need to hear it."

Grant hugged me tighter. "Things just spiraled from there. Jake lost his job and took up day trading to try and pay the bills. I don't think it's going well for him, because David called to tell me that if someone didn't get Jake under control, he was kicking him out. I tried to talk to him, even offered to get him a job in our financial department. He said he was fine and that I needed to stop worrying about him and stay focused on finding you."

"How long ago was that?" I whispered.

"Three weeks ago. I haven't heard anything since, but I guess that's a good thing."

My stomach turned again. Jake and I had been connected for years, and now he felt so far away, I wondered how our relationship would ever recover. Grant squeezed my hand in support, reminding me he was still there. "Where were you all that time?" I asked.

"I was in New York, making appointments with every investor I knew. Somehow, I got them to hand me thousands of dollars for my software. I used every tactic you taught me and it worked. It wasn't until the fifth one that I heard about the recommendation letters your father had sent."

"Did they help?" I asked softly.

"Yes, baby, they made all the difference in the world," he assured me. "In just a few days, I had all the money I needed to test the software and that is when I first approached Mark Stonewall. Your father's stock had been soaring ever since you and Robbie started making the papers, so Mark was eager to have something that could help them compete. We did the test run on his system and it was a complete success. Mark offered to buy the software for millions, but I knew better. I wasn't going to be someone's paperboy anymore. I offered him a deal. I'd sell him 49% ownership of the technology, and he had to make me vice president of the new division. He was already so impressed with me that he took the deal, and it's been remarkable. I've made more money in two months than most people do in a lifetime, Issy."

"Grant, you know I don't care about that."

Grant reached out and touched my face, assuring me that he understood. "It's not the money, Issy. It's the freedom. We are no longer dependent on your father. You can go back to Winsor and finish your school. I have the freedom to work anywhere I want to, but mostly, we can be together."

Grant's words sent warmth through my body, but it felt wrong to be happy when everyone else had suffered because of me. "What about my mom? My father threatened her too."

"Your mom is in rehab. She admitted herself a week after you disappeared. Jake said he had been taking her pills away when he found them, but she always found a way to get more. But your dad did take possession of the house. I'm not sure if she's still hospitalized because she needs to be or if she's there because she has to be."

I stood up from the couch, fury starting to flood my stomach. "How is it possible that he gets to win, when all of us suffer?" I demanded. Grant tried to console me, but I was too angry. "You have no idea how much I hate him…how much I want to make him suffer the way I have."

"I think he is suffering. I ran into him two weeks ago. His company is a mess, Issy. Stock prices have practically bottomed out and it doesn't look good for recovery. I didn't realize how much I actually did for him until I left. Your father never knew the computer stuff. That was all me. I was the interpreter for him, which explains why he never was willing to let me go."

I walked towards the window, staring out across the city lights. "I don't feel sorry for him. He deserves everything he gets," I stated coldly.

Grant wrapped his arms around me and I leaned into him, feeling the anger start to dissipate a little. "One day, you're going to have to forgive him, Issy, for your own sake. Bitterness is no way to live, and I want you to live the life you've never been free to have."

I turned around and threw my arms around his neck pulling him towards me. The fire that had been ignited earlier raged with new fury as we consumed one another. We somehow managed to stop before it went too far, even though both of us we breathing heavy when we separated.

"Stay here," he said, kissing my hand with a grin before running back to his bedroom. He was back in seconds and carrying a small black box. "You once asked me to give you the names of two couples that were happily in love." Grant opened the box and watched for my reaction. I didn't move. The box held a gold ring with a larger square diamond in the middle and two smaller, round diamonds sitting beside it. "These two diamonds are from my grandmother's and great grandmother's wedding rings. Together they represent over a hundred years of marriage, commitment and love. The middle one is for us."

I stared at the ring, unable to find the words. Grant took it out of the box and slipped it on my finger. "Say yes," he whispered as he put his forehead to mine.

What else could I say? He had stolen my heart and I never wanted it back. "Yes."

I watched Grant close his eyes and finally breathe again before bringing me in for a kiss so tender and intimate that my knees would have buckled if Grant hadn't had me cradled in his arms.

"Grant?" I whispered as he kissed me, his lips trailing down my neck.

"Yes baby?" he answered, never stopping the fire he was sending down my body.

"I know this seems crazy since I've never wanted to wait before, but I kind of feel like we've been given a second chance, and I want to do things right." My voiced trailed off as he kissed me, my resolution already starting to wane.

Grant took my face in his hands and stared lovingly in my eyes. "Sweetheart, I'd wait for you forever."

I grinned at him and then moved as close as I

could, "Well, I'm not as patient as you," I whispered, kissing his ear. I felt his breath catch in response. "I was thinking Vegas."

He jerked back and stared at me is disbelief. "Are you serious?"

"You're not planning on changing your mind are you?" I asked with my eyebrow raised, my mischievous grin already consuming my face.

"Not in a million years," he assured me before picking me up and spinning me around. I felt the laughter echo through my entire body as we collapsed on the floor. My wish had finally come true. The life I always wanted was here.

EPILOGUE

I woke up with a smile on my face. Grant was still sleeping peacefully next to me, and I took in his flawless face. I glanced at the gold band adorning his finger and sat in amazement that this wonderful man would be mine for the rest of my life.

We had said our vows on a beach in the Virgin Islands right as the sun began to set. It was fitting to marry on the beach since that's where it had all started for us.

I thought of our first night together and blushed. I never understood why Parker and Avery wanted to wait, but now I did. Everything about the night had been beautiful. There was no insecurity in his touch. We were one flesh under God and able to express that love to each other without regret or fear. I softly kissed my sweet husband before dawning my robe.

The smell of salt water assaulted me as I stood on the balcony holding Grant's phone in my hand. I still hadn't called Jake. It had been three days since Grant found me, and I didn't know why I was waiting. I took a deep breath and sent him a text.

Me: This is Issy. When I call, please pick up.

Jake picked up on the first ring. "He found you," he cried, his voice shaking. "I've been going out of my mind, Issy!"

Then he started ranting. First at me for not calling him, then at Grant for not telling him right away that he found me. Finally, he started cursing my father and threatening to hurt him even more. Once he finally calmed down, he asked, "Where are you? I'm coming to get you."

I let out a sigh, not sure why I felt so nervous. "I'm in the Caribbean, Jake. Grant and I got married last night."

There was silence on the other end until I heard an echoing click.

"Jake?" I asked, but it was too late. The line was already dead.

TO MY WONDERFUL READERS

I hope you enjoyed Issy and Grant's story. Please take a moment to leave a review on Amazon.

To see how it all began, check out the first book in the Winsor Series, *Shattered Rose*. Available now on Amazon.

The final book in the series is Jake's story, coming early 2014.

I'd love to hear from all of you. Connect with me on Facebook to hear all about my upcoming projects:

https://www.facebook.com/tlgraybooks

Or sign up for updates on promotions and new releases via my newsletter at http://www.tlgray.com

ABOUT THE AUTHOR

T.L. Gray is a freelance writer who also serves as a pastor's wife in Ennis, Texas. It was her desire to see young girls know and experience Christ's unconditional love that led her to write her debut novel, *Shattered Rose*. She strongly believes that sometimes the greatest stories are told from the heart of those who have lived them. T.L. Gray is currently working on Book 3 in the Winsor Series which is set for release in early 2014.

Made in the USA
San Bernardino, CA
08 August 2013